To my ... thank... Sally.

Never Say Sorry

by

Suzie Peters

So glad I met you.
and so glad we are
still there for
One another !!
love
Donna x y

2020·

GWL
PUBLISHING

First Published in 2019
by GWL Publishing
an imprint of Great War Literature Publishing LLP

Produced in United Kingdom

ISBN 978-1-910603-74-1 Paperback Edition

GWL Publishing
Forum House
Sterling Road
Chichester PO19 7DN

www.gwlpublishing.co.uk

Also by Suzie Peters:

Escaping the Past Series
Finding Matt
Finding Luke
Finding Will
Finding Todd

Wishes and Chances Series
Words and Wisdom
Lattes and Lies
Rebels and Rules

Recipes for Romance Series
Stay Here With Me
Play Games With Me
Come Home With Me

Believe in Fairy Tales Series
Believe in Us
Believe in Me
Believe in You

Never Say Sorry

Dedication

For S.

Part One

Chapter One

Abbie

I was seven years old when we moved to Porthgowan.

Before that, we'd lived in London; in a house in Wandsworth. I don't remember either the house, or the road we lived in, or London itself; not very much. I remember my bedroom had wallpaper with small blue flowers on an off-white background, and the curtains were plain and cream coloured, and I used to like sitting up there, drawing and reading, and looking out at the garden, and the small square of sky above. I remember the view was limited by the width of the window, and that I could see into the garden of the house behind ours. It was owned by an elderly couple and the woman, who had silver coloured hair, and always had an apron tied around her waist, used to wave at me sometimes, when she was hanging out the washing, or weeding the flower beds. We didn't have flower beds. Our garden was a patch of concrete, with some pots of herbs and shrubs scattered around. Mum and Dad would sometimes sit out there with a glass of wine in the evenings, but it wasn't much good for playing.

As for Wandsworth itself, I don't recall any redeeming features. My school was a ten minute walk away, and really the extent of my knowledge was the few short streets between our double glazed front door, and the school gates, where my mum would take me every morning, before going on to work.

Mum was a teacher. Not in my school, but in a secondary school in Putney. And Dad was a graphic designer. Dad liked his job, although the hours could be a bit unpredictable. He'd sometimes have to work evenings and weekends at short notice, and Mum would get cross about that, and they'd argue – that's to say, Mum would shout at Dad, and he'd sit there and listen – and then long silences would follow, broken only when Dad apologised. There were a lot of long silences in our house. There were also quite a lot of loud whisperings too. This was an annoying thing my parents sometimes did, when they were having an argument, but they didn't want me to overhear, so they would whisper really loudly – not quite loudly enough for me to actually hear what they were saying, just loudly enough for me to notice.

The news that we were moving came as a surprise to me. My parents broke it to me over dinner one evening in the May half-term. I was still six at the time, not being due to turn seven for a couple of months, and I remember we were having spaghetti bolognese. I was struggling to twirl the pasta around my fork and get it to my mouth before it all fell off again, when Dad took my plate away and cut it up for me, while Mum explained that they were going to be moving... to Cornwall.

I didn't even know what Cornwall was, but Mum explained it was a place in the West Country – which didn't help at all – and that there was village there called Porthgowan, which she'd been to several times as a child, when her family used to go on camping holidays nearby. She said it had a lovely beach, lots of pretty houses, a few shops... and a pub. And that was where we were going to live. I had hundreds of questions – literally hundreds. To start with, what was a pub? Would I have my own bedroom still? Where would I go to school? Could I take all my books and drawing things? And what about my teddies? And my clothes? The list was endless. They answered a lot of my questions, telling me they'd looked into a school for me already, and I could take everything with me, because I'd have my own bedroom in the flat above the pub. We'd be moving at the end of the summer term, in the last week of July, so the next few weeks were going to be busy with packing. To some of the things I asked, however, they just said 'don't worry about it', which was quite worrying really. After all, how was I to know what was happening? I was only six years old.

*****

The pub was called The Lobster Pot and on first inspection, it wasn't inspiring. Admittedly, it was right on the beach, with just a low wall between it and the sandy cove, but other than that, it had little going for it. The paint around the windows and doors was chipped and flaking, the sign was hanging on one hinge, all lopsided. There was a car park to one side – the side closest to the sea, beyond the building itself – but it was full of wood and piles of bricks, and rubble, and an old toilet, tipped on its side. That made me worry that there wouldn't be a toilet inside and I gripped Dad's hand a little tighter. Had we really left our small but comfortable home in London... for this? Were my parents mad? I looked up at them. Mum was smiling, looking pleased. Dad was scratching his head, until he glanced down at me, and planted a grin on his face.

"Don't worry, poppet," he said. "It's not as bad as it looks."

Mum slapped his arm. "It's not bad at all," she said. "It's perfect... well, it will be when we've finished with it."

At that moment, a man came out of the building beside the pub, which had a sign that read 'Porthgowan Arts'. He was tall, with reddish-brown hair and tanned skin, and he walked over, his hand outstretched.

"I'm Devin Kellow," he said, with a strange, lilting accent that I rather liked. "You must be the new owners." He nodded towards the pub.

"Yes," my dad replied, shaking his hand. "I'm Robert Fuller, and this is my wife, Sandra." Mum stepped forward and shook Mr Kellow's hand as well. And then my dad put his hand on my head. "And this is Abbie," he added.

Mr Kellow crouched down in front of me, smiling. "Hello," he said. I felt shy at the time, so I didn't reply, although he didn't seem to mind and stood up again, looking at my dad. "I've got a daughter as well," he explained. "About the same age, I should think."

"Well, Abbie's seven," my dad said – because I was by then, being as I'd had my birthday two weeks beforehand.

"Oh… so's Tara." Mr Kellow smiled down at me again. "She's at school at the moment. They don't break up until tomorrow. But she'll be back this afternoon. Perhaps Abbie can come round later? I'm sure Tara would like to meet her."

"Abbie would love that," my mum replied, although I didn't feel so sure about it myself. I was feeling a bit uncertain about the whole thing, and really I just wanted to stay with my parents. "We left London last night and broke our journey half way down," my mum continued. "That's how we could get here so early. But our removal van isn't due to arrive until this afternoon." She glanced at Dad. "It'll be useful to keep Abbie out of the way for a few hours, won't it?"

Dad nodded, but didn't say anything, and kept his hand on my head.

"Well, I'll let you know when Tara gets back, shall I?" Mr Kellow suggested and my mother agreed.

"Are there many other children here?" my dad asked and I listened up, wanting to know.

"Not many," Mr Kellow replied. "There's Tara, Josh and Simon. They're all the same age and they do almost everything together. Simon has an older brother, Andrew. And then there's Sara and Melanie Towers. Sara's a year younger than Tara, I think, and Melanie's only three."

"That's it?" My dad seemed surprised.

"For this age group, yes. I'm not counting the teenagers." Mr Kellow smiled, and then said he'd better let Mum and Dad get on. They thanked him and he went back into his shop. I watched him go, and then allowed my gaze to wander to the display in the window. There were two paintings – both of coves, rather like the one we were standing in and, although they didn't look exactly like Porthgowan, I liked them.

"He was nice," Mum said.

"Yes. Friendly chap. I wonder where his wife is," Dad replied.

"He wasn't wearing a ring. Maybe there isn't a wife," Mum murmured, although I could hear her quite clearly.

"You noticed that?" Dad said, letting go of my head now and turning to her.

"It pays to notice things. We're going to be..." I stopped listening, her voice trailing off, as I wandered over to the art gallery – Mr Kellow's shop – which was painted a sort of mid-blue, with the name scrolled in white lettering above the large bow-fronted window, through which I stared, desperate to discover what was on the inside. From what I could see, the walls were lined with paintings and sketches, some in frames and some not, and I started to think that maybe an afternoon spent in there wouldn't be so bad after all.

Tara had the same accent and the same colour hair as her father, only hers was tied up in a pony tail, with a dark red ribbon that matched the stripes on her school summer dress. She had pale blue eyes and freckles, and when Mum took me round to the art gallery later that afternoon, and Mr Kellow opened the door, she greeted me with a smile and held out her hand. I looked up at my mum and she nudged me forward, so I took Tara's hand, and she led me through the shop, leaving my mum and Mr Kellow talking, my mum telling him how the removal men had struggled to get the van down the lane, and had spent the first half hour moaning about it, but had calmed down after a cup of tea and some chocolate digestives. She hoped they'd be finished unloading in a couple of hours, evidently.

The shop was long and narrow, and there were steps leading down to a lower level, where there were a few artists' supplies for sale – just basic paints, pencils and sketch pads. Beyond that, through a door that had a sign on it, which said 'Private', there was a small kitchen with a two-ring hob, a sink, and a table in the centre with a red Formica top, and two chairs.

"We don't live here," Tara explained, even though I hadn't asked, as she held out a chair for me to sit on. "We live on East Street." I had no idea where that was, but assumed it was somewhere in the village. "Dad closes the shop for ten minutes in the afternoons and comes to meet the school bus, then he brings me back here until it's time for us to go home."

"What about your mum?" I asked, leaning on the table.

"She died," Tara said in a very matter of fact way. "I don't remember her." She opened a small fridge, checking inside. "Would you like some apple juice?"

I nodded my head and she pulled out a carton of juice and fetched two small glasses from the cupboard above the sink, standing on a low stool to reach, and then poured us out a measure each, before bringing them over to the table and sitting down opposite me. "We'll have these," she said, "and then we'll go exploring, shall we? I'll show you the village… and maybe we'll see Josh and Simon."

"Who are Josh and Simon?" I took a sip of juice.

"They're my friends."

"Does your dad just let you go off by yourself?" I asked her.

"Yes." She seemed surprised by my question. "Don't your parents?"

"Not in London, no."

She swallowed down the last of her drink and I did the same, not wanting to hold up the next part of the afternoon – not from any particular desire to see the village, or because I was keen to meet Josh and Simon, but just because I didn't want her to think I was being stuffy or aloof.

"Shall we go?" As she spoke, she got up and held out her hand. She seemed keen on holding hands, so I took it, and then she smiled at me and led me back the way we had just come, where we found my mum and her dad were still standing at the front of the gallery, talking.

"Where are you off to?" Mr Kellow asked.

"I'm going to show Abbie the village," Tara replied.

"Well, make sure you stick to The Street and the beach," he said, frowning slightly. "No wandering off."

"Yes, Dad." She turned and rolled her eyes at me and then we headed out of the door.

"Which part is The Street?" I asked her.

"You're standing in it," she replied. "The Street is the name of this road." She pointed to the narrow lane we were standing at the edge of, which I knew from our arrival that morning, started at the top of the hill and wound down, past the prettily painted houses, to the pub, and the cove. "It leads around the corner and back up to the main road again," Tara said, indicating the curve where The Street seemed to disappear. "I'll show you the beach first."

Without waiting for me to reply – although I'm not sure whether she expected me to – she pulled me along the edge of the road, away from the pub, keeping us right by the low wall, until we reached the gap, which she walked through, guiding me across the small car park, to another gap in a second wall of similar height, and on to the beach itself.

"Take your shoes and socks off," she instructed, as she let go of my hand, bending down to undo the buckles on the sides of her school shoes and pull off her white socks. I knelt down and took off my trainers, copying Tara by tucking my socks inside and holding them by the heels, before she ushered me onto the sandy shore.

I'd never felt sand between my toes before. It was strangely warm, in the late afternoon sun, soft and rather soothing, and it tickled, just slightly as we walked along beside the wall to an area of rocks, where two boys were sitting. They glanced up as we approached and then slowly got to their feet, looking inquisitive.

"This is Abbie," Tara announced, waving her arm in my direction.

The boy on the left, who had blond hair, nodded his head, but didn't say a word. The other one, smiled and said, "Hello." He had much darker hair and deep brown eyes. It turned out his name was Josh Brewer, and the other, more shy boy, was Simon Trelawny.

That summer went so much better than I'd imagined.

The pub became a building site as Mum and Dad's plans came to fruition. Obviously, I'd known nothing about their intentions, but it soon became clear they had big changes in mind. My initial fears about the sanitary facilities turned out to be unfounded. There was indeed a working toilet in the upstairs flat of the pub, along with a kitchen-dining room, three bedrooms and a large lounge. They made very few changes to the living accommodation, other than repainting some of the rooms to suit their own tastes – and my own, being as I was given free rein to choose the colour for my bedroom, which soon became a pale pink, with a frieze of painted butterflies stuck about halfway up the wall.

Where they did most work, was downstairs, in the pub, which they refurbished and extended, adding a huge conservatory, beer garden and children's play area, which were all built on the space that the car park had once occupied. My parents' thought process was that, there was a perfectly good public car park just a few feet away, by the beach, and being able to serve food and cater for families at the pub was more important than providing parking – especially when that facility was already available so close by.

The work took a couple of months, but by the time I started school in the September, the interior was almost finished, with just the conservatory to be completed.

In the meantime, I'd kept out of the way – much to everyone's relief, I think – and spent almost every day at the beach with my friends. It may seem odd that four seven year olds would be allowed the freedom to wander on the beach by themselves – and these days, I imagine most parents would blanche at the prospect – but Josh's mum ran the post office, which was on the opposite corner of the bay to the pub, just on the point where the road curved upwards again. Between her, my parents, and Tara's dad, we were within sight of at least four adults most of the time. Simon's dad was the village doctor, and they lived further up the hill, in a big house, but there were other adults around too, who kept a watchful eye. There was Henry, who owned and ran the pottery, which was beside the post office, and then there was Mr Gregg, who kept the general store, where we'd sometimes be allowed to go and buy an ice cream.

It was an odd feeling, being safe and watched-over, and yet completely independent at the same time. Once I'd got used to it though, I found I liked it.

Luckily, I could already swim. There had been a leisure centre with a pool not far from where we lived in Wandsworth, and my dad used to take me there on Saturday mornings while Mum did the housework. When we'd finished splashing around, we used to have a hot chocolate and a doughnut in the cafeteria, my clothes still sticking to my skin, just slightly, where Dad hadn't completely dried me off. I didn't mind though; I enjoyed the creamy, frothy hot chocolate and I liked licking the jam out of the doughnut, once I'd taken that first heavenly bite. Even as an adult, those Saturday mornings remain one of my fondest memories of my early childhood, before we moved to Porthgowan.

Of course, swimming in the sea was quite different to being at a pool – there were waves to contend with for one thing. But they were never high. The cliffs surrounding the cove protected us from the worst of the ocean's moods. The scarred rocks, and the way they almost encircled us, with just a narrow opening leading out to the wider sea, was another thing that gave me a feeling of security.

Safety and freedom – they were strange and yet ideal bedfellows.

All too soon though, the summer was over. My mum had taken me to Helston at the end of the holidays and bought me a school uniform, which for the winter term consisted of a grey skirt, white polo shirt and deep red sweatshirt, and on my first day, she took me, in the company of the other village children, to the bus stop at the top of the lane. The bus collected children from lots of outlying villages, but it couldn't come into ours. The Street was too narrow for it to pass, and too tight for it to turn at the end, and so every day, we walked up the hill and waited. Some of the children – like Josh and Simon – walked by themselves. Others, like Tara and I, were taken by our parents, and Mum and Mr Kellow chatted while we waited for the bus to arrive.

I felt nervous, worried about school, about whether I'd be behind the local children in my studies, about meeting lots of others and what they'd make of me.

Sitting on the bus, I waved to my mum and she waved back, still talking to Mr Kellow at the same time, before they turned away and started back down the lane. The journey was a long one – about twenty minutes, I suppose – but it seemed longer. Some of the other children stared at me, as though I were an alien from another planet, but Tara stuck by my side, with Josh and Simon on the seats in front.

I was in Miss Penhallow's class. Class 3P. And Tara, Josh and Simon were all with me. The first part of the morning, until break, was spent giving out books, and getting to know the classroom and where everything was kept. After break, we had maths. All my life, I've never been very good at anything to do with numbers, but it wasn't as hard as I'd thought it would be. I certainly wasn't behind the other students, anyway, and that was a relief.

At lunch, I ate with my friends, pleased to discover that school lunches were quite nice – much better than they'd been in Wandsworth – and then we had half an hour to play outside.

And afterwards – to my absolute delight – we had art. All afternoon.

Miss Penhallow wanted us to draw something that represented our summer holiday. So I drew the cove. I sketched the tall cliffs, dominating the village, with the pub, the art gallery, the post office and the sandy beach, showing low waves lapping on the shore, and the sea fading off into the distance. I sat quietly, even when some of the other children were being naughty, and just focused on my drawing. At the end, Miss Penhallow gathered up the pictures, telling various children to put away the pencils, or pack up the spare paper, while reminding others that the bell hadn't gone yet, and they needed to be quiet until it did.

"Why, Abbie," she said, stopping as she got to me, "that's beautiful."

"Thank you, Miss." I felt myself blush as the other children turned to stare.

"I think we'll put it up on the wall, shall we?" Miss Penhallow added, smiling. I smiled back, but my smile faded, replaced by crushing disappointment, when she just picked up my drawing and placed it with the rest, and then walked to the front of the class and dismissed us for the day.

Standing at the bus stop, a boy whose name I couldn't remember leaned over to me.

"Where you from, then?" he asked, looking at me suspiciously.

"Porthgowan," I whispered.

"No y'aren't. Y'aren't from round 'ere. You talk funny."

A few of the other children laughed and I felt myself blush – again.

"You're the one who talks funny, Billy." Josh was standing beside me, even though I was sure he hadn't been there a moment ago.

"Wossit gotta do with you?" the boy named Billy said, his eyes darkening.

"Everything." Josh moved forward and Billy backed down, moving away.

Once I was sure he'd gone, I turned to Josh, and whispered, "Thank you," very quietly.

He smiled at me. "You don't need to thank me," he replied. "We're friends."

The next morning, when we got into school, Miss Penhallow had stuck my picture up on the wall for everyone to see, and a group of children, including Josh and Simon gathered around it, staring at it, and then looking at me. Josh broke away from the group first, and came over to where I was sitting. He leant on the table beside me.

"You really drew that?" he said, pointing to the picture everyone else was still seemingly admiring.

"Yes."

He nodded his head, and without saying a word, went and sat in his own seat. Once the other children had settled and Miss Penhallow started reading the register, Josh turned, looked at me, and smiled.

Together, we passed through several such school terms, Easter, summer and Christmas holidays. When the weather wasn't good enough to be outdoors, we'd either go upstairs at the pub, or to Simon's house, which was a large, double-fronted property halfway down The Street, with roses growing up a trellis around the front door, and orderly flowerbeds, with well pruned shrubs, where a weed wouldn't dare to rear its ugly head. I don't think Mrs Trelawny followed the philosophy that weeds are just flowers growing in the wrong place, and she could often be seen squirting something toxic onto her herbaceous borders to keep them free from unwelcome invaders.

Before long, we progressed to secondary school. A longer bus ride, and different uniforms were required, but other than that – and the addition of homework to spoil our afternoons – our lives didn't change very much.

It was at the end of year eight, as the long summer holidays approached once more, that something happened which would alter our friendships forever, although as is often the way with such events, we weren't aware of that at the time; we were too caught up in the drama of it all to notice.

Tara, Josh and Simon were all thirteen by then. I was still twelve, but I was looking forward to my birthday, and becoming a teenager at last. That particular Friday afternoon was overcast, but warm, and we'd come home together on the bus as usual. Mum and Mr Kellow had given up meeting us long before – when we were in year six at primary school – deciding we were old enough to walk home together, with Josh and Simon. As we approached Simon's house that day though, we were surprised to see Doctor Trelawny standing outside, looking up The Street, watching for us.

"Simon?" he called as we drew nearer.

Simon didn't reply, but nodded and veered in the direction of his father, leaving us to carry on, although we slowed our pace slightly, intrigued by this unusual turn of events. Doctor Trelawny, a man who was older than my father, and Mr Kellow, with a receding hairline, and metal rimmed glasses, would normally have been in his surgery at that time of day, but he leant down and spoke quietly to Simon, who then turned to us and called out that he had to go in; he'd come and find us later. Doctor Trelawny frowned and gave us a half-hearted wave, and then ushered Simon into the house, closing the door behind them both.

"That was odd," Tara remarked. "What do you think it was about?"

"It's none of our business," Josh replied, and we continued down the lane.

Simon didn't come and find us that afternoon. In fact, it wasn't until much later the following day that we saw him again, looking puffy eyed and pale.

We were sitting in our usual spot by the rocks, and he sauntered over and plonked himself down next to Josh and opposite me, his knees bent, his arms resting on them.

No-one said anything for a minute, and then Tara broke the silence.

"What's happened?" she asked, leaning forward and placing her hand on his arm. He glanced across at her, frowning, as though he'd forgotten she was there, and sighed deeply, biting at his bottom lip. I wondered for a moment if he was going to cry and what we'd all do if he did; but fortunately he didn't, which saved me having to worry about it. Instead of crying, he shook his head and looked out to sea.

"Mum's got cancer," he mumbled.

They were three simple words, but they fell on us like waves crashing on the shore, washing over us and sucking the breath from our lungs.

"Christ, mate," Josh said, speaking where I couldn't, and it seemed neither could Tara, and I watched, dumbstruck as Simon slowly opened up, encouraged by Josh's gentle questioning, telling us how his father had sat him and Andrew down in their dining room and had told him and his brother about their mother's breast cancer, how she'd found a lump and his father had confirmed it, and she'd been to the hospital already and had tests. She was going to need surgery and treatment. He leant back on his elbows as he spoke, separating himself from us, it seemed, but Josh copied his action, going with him, staying by his side.

"Do you think she'll die?" Tara's words split through us, like a cleft opening up in a rock.

"Tara!" Josh and I both spoke at the same time. "Be quiet," I added under my breath, and she turned to me.

"What?" she said, shrugging. "We're all thinking it."

"Are we?" Josh retorted.

An awkward silence followed before Simon replied that his dad had told him and Andrew that their mum was going to be fine. The surgery would be hard; the treatment would be harder, and they'd have to help out around the house while she recovered. But she was young – younger than their dad, at any rate – and she was strong and fit. Of course she'd be fine. Simon sighed and said the problem was, his dad kept repeating that phrase so often, he wasn't sure who Doctor Trelawny was trying to convince – himself, or Simon and Andrew. It was hard not to see his point.

Things changed from that day onwards. Simon spent more time at home, helping out, like his dad had asked him to. Doctor Trelawny had to work, and Andrew wasn't much use, so Simon tried to do what he could. Josh and I called round from time to time, and on one occasion, we caught sight of Mrs Trelawny, sitting in the living room, her feet up on the sofa, her skin pale and pasty, her head covered with a scarf to hide the fact that her hair had fallen out. She'd lost weight and looked like a shadow of her former, formidable self. She didn't look up, didn't seem to even notice we were there.

Tara still came out with us sometimes, but her outburst, and her insensitivity towards Simon had altered our perspective of her.

"Maybe she doesn't understand Simon's attachment to his mother, because she's never had one herself," I reasoned to Josh one Saturday when he and I were sitting on the climbing frame in the children's play area behind the pub. It was several months after Mrs Trelawny's diagnosis, and the weather had turned much colder – too cold to sit on the beach, although we didn't want to be indoors.

"You think that's a good enough reason for her being so… so rude?" Tara had made a comment about Simon being 'pathetic' just that morning, which was why she wasn't sitting with us. She'd stormed off after Josh had picked her up on it, and we hadn't seen her since.

"No," I mused.

"Let's face it," he said, plucking at the hem of his denim jacket with his fingernail, "I don't have a father, and I probably have one of the worst mothers in the world, but I can still try and understand how Simon feels."

I reached over, trying not to lose my balance, and rested my hand on his arm. "You're a good friend to him."

He turned and smiled, and for the first time since I'd known him, I was truly aware of the sadness in his eyes. And I wanted, more than anything, to hug him.

By the following summer, Simon's mother had recovered – well, she'd been told she was in remission. I had to ask Mum and Dad what that meant and Dad explained that she wasn't cured, but the cancer had gone away for now. To me that seemed like a mere postponement. If it had only gone away 'for now', then surely, it could come back? Simon and his dad were relieved though, and even I had to admit, his mum did look a lot better than she had on that day when Josh and I had caught a glimpse of her illness through that half-open door.

Simon slowly re-introduced himself into the group, but he'd fallen behind with some of his school work – as had Andrew, who was taking his GCSEs that year – and he spent a lot of time studying and catching up. Tara had drifted away slightly, so often my evenings and weekends were spent with Josh. Just the two of us. I'd usually find him sitting on the beach in our spot, and I'd join him. Simon would occasionally be there too, and I'd fetch us cans of coke and packets of crisps from the pub. We'd gaze out to sea and talk; sometimes I'd sketch and just listen to them.

"Why do you keep drawing?" Josh asked me one day, when it was just the two of us. "Don't you get bored of the view?"

I looked up and smiled at him. "No. It changes all the time. The light is different, the way the sunlight plays on the water, the shadows under the rocks." I pointed to the area at the bottom of the cliff as I was talking, and then turned back to him. "But why do you keep coming down here? Don't you get bored of the view too?"

He smiled and said, "No," and then looked away again, tracing circles in the sand with his fingertip. "And anyway, it's better than being at home."

I'd seen his sadness several times by then and I knew things weren't right, but Josh had never really spoken about it, not to me, anyway, so I sat in silence and waited.

"Nothing I ever do is good enough," he said eventually, leaning back on his hands and gazing out to the horizon. "She shouts at me all the time these days... even more so than before."

"What does she shout about?" I asked him, putting down my sketch pad and pencils.

"Everything," he replied a little evasively. "I can't wait to be old enough to leave home."

That shocked me. "Leave home? You mean you'd leave the village?"

"Not out of choice, but if it meant getting away from her, then yes." His voice was determined, with a tinge of bitterness, and I knew he'd thought it through, probably over many years, even though he was only fourteen.

That made me sad, although I didn't say anything. Somehow, I knew I didn't need to, and instead we sat together, our shoulders touching, our heads bent close, and watched the sun set.

We drifted for a while in that sanctuary, that no man's land between the sheltered innocence of our childhood and the boundless uncertainty that awaited us as adults. 'Coming of age', I suppose they call it, but the thing is, when you're the one who's living it, you're not really aware of the stages of your own development, not until it's too late to appreciate them, anyway. They just seem to happen around you, in a myriad of changes and experiences, and then, before you know it, the window of your childhood is suddenly closed for good and all you're left with is memories.

For me, that moment of closure arrived during the Easter holidays of year eleven. Everyone else was sixteen by then, although I was still fifteen, and we were about to face our first real test in life – or at least, it felt like that to us. Our GCSEs were imminent. Simon's brother Andrew had failed his dismally a couple of years earlier, blaming their mother's illness for his shocking results. He'd been offered the chance to re-sit them, but had declined and managed to find a job in the packing house of the local brewery. The rest of us saw this as a lesson to be learned, and we knuckled down to revise, seeing less of each other as the exams drew nearer and nearer. That applied to all of us, except Tara, who'd rejoined us by this stage – albeit not with the same close attachment as before – and who was one of those super-bright students who never seemed to have to work too hard to over-achieve. She barely even paid attention in classes, completed her homework in minutes, rather than hours, never bothered to revise for tests, and yet always scored top marks in everything. I'd like to say it made me sick, but despite our differences, we were still friends and I couldn't dislike her – not even for being so annoyingly clever.

The Easter holidays gave us a chance to unwind just a little, to mix our revision with the odd trip to the cinema in Helston, or an hour on the beach, if the weather permitted, which it did on most days, because Easter fell late that year.

It was the day before Good Friday. We'd been off school for a week already, and I was feeling okay about how my revision was going... with the exception of science, that is, because it was never my strong point, along with maths, which had remained a thorn in my academic side. I'd spent the morning looking at my history notes, trying to take in various facts and figures about the Industrial Revolution, and was about to put everything to one side and stop for lunch, when my mum stuck her head around my bedroom door.

"Can you come into the kitchen for a minute, Abbie?" she asked. She looked pale and I thought she might have been crying, and I felt my stomach churn and my palms start to sweat as I got up from my small desk, and followed her into the kitchen at the opposite end of our flat.

Dad was already there, sitting at the dining table in the middle of the room and for a moment, I wondered who was downstairs, behind the bar. It was twelve o'clock, after all. Then I remembered Josie worked on Thursdays. She lived in West Street, on the opposite side of the village to Tara and her dad, and had been helping out a few lunchtimes during the week since her little boy, Evan, had started school. Even so, for both of my parents to be absent from the bar was unheard of. This had to be serious.

"Sit down, poppet," my dad said, pulling out the chair beside him. He'd never stopped using my pet name, and although it sometimes made me cringe, deep down, I quite liked it.

I sat and waited while Mum took a seat opposite. The silence was deafening and my nerves almost got the better of me as I recalled Simon telling us how his father had sat with him and Andrew at the dining table and told them about his mother's cancer. This was it; they were going to tell me one of them was ill... maybe even dying. Oh God...

"Your mother's got something to tell you," Dad said at last and I looked up. She was glaring at him, with a look I didn't understand, but then she softened slightly and turned to me.

"There's no easy way to say this," she began, and I braced myself. "Your dad and I are splitting up. We're getting a divorce."

I was almost relieved. They weren't ill. Neither of them was going to die.

Then it dawned on me. A divorce…

"What's going to happen?" I asked, looking from my mum to my dad. "I mean, what's going to happen to us?" Were we going to move again? Were we going to have to leave the village? I didn't want to. I liked it here; I felt like I belonged. And I had friends. Real friends.

My dad sighed and looked away, so I turned back to Mum again. "I'm leaving," she said, quite simply, as though she was telling me she was going to the shops, or to get the car serviced.

"You're leaving?"

That struck me as odd. I'd always known – I think right from the word 'go' – that it had been Mum's idea to move to Porthgowan. Why would she be the one to leave?

"Yes." Her voice dropped a little now, and I knew instinctively there was something more to come – something worse, perhaps. But what could be worse? "I'm moving to North Cornwall." Well, that didn't seem too bad. "With Devin and Tara…"

I stared at her, trying to take it in. "Devin?" I repeated. "Devin Kellow… and Tara?" She nodded her head and I felt tears welling up in my eyes as the realisation of what she was saying dawned on me. "Does this mean…?" I couldn't get the words out, so I paused and tried again. "Does this mean you and Mr Kellow…?" I still couldn't say it, and neither could I say his name, it seemed. He'd gone back to being the 'Mr Kellow' of my childhood, not the 'Devin' of my teenage years. I stood up, the chair scraping on the floor as I pushed it back. "Are you sleeping with him?"

My mother looked away and it was my father who slowly got to his feet and put his arms around me. "These things happen, poppet," he murmured, giving me a hug. "You can't help who you fall in love with." I leant back, pulling way from him and looked up into his face. His eyes were sad, rather lost, I thought, and he shrugged his shoulders. "Your mother has fallen out of love with me and in love with Devin. It can't be helped."

Part of me wanted to shout at him, to ask him why he wasn't fighting for her, why he wasn't even trying to keep their marriage together, to keep us together. But I didn't. I could see the pain on his face and I couldn't make it worse. I turned back to my mother, who was still sitting at the table, her hands clasped tight in front of her.

"So, you're leaving?" My voice sounded harsh, even to me, and she looked up sharply as though *I'd* wounded *her*.

"Yes," she replied. "But you can come with me, if you want."

For a moment, I couldn't even think, let alone speak, and I sat back down in the chair, just to steady myself. My dad sat too, moving closer and facing me, then taking my hands in his. "I know this is a lot to take in," he said, "and you don't have to decide right now."

"So Mum's not leaving yet?" I was trying to get my head around what they were saying.

"No, Mum's leaving tomorrow."

"Tomorrow?" I almost shouted the word. "So, when you say I don't have to decide 'right now', what you mean is you want me to decide by tomorrow… you want me to choose between you? And… and you want me to do it by tomorrow?" I spoke slowly, trying to get them both to understand how completely unreasonable they were being.

Dad shook his head, gripping my hands a little tighter. "No, poppet. That's not what I'm saying at all." He took a breath, closing his eyes for a moment, before opening them again and looking right at me. "Your mum and Devin came to me yesterday evening, after the bar closed, and told me of their plan. Devin's already sold his house and the art gallery and bought a new shop in Padstow. It's got a flat above it and he and your mum explained that they wanted to make the move quickly, rather than hanging it out any longer."

I turned to look at my mum. "You planned this all very neatly." I couldn't hide the bitterness in my voice. "Dropping it on Dad like that… didn't you think—"

"They didn't drop it on me," Dad interrupted and I turned back to him again. "Not exactly."

"What are you saying?" I felt like I was lost on a churning tide, being swept one way, and then another, rudderless.

"I—I've known about your mum and Devin for a while," he said, looking down at our clasped hands.

"You have?"

"Yes. We've done our best to shield you from it. And I've been trying to work things out."

"That's my point. *You've* been trying to work things out… while mum and Mr Kellow have been planning this behind your back."

Neither of them bothered to deny it and we sat for a few minutes in complete silence, other than the sound of our own breathing. It was Dad who finally spoke. "I've told your mum that I'm not letting you go with her," he said. "Not yet, anyway. It's too close to your exams. I've told her that you're staying here until you finish school. Then, if you want to, you can go and spend the summer holidays with your mum, and Devin, and Tara in Padstow, and after that, we can all sit down and discuss what you want to do."

"But I'm going into the sixth form. It's already been decided."

"There are colleges there too," Dad pointed out, although I wasn't very interested.

"What about Tara's exams?" I queried, the thought suddenly hitting me that she'd be going too. The very next day.

"Devin's made the arrangements with her new school for her to sit the same papers as she would have done here, and Tara's bright enough to cope with the move," my mum replied, speaking for the first time in ages.

"Whereas I'm too stupid, I suppose." I couldn't help myself.

"No-one said that," Dad reasoned, although my mum just looked away.

"Have you told Tara?" I asked, waiting for her to turn back. She did and nodded her head.

"Well," she said quietly, "Devin's telling her now."

I wondered how Tara would be reacting; how she'd feel about all this, and I turned and looked at my dad again. "I can't choose," I whispered, the tears building again. "I can't."

"You don't have to. Not yet. And in any case, whichever one of us you live with, you'll still be able to see the other one as often as you want. Padstow's only an hour and a half away. We both still love you, and us splitting up won't change that. It won't change anything."

How could he say that? "It changes everything!" I blurted out and stood, yanking my hands from his and running from the room, down the stairs and out of the back door.

"So? What do you think then?" Tara's voice brought me to a standstill. She was sitting at one of the picnic benches in the beer garden, her slim legs clad in tight faded jeans, a shirt tied at her waist, with a thin vest beneath, and her wavy hair hanging loose around her shoulders.

I strolled over and sat opposite her. "It's awful."

"Really?" She twisted to face me, leaning forward and resting her elbows on the table. "I think it sounds perfect." She beamed a smile at me, her eyes sparkling with excitement. "We've always been friends." That wasn't strictly true, but I wasn't in the mood to pick her up on it. "And now we can be sisters. Just think of the fun we'll have together."

"But I'm not coming with you," I pointed out.

"Well, not yet maybe, but you will be in the summer." She leant back slightly, flicking her hair behind her shoulder and smiling. "I went to Padstow with dad a couple of months ago. Obviously I didn't know he was checking out the new shop at the time. He just told me we were having a weekend away… And I've got to say, it's so much nicer than this dump. It's not like a big city… it's not London or anything, but it's got a lot more shops, and things to do… and there are so many more boys there." She almost swooned and then giggled. "It'll be brilliant." That was one of her 'in' words at the time. One of many.

"How can you say that?" I stared at her, anger building inside me. "My parents are getting divorced. I'm supposed to choose between them. Do you have any idea how that feels? Whatever I decide, one of my parents is going to feel rejected. I don't want to be responsible for that."

She sucked in a long breath, and let it out again slowly, almost like I was boring her. "It's not your job to worry about your parents, Abbie.

Do you think your mum was worrying about you – or even thinking about you – when she started shagging my dad?"

"Don't!" I put my hands over my ears, although I wasn't really sure why. It wasn't like it blocked out the words, or the images they conjured up.

She stood up, looking down at me. "It's no use trying to pretend it's not happening," she said harshly, and I was reminded at once of her attitude towards Simon when his mother was ill. It made me wonder if I'd ever really known her at all. "And it's no use worrying about your parents. They made the problem, not you."

I stood as well now. "My dad didn't." I raised my voice. "Unlike yours, *he* didn't sleep with someone else's wife."

She stilled, her eyes flashing with rage, and then turned and walked away.

I took a breath and looked up at the pub, but I couldn't face going back inside. I didn't want to see either of my parents at that point. I was too angry and disappointed with my mother, and too confused by my father. How could he just let her go like this? How could he let her break us up, and tell me it didn't change anything? Why wasn't he fighting harder?

With tears pouring down my cheeks now, I went around the side of the building and out onto the beach, almost feeling the relief wash over me as I spotted Josh, sitting in our usual spot. He wasn't on the sand, because it was cold and damp, but he'd perched himself on the rocks above, his broad shoulders hunched over, as he stared out to sea. Even through my tears, I could see his dark hair, the back of which touched the collar of his denim jacket, and I knew his deep brown eyes would be tinged with that familiar sadness.

He looked up as I approached and I saw the way his head tilted to one side, just before he clambered down off the rocks and walked over.

"What's happened?" he said, looking down at me.

"It… it's awful," I murmured, sniffling.

"What is?" He ran his fingers through his hair. "Tell me, Abbie."

"My parents are getting a divorce," I wailed. "My mum's been… been seeing Tara's dad. They're leaving together, all three of them." I covered my face with my hands, sobbing loudly, and then felt his arms come around me, his hand on the back of my head. He held me against his chest and I moved my hands away, putting them around his waist and hanging on to him for dear life, because at that moment, it felt like he was my anchor and I needed him to stop me drifting off into oblivion.

After I don't know how long, I leant back again, letting my hands drop to my sides, and looked up into his face. His eyes weren't sad anymore. They were filled with concern, and something else I didn't immediately recognise. It looked like fear, but that didn't make sense to me.

"Are you going too?" he asked.

I shook my head. "Not yet."

He frowned as the wind caught my hair, blowing it across my face, and he brushed it away with his fingertips, still staring at me. "What does 'not yet' mean?"

"It means I'm staying here until I've done my exams. Then I'm supposed to go to my mum's for the holidays, and after that I'm meant to decide where I want to live."

He sighed and nodded his head. "You don't sound very keen on the idea."

"I'm not." I lowered my head. "Tara thinks it's going to be fun... that we'll be like sisters. She doesn't seem to understand how it feels."

"That's because Tara only ever sees things from her own point of view," he replied.

"Doesn't everybody?" I looked up at him again.

"No." He put his hand in mine and led me over to the rocks, where we sat down and he took off his jacket, putting it around my shoulders. "You're cold," he murmured.

"I ran out of the flat in such a hurry, I didn't think to bring a coat."

We stayed like that for a while, just sitting together, neither of us speaking, or even feeling the need to. Eventually, though, he turned to me. "What do you think you'll do?" he asked.

I shrugged. "Get through my exams, I suppose."

"And then?"

"At the moment, I'm not sure. I don't really feel like I even want to visit them. It seems to me that Mum and Mr Kellow have been so selfish in all of this. They haven't thought about what their actions will do to anyone else… not Tara, not my dad, and not me. Tara's okay with it, but…" I stopped talking, feeling the tears starting up again.

"You're not." Josh finished my sentence for me.

"No."

"No-one says you have to go." I turned to him and he was looking right at me. "You can delay visiting your mum, or you can just say you don't want to go. It's up to you."

"Is that what you think I should do?" I asked, looking for guidance. He gave me a very slight smile. "I can't tell you what to do, Abbie."

"I wish you would." I sighed. "I wish someone would."

"You have to decide this for yourself," he said gently, putting his arm around me again. "And you have to do what's right for you. Not for your dad, or your mum, or Tara… or me." I looked up at him again. "Because, whatever they all think, this is about you."

Chapter Two

Josh

That was the moment. At least, that was the moment I knew for certain. I'd suspected for a while – quite a long while really. Maybe even years. But that was the moment I knew. I was in love with Abbie Fuller.

Just the thought of trying to live without her was like having my heart ripped out and stamped over – by a herd of charging wildebeest. The reality of her leaving, I knew, would be so much worse.

And yet, I couldn't tell her to stay. I couldn't even ask her to… for all kinds of reasons.

First and foremost, there was the reason I'd given her. She had to decide for herself what to do, and that choice had to be right for her, and no-one else. Me asking – well, begging – her to stay and telling her why I needed her to wasn't going to help, and besides, I wasn't ready to tell her how I felt. I was too scared of having my feelings shot down in flames.

There was also the fact that she was angry. She didn't actually tell me that, but it was obvious – at least, it was to me. She was angry with her mum for betraying her dad, and with Devin too. She was angry with her dad for not trying harder – or that's how she saw it, anyway. And she was angry with Tara for being so indifferent to everyone's feelings but her own. Abbie needed to calm down, to put those dark feelings behind her, before she made the decision. She needed to take some time and take stock, and maybe letting her mum leave and putting some distance between herself and the 'problem' was a good idea.

It certainly felt like it at the time.

We made it through our exams, although how Abbie managed to focus, I don't know, considering what she'd gone through. But she did.

And then she made the decision that she wasn't going to visit her mum. She was going to stay in Porthgowan. We didn't really talk about it that much, she just came and found me one day right at the beginning of that long summer break between school and college, and told me. She didn't seem to want to explain, and I didn't ask. I just offered up my thanks to anyone who happened to be listening. She was still here. She wasn't leaving. Everything was right with the world.

I questioned the 'why'. Of course I did. In my own head, that is. I didn't think for one second that her decision had anything to do with me, but I reasoned that maybe her anger with her mother hadn't died down, maybe she felt guilty about leaving her dad. Maybe she was even worried she'd prefer Padstow, and she'd want to stay there, but that abandoning him would be too hard. As I say, we didn't discuss it.

In her shoes, if someone had given me a way to leave, I'd have been packing my bags and running for the hills, providing I could have taken her with me, of course. Because, all my life, as far back as I could remember, I'd wanted nothing more than to get out of the village.

That probably makes it sound like I hated the place. I didn't. I actually really liked it. I liked the quietness, especially out of season, when there weren't so many tourists around, and we had the village to ourselves. I loved the beach, the seclusion, the sound of the waves, the security and solitude of just 'being'. I liked the quaint layout, the way the tiny lane – The Street – led off of the main road at the top of the hill and meandered down to the cove, with the pub and the art gallery at the bottom, bypassing a few houses en route, some in Cornish stone, and others rendered and painted in pastel tones. At the bottom of the hill, were the art gallery and the pub – The Lobster Pot – and beyond that lay the tiny cove, its sandy beach surrounded by high, ragged cliffs, and the small car park, housed between two low walls, providing spaces for about a hundred or so vehicles. During the winter, it was empty most of the time, but in summer, it was packed, with cars sometimes queuing down The Street, their exhaust fumes belching, their occupants hoping in vain that a space would miraculously appear upon their arrival. There were three shops behind the car park, on the opposite side of the road: a chemists, which did a roaring trade in sun lotion, bite cream and plasters during the summer, and survived on local prescriptions and the need for paracetamol and cough medicine for the rest of the year; a gift shop, which sold everything from long sticks of pink rock, to sun hats and buckets and spades, as well as an array of some of the ugliest porcelain figurines, with the word 'Porthgowan' painted on them, as evidence of a visit; and finally, there was a general store, where you could purchase most basic food items, from a small selection of fresh fruit and vegetables, to milk, cream and the local papers… not to mention ice cream, from a freezer cabinet, kept just inside the front door. On the opposite corner to the pub, was the post office, which was run by my mother. We lived above the 'shop', which also sold stationery supplies, wrapping paper, greetings cards and, in the summer months, had a display of postcards for sale outside, showing Porthgowan, and the surrounding area to their best advantage. Beyond the post office was probably my favourite shop in the village. Not that it was really a 'shop'. It was a pottery, run by Henry Kemp, and it was made up of his workshop at the rear and a small showroom at the front, where he displayed his wares. Unlike a lot of similar places in seaside and tourist resorts, Henry didn't go for outlandish designs and unnecessary frippery. He produced useful things: plates, cups, bowls, dishes… things you could actually eat off of, and cook with. As long as you didn't mind the fact that no two items were ever the same, even when they were meant to form part of a supposedly matching set, then Henry's pottery was perfect. For myself, I didn't mind at all. I loved its originality, its quirkiness and the way it felt in my hands… the rough and the smooth, the irregular surfaces and uneven finish. I loved the imperfections.

So what was it that made me want to leave this idyllic place, where I felt so at peace, so at home and so calm? The simple answer was… my mother.

She'd resented me since the day I was born. I was her 'mistake', her 'embarrassment'. I should never have happened. But I did, and the man involved did what a lot of men do in similar circumstances and disappeared into thin air, almost the moment my mother told him of my anticipated arrival. From that day on, she blamed me – seemingly for my own conception, and everything else that she could think of.

By the time I reached the age of ten, she'd verbally beaten the confidence out of me, to the point where my teenage years were always destined to be filled with even more angst and confusion than even the average hormonally charged young man, trying to find his way.

My one salvation throughout all of that, was my friends – and in particular, Abbie. She arrived in the village when I was nearly eight; herself confused and bewildered by the changes being forced upon her. She'd come from London and, although I'd never been there, I'd seen it on television, in detective dramas and on the news, and I couldn't imagine anywhere more different from Porthgowan. To her, it must have seemed as though she'd been dropped on the moon.

She adapted though, and quickly became part of our little group. Unlike Tara, who I always thought of as a bit bossy and self-opinionated, Abbie was quiet and shy. She liked to draw and was very good at it. I remember once, when we were sitting on the beach – we were probably eleven or twelve at the time – and she was sketching something in pencil, she looked over at me and smiled, and said she loved it here. I asked why, and she said, "Look…" and pointed upwards with her pencil, waving it around, "… there's so much sky."

That seemed like such an odd thing to say. There's sky everywhere, after all, but I had to smile back at her, just because of the way she said it. Abbie had that effect on me, even then.

So, she stayed. She didn't leave; not even for a short visit to her mother in Padstow, and to me, that felt like a miracle… like deliverance.

Of course, lacking in self-confidence and living in the certainty that she could never be interested in someone like me, I didn't act on it. I kept my feelings to myself and we continued to spend our days on the beach, recovering from the excesses of revision and stress, wallowing instead in the breathless delight of doing absolutely nothing, or in reading, just for the sheer pleasure of turning a page, without having to worry about remembering every little detail that he been printed on its predecessors.

I'd sit and watch Abbie for hours, content just in those moments, taking in the way the sun shone on her chestnut coloured hair, her amber eyes sparkling when she smiled, the little furrow above her nose, that formed when she was concentrating on something, and how, when she clasped her pencil between her teeth, which she sometimes did, her lips would touch it gently, briefly, just for a second, before she'd release it and start to draw again.

We didn't just sit. We'd swim together too – like we always had. Only now it wasn't about races, and ducking each other under the waves, and who could splash who first; now it was a struggle not to get caught gazing at her perfect figure, at the way her costume hugged the contours of her body. Now I had to hold myself back from caressing her soft tanned skin, especially when she sat beside me, water droplets spilling down her long legs, urging me to lick them.

It wasn't an urge I could act on. Fear of rejection saw to that. But that didn't mean I was going to give up the pleasure and torment of spending every second of my spare time with her.

I soon had less spare time than before though, because I found myself a job. Well, that's not strictly true. The job found me. Abbie's dad came into the shop one day, to give my mum a postcard that he wanted put in the window, to advertise for someone to help out in the kitchens at the pub. I saw it, and when he left, I followed him and walked back to the pub by his side, asking him about the vacancy. He was looking for someone to help with washing up – nothing difficult or strenuous. I was already sixteen, due to be seventeen in the October after we started at college, and my time was free. Before we even arrived back at the door of The Lobster Pot, we'd shaken hands and I had a part-time job, working lunchtimes at the weekends and on Tuesdays and Thursdays.

In my own mind, I thought it might mean I'd see more of Abbie. In reality, my decision had the opposite effect. Of course, she wasn't going to hang around the pub kitchens, just because I was there. So, while I was up to my elbows in greasy pots and pans, she was keeping herself entertained elsewhere, as I discovered when I came out of the pub one Saturday afternoon late in August and saw her walking up the hill, holding hands with Andrew Trelawny. They may have had their backs to me, but I'd have known Abbie anywhere. I think I'd have known her even if I was wearing a blindfold. And as for Andrew, there was no mistaking him. He was very different to Simon… Tall, dark, with pale skin and slightly brooding eyes, he was probably my worst nightmare. Not only was he older than me, and therefore probably more interesting and attractive to Abbie – and every other girl in the village – but he had a car. It may only have been a second hand Ford Fiesta that had definitely seen better days, but it was still a car, and that meant freedom. The freedom to go anywhere and do anything, without relying on the hourly bus service to Helston.

I swore under my breath and wandered down to the beach, sitting on the rocks and staring out to sea, trying very hard not to imagine Andrew's lips on Abbie's, his hands on her soft skin, touching her in the places I'd only dreamed of. My plan didn't work very well, however, and my mood deepened.

I suppose it was a couple of hours later when I became aware of a shadow, blocking the sunlight and glanced up. For a moment, I was blinded by the setting sun and thought it was Abbie standing in front of me, but then I realised the shape was all wrong. Abbie was taller than this girl, and her hair was straighter. I focused and recognised Sara Towers.

"Hello," she murmured.

"Hi." She stood for a second or two, and then dropped down and sat beside me. I wondered why. She'd never done that before, and it wasn't like I'd invited her to.

She was wearing skimpy shorts and a top, and her legs were tanned, but they weren't as long and shapely as Abbie's. "What are you doing?" she asked.

"Nothing."

"Do you often sit here doing nothing?" I turned to look at her, noticing the change in her voice. It was quieter all of a sudden, and a note or two lower.

"Yes."

She let her eyes settle on mine. "How about we sit and do nothing together?" she suggested.

And, as the memory of Abbie and Andrew walking hand-in-hand together flashed across my brain, I couldn't think of a single reason not to say, "Alright then."

I didn't actually ask Sara to go out with me, we just sort of ended up together, and for the next week or so, it seemed that every time I turned around, she was there. She was like a constant shadow – and not in a good way. She held my hand whenever we walked anywhere, sat right next to me if she got a chance, waited for me outside the pub when I finished work. We didn't kiss though. I got the feeling she wanted us to, but I was a lot less sure about that. After all, she wasn't Abbie. And I always felt as though I'd been saving my first kiss for her.

I barely saw Abbie in those last few days of the holiday, as August became September and the beginning of term beckoned. If I wasn't working, she was with Andrew – or so it seemed to me. We met up a couple of times on the beach, but then it seemed Sara would come along and drag me off somewhere, almost like she had a sixth sense for Abbie's presence – and my enjoyment of it.

I did see Abbie on the last Friday of the holidays and we managed to have a drink together, in the new coffee shop that had opened up where the art gallery used to be, next door to the pub. Andrew was working and I had no idea where Sara was – I didn't care either. Abbie was sitting opposite me, and that was all that mattered.

We talked about college for a while. She seemed enthusiastic about going and I wondered for a minute if she was bored. I knew I was. Sara was driving me insane.

Abbie was going to be studying Art, English and History, while I was doing Media Studies, Business and Economics. We wouldn't be seeing much of each other during the day, but I had high hopes for our lunch breaks. I knew the bus ride might be awkward, being as the college was on the same campus as our old school, and Sara – who was a year younger, and just going into year eleven – would be riding to and from school with us. But lunchtimes together were better than nothing – or so I kept telling myself.

"How are things going with Sara?" Abbie asked out of the blue and I nearly choked on my coffee, putting the cup down carefully.

"Okay." I wasn't about to ask the same question of her and Andrew. I didn't want to know the answer.

"She likes you," she said, looking down at her cup.

"Does she?" I didn't think I could have sounded more bored if I'd tried. It wasn't an act either. I wasn't bored with Abbie, but talking about Sara wasn't my idea of fun.

"I saw her earlier. She said you're taking her to the pictures tonight."

I'd forgotten about that. "Yes."

"I went with Andrew last weekend," she remarked, twirling the spoon in her saucer now. "We saw *The Mummy*, but if I'm being honest, I didn't like it very much."

I wanted to ask if she was referring to the film, or seeing it with Andrew, but then I didn't want to know that either. I could only imagine the sort of things Andrew got up to at the cinema – and I doubted they had very much to do with watching movies.

"I don't know what we're going to see," I replied, avoiding the question. "I told Sara she can choose."

"That's nice of you." She looked up and smiled, and I wished things could be different.

Sara chose a movie called *Never Been Kissed*, which struck me as slightly ironic, being as I hadn't been, although I wasn't sure I could say the same about Sara; but then I wasn't interested enough for it to worry me. I should have known she'd choose something romantic though, and my only saving grace was that there was an element of humour to the film as well, so it wasn't all hearts and flowers, thank goodness.

We caught the bus home afterwards and she spent the whole journey talking about the film, about how wonderful it had been, how romantic it was when Sam finally appeared at the end and granted Josie's wish, kissing her in the middle of the baseball field. I nodded my head when it seemed appropriate and tried to make the right noises, helping her off the bus and letting her take my hand when we walked down the hill.

Sara lived in one of the last houses before the bend in the road, just a couple of doors up from the pub, and I walked her to her gate. Outside, she turned and looked up at me.

"I've had a lovely evening," she said, doing that thing with her voice again.

"Me too." It had been better than sitting at home with my mother, being shouted at, but 'lovely' was probably stretching it. Still, she didn't want to hear that.

I was about to move away, when she put her hands on my upper arms and leant up, attaching her lips to mine. She held them there for about ten seconds, seemingly expecting me to do something, and then she pulled back again. My initial reaction was one of relief, mainly that she'd stopped kissing me, but also that we hadn't butted heads, or clashed teeth. I hadn't made a fool of myself, thank God. Even so, it wasn't what I'd wanted from my first kiss. Not in the slightest. There was no passion, no romance. There was no Abbie.

"I've been longing for you to do that," Sara whispered.

I wanted to point out that I hadn't done anything, that she'd kissed me, not the other way around, but at that moment, I turned and noticed Abbie, sitting on one of the benches at the front of the pub. She was staring at us and, in the lights that hung from the outside of The Lobster Pot, I could see an odd expression on her face. It looked like she was angry, or upset maybe, but that didn't make sense to me. Why would she be either of those things, because I was kissing Sara? Or because Sara was kissing me, to be more precise. She was dating Andrew. Even as I was trying to work that out, Abbie stood up and disappeared around the corner of the building, and I looked back at Sara again. She was staring down the hill too, the expression on her face one of sheer satisfaction. It was an unmistakeable smugness. And it was ugly.

"I'm sorry," I said, taking a step back.

"What for?" She tilted her head and looked up at me, evidently confused.

"I can't see you anymore."

Her mouth dropped open. "What do you mean?"

"Just that. I don't want to keep seeing you."

"But why, Josh?"

I wondered what to say, whether to try and sugar coat it, but then I decided on the truth and lowered my voice, whispering, "Because I'm not into playing games."

She swallowed hard and looked down at the space I'd put between us, and I knew I was right. For some reason she wanted to score points over Abbie, or detract from our friendship. And I wasn't about to let that happen. Even if all we ever had was friendship, Abbie meant more to me than anyone else ever could. I shook my head and turned around, walking away from Sara and feeling the relief wash over me.

The next day, Abbie was already on the beach when I got there. She was sitting in our usual spot, on a rug, laid out on the sand, her bag by her side and her sketchpad resting on her knees.

She didn't glance up as I approached, or even acknowledge me when I sat down beside her. Was she still angry?

"I've broken up with Sara," I whispered, keeping my gaze fixed on the horizon.

"How?"

I turned to her. Her question seemed odd. "I just told her," I said.

"Just like that?"

"Yes."

"Why?" She was staring at me now, those two little furrows settled on her brow, above her nose, like it was me she was concentrating on, me she was trying to read and fathom out.

"She was playing games." I had to be honest. "I didn't like it."

Her face cleared and she turned, reaching into her bag and bringing out a can of cold coke, which she handed to me. "I brought this for you," she said, and I remembered all the times she'd done that before, going right back almost to when she'd first arrived in the village.

I opened the can and took a long drink, wondering how she'd known I'd be there. It wasn't like we met regularly anymore. But then I realised it didn't matter. The point was, she was there, and so was I. And everything was right with the world. Again.

"What are you drawing?" I asked her and she tilted her sketchpad in my direction and leant into me slightly, stealing my breath as she showed me an unmistakeable image of myself.

"You've drawn me?"

She nodded. "It's not very good. I don't usually draw people."

"It is good," I replied. "Well, it looks like me, anyway."

She turned the pad back around. "Oh, I'm not sure," she said, sounding doubtful. "I don't think I've got your nose quite right."

"Well, you haven't made me look like Pinocchio, so that's alright."

She giggled and went back to shading and I sat there watching, comfortable in her presence, as usual, as though my time with Sara, my temporary insanity, had never occurred.

Of course, she was still seeing Andrew, and on our first day back at college, that fact reared its ugly head for all to see. With hindsight, I suppose it became the day that changed everything between Abbie and me – but at the time I didn't appreciate that.

Simon took the bus with us. We hadn't seen much of him over the summer; he'd got work at a nearby campsite over the holidays, cycling there in the mornings and coming back late in the afternoons. It seemed that whenever he was free, I was working, and then later on, I think he felt awkward spending time with Abbie when she was going out with Andrew – that certainly seemed to be the case, based on his comments when we boarded the bus that first morning.

"What on earth are you doing going out with my brother?" he asked, sitting down in the seat in front of us and turning around, his eyes fixed on Abbie. She blushed and shrugged her shoulders, not replying. "You know he's a loser, don't you?" I wondered if he was talking out of concern for her, or a sense of superiority, that he'd managed to pass his GCSEs, when his brother had failed so badly.

Again, Abbie didn't respond and, after Simon's third question, I told him to leave her alone. I wasn't defending Andrew and I didn't like the idea of Abbie seeing him any more than Simon did, by the sounds of things, but there was no point in browbeating her. She'd decided to go out with him, and that was that.

That afternoon, Andrew was waiting at the gates, in his old Ford Fiesta. It felt as though he was staking a claim; reminding us that Abbie was his… and that there was nothing any of us could do about it. And as Abbie walked over to him, it seemed like he was right.

Chapter Three

Abbie

Taking the decision to stay in Porthgowan and not go to even visit my mother, Devin and Tara in Padstow, was really hard. It was one of the hardest things I'd ever had to do. But when the time came, I knew I wasn't ready. I was still too angry with Mum. I was even angrier with Devin. And I wasn't especially pleased with Tara. I wasn't ready to forgive either, and I sat down with my dad and explained it to him, the day after I finished my last GCSE. I might not have put it in those exact words, because I knew he'd probably try and tell me it wasn't Mum's fault. But after I'd said my piece, he told me he understood, and said he'd go and phone Mum, and let her know. Twenty minutes later, he came back. He said he'd made the call, and then said he had to get down to the bar to open up. I didn't ask how Mum had reacted. I assumed if it had been good, he'd have told me. And if it had been bad, I didn't want to know.

I went and found Josh after that. He was on the beach as usual and I told him I was staying. He didn't ask why and I was grateful for that. I didn't want to talk about it anymore. Talking about it wasn't going to solve anything, and I didn't want him to think badly of me for being so cross and unforgiving. They're not very attractive character traits, after all.

We spent most of the summer together, Josh and I. Simon had taken a job at the campsite just outside the next village. He could cycle there and back, and the pay was good, evidently. Tara was gone of course.

It ought to have felt different with it just being the two of us, but it didn't. Josh and I had been thrown together during the summer of Mrs Trelawny's illness and it felt like we'd been best friends ever since.

We swam, we sat, we talked, Josh read, I drew. It was relaxing after the stress of revision and exams. And then, about half way through the holidays, Josh started working at the pub. That meant we spent less time together, because he was working – and I missed him. I missed him more than I was willing to admit to anyone; even myself. I couldn't tell him, of course. I think he was enjoying his first taste of independence and I wouldn't have done anything to jeopardise that.

It was during one of my solitary lunchtimes on the beach, that Andrew Trelawny came over to me. He was with another boy I didn't know. I'd seen him around with Andrew a few times, but I had no idea of his name, or how they knew each other. I assumed they probably worked together at the brewery, but why they'd come to see me, I had no idea. I wasn't sure I'd spoken more than a dozen words to Andrew since I'd arrived in the village ten years earlier.

They stood for a few moments, with me looking up at them, shielding my eyes from the sun, feeling confused by their presence. Then Andrew took a half step forward.

"D'ya wanna go out wi' me?"

To start with, I wasn't sure what he'd said and I wondered about asking him to repeat himself, but then it dawned on me. He was asking me out. His friend was standing behind him, looking expectant.

"Um… okay."

The words were out of my mouth before I had the chance to stop them.

"Pick you up later," Andrew said. "Seven o'clock."

And with that, he was gone.

I thought about calling him back and telling him I'd made a mistake. But he was already half way back to the sea wall, his friend laughing beside him. I felt uneasy about that, but then it wasn't his friend who'd asked me out. It was Andrew.

That evening, he picked me up as promised, and drove us to a pub in the next village. I wasn't old enough to drink, but we sat outside and he bought me a coke, having a pint of beer himself. A couple of his friends were there – although not the one who'd been with him earlier, I was pleased to say. These two were no less juvenile though, and they all spent the evening joking and fooling around. Luckily, Andrew didn't drink too much and drove me home safely. My dad was clearing the tables when we got back, and I jumped out of the car before Andrew had the chance to kiss me.

"I'm working tomorrow," he called as I ran inside. "But I'll see you Saturday?"

I wasn't sure I wanted to, but I waved over my shoulder, just to be friendly.

On Saturday, Andrew came and found me on the beach. "I just called at the pub. Your dad said you'd be here," he murmured, sitting down beside me. "What're you drawing?"

"Nothing." I closed my sketchpad and put it away in my bag.

"Let's go for a walk then." He jumped back up to his feet again, and held out his hand. It seemed rude to ignore him, so I took it and we walked hand-in-hand back past the pub, which just reminded me of Josh and how I'd much rather have been spending my Saturday afternoon with him, once he'd finished work. Not surprisingly, we didn't stop, and continued on up the hill, until we got to Andrew's house, which didn't strike me as much of a 'walk'.

"Why are we stopping?" I asked him.

"I thought we could get a drink."

He opened the garden gate and walked through, leaving me to follow. Feeling doubtful, I hesitated but then stepped in behind him, just as the front door opened, and his mother stood, facing us.

"What are you doing here?" Andrew said. "I thought you and Dad were going into Falmouth today."

"We were, but I felt tired, so we decided to leave it until next weekend. I saw you coming in the gate and thought I'd open the door for you." She glanced over his shoulder at me, and smiled. "Hello, Abbie. How are you?"

"I'm very well, Mrs Trelawny. How are you?"

"Not too bad." She stood to one side. "Are you coming in?"

"No," Andrew said, turning.

"But I thought…" I looked up at him, his dark eyes blazing beneath his thatch of almost black hair. I closed my mouth. "I've got to be getting back," I murmured.

"Oh." Mrs Trelawny seemed confused – but nowhere near as confused as I felt.

Once she'd closed the door and we were back on The Street, I turned to Andrew. "I thought we were going to get a drink," I remarked.

"We were. But I didn't want to sit with my mother."

"Why not? There's nothing wrong with your mother."

"You don't have to live with her," he mumbled and we walked back down the hill. He left me by the pub and I stood watching him amble away, wondering why he'd bothered coming to find me in the first place.

Although Andrew continued to call every so often, and we went back to the pub in the next village a couple of times, I can't say I ever looked forward to our time together and was starting to wonder how I could tell him I didn't want to see him anymore. He wasn't the easiest of people to speak to though and, in all honestly, I couldn't complain about his behaviour. He hadn't even tried to kiss me, which I have to say was a huge relief, because I wasn't looking forward to the time when he did.

I was seeing less and less of Josh by then, although we did find time for a coffee on the Friday before we started at college. He'd been going out with Sara Towers for about a week by then, I suppose. I was surprised by that – well, to a certain extent, anyway. Sara had been keen on Josh for a while and had made no secret of it, but that he should have asked her out threw me a little. Sara could be quite manipulative and had a bit of a reputation in school for playing people off against each other. I wouldn't have thought Josh would go for a girl like that, but then I figured he was probably just as surprised that I'd said 'yes' to Andrew as well. I still hadn't worked that one out for myself, even though I'd been seeing him for a couple of weeks.

That evening, I knew Josh and Sara were going to the cinema. Andrew had been going out with some of his friends from work – which I wasn't complaining about – and I'd spent some of my time watching television. It was warm though, so I'd come downstairs and was sitting on one of the benches outside the pub, when I saw Josh and Sara coming down the hill. They were holding hands and, although I don't know why, I couldn't take my eyes off of them.

They reached Sara's house, which wasn't too far up the hill from the pub, and even as I sat there, staring, they moved closer together, and then they kissed. In the darkness, it was hard to tell who kissed who, but it didn't matter – not to me. For some reason that I couldn't fathom, it hurt to see them like that. It felt like I'd lost a part of myself, like it had been cleaved from me, leaving a gaping chasm, a wound I felt would never heal.

It wasn't a long kiss, and as they parted, Josh turned. I don't know why, but he did, and our eyes seemed to meet. I couldn't see him clearly, but I imagined with me sitting under the outside lights of the pub, he'd be able to see me well enough, and the last thing I needed was for him to notice me crying, because I was by then. Even though it made no sense – I was going out with Andrew, after all – the sight of him kissing Sara, was more than I could handle. I got to my feet and went around the side of the building, leaning against the wall, clutching my arms around my stomach and sobbing, long silent tears.

A while later, I heard footsteps walking past. I wondered if it was Josh and prayed he'd keep going; that he wouldn't find me crying over something that even I didn't understand.

The next day, I went to the beach early, wanting to make that connection with the place I'd come to love so much, to feel its warm embrace, its comfort and security. I sat for a while and, although I usually drew something scenic, I found myself sketching Josh's face, tracing the lines of his high cheekbones, his square jaw, his straight nose – although I struggled with that and had to keep going over it. I wished I could have done justice to his features, but I wasn't sure that was even possible. After all, you can't recreate perfection, can you?

I was concentrating hard, trying to shade around his eyes, when I felt him sit beside me. I knew it was him without needing to look up.

He told me he'd split up with Sara, and I instantly knew I'd found the missing part of myself again. In that instant I was mended; I was whole once more.

I asked him how he'd done it; how he'd broken up with her, and he said, "I just told her." And I wanted to ask him if he thought that would work on Andrew too. I didn't. I didn't want to talk about Andrew. Josh asked about my picture and seemed surprised I'd drawn him. I suppose it ought to have been embarrassing, but it wasn't. I'd never been embarrassed with Josh, not properly, anyway, and we sat there together, while I sketched and he watched me… just like we always did.

Our first day at college was different to anything I'd expected, and it was a day I'll never forget.

I really enjoyed my lessons. I was studying Art, English and History – the first of those being a necessity as far as I was concerned, and the second two having been my favourite subjects at school. I still found the art classes a little restrictive, but Miss Grady was a better teacher than Mr Dodds, who'd taught us for years ten and eleven and had very limited ideas as to creativity. He seemed to spend most of his time trying to get us to rein in our imaginations, instead of letting them go.

The other big change was that Josh, Simon and I saw so much less of each other. We were all studying different subjects, so we only met up on the morning bus ride and at lunchtime. We should have been able to ride home together as well, but much to my surprise, at the end of our first day, when we reached the school gates, Andrew was waiting for me. Well, I say 'Andrew'… what I actually mean is, he was in his car, waiting for me. He hadn't got out, or anything, and as I appeared, he tooted his horn, attracting everyone's attention, including mine.

I wanted to die of embarrassment, especially as Simon and Josh were with me. Simon had only been questioning my sanity that morning on the journey into college, asking why I was seeing his brother, and I'd found it hard to justify myself to him. It wasn't that I thought he had no right to ask, but that I genuinely couldn't think of a reason why I was still dating Andrew – other than the fact that I was too much of a coward to end it, of course. Simon seemed just as bemused as myself and kept on about it, until Josh told him to leave me alone. I was grateful for that, mainly because I didn't have any answers.

I left Josh and Simon at the gates, and went over to Andrew. What choice did I have? I was worried that if I didn't, he'd eventually get out and come over, and probably make a scene.

"Get in," he said, without so much as a 'Hello,' or a 'How was your first day?'.

"Shall I get Simon and Josh?" I asked.

"Why?" He seemed perplexed by my question.

"Well… if you're going to take me home, we can take them too, can't we?"

He hesitated for a moment. "They're big enough to make their own way." He glanced up at me, putting the car in gear already. "Get in."

I looked back at Josh and Simon, and waved, giving them a smile. Josh smiled back. Simon didn't, and I got into the car just as Andrew drove away with an unnecessary screech of tyres, forcing me back into my seat.

"Slow down," I urged.

"I'm only doing thirty." He wasn't; he was doing at least forty-five.

I put my bag down into the footwell and tried to get comfortable for the twenty-five minute journey home – although if he continued to drive so fast, I doubted it would take that long to get back to the village. I realised though that I wasn't sorry about that, and decided to keep quiet about his speeding.

"Why aren't you at work?" I asked.

"I got the afternoon off," he replied as we came up to the mini-roundabout, and he indicated left instead of right.

"Um… where are we going?" I looked across at him as he took the turning.

"It's a surprise. That's why I took the afternoon off." He glanced over at me and placed his hand on my leg, and for the first time I felt a frisson of fear. My dad had bought me my first mobile phone for my birthday the previous July, but I didn't take it into college – phones were strictly forbidden on the premises and I didn't want to have it confiscated. However, at that moment, I wished I'd had it with me, even if only so I could have threatened to use it if he didn't take me home. As it was, I felt powerless… and increasingly scared, as Andrew drove me away from the village.

"W—Where are you taking me?" I stuttered.

"Somewhere nice," he replied. "Don't look so worried. You'll like it."

I didn't feel reassured by that, but other than jumping from a moving vehicle, I didn't see what else I could do, apart from wait to see where we were going, and hope for the best.

We'd only been driving for about ten minutes when he slowed down and indicated right, stopping to allow two cars to pass, before turning into a holiday park. At the front, near the road, was an office and a shop, with a few parking spaces. We drove straight past those and on into the main body of the park, which featured static caravans and mobile homes, and a few log cabins.

"What are we doing here?" I felt my stomach lurch and my palms dampen.

"A friend of mine rents a caravan here," he replied, as though that was a sufficient explanation. I wondered why someone who he knew, and who presumably lived or worked in the area, would need to rent a caravan… and then I realised how naive I was being and I shifted in my seat, moving closer to the door.

"Stop the car," I said, raising my voice.

"I will," he said, grinning. "In a minute."

He drove through the centre of the park, checking the numbers on the sides of the static holiday homes, until he clearly found what he was looking for – a large green painted caravan, with a cream coloured stripe around the centre. The curtains were drawn across the windows and, unlike a lot of the other caravans and mobile homes surrounding it, this one looked rather unloved. There were no flowers planted in raised tubs, no small picket fences, no tables and chairs. It looked depressing and, to me, absolutely terrifying.

"I don't know what you've got in mind…" I did. I knew exactly what he had in mind. I just wasn't brave enough to say it. "But I want to go home."

"You know you don't mean that." He smirked and got out of the car, coming around to my side. He'd chosen today of all days to be a gentleman and open the car door for me. Well, I wasn't getting out, not if I could help it, so I sat on my hands, clamping them beneath my thighs. The only way he was going to get me out of there was by dragging me… and I wasn't going to go quietly, either.

"C'mon then," he said, his arm resting on top of the open door. I shook my head. "Abbie, c'mon… I don't have all day." He stepped forward and leant into the car.

"I'm not getting out."

"Yes, you are." He started to tug on me and, despite my determination not to move, I could feel his weight shifting me. I pulled the other way, fear giving me strength, but he re-doubled his efforts. "Stop fucking around, will you?" He raised his voice.

"No!" I yelled.

"What's going on here?"

Andrew stopped dead and stood up, and I glanced out of the windscreen, looking at the man who was walking towards us; the man who'd just spoken. He was well-built, probably in his mid-thirties, with dark hair and a concerned expression on his face.

"Nothing," Andrew replied.

"It doesn't look like nothing," the man said, approaching the car now. He looked at me. "Are you alright?"

I shook my head. "No."

"I think you should step away from the young lady," the man said, looking back at Andrew now.

"And I think you should fuck off and mind your own business," Andrew replied.

"What's wrong, Matt?" A woman appeared from around the next mobile home, carrying a small child.

The man didn't answer her. He didn't even turn around. Instead, he kept his eyes on Andrew. "Step away from the young lady and let her get out of the car," he said, his voice still and calm.

"And if I don't?" Andrew's voice was shaking, although I'm not sure why. He may have been afraid, or just unsure of himself, faced as he was with two adults who seemed to have worked out that he was up to no good.

"Then I'll call the police," the man replied, pulling a mobile phone from his pocket at the same time.

"For fuck's sake." Andrew paused just for a second, and then leant into the car. The man stepped forward, but he was too late and I felt myself being hauled out and dumped onto the ground, my bag thrown down beside me. "She's not worth it anyway," Andrew shouted, and then jumped back into the car and drove off, kicking up mud and grass at me as the tyres spun.

The man and woman were beside me in moments.

"Matt," the woman said, "take Oliver." The man took the child – who I now presumed to be his own son, while the woman knelt down next to me. "Are you alright?" she asked. "Are you hurt?"

"No." I wasn't hurt, but I wasn't alright either. I was scared and shocked.

"Let's get you up," she said and got to her feet, helping me to stand. My legs felt wobbly, but I managed, and looked around me, I think to make sure Andrew had really gone. There was no sign of him, and while I knew I should have felt relieved, I just wanted to go home.

As though she sensed that, the woman came and stood in front of me, leaning down slightly, as she was quite tall. "Where do you live?" she asked. "Are you local, or on holiday?"

"No, I'm local. I live in Porthgowan."

"That's the pretty village we went to the day before yesterday," she said, smiling. "The one with the nice pub right by the beach?"

I nodded my head. "I live at the pub."

Her smile broadened. "Well, what a small world. We had lunch there. The landlord was very friendly. It's our first time in Cornwall and he suggested lots of places for us to visit."

"That's my dad," I replied, feeling tears pricking behind my eyes and wishing I could be with him, could feel his arms around me, knowing he'd keep me safe. The problem was, I could never tell him about what had just happened. He'd probably want to kill Andrew – or at the very least do him a few serious, permanent, life-changing injuries.

"I can take you home, if you'd like?" the woman said. "My name's Nicky. This is my husband, Matt… and our son, Oliver."

"Nice to meet you." I nodded my head.

She held out her hand, although I don't think she expected me to take it. "Come with us," she said. "We're staying in one of the log cabins. Our car's parked just outside it, and I'll take you home… unless you'd like to stay and have a drink or something first?"

I shook my head. "No, thank you. I—I'd rather just get home. Sorry… I…"

She smiled. "There's no need to apologise. In your shoes, I'd feel the same way."

Matt turned and started walking, and Nicky followed. I picked up my bag and went with them, thankful that they'd been there to save me.

Nicky drove me back, only needing a couple of reminders for which directions to take. On the journey, she told me that I could still call the police if I wanted to – especially if Andrew caused any trouble.

"Have you got some paper in your bag?" she asked. "And a pen?"

"Yes." I wasn't sure why she was asking, but I pulled out my English folder and a biro.

"Write this down…" She proceeded to give me an address in West Sussex, and a telephone number. "That's where we live," she explained. "And that's our home number." I was staring at her, and I must have been looking confused, because she glanced over at me, and smiled. "If you do decide to go to the police and you need a witness, or anything, give them our details."

I felt the tears forming again, but managed to whisper, "Thank you," to her.

"I was your age once too," she said, as though that was meant to mean something. It didn't – not to me – and she didn't explain it either.

When we got to the turning into The Street, the one that led down into the village, I asked her to let me out.

"Here?" she asked, seemingly surprised as she checked her mirror and pulled over to the side of the road.

"Yes. I think I'd rather walk back from here, rather than have anyone see me being driven back by a stranger. I'm ever so grateful, but…"

"I know," she said, smiling. "People talk in small villages, don't they?"

"Yes." I picked up my bag. "Thank you again for everything you've done for me. You, and your husband."

"It's nothing," she said. "And remember, don't take any nonsense from that boy. And if you do decide to go to the police, you know where we are."

"Thank you."

She nodded her head and smiled, and I climbed out of the car. With a wave, she drove off, and I crossed the road, about to start walking down the lane into the village, my thoughts elsewhere, my mind whirling with images of what might have happened if Matt and Nicky hadn't arrived when they did.

"Abbie?" I looked up at the sound of my own name being called, feeling a chill run down my spine, and then relief washing over me when I saw it wasn't Andrew; it was Josh, sitting on the bench by the bus stop. "Where have you been?" He stood up and walked over to me. "And who was that woman in that car… and what happened to you?" He picked some of the grass from my top, although I hadn't even realised it was there and I looked up at him, at the concern in his eyes, and burst into tears.

He didn't hesitate, not even for a second. He just pulled me into his arms, holding me tight to him and stroking my hair as I rested my head against his chest.

"I was so worried about you," he murmured. "You didn't come back…" I shook my head and he pulled away, looking down at me.

Then he frowned and whispered, "Come with me," and he took my hand in his, leading me down the hill.

As we passed Andrew's house, I felt myself tense, even though his car wasn't there, and Josh gripped my hand a little tighter. I wondered if he knew what had happened – or if he'd guessed, because he couldn't possibly 'know', could he?

We walked straight past the pub and out onto the beach, along to our favourite spot, where we sat on the rocks. Josh took my bag from my shoulder and put it behind me, then held my hand again and turned to me.

"Did Andrew do something to you?" he asked.

"No." I heard his sigh of relief. "But he tried to." I started crying again and he put his arm around my shoulders, holding me as I told him what had happened. I felt his grasp tighten a couple of times, his muscles tensing against me when I told him the things Andrew had said, and the way he'd tried to pull me out of the car. By the end, I was crying again, more out of relief and gratitude towards Nicky and Matt, than anything else, I think.

"It'll be okay," Josh murmured and held onto me until I'd calmed.

"I'm sorry," I whispered eventually.

"What on earth for?" He seemed surprised.

"Crying all over you."

He smiled. "You don't have to say sorry to me."

I looked up at him. "Why not?"

"Friends don't have to say sorry, Abbie. Ever." I put my arms around his waist and held onto him, and he hugged me back.

After a while, I felt him shift slightly and looked up. His face was serious. "What's wrong?" I felt nervous all of a sudden.

"Can I ask you something?" he said and I nodded. "Did Andrew touch you?"

"No," I replied. "I told you what happened."

"I don't mean today," he said, looking into my eyes. "I mean in the past... has he ever touched you, or done anything you weren't comfortable with?" He hesitated, but before I could answer, he went on, "Because, if he has, we need to tell someone."

"He hasn't," I replied.

"Promise?"

"I promise. We hadn't even kissed. That's why this came as such as shock. It just came out of the blue."

He sighed and nodded his head. "Okay."

A thought struck me and I put my hand on his arm, making sure I had his attention. "You can't tell anyone."

"What about your dad?"

"No. Especially not my dad. He'll probably want to kill Andrew…"

"You think I don't?" He stared at me for a moment and then turned away and I jumped off of the rock, moving in front of him and looking up into his troubled face.

"You won't do anything, will you?" I could hear the desperation in my own voice and Josh slid down too, and stood before me. "Promise me you won't…"

"I won't. I promise."

"And you won't tell anyone either? Not my dad… and not Simon."

He paused. "If that's what you want."

"It is. I just want to forget it ever happened."

"And what if Andrew doesn't?" he said. That thought hadn't really occurred to me, despite everything Nicky had said, but it did then and I felt a real, genuine terror creep down my spine. Josh took a step closer. "Don't look so scared," he murmured.

"But, what if he… w—what if he tries again…?"

He shook his head. "Nothing's going to happen to you. I promise."

It was strange, but the fear vanished as quickly as it had come. Josh's words, and the way he'd said them, made me feel safe, just the same as his arm did when he put it around me and walked me home, carrying my bag for me.

The next day, I woke with a start, cold with sweat, my heart pounding with fear. It was all well and good Josh saying nothing would happen to me, but he couldn't guarantee that, could he? He couldn't be by my side, all day every day, ensuring my safety. It simply wasn't practical.

Except, it seemed it was. Because from that day on, when I opened the back door each morning to leave for college, Josh was waiting for me and we walked up the hill to the bus stop together. At lunchtimes, he somehow managed to be outside my classrooms – no matter what the class was – and he'd walk with me to the cafeteria, and sit with me while we ate our lunch. Then, after school, he'd meet me and we'd walk up to the school gates. He'd stand with me, waiting for the bus and sit with me all the way back to the village, then walk me home again.

It was during the second week of term, while I was doing some English homework in my bedroom, that I received a text message on my phone. I rarely received messages, because hardly anyone knew my number and to start off with, I was worried Andrew might have found it out somehow. My hands were shaking as I opened it up, to find it was from Josh.

— *I got myself a phone, so you can call me if you need to. Your dad gave me your number. If you add mine to your contacts list, then you'll know it's me. Josh*

I added his number and then sent him back a message. It just said 'Thank you'.

Josh and I became inseparable over the coming months and and I didn't mind one bit. Maybe that was because I'd realised by then that I was in love with him. I don't know exactly how that came about. It wasn't like a thunderbolt moment or anything. It was just like a slow, steady understanding that I loved him, and that I probably always had done. And it wasn't just because he protected me and made me feel safe – although they were fairly big factors at the time – it was also because he cared and he always put me first. And I wanted to do the same for him. And in my mind, that was what love was about.

We made it through our first year at college, our friendship stronger than ever, our time shared between studies and each other; my heart lost to him. During the summer holidays, Josh increased his hours at The Lobster Pot, still working weekends but also four lunchtimes during the week. He told me, on one of our quiet afternoons, that stretched into early evening, while we were sitting on the beach together, that he'd taken the extra shifts at the pub for two reasons: one was because he'd learned to drive that previous spring and wanted to save up some money to buy a car; the other was because his mother was becoming even more intolerable than usual and he needed to get away from her. He said he knew that working meant he'd see less of me, but he hoped I'd understand. I did. And to make up for it, I helped out occasionally in the kitchens at the pub. The look on Josh's face when I first walked in wearing a 'Lobster Pot' apron, my hair tied up into a white cap, with the pub's logo printed on the front, was an absolute picture – and made up for the fact that I really didn't enjoy working there. Not compared to sitting on the beach and drawing, anyway. Still, it was worth it, just to see the smile on his face.

Simon disappeared from our lives again, taking holiday work at the campsite, just like he had the previous year, so the private time that Josh and I did get, was spent alone, usually on the beach, with him reading and me drawing, sometimes swimming, and sometimes just lying back and looking up at the sky, not even feeling the need to talk, if we didn't want to. As much as I liked Simon – and I did – I wasn't complaining about his absence; not if it meant I got to be with Josh.

I suppose we were about half way through the holidays, when I was woken early one morning by the sound of my mobile phone beeping. I'd forgotten to turn it off the night before and I fumbled, bleary-eyed, in the semi-darkness of my bedroom, trying to find it before it beeped again.

It was in my art bag, which I'd had at the beach the day before, and as I sat back down on the bed, I saw there was a new message for me, and I wondered who on earth could be sending me a text at, what the phone told me, was just after five o'clock in the morning.

I focused on the screen, rubbing the sleep away, yawning, and read:

— *Meet me on the beach, please? J*

I wondered if there had been an argument with his mother, and if he perhaps wanted to meet up and talk about it before his shift at work, so I sent a text back straight away.

— *When? A*

His response was immediate.

— Now.

I was a little disturbed by that response. He obviously didn't want to tell me what had happened in a text, and neither did he want to call me, but whatever it was must be bad if he needed to see me so early in the morning.

I jumped off the bed and dashed to the bathroom, having a quick wash and brushing my teeth, knowing I could shower properly later. Then I went back into my bedroom, pulled on some underwear, together with shorts and a t-shirt, put my hair up in a ponytail and ran out of the door.

Outside, it was a perfect morning. The stillness was breathtaking; everywhere was silent, not a soul having stirred from their beds. The cove was bathed in a pinkish-purple hue, as the night waned and the sun started to rise, seeping through the fragility of the breaking day.

I went down onto the sand and walked along to our spot, where Josh was standing and, as I approached, he turned – almost as though he knew I was there – and started walking towards me. It was hard not to smile, as I took in his dark hair, broad shoulders, hidden from view by a white t-shirt; his narrow hips and long legs, encased in stonewashed jeans. His stride was purposeful and, as he came closer, I saw the intensity of his deep brown eyes.

I stopped and looked up at him, waiting for him to speak, to tell me what had happened.

He didn't. Instead, he reached out with both of his hands, cupping my face and taking the final step, so we were almost touching. So close…

He leant forward and brushed his lips gently against mine, their softness capturing my breath, the contact sparking across every nerve in my body.

Then he pulled away again, gazing into my eyes, and whispered, "Be mine?"

Chapter Four

Josh

She stared up at me and nodded her head, and I bent again, kissing her once more, my tongue flicking against hers, and hers caressing mine in return.

She'd said 'yes' to being mine. I felt as though my happiness was complete, as though my life couldn't possibly get any better than it was at that moment – even though my body was telling me it could. It most definitely could.

Eventually, we broke the kiss, mutually I think, both of us a little breathless, and I looked down into her shining eyes, her cheeks a little flushed, her lips slightly swollen from my kiss. "Mean it?" I asked, just to be certain.

"Yes." She smiled, and I took her hand, leading her back to the rug I'd laid out on the sand and sitting down with her. Without waiting to be asked, and with not a word of encouragement from me, she crawled between my parted legs and leant against me, her back against my chest, my arms tight around her, holding her close, her hands resting gently on my forearms.

"I've wanted to do that for so long," I murmured, kissing the top of her head.

"Which bit?" she asked, twisting and looking up at me, a smile settled on her lips.

"All of it." She grinned and snuggled down again. "I've wanted to ask you to be mine since… since I can't remember when. And I think I've wanted to kiss you for even longer."

She shook her head slowly. "I wish you had," she replied. "I wish you'd asked me before Andrew did…" Her voice faded and I reached down, clasping her chin and turning her to face me. The sadness in her eyes was unmistakable, as was the pain it caused deep in my chest.

"I've never wanted anything more than to take that memory from you," I whispered, cradling her and leaning down, kissing her still swollen lips. "And I will."

"How?" She looked up into my eyes.

"By making you so happy, you can't help but forget it."

She smiled again, her amber eyes sparkling in the early morning light, and I knew I'd never love another woman for as long as I lived, for the very simple reason that she'd filled my heart, and there wasn't room in there for anyone else.

By that stage of the holidays, I was working four weekday lunchtimes, plus weekends in the pub kitchen. I'd needed to escape my mother, who was dropping hints about me leaving home as my eighteenth birthday approached, as though my age made a difference; as though I'd suddenly be able to afford to live by myself somewhere, regardless of the fact that I still had another year of college to see out. I also wanted to save up to buy a car. I'd passed my test in the April, and knew that at least having a vehicle of my own would mean I could escape for afternoons, evenings, and even weekends, to get away from my mother – and I could take Abbie with me, now she'd said she was mine.

Abbie was also working a couple of shifts in the pub kitchen as well, which was a real bonus – because it meant I got to see her, even when I was at work. Our next problem, however, was to decide whether to tell her dad that we were seeing each other, or to try and keep it a secret from him. We both decided, on the slow walk back to The Lobster Pot, as the sun came up and I held her hand in mine, rubbing my thumb along her soft skin, that we didn't want there to be any secrets – we had to tell Robert.

"I'll talk to him," Abbie said, as we reached the back door. "It'll be better coming from me."

"Are you sure? We can do it together."

She shook her head. "No. I'll tell him."

She stood up on the back step, making her the same height as me – well, nearly – and put her arms around my neck, leaning in and kissing me. It was a funny feeling. I'd dreamt of being with Abbie for so long, fantasised about kissing her and holding her until those were the only thoughts in my head, and yet the reality was so different, so much better than even my wildest hopes. She seemed to kind of melt into me, her soft moans reverberating through my body. My reaction to her was physical and sensual, but it was also emotional, and there was something almost mystical about it as well. It was as though we were meant to be, like nothing and no-one could ever part us. We belonged. It was as simple as that. We just belonged.

"I'll see you later?" she whispered, pulling back at last.

I nodded. "I'm due in at eleven-thirty, so I'll see you then."

I kissed her this time, hearing my own groan as I flattened my hand on her back, pulling her closer to me. She felt better than anything I'd ever touched; and she tasted like heaven.

"Bye," she murmured, breaking the kiss once more. "I'd better go."

I was reluctant, but released her, and she ducked inside the pub.

I went back to the beach, picking up the rug I'd left lying there and folding it up, placing it on the top of the rocks and sitting down. Was it even possible to be this happy, I wondered. Was it possible to be this much in love? I hadn't told her that was how I felt, but I would – when the time was right. I felt certain of that. I was still sitting there twenty minutes later, a smile plastered to my lips, when my phone buzzed. I had it in my back pocket and pulled it out, checking the screen to find I had a message. It was from Abbie, and I opened it up, my heart leaping into my mouth, just as I jumped down from the rock and grabbed the rug, running to the pub, her words echoing in my head.

— *Can you come back here? Please. A x*

I went around the back, and knocked, waiting, until Robert came to the door, looking through the glazed window, a frown settling on his face, as he paused before letting me in. He was still a young man, around forty, with hair that was a shade or two darker than Abbie's, and rather sad grey eyes.

He stood to one side in silence and I walked past him, looking for Abbie, who was nowhere in sight. My heart was beating loud in my chest as I turned to face him.

"Abbie sent me a text message," I explained. "Is she okay?"

He sucked in a breath and let it out slowly. "Come with me," he said, his voice more gruff than I'd ever heard it, and I followed him into the small lobby, through the door marked 'Private', and up the stairs into the flat above the pub. He went straight into the kitchen, where Abbie was sitting at the table, her phone clutched in her hand. She looked up as she saw us enter and, the moment her eyes settled on mine, she smiled, then stood and ran to me, throwing herself into my arms. I dropped the rug I was still carrying and caught her, holding on and trying not to let my fears overwhelm me.

"Sit down." Robert's voice intruded into our moment and Abbie pulled away from me, taking my hand and leading me back to the table, where we sat next to each other. Robert remained standing, leaning back on the work surface beside the cooker and looking down at us. "Abbie's told me you've asked her to go out with you," he said, eyeing me with something a little less than enthusiasm.

I wanted to correct him and tell him that I hadn't asked Abbie to 'go out with me' at all, I'd asked her to 'be mine'. I hadn't been careless with my choice of words. But I thought better of it, being as his reaction wasn't entirely promising, which surprised me, considering that he'd always been quite friendly towards me.

"Yes," I replied simply.

"Do you think that's wise?" he asked.

"Yes. It's the wisest thing I've ever done," I said. His eyes widened just a fraction when I said that, but then his frown settled again.

He sighed and stepped forward, pulling out the chair opposite us and sitting down. "Look…" He sounded more reasonable now, less pessimistic, although I still got the feeling he wasn't on our side. "I know you think this is all that matters, but it isn't. You've both got your A-Levels next year. Don't you think you should be concentrating on that at the moment, rather than getting involved?"

"I wasn't aware the two things were mutually exclusive," I reasoned. "I don't see why we can't study, and go out with each other." I paraphrased his words.

"Abbie wants to go to University," he said, as though I hadn't spoken.

"I know, and so do I."

"Yes, but she wants to study art. It's likely she'll go to Falmouth. And you can't study there, can you? Unless you've suddenly developed an interest in creative arts."

"I'm aware of that," I told him, sitting forward, fighting my own corner. "I know what Abbie wants to do, and I'm aware that Falmouth is her only real option." As a university specialising in creative arts, it made sense for her to go there. "I have no intention of standing in her way, if that's what you're suggesting, and I realise that her decision means we'll be studying at different universities, but that doesn't mean we can't make this work."

"You really think you have a future together?" he said, waving his hand between the two of us. For a moment, I ignored the situation and the negativity, and contemplated the fact that Abbie must have discussed having a future with me, must have told him she was serious about us, otherwise why would he have brought it up? Why would he be so worried? He wasn't thinking about our relationship as a brief fling that would be over and done with before the leaves had changed their colour, and that meant she couldn't be either. I smiled at that thought, and he stared at me, looking confused.

"Yes, I do," I replied, remembering to speak at last.

"Even though you're so young; even though…"

"This is about Mum, isn't it?" Abbie interrupted suddenly, raising her voice. "Just because you and she met when you were our age doesn't mean either of us is going to turn out like her." She froze and then blushed. "I'm sorry," she murmured. She looked from her father to me, then got up, the chair scraping on the floor, as she ran from the room.

A part of me wanted to go after her, but I knew I had to deal with Robert first. I had to convince him to let me be a part of Abbie's life, before I could hope to offer her any kind of comfort.

"She didn't mean that," I said quickly.

He tilted his head to one side. "You think?"

"Her mother hurt her when she left," I explained.

"Nowhere near as much as she hurt me," he murmured.

"You think?" I echoed, then I went on, "She hid it from you," before he could say anything. "She came to me."

"She did?" I could see his surprise as well as hearing it.

"Yes. She was angry."

"With her mother?"

I wondered whether to tell him the truth, and decided I might as well. At that point, what did I have to lose? "Yes. And with Mr Kellow, and Tara... and you."

"Me?"

"Yes."

"Why me?"

I sighed. "Because she didn't think you were fighting hard enough for her mother, or for your marriage."

He stared at me for what seemed like a very long time, and then shook his head, before lowering it into his hands. "I probably should have explained it to her." His voice was a gentle murmur, but I could still hear him clearly. "I just didn't want to admit it. I didn't want to talk about it." He looked up and I tried very hard not to react to the bleakness in his eyes. "It wasn't the first time," he whispered.

"Sorry?" I'd heard what he said, I just didn't know what he meant by it.

"Abbie's mother," he replied, "she had an affair before..." I had no idea how to respond to that, so I sat in silence and watched him. "It was the reason we moved here," he explained, then turned and stared out of the window. For a moment, I thought perhaps he wasn't going to speak again, but suddenly he started to talk. "She was screwing some

61

bloke at work," he said. "A geography teacher, of all things." It struck me as curious that the man being a geography teacher seemed to make a difference, and I wondered whether it would have been better if he'd taught French, or Physics… or even P.E. "Their affair went on for about four months, or at least that's what she told me…" He stopped talking, then continued, after a pause, "He ended it when his girlfriend found out, and Sandra decided she needed to get it off her chest, to make peace with herself, by telling me. So she did."

"What happened?" I asked, when this particular pause became long enough for me to realise he wasn't going to add anything.

"She told me it was a mistake; she begged me to forgive her," he replied. "And I did. It took time, but I did. I told her I wanted her to leave the school, to get a job somewhere else. She agreed to that, and then a few days later, she came to me and suggested we should move down here. She said it would be a fresh start for all of us… and I was stupid enough to believe her." He turned back and finally looked at me again. The pain was still visible in his eyes, even all this time later. "She started sleeping with Devin about six or seven months after we moved here."

That came as a shock. I had no idea their affair had been going on for so long, and I was sure Abbie didn't either.

"There was no point in fighting for her, or for our marriage," he continued. "She didn't want me, and she didn't want to be married to me. Not anymore. Even I managed to work that out. How does that saying go…?" He stared at me and I shrugged, because I had no idea what he was talking about. "Hurt me once, shame on you. Hurt me twice, shame on me."

I could understand the sentiment… sort of. The thing was… "Abbie didn't know about that," I reminded him. "The way she saw it, you didn't care enough to want to keep your family together."

"I know," he sighed and stood up, wandering over to the window this time and gazing out at the view of the bay below. "I'll speak to her. I'll try and explain it." He turned back. "What are you going to do?" he asked. I wasn't completely sure what he meant, but even so, I knew what my answer was going to be, without even thinking about it.

"I'm going make Abbie happy."

He looked at me for what seemed like forever and then came back across to the table. "If you hurt her, I'll…"

"I won't," I interrupted. "I'll never hurt her. I couldn't." I wasn't about to tell him that I was in love with her – not when I hadn't told Abbie herself.

"Okay," he said eventually. "I won't stand in your way."

If he'd been less upset about his own situation, I might have taken the time to explain to him that he couldn't have done; that the only person who could stop me from being with Abbie, was Abbie herself, and that as long as she wanted me beside her, no-one could keep me from his daughter. No-one. Not even him.

Robert spoke to Abbie later that day, and told her everything he'd told me, and they talked it through. She came to me afterwards and cried, and we talked it through too. She was angrier than ever with her mum, but once she'd finished crying, I think she felt better, and over the coming weeks, her relationship with her dad definitely improved. She understood him more. After that, Robert positively welcomed me, like I was part of the family. That was an unusual feeling for me, but I liked it.

Abbie and I spent the rest of the summer together, taking picnics on the cliffs above the village, sitting on the beach, walking in the moonlight, swimming in the sea, just being together as much we could. Aside from all of that, we kissed – a lot. We got good at it too. Really good.

And every single day, I fell more and more in love with her.

It was a perfect summer and my only regret was that it had to end. And end it did, when we went back to college.

I missed her, more than I could hope to put into words. Abbie was studying hard. I was too, obviously, but she was serious about it, desperate to earn her place at Falmouth University. I'd hunted around and the nearest uni I could find where I could study the right kind of marketing course – one I was really interested in – was at Plymouth. It was a two hour drive from Porthgowan and when I told Abbie that, she burst into tears.

"Two hours?" she sobbed as I held her, while we sat on the sofa in the living room above the pub one evening. It was a Friday night in the middle of October – a few days before my eighteenth birthday.

"Yes. It's not far."

She turned and looked at me. "Not far? What about if I lived at uni, rather than commuting from here? Would that help?" It was an option she'd talked about, but hadn't decided on yet. She loved the village, but part of her wanted to get the experience of university life. There were advantages and disadvantages to both choices and every time we discussed it, she ended up still unsure as to what she wanted to do.

"Well, it'd make the journey a little shorter, but either way, I can still drive back down to see you every weekend," I reasoned, wiping away her tears with my thumbs and kissing her.

"How?" she said, trying not to cry again. "You don't have a car."

"I will do. I've saved quite a lot of money now." I kissed her again, because I liked kissing her. "I'll work it out. I promise."

The next day, my Uncle Tim arrived. He was an infrequent visitor and, judging from the expression on my mother's face when he turned up immediately after breakfast, he wasn't expected. He'd stayed at a hotel in Helston, and travelled down early, he explained.

"Why?" my mother asked, looking at him suspiciously. Uncle Tim was a tall man, someone who tended to dominate a room, and for as long as I could remember, although I'd only met him on a handful of occasions, I'd always been struck by how well dressed he was. He possessed some of the finest suits I'd ever seen, and even on a Saturday morning, he stood in our kitchen, dressed in designer jeans, with a pale pink shirt and a dusky blue sweater tied around his shoulders, positively oozing style. His dark hair was pristine, despite him having arrived in his open topped Jaguar, which was parked outside the Post Office, and he had a pair of Aviator sunglasses perched on top of his head. I was pretty sure that every female head between here and Helston would have been turned in his direction as he'd driven down.

"I wanted to see my nephew," he replied and I looked up at him from the breakfast table.

"You did?" I was surprised, and so was my mother. She certainly looked it anyway. She wasn't close to Uncle Tim. I don't think she'd ever been close to anyone – including my own father – but she'd always told me she had 'expectations' of Tim. I had no idea what that meant, and I didn't want to either. Knowing her, it wouldn't be good.

"Yes. You're going to be eighteen on Monday," he said, as though I'd forgotten my own birthday. "So I've come to give you your present."

"You've driven all the way down here, just to give me a birthday present?" Now I was really astonished. Uncle Tim was rich – a self-made millionaire, if my mother was to be believed – and he'd always been generous in his birthday and Christmas gifts. But they were usually in the form of cheques, stuffed inside greetings cards and sent through the post. A personal visit, just for the purposes of delivering a birthday present… this was something very different.

"Have you got your shoes on?" he asked me.

"Yes. Why?"

"Because I'm taking you to Truro."

"Now?"

"Yes." He grinned.

"But you can't. I'm due at work in…" I checked my watch. "Three hours. We won't get to Truro and back."

"Yes we will. Well, we will if you stop talking and hurry up. It's only forty minutes to Truro."

I stood up. "No, it's not…"

"It is in my car." He chuckled and held the door open, ushering me out. "Back soon, Mary," he called and closed the door behind him.

I climbed into the passenger seat of his dark blue Jaguar XK8 convertible, did up my seatbelt and looked over at him. "Where exactly are we going?"

"That would be telling," he said, smiling as he started the engine.

He drove along the sea wall, preparing to turn the corner to climb the hill back up to the main road, but as we passed the pub, I saw Abbie, watering the tubs of flowers by the front door.

"Can we stop, just for a second?"

"We've only just started," he replied, although he pulled over, as requested.

"I won't be a minute." I jumped out of the car again, and ran over to Abbie, who looked up at me enquiringly as I came to a halt right in front of her.

"Who's that?' she asked, lowering her voice.

"That's my Uncle Tim."

She smiled. "Oh?"

"He's just taking me to Truro."

"He is?"

"Yes. It's something to do with my birthday. He's got a surprise for me, or something."

She nodded. "Sounds like fun."

"Hmm…" I'd never been keen on surprises, so I was reserving my judgement on that. "The thing is," I continued, "he may be certain he'll get me back by eleven-thirty, but I'm not so sure. So, just in case I'm not, do you think you could let your dad know?"

She smiled again and placed her hand gently on my chest. Abbie had taken to touching me more and more over the previous few weeks; just simple, spontaneous gestures like this, which she did almost subconsciously, and I cupped her face in my hand, my thumb brushing her cheek as she looked up at me. "I'll go one better," she said softly. "I'll cover for you until you get back."

I leant down and kissed her, regardless of Uncle Tim sitting in the car behind me. "What did I do to deserve you?" I whispered, breaking the kiss.

She shrugged, playfully. "I don't know, but do you think you could keep doing it?"

"With pleasure…"

She gave me the most perfect smile and I kissed the tip of her nose, before letting her go and running back to the car. Tim had us underway again before I'd even re-fastened my seatbelt and he didn't say a word until we were on the main road, heading in the direction of Truro.

"Was that your girlfriend?" he asked.

"Yes."

He glanced at me, just quickly and then nodded his head. "Well, you have excellent taste, Joshua."

Hardly anyone ever called me by my full name and I smirked.

"Thank you, Uncle Timothy." I returned the compliment and he grinned.

"What's her name?" he asked.

"Abbie, although I suppose it's probably Abigail, if we're using proper names. I've never known her as anything but Abbie though."

"From what I could see of her, she's very beautiful," he remarked.

"Yes, she is. And she's far too young for you." He laughed then, throwing his head back. "Now, where are you taking me?"

He looked at me again. "You'll just have to be patient," he said, then changed down and floored the accelerator, tearing up the country roads.

Where he was taking me was the BMW dealership in Truro, and once there, much to my astonishment, he proceeded to order me a brand new 325i. I was allowed to choose the colour for myself, and went for a smokey grey, with black interior.

It was only when Uncle Tim was completing the paperwork that I realised the full implications of what was happening, and that I had to stop it.

"You can't do this," I said, putting my hand on his arm to halt the process of him signing my life away.

"Why not?" he replied, looking at me with a bemused expression on his face.

I closed my eyes for a moment, then opened them again and turned to Uncle Tim, before I stood up and nodded my head towards the door of the showroom, indicating I wanted to talk to him outside. He put the lid back on his fountain pen and got to his feet, much to the alarm of the salesman.

"We'll be back in a minute," Uncle Tim said, allaying the man's fears that he was about to lose a sale, and he followed me out of the glass doors. "What's wrong?" he asked the moment we were outside. "And don't give me any crap about it being too much money. I earn it and I'll spend it however I see fit."

"It's not that," I replied, stepping further away, so no-one inside could hear.

"Then what is it?" Uncle Tim asked, following me.

"Well, I do think it's too much, if I'm being honest… but the real problem is…" I let my voice fade, wondering how to admit the problem to a man who was just about to spend tens of thousands of pounds on my birthday present.

He looked at his watch. "You're the one in a hurry to get back home, Josh," he said. "Just tell me what the problem is."

"I can't afford it." I blurted out the words.

"In case you haven't noticed, I'm paying," he replied, rolling his eyes.

"I know, and I really do appreciate it. But I'd still have to pay for insurance, and in case you haven't noticed, I'm not even eighteen yet. It'll cost a fortune. A fortune I don't have."

He paused, then chuckled and put his arm around my shoulder, turning me and walking me back towards the showroom. "I'll pay for that too," he said. "And I'll get them to send the renewals to me. You can call it your birthday present for the next few years, until you've built up some no-claims discount, and you're working and can afford to pay for it yourself." I looked up at him, shaking my head. "Now, stop arguing and get back in here," he said, holding the door open. "Otherwise you're never going to get back to that beautiful girlfriend of yours."

I had to smile. What else could I do? I had a lot to be grateful for.

The car was delivered, as promised, six weeks later, much to my mother's surprise. Obviously, she'd been expecting a car of sorts; we'd told her about it on our return from Falmouth, immediately before I'd run over to the pub to start my shift. But what she hadn't expected was something so sleek, so refined and – frankly – so pretty. She kept frowning at me, and asking what I'd done to deserve it. I didn't reply, because as far as I was aware, I hadn't done anything.

Abbie liked the car almost as much as I did, and for very similar reasons. It gave us freedom. Even though it was winter, I could take her to places we'd never been before – well, not together, anyway. I drove us out to abandoned tin mines, remote beauty spots and small uninhabited coves, where we'd walk if the weather permitted, and sit in the car if it didn't. Those quiet times alone were the only chances we really got to talk about the future – and we did. Abbie wanted to paint, or to draw, I knew that much already, and her telling me didn't come as any surprise. She hadn't worked out how to make a career of it yet, but she hoped to discover that while she was at university. I wanted to go into PR, or marketing, to get some experience working for someone else, and then to start my own business. Abbie listened intently to my plans, asking questions, showing an interest. We didn't discuss how we'd fit our lives together around our individual ambitions, but we both supported each other's hopes and dreams. I suppose that out of those conversations came my only moments of concern. As time progressed, I was becoming more and more convinced that my career would pull me away from the village, and probably from Cornwall too. But Abbie loved Porthgowan with a passion I'd never been able to feel, and I sometimes lay awake at night, wondering how we'd make that work; how she'd feel if I followed my dreams, and whether she'd be willing to come with me. I knew we were going to have to talk about it at some point, but I was putting it off. We had three years of university ahead of us. A lot could change in three years, so there was no point in looking for trouble where it didn't exist. Not yet.

Just before Christmas, while I was at work, Robert came to see me. He asked if I'd go into the bar before leaving for the afternoon and I wondered if something was wrong; whether Abbie had said something to him about the future, and he wanted to speak to me about that. By that time, she'd applied to Falmouth and I'd put in my application to Plymouth. It was risky, putting all our eggs in one basket, but Falmouth was really the only place for Abbie, and I wasn't going to look any further afield than Plymouth – not after the way she'd reacted to discovering that we'd be two hours apart. If I didn't get in, I'd just have to think of something else. We'd done our applications together and afterwards, she'd thrown her arms around me, seemingly upset, even though I'd told her over and over that I'd see her every single weekend, and we'd talk all the time on the phone.

I saw out the rest of my shift feeling nervous and unsure about what Robert might want to say to me, even wondering whether perhaps he intended to have a 'man-to-man' talk about my behaviour at university, warning me maybe that the freedom I was bound to feel on leaving home did not extend to cheating on his daughter. As if…

It was with some trepidation that I went through to the bar after closing time, the last of the lunchtime customers having already left. The place was decorated for Christmas, and had been for a couple of weeks, and Robert was collecting glasses from the empty tables. When he saw me, he looked up and smiled.

"Ah…Josh." He seemed cheerful and I felt myself relax. "Let's have a seat, shall we?"

I went over to where he was standing and we sat down at the table. It was in the front window and we looked out over the cove, the car park deserted and the wind whipping in off the sea.

I looked over at him, hoping he'd put me out of my misery quickly. "I want some advice," he said, and you could have knocked me down with a feather. That wasn't what I'd expected at all.

"What about?" I asked.

"How to get more customers through the door of this place." He looked around. "We do alright in the summer months, but in the winter…" He stopped talking and picked up a beer mat from the table, resting it on its end.

"I see…" I mused. "So, you're looking for something to incentivise the locals to come in here?"

He nodded. "I'd like to help Abbie get through uni," he said, looking shy. "I don't want her having to work her way through the next three years, not if I can help it, or at least not all the hours God sends. But if I'm going to do that, then I need to get the takings up."

I sat for a moment, thinking. If this was about Abbie, then I'd do whatever it took. "Well, you could consider extending your opening hours."

He frowned. "How is that going to help?"

"You'd have more chance to get people in the door?" I felt like I was stating the obvious.

"Yes, but I'd be paying higher wages to cover the extra hours."

He had a point. "Okay, what about having special events then… ones the locals can get involved with."

"Such as?"

"You could have a Karaoke evening."

He smiled. "Have you heard how badly they sing in church? I don't go myself, but the vicar tells me he wears earplugs for the Sunday morning service."

I didn't know that. But then, I didn't go to church either. My mother did, although she'd never mentioned the earplugs. She was usually too busy gossiping about someone or other, more often than not in an effort to cause trouble.

"What about a quiz night?"

"A quiz night?" he repeated.

"Yes." I started to think on my feet. "You could charge a small fee to cover any costs, and then get people to enter as teams… build up some friendly rivalry."

"What about a prize though?" he asked. "People would expect a prize."

"Why not offer a voucher? The winning team get a free dinner each." He looked at me a little sceptically. "You could set a cap on the number of people in each team – of say no more than four. That way, you'd only be giving away a meal, to maybe three or four people. But they'd probably bring someone else with them, and unless that person was also a winning team member, they'd have to pay full price for their food, and they'd both have to buy drinks."

He looked at me long and hard. "I think you might have an idea there," he said, letting the beer mat drop to the table.

He got to his feet. "Well, if you're going to do it," I replied, standing myself, "I'd suggest you try and start in January. It's the quietest time of year."

"Don't I know it."

"You'd be bound to get people interested." I tried to sound enthusiastic and he smiled at me.

"Thanks, Josh. You've been a great help."

I shrugged, feeling embarrassed, and picked up the last remaining glasses from the table behind us, carrying them over to the bar for him, before saying goodbye.

After a few weeks of sticking up posters, doing leaflet drops and generally spreading the word to anyone who would listen, the first quiz night was held on the second Wednesday in January. The turnout was remarkably good, proving the point that life in the village had little to offer during the winter months. Fourteen teams were entered, one of which included my mother, who'd paired up with two other women she knew from church. Abbie and I went along, just as observers; we had, after all, been involved with the creation of the quiz and, although Robert had devised the questions himself – with the help of many reference books – we didn't want there to be any cries of 'foul', by us entering ourselves.

The evening was a huge success, the bar was busy and takings were up enormously. It was the first piece of proper promotional advice I'd ever given anyone and it felt really satisfying to see it come to fruition.

Much to my surprise, my mother and her friends won the prize that first week, thus ensuring they would return every other week thereafter, in the hope of repeating their success. They bought plenty of drinks and, even though they didn't win again – at least not for a couple of months anyway – they usually went along early for a meal beforehand, as did several others. All in all, Robert was very pleased.

He wasn't as pleased as I was though. And the reason for that? Well, after the first couple of weeks of the quiz night, Abbie and I no longer felt the need to attend. It wasn't really our 'thing' anyway, and we'd only been there to start with for moral support. Besides, Robert had regular staff who were helping out, and our presence really wasn't required.

Instead, we took advantage of my mother's flat being empty for a few hours, and started going there instead. Obviously, we could have gone out in the car, or upstairs to the flat above the pub, where we spent most of our evenings, but being completely alone, without fear of interruption or intrusion, was novel, and exciting, especially as over the previous weeks and months, we'd honed our kissing techniques to perfection, and had added a few other skills into our repertoire. Somehow, we'd managed to keep our clothes on, but I think we both knew that was a situation that wasn't going to last much longer.

So, on that particular early February evening, we were lying on the sofa, our bodies entwined, Abbie's beneath mine, our lips crushed together, tongues clashing, my hand on her firm breast, while hers rubbed my back, beneath my t-shirt, when all of a sudden, we stopped, our breathing hard, as we stared at each other. The atmosphere had changed. It was like the flick of a switch, and even though neither of us said anything, we just knew. We knew this was it. I leant up slightly, resting on one elbow, and looked down at her, letting my fingers drift to the hem of her jumper, raising it a few inches to reveal her perfect flat stomach. She sucked in a breath as I traced a line upwards, gingerly uncovering her white lace bra, before leaning down and kissing her through the thin material. She moaned just softly and, after a few minutes, I knelt up, moving between her legs, and without taking her eyes from mine, she sat, lifting her jumper over her head and dropping it down onto the floor beside us. I moved forward, kissing her and undoing her bra at the same time, releasing her full breasts into my waiting hands, before lowering my mouth and kissing her soft flesh, marvelling in her delighted squeals when my tongue found her hardened nipples, at least until she suddenly stopped me, grabbed my t-shirt and pulled it over my head, running her hands across my chest and down to my stomach, her eyes widening as I lay us both back down and we touched, caressed, stroked, and whispered gentle words of praise and pleasure. I longed to see her though, and when I knelt up again and gazed down at her, reaching out and slowly undoing her jeans, she didn't object. She bit her bottom lip, her eyes on fire. It was kind of awkward, working out how to pull her jeans off while I was kneeling in the way, and in the end, I stood up and yanked them down, which made her giggle as I nearly pulled her off the end of the sofa.

"Sorry," I mumbled, helping her back up again.

She shook her head and put the tip of her forefinger in her mouth, and I wondered if she had any idea how adorable she looked, lying there like that.

I bent and put my fingers inside the top of her cotton briefs, not taking my eyes from hers. "May I?" She nodded and I pulled them down, more gently this time, lowering them and dropping them to the floor, before straightening and gazing down at her perfect naked body. "God, you're beautiful," I whispered and reached for the buckle of my belt. She sat up then, grabbing my hand, halting me. "What's wrong?"

"I'm sorry," she murmured. "I'm not... I'm not..."

I understood straight away. "You're not ready?"

She gazed up at me. "I'm sorry," she repeated and I smiled.

"Don't be. Remember? Friends never have to say sorry."

"Friends?" She looked surprised.

"Yes. Friends." I leant down and kissed her, tilting my head and deepening the kiss, before taking hold of her legs and twisting her so she was sitting, facing me, with her feet on the floor. When I broke the kiss and stood upright, she looked disappointed, until I knelt in front of her and pulled her closer to me, keeping my eyes fixed on hers as I moved between her legs again, my hands on her knees, parting them wider.

"Lie back," I whispered, hoping to God this was going to work. I'd never done any of this before, so I was going with my instincts, banking on natural intuition... and deep, ingrained love.

She gazed at me and relaxed back into the cushions behind her, as I looked down at the neat triangle of hair at the apex of her thighs, her lips already swollen, and glistening with anticipation, and I slowly ran my fingertip from her entrance upwards through her delicate folds, until I reached that perfect spot, and she shivered, moaning my name. That sounded so good, I leant down and repeated the process, but with my tongue this time, tasting her. She was sweet, like honey, except she wasn't, because she wasn't like anything else I'd ever tasted in my life and as I knelt forward and started to lick her, I knew I'd never be able to get enough.

I allowed my tongue to roam freely over her, and it didn't take long before her breathing changed, her thighs started to quiver and I felt her hand on the back of my head, holding me in place as she ground her hips into me. Then suddenly she cried out, my name a mantra on her lips as she let go wildly, thrashing beneath me, while I drank from her.

I gave her a few minutes to calm, but before she could say anything, I changed position just slightly and repeated the process, only with my fingers this time, and I watched her as she writhed and bucked, her head thrashing, until she came apart a second time, her eyes fixed on mine, her beautiful body yielding to pleasure.

"Oh God…" she murmured once she'd got her breath back. "That was…"

"Incredible." I sat up beside her and pulled her soft naked body into my arms, where she nestled, spent, curled into me.

"Yes, it was." She sounded a little drunk and I smiled, just as she twisted slightly and looked up at me. "Only now I feel even more guilty," she murmured.

"Why?"

She hesitated and bit her bottom lip, and then whispered, "What about you?"

I shook my head. "That doesn't matter," I replied and she leant back, looking confused. "You've given me so much this evening."

"*I've* given *you*?" she said, frowning.

"Yes." I ran my fingertips down her cheek and across her lips. "You let me see a side to you that no-one else has ever seen before." She lowered her eyes, like she was embarrassed, and I placed my finger beneath her chin and raised her face to mine. "I think, because you're quite shy, you hold something back when you're with most people, don't you?" She paused for a second and then nodded her head. "But watching you just now," I added, gazing into her amber eyes, "I know you weren't holding back at all. What I saw; what I felt; that was all of you. That's what I meant when I said you'd given me so much… you gave me all of you."

She sighed and rested her head on my bare chest, her arms tight around me. "Of course I did… I'm yours."

Over the next few weeks and months, our Wednesday nights took on a greater significance than ever. We moved things from the living room to my bedroom, just for the comfort of a double bed, if nothing else, and I explored her body, discovering every inch of her, savouring her soft, delicate skin, her sweet, perfumed taste, getting to know the signs of her building orgasms, the unique noises she made in her deepest moments of pleasure. She always asked me to keep my jeans on, apologetic, but wary of taking that 'final step', as I'd come to think of it. I didn't mind though, because I knew we'd get there one day, and waiting for her was the most self-indulgent form of denial I could have imagined.

There were other things happening in our lives too. It wasn't just about the hedonistic delights of having my every fantasy fulfilled by the girl I loved more than life; more than breath.

We studied. We studied hard, and I received a conditional place at Plymouth University, dependant on my A-level results. Abbie had to wait a little longer, because she'd had to submit a portfolio of her work, but eventually, she heard that she'd got an unconditional offer from Falmouth. She was delighted and relieved, and so was I. Our futures were set, it seemed, and Abbie was even growing accustomed to the idea that we'd only see each other at weekends, consoled by the fact that the long holidays would be ours entirely.

We both took our A-Levels, the studying seeming to pay off, as we both came out from our separate exams feeling confident that we'd done our best – and that at least we'd never have to do that again. Abbie's History paper was the last one, and I met her by the gates, walking her over to the car and opening the door for her. As she sat down, she looked up at me.

"Now all we have to do is wait," she said, smiling her satisfaction.

We also continued to go out in the car – enjoying picnics and longer walks in the warmer weather. Some of the places we went to were very remote, and we didn't see another soul, and it sometimes occurred to me that no-one would have been any the wiser if we'd gone beyond the hand-holding and kissing that had become a feature of our outings. The problem was, to me, that seemed cheap and sleazy, and Abbie was neither of those things, so to treat her as such, was wrong. I didn't care about waiting, or being patient, or how long it took. As far as I was concerned, she was worth it.

The summer soon beckoned, and Robert announced at the very end of June that the following quiz night would be the last for the time being; he needed to get the pub ready for the holiday season. This declaration was met with howls of disappointment, which were only just appeased by him pointing out that normal service would resume in the autumn – just a few short months away – giving the teams time to read up on their general knowledge.

Abbie was upset by this news and I honestly thought she was going to cry when Robert told us, but she held it together and, once we were alone, we agreed to make our last Wednesday night really special. I had no idea what Abbie had in mind by that. As far as I was concerned, she just had to turn up and the evening would be 'special', but for myself, although it may have been presumptuous of me, I decided to go into Helston and visit the pharmacy. I didn't want to go to the one in the village, in case anyone saw me there, and started to gossip about Abbie, but it seemed like the right thing to do, to be prepared, to be responsible. And if nothing happened? Well, there was always another time…

My mother left early to meet her friends, and I sent Abbie a text to let her know the coast was clear. She arrived within five minutes and, without a second's hesitation, we kissed, deeply, as I cupped her face with one hand, the other resting in the small of her back, while her hands wandered up my arms, and around my shoulders, her fingers knotting in my hair.

"Hello," I said, when she finally broke the kiss and leaned back.

She blushed and lowered her eyes, looking embarrassed. "Hello."

Further speech seemed unnecessary and, with my heart beating loudly in my chest, I took her hand, leading her through the flat and into my bedroom. We stood together and I slowly undressed her, removing her shorts and t-shirt, her bra and knickers, sucking in a sharp breath, when she was finally revealed.

"You shaved?" I whispered, looking up from my kneeling position in front of her.

She nodded, blushing, and I stood. "We said 'special'," she whispered, and I smiled.

"You were always special," I murmured.

"Do... do you like it?" She seemed doubtful all of a sudden.

"I've never seen anything look more perfect..." I leant forward and kissed her gently, my tongue finding hers, then I walked her backwards to the bed, lying her down and gazing at her for a second, before parting her legs and admiring her. "I want to taste you." I could hear the emotion in my voice, and she sighed and smiled as I edged between her thighs, my tongue finding that tender spot. She raised her hips to my relentless touch, her hand on the back of my head, and soon she cried out my name, the waves of pleasure overwhelming her, crashing through her quivering body.

As she calmed, I planted gentle kisses over her naked mound, then once her breathing had returned to normal, I knelt up, and she sat, reaching out with a beguiling timidity, her shaking fingers fumbling with the buckle on my belt. I placed my hand over hers and she glanced up at me, her eyes alight.

"You're sure?" I whispered, knowing we were crossing a boundary. "We don't have to..."

"I want to." Her voice was strong and firm, and I took over, loosening the belt, undoing it and the button, then letting my hand drop to my side, and allowing her to decide the next move. She sidled forwards slightly and lowered the zip of my jeans, before she tried to pull them down. They were tight fitting and unwilling to budge, so I stood, taking them off myself as Abbie moved to the very edge of the bed, sitting before me. She reached out and I stepped closer, letting her pull down my trunks, releasing my rigid erection, her widened eyes fixed on it, her tongue subconsciously grazing across her bottom lip.

I lifted her, moving her back onto the bed again and kneeling between her parted legs. She gazed up at me, and I placed my hands either side of her head, leaning down and kissing her. She groaned, her fingers twisting into my hair, her tongue clashing with mine as her legs came around my hips, entwining me, pulling me closer already, the head of my erection instinctively finding her entrance, nudging against her.

Suddenly, she broke the kiss. "Wait!"

"What?" I leant back.

"We can't," she wailed. "We don't have any… um…" Two spots of red appeared on her cheeks as she blushed, and I realised what she was saying.

"You mean we don't have any condoms?"

She nodded, tears forming in the corners of her eyes. I leant down again and kissed them away, tasting the saltiness on my tongue, before I knelt up and reached over to the bedside cabinet.

"It may have been a bit arrogant of me," I murmured, feeling embarrassed myself now. "But I thought I'd better be prepared." As I said the words, I recalled my fumbled attempts a couple of hours earlier, when I'd been trying to work out how to use a condom, just to avoid making a prat of myself in front of Abbie.

She leant up on her elbows and watched me remove the cardboard box from the drawer, opening it and pulling out a foil packet. "Prepared?" she echoed, her voice a mere whisper.

"Yes." I dropped the box and moved over her again, our lips almost touching. "It's my job to take care of you, even if I was so wrapped up in the idea of making love to you, that I'd temporarily lost my mind, and had forgotten all about the fact that I'd bought these."

She giggled, her eyes sparkling again, but not with tears this time, as I knelt back, opened the foil packet and carefully unrolled the condom down my erection, like I'd been doing it for years. I felt rather pleased with myself as Abbie watched me closely and, when I was ready, I looked back up at her.

"Have you done that before?" she asked.

I felt my shoulders drop slightly and knew I had to be honest. "Yes." She pulled away from me, trying to close her legs. "No, wait," I cried out, resting my hands on her thighs, holding her still. "You don't understand."

"Really?" The tears were back in her eyes again.

"Yes, really. I—I practiced it, earlier this evening, before you came over."

"On whom?"

"On myself, of course. I didn't want to mess it up in front of you."

She smiled and relaxed back into the duvet. "And how did you get... um... aroused?" she asked, teasing.

"I thought about you for... oh, about ten seconds," I replied and she giggled.

Looking down at her, I wanted to take that moment to prepare her; to tell her that I may not have messed up the condom thing – well, not in its execution, anyway – but that I was quite likely to mess up everything else. After all, the next part of what we were about to do wasn't something I could practice in advance. I wondered if should warn her that I'd never done anything like this before, and that there was every chance it would be over a lot quicker than either of us would like. I wanted to apologise in advance, I suppose. But as I moved into position, my erection nudging against her again, I realised that although it may have been my first time, this wasn't about me. Not in the slightest.

"Relax," I whispered softly and she took a breath, letting it out slowly as I entered her. She felt tight, her walls gripping me as I pushed slowly inward, keeping my eyes locked on hers, our lips just a breath away. I felt something stopping me, a barrier, and I leant down and kissed her, swallowing her cry as I pushed harder and took her virginity, in the same instant as I gave her mine. We stilled, absorbing the moment, until I broke the kiss and looked down at her serene, smiling face and knew that she really was mine. Completely.

She smiled, touching my arms and raising her hips just slightly, inviting me in. "I'll never leave you," I whispered. I don't know why, but it felt important to say that, just as I moved again, taking her slowly and tenderly, filling her until our bodies were locked. I couldn't get any deeper inside her and I paused to take in the beauty of her body, the sound of her breathing, the touch of her fingers on my arms, and to acknowledge the deep ache within myself that was about to be fulfilled. As I started to move, she moaned softly and let her hands drop down beside her head, so I grabbed them in my own, holding them in place, pinning her, claiming her, and she gasped, raising her legs, wrapping me up in her, our bodies bound.

The room filled with the sounds of our lovemaking; sighs and moans, and incoherent words. She matched my rhythm, her hips grinding into me, a sheen of sweat forming on our bodies as the intensity built.

"Please, Josh," she murmured and I instinctively changed the angle, going deeper and harder, until she cried out, throwing her head back and clamping around me in ecstasy, and then I felt it… that crescendo, that longed-for moment of my own release, my heart pounding, my nerves on fire as I poured myself into her.

"I love you so much," I whispered, looking down into her shining amber eyes. They sparkled and her lips parted, and for a brief moment, I wondered if I'd said the wrong thing, if she was going to cry, but then a slow smile spread across her face and she pulled one hand from mine and reached up, tracing a line around my lips with her fingertip.

"And I love you."

I held her in my arms, our breathing synchronised, our bodies locked, our hearts entwined. One.

After that, the real struggle became keeping our hands off of each other. Not to mention our lips, our tongues… and our mouths. And what Abbie could do with her mouth defied description.

We still had plenty to do, of course. Between working, and dealing with the tourists, who seemed to have invaded the village in their droves that year, not to mention Abbie's eighteenth birthday, and then getting our exam results, confirming that my place at Plymouth was secured, there wasn't a dull moment, but the moments we did have, were spent with each other. We still went for walks, we still went to the beach and just sat together and talked, or sometimes I'd feed Abbie strawberries, watching the way her lips caressed the soft fruit as she took each bite, and unable to resist, I'd kiss her and taste that summer sweetness. Occasionally, I took her out to dinner, although we always came away feeling that the presence of other people had somehow spoiled our evening. But regardless of all of that, whenever possible, wherever possible, we made love.

I still drew the line at the back seat of the car – or even the front seat of the car – but we took advantage of my mother being a regular churchgoer and found a great way to spend our Sunday mornings. We also worked out that, in all the time we'd been together, Abbie's dad had never once come upstairs during the evenings we'd spent together. And over the summer months, we were safer than ever, because the pub was popular with holidaymakers. So, we took to spending our evenings in Abbie's bedroom, in Abbie's bed.

One evening, after I'd already made her cry with pleasure, by a combination of my tongue and my fingers, and had held her in my arms until she calmed, I reached into my jeans, which were lying on her bedroom floor, looking for a condom.

"Josh?" she said from her prone position on the bed behind me.

"Yes?" I turned to look at her, my jeans still in my hand.

"You don't need one of those."

I stared down at her, dropping my jeans. What was she saying? "Sorry? Don't you want to make love? Is something wrong?" Had I hurt her?

"No, nothing's wrong, and yes, I want to make love, but you don't need one of those." She lowered her eyes to the foil packet in my hand and, despite my confusion, I crawled up her body, raising myself above her. I tried to ignore the alarm bells that were ringing in my head, because in my mind, if there was nothing wrong, and she still wanted me, then her words could only have one other meaning, and I really wasn't sure how I felt about that. It wasn't something I'd ever really thought about – even though she clearly had.

"I—I don't understand," I stuttered. She was eighteen. So was I – at least for another couple of months. We were too young for this. We both had places at universities - different universities, nearly seventy miles apart. Neither of us had any money. Obviously, I loved her with all my heart, and I'd give her anything she wanted, but we were barely adults ourselves. How could we…?

"Don't look so scared," she whispered, interrupting my thoughts.

"Scared?"

"Yes. You look terrified."

I tried to change my expression. "I'm not terrified. I'm confused."

She rested her hands on my arms. "Why are you confused?"

"Because I don't understand." It was no good. I had to ask her. "Are you saying you… you want us to have a baby? Is that it?" Another thought struck me and I almost shivered, but tried to control it. "Or are you trying to tell me you're already pregnant?" I couldn't see how that was possible; I'd been so careful, but…

She gazed up at me, then covered her face with her hands, her body shaking. I couldn't tell if she was laughing or crying, and I wasn't sure that either of those reactions was very good, in the circumstances. I was beyond confused now.

"Abbie?" I leant on one arm and used the other hand to remove hers from her face, relieved to see she was giggling.

"I'm sorry," she murmured.

"Why?"

"I couldn't resist."

"Couldn't resist what?" I knelt back, releasing her, and looking down at her as she leant up on her elbows.

"I should probably explain," she said softly.

"I wish you would."

"Well…" She sat up now, so we were facing each other, the condom still gripped in my hand. "I decided I didn't really like you having to use these." She pulled it from me, holding it between us.

"You didn't?"

She shook her head. "No. So I got the bus to Helston a couple of weeks ago and went to the clinic there." She paused and, even though I thought I knew what was coming, I let her finish, her eyes dropping, focusing on my chest. "I've gone on the pill," she whispered.

I knelt in silence, until she raised her face, looking up at me, filled with uncertainty for some reason.

"I see," I murmured.

"You're not cross, are you?"

"Why would I be cross?"

"Because I didn't talk to you about it first," she said. "I—I wanted it to be a surprise." She bit her bottom lip.

I reached out, releasing it with my thumb. "It's your body, Abbie…"

"It's yours too," she said and I leant down and kissed her passionately, showing her my love, even if the lump in my throat had rendered me temporarily incapable of expressing it.

We pulled apart and she looked up at me, her eyes sparkling with mischief now. "But as for letting me think you wanted to us to have a baby, or that you might even be pregnant…" I loaded my voice with a warning tone and she gazed up at me.

"But I do want us to have a baby," she interrupted, completely serious.

"You do?" I felt the confusion returning again.

"Yes." She nodded her head for emphasis. "One day."

"One day," I murmured, relieved, and I kissed her again as she laid back down, pulling me with her.

"We won't be needing these again," she said, breaking the kiss and throwing the condom across the room.

"No, we won't."

And as she raised her hips to mine, her legs wrapping around me, I felt her for the first time, all over again.

It was only a few days later, one Sunday morning, while my mother was at church, that Abbie joked with me that I'd unleashed a monster in her.

"How do you work that out?" I asked, cradling her soft, silken body in my arms, propped up on the pillows on my bed, enjoying the afterglow.

She looked up at me. "You showed me how to love," she whispered, tracing tiny circles on my chest with her fingertips, moving slowly downwards, her touch arousing me anew.

"And how does that make you a monster?"

She smiled and pulled away, kneeling up and straddling me. "Because now I know what it's really like, I want more," she said, raising herself up, then lowering herself onto me and sighing, her eyes closed as she felt the welcome intrusion.

I clutched her waist, holding her in place. "You think I don't?"

She smiled. "I know you do." She ground her hips, feeling the evidence of her statement buried deep inside her as she started to move. "Give me more, Josh," she urged, her hands resting on my chest, as she rose and fell, her head rocking back

I sat up, our bodies touching, capturing her head and kissing her. "Take me," I whispered into her mouth. "I'm all yours."

It was true. I was all hers… body, mind, and heart. And even as we rushed to get dressed, giggling and kissing, I cherished every second of my time with her.

Abbie had only been gone for a minute or two, the moans and sighs of her goodbye kiss still a very recent echo, when my mother came in from church. I was standing in the kitchen, having just put the kettle on to boil.

"What was that girl doing here?" she demanded.

"I assume you mean Abbie?" I turned, taking in her narrowed eyes and tight lips, sensing that something was brewing.

"Of course I mean Abbie. I've just seen her leaving as I was walking down The Street."

"So?" I raised my voice slightly.

"What was she doing here at this time of the morning?"

"What do you think?" I couldn't see that it was any of her business, but there was also no point in pretending either.

"You're screwing her?" she shrieked, surprising me with her crude language.

"That's none of your business."

"You are, aren't you?" She glared at me. "You bloody fool."

I'd never yet won an argument with my mother, and I didn't intend getting into one with her about Abbie, so I shook my head, shrugged my shoulders and walked away.

My mother's reaction didn't surprise me. I hadn't really expected her to be overjoyed at the discovery that Abbie and I were serious about our relationship. Let's face it, she'd never been overjoyed about anything related to me. But whatever her opinions might have been, I wasn't going to let her stand in our way.

I met up with Abbie again later in the day, after my lunchtime shift at the pub, but didn't tell her about my argument with my mother. It was only one of many, and I didn't want her to think she'd somehow been the cause of a problem. My mother was the cause, not Abbie.

It was the bank holiday weekend, at the end of August, and the village was hectic, so that afternoon, we drove out to one of the abandoned tin mines – a really remote one – and went for a walk, staying there until the sun was starting to set. I felt a really special connection to Abbie that day, like we'd somehow broken down a barrier – not that there had been any noticeable barriers between us. But for some reason, when I looked at her, when I held her and kissed her, and told her how much I loved her, it felt different.

Two days later, on the Tuesday, Uncle Tim arrived in the village, unannounced. I'd just finished work, and had dashed home to change, surprised to find the familiar dark blue Jaguar parked outside the Post Office.

My mother had barely spoken to me in the two days since our confrontation over Abbie, but on that afternoon, she was serving behind the counter, and she managed to string together enough words to tell me that Uncle Tim was in the kitchen and that he wanted to see me. Impatient to get back out to see Abbie, I went through, and sure enough, he was sat at the kitchen table, a half drunk cup of tea in front of him.

"Josh!" He glanced up, a smile on his face. "You're looking good."

"Thanks. So are you." It was true. He had a fantastic tan, and looked as smart as ever, in jeans and a short-sleeved check shirt.

"How's the car running?" he asked and I wondered if he'd come all the way down here just to make conversation. It seemed improbable, but he was taking his time getting to the point.

"Like a dream."

He nodded and sat forward, indicating the chair opposite him. "Have a seat," he suggested, which seemed an odd thing to say, considering this was more my home than his. Even so, I sat down and waited. "I've got a surprise for you," he said.

"Another one?"

He smiled. "Yes. And I think you'll like this even more than the car." I found that hard to believe, but didn't interrupt. I was intrigued. "I have a friend," he said a little pensively, as though he was thinking this up as he went along. "He owns a large PR company in London."

This was news to me. Obviously, I didn't see that much of Uncle Tim, but I knew he was something big in the city – hence the bank balance, the car, and the address in Notting Hill. But to discover that he had connections in the very industry I was looking to enter came as a surprise to me.

"I've spoken to him about you," he continued and I became aware that my mouth had fallen open, and made a point of closing it. "He's agreed to give you an interview."

He may as well have told me we were moving to Pluto. "You are aware that I haven't taken my degree yet," I pointed out, despite the bombshell he'd just dropped on me.

He smiled. "Of course. I told Charles that, and he said that's not important. He owes me a favour or two."

"Charles?" I queried. "Charles who?"

"I'm not sure if you'll have heard of him," he said. "His name's Charles Tatnell."

We weren't moving to Pluto at all. I was already there. "D—Do you mean *the* Charles Tatnell, of Tatnell, Burns and Chattaway?"

"That's the one."

I'd just named the biggest PR and marketing agency in London, probably in the country. The idea of interviewing with them was like a dream come true. Just the experience of spending some time with Charles Tatnell would be a godsend. It wasn't something that happened to people like me, from a small village in Cornwall, that no-one had heard of.

"He wants to interview me?" I needed to make sure I hadn't misheard.

"Yes. He's hiring at the moment for a new department, or something, so if he likes you, he wants to offer you a job."

"A job?"

"Of course. Why else would he be interviewing you? He hasn't got time to sit around chatting just for the sheer hell of it."

No, of course not. What had I been thinking?

A job?

A job with Tatnell, Burns and Chattaway?

"Um... okay," I said slowly. "When can he fit me in?"

"Well, that's the thing," Uncle Tim replied. "He's going abroad for a while at the end of next week, so he's said that if you're really interested, it'll have to be in the next day or two. He's got things to prepare for his trip."

"The next day or two..."

"Yes... if you're interested." He looked at me, his eyebrows raised expectantly.

"Oh, I'm interested. I'll have to look into the trains." I didn't relish the idea of driving in London.

"I can take you back with me, if you want," he offered.

"You can?"

"Yes." He nodded, smiling again.

"When are you leaving?"

He shifted in his seat. "This is a flying visit, Josh. I'm going back straight away." I stared at him. "Of course, if you've got more important things..."

"No," I interrupted. "I'll come with you."

He nodded. "You'd better pack an overnight bag."

"Yes... yes of course." I got up, almost knocking the chair over, in my excitement. "I'll... I'll..." I felt flustered, almost panicked.

"Calm down." Uncle Tim stood and walked around the table, taking hold of my shoulders and calming me. "Take a deep breath." I did as he said. "Now, go upstairs, find a bag and pack it with some clothes. You'll need something smart for your interview tomorrow, don't forget."

I nodded and he released me, smiling as I ran up the stairs and into my room, trying to control my breathing as I pulled out a holdall from the bottom of my wardrobe and put in the clothes I thought I'd need for an overnight stay in London. I didn't own a suit, but I did have a smart pair of black trousers and a white shirt, which I folded as carefully as I could, hoping they would survive the journey, and then I zipped up the holdall and ran back downstairs.

"Ready?" Uncle Tim said, my mother standing in the doorway that led through to the shop, her arms folded across her chest.

"Yes," I said, then, "No."

"What's wrong?" He looked at me, seemingly surprised as I dropped the holdall and bolted for the back door.

"Abbie," I called over my shoulder.

In the haste, the excitement, the thrill of it all, I'd almost forgotten her. What was wrong with me? I wanted to kick myself, but I didn't have the time. So instead I ran across the road. She was sitting on the sea wall where we'd agreed to meet and she stood as I approached.

"Hello." Her voice was soft and I leant down and kissed her.

"Hi."

"You look a bit out of sorts."

"I feel a bit out of sorts."

She tilted her head to one side. "Is there a reason for that?"

"Yes." I held her hands in mine and explained, telling her about Uncle Tim's sudden arrival, about his friend, Charles, and the interview.

"A job?" she said, cottoning on a lot quicker than I did. "In London?"

"Well, yes… but, no. I won't get it."

She frowned. "Why not? You're good at this… and you're enthusiastic. You believe in what you're doing. That's half the battle I would've thought."

"I know, but…"

"Then stop doubting yourself." The sincerity in her voice was breathtaking. She believed in me, even if I didn't.

I saw her glance over my shoulder and turned, to see my uncle loading my holdall onto the back seat of his car. "I should probably go," I told her, leaning down and kissing her again.

"When will you be back?" she asked.

"Well, it depends on when the interview is," I replied. "Either late tomorrow, or sometime on Thursday." A sudden thought struck me. "Can you let your dad know I might not be here for my Thursday shift?" She nodded her head. "I'll call you." I kissed her again and then moved away, holding her hand until our arms were outstretched, then our hands, and then our fingers. Then we were parted, and I turned and ran back to Uncle Tim's car, climbing into the passenger seat.

"Alright?" he asked.

"Yes."

"She doesn't mind you going?" He nodded towards Abbie.

"No, of course not." It seemed like a strange question to me, especially as Abbie had just been so supportive and encouraging. Why would she mind? She loved me.

I sailed through the interview the following morning, getting on really well with Charles Tatnell, who was a larger than life character, flamboyantly dressed in a loud check suit and scarlet shirt, with no tie.

He offered me the job there and then, explaining that he'd been given a similar chance at the beginning of his career and had seen 'something' in me the minute I'd walked into his office. I hoped it wasn't a shared taste in fashion, and accepted his offer, agreeing to start the following Monday.

As he walked me to the door of the plush offices, he explained to me that the new department he was in the process of setting up would be working exclusively with publishing companies. He wanted me to be part of that team, starting at the bottom, of course. My salary would be small – although to me it seemed quite large – but he promised a shining future, if I was willing to put in the hours.

I caught the underground back to Uncle Tim's flat in Notting Hill, feeling elated, and relieved it was less busy than it had been on my early morning journey.

"How did it go?" Tim asked, opening the door to me. He was working from home, his study being set up in one of the six bedrooms in his luxurious mansion house apartment.

I teased him, tilting my head this way and that before announcing, "I'm gainfully employed… so…"

He slapped me on the arm. "Well done!"

"Thanks."

We walked through into the kitchen, which was very modern, filled with every gadget imaginable, and he poured me a coffee from the machine, passing it over the granite topped kitchen island.

"You'll stay here, won't you?"

"When?" I took a sip of coffee, and looked at him, feeling confused.

"When you move up to London, of course. You weren't thinking of commuting from Cornwall on a daily basis, were you?"

"No… Um, thanks. That's really kind of you."

He smiled at me again, and then wandered back to his study, leaving me in the kitchen, with the numbing thought that had just entered my head.

How on earth was I going to break the news to Abbie?

I managed to catch the two o'clock train from Paddington, which got me into Falmouth at seven-thirty. It was then an hour's bus ride home, but at least I was back, and I had until Sunday afternoon before I had to leave again.

I didn't even go home to dump my bag, but took it with me to the pub, going in through the front door and straight up to the bar. Robert was serving someone – not anyone I knew, presumably a tourist – but once he'd finished, he turned to me.

"Abbie's upstairs," he said, opening up the hatch in the bar and letting me through.

I thanked him and went straight up the stairs, leaving my bag at the top. She wasn't in the living room, so I knocked on her bedroom door, which she opened, a smile forming on her face the moment she saw me, right before she threw her arms around my neck and kissed me.

"Well, if that's the sort of greeting I'm going to get when I go away, I'll have to do it more often," I said, making light of things, as we broke the kiss.

She stared up at me. "And will you be?" she said, sounding nervous.

"Will I be what?"

"Going away more often."

I took her hand and led her back into her room, closing the door behind us and leading her over to the bed, sitting us both down. "Yes," I said softly, and she nodded her head.

"You got the job?"

"Yes."

She smiled, a real, proper, genuine smile, that touched her eyes and everything. "Well done," she beamed. "I knew you could do it."

I cupped her face in my hands, focusing on her. "You do know this doesn't change anything, don't you?"

The furrow appeared above her nose. "It changes everything, Josh." Her voice was disarmingly honest and I shook my head.

"No, it doesn't. It just means my drive back here will be four hours longer than we thought it would be."

She sighed. "You can't drive back here every weekend."

"Why not? I can leave London at about six on a Friday evening and be back here by midnight. We'll have all weekend together."

"But you'll be exhausted." She was trying to sound reasonable, but she sounded upset too.

"So what if I am? I'll have you." She put her arms around my neck and buried her head on my shoulder. I felt the dampness of her tears through my shirt and held onto her. "I'll make it work," I whispered into her ear. "Please don't be scared, and please don't cry. I promise, I'll make it work."

I loaded up the car with all the things I wanted to take, except for Abbie.

"Call me when you get there," she whispered as I held her.

"Of course. I'll call you all the time."

She smiled, leaning back. We'd said our proper goodbyes in her bed the previous evening. This was the public version, but even so, I kissed her deeply, holding her close, imprinting the feeling of her on my brain, because I was going to have to survive for five days without her.

"I'll be back on Friday," I said and she nodded as I got into the car, Robert putting his arm around her and giving me a wave as I drove off up the hill, looking in my rear-view mirror and seeing her turn to him, and nestle against him. She was crying. I knew that. And I wanted to go back and hold her myself, rather than leaving it to her dad to comfort her. But the thing was, if I did that, I'd just be prolonging the agony.

"I'll be back on Friday," I repeated to myself, through the lump in my throat, putting on my sunglasses and concentrating on the long drive ahead.

London traffic was easier than I'd thought, but then I reminded myself that, by the time I got there, it was Sunday evening, not the dreaded Monday morning rush hour. Still, I'd be doing that on the underground, not in the car, which I parked at the front of Uncle Tim's apartment block in a designated space, alongside his Jaguar.

Upstairs, he showed me to my room; which was different from the one I'd slept in before. This was larger, with a wet room and dressing area adjoining, and it was on the opposite side of the flat from his.

"I use the other room for overnight guests," he explained. "You can make yourself more at home here."

I nodded, looking around at the sumptuous furnishings, the fur throw on the end of the extra wide bed, the lush, thick carpets and expensive, original wall hangings.

"I'll leave you to unpack," he said, and smiled, leaving the room. I glanced at my two suitcases, which contained most of my clothes, except for the few things I'd left behind, having reached the conclusion that I didn't really need shorts, or numerous pairs of swimming trunks in London, and decided that unpacking could wait. Instead, I pulled out my phone and called Abbie.

"Hello," she said, and even though she was trying to sound cheerful, I could hear her tears.

"Tell me you haven't been crying for the last six and a half hours," I replied, but she didn't answer, which I assumed meant she couldn't tell me that – not without lying, anyway. "Abbie," I said softly, and she sniffled. "Please don't."

"Sorry," she murmured. "I just miss you."

"I miss you too."

"How's London?" she asked, making an effort not to cry, although I could tell it was a struggle.

"I haven't seen much of it yet… but I don't want to talk about London."

"Oh?" She sounded intrigued, which was much better than hearing her tears. "What do you want to talk about?"

"You."

"Me?"

"Yes."

"What about me?"

"I want to tell you how much I miss touching your soft skin, and holding your hand and looking into your eyes, and seeing your perfect smile when I tell you how much I love you. Because I do, Abbie. I love you so much."

"I love you too."

"And I don't want you to cry all the time."

"How can I not cry?" she said, and it sounded like she was about to start again. "It's a whole five days until I'm going to see you again."

"I know, but if you spend those five days crying, you're going to wear yourself out, and that won't be any good at all."

"It won't?"

"No."

"Why?" There was just the hint of a tease in her voice now and it made me smile.

"Because when I get back there on Friday, I don't intend letting you sleep for the whole weekend… so you'd better conserve your energy while I'm away."

She sighed. "Well, when you put it like that," she murmured, "I suppose I should."

I laughed, and after a moment, so did she, and then we talked for another twenty minutes about everything and nothing. She seemed more cheerful by the time we hung up, and we arranged that she would phone me in the morning.

Although it was late, Uncle Tim had ordered in a curry and he called me through when it arrived, a few minutes after I'd finished my call with Abbie. We sat together at the kitchen island, surrounded by take-away cartons, and we both had a cold beer to go with it.

"I keep odd hours," he said, helping himself to more Chicken Madras, which I found a little hot and spicy for my tastes. "And I travel a fair bit. You may go for days without seeing me… sometimes weeks. So, just make yourself at home."

I nodded and looked around at the sheer luxury of it all, wondering if I'd ever be able to feel 'at home' here.

When I got back to my room, I found a text message on my phone, from Abbie, and I sat down on the edge of my bed to read it:

— Thank you for saying all those lovely things and for cheering me up, and I'm sorry for crying so much. I promise not to do it all the time – because I want to have a thoroughly exhausting time with you next weekend. Please don't forget, I love you. A xxx

I typed out a reply.

— You don't have to thank me. I meant every word. I apologise for taking a while to reply; we were just having dinner. I'm already looking forward to next weekend, and believe me, I will never forget that you love me – almost as much as I love you. J xxx

Her reply was instant.

— Don't apologise – remember? Friends don't have to. I'm just going to bed now. I'm tired and I need to conserve my energy. Evidently. I'll call at 7 tomorrow. Love you A xxx

I smiled as I typed out:

— I wish I could be with you right now, but I can't, so dream of me instead. Love you more J xxx

I put the phone down, but it beeped again, and I picked it up and read:

— *I always dream of you. A xxx*

It went without saying that I did too.

The next morning, after a night spent dreaming about doing all kinds of highly erotic things with Abbie, and a twenty minute phone call telling her about them, which made her sigh and moan more than ever, I made my way to my new job, where I was introduced to the three other people in the team, with whom I'd be sharing an office. Stacey was in charge. She was probably in her late twenties, with red hair – albeit not natural – and it only took me ten minutes to establish that she really liked the sound of her own voice. Ant – which I assumed was short for 'Anthony' – and Elena were in their early twenties and, while Ant was fairly laid back, Elena was one of those people who claimed to thrive on stress. She shared this trait with Stacey and between them, they ran around, shouted a lot and Elena occasionally burst into noisy tears, which I found utterly pointless. I liked the atmosphere of the place though. It may have been an office – one set in a huge five storey house just off of Sloane Square – but there was no formality. We could wear what we wanted, as long as it was 'decent', and a lot of the employees seemed to share Charles Tatnell's tastes for bright colours and exuberant styles. My own preference soon became for jeans (always blue), a shirt (usually white) and a jacket (either a grey or blue blazer-style), the latter of which I'd take off almost the moment I entered the building. The work itself was easier than I'd expected and consisted mainly of making phone calls to book reviewers and magazines, and sending out press releases, as well as helping to set up a huge launch, which one of the new publishing company clients had dropped on us, with just a couple of weeks' notice, having been let down by their previous PR agency, which was the main reason they'd transferred their account to TBC. They had a celebrity author, who'd written a kiss-and-tell biography and they wanted everyone – and I mean *everyone* – to be there to see it hit the shelves. Having taken an advance copy and spent an evening reading it, after I'd finished my nightly call to Abbie,

I thought it deserved a place in the bin, rather than on the bookshelves, but that was just my opinion, and as the office junior, I wasn't really entitled to one of those.

I made it through to the end of my first week though, and feeling tired but pleased with how things had gone, I drove down to Cornwall. It was exhausting, and took me longer than I'd anticipated, so I stopped about two hours from home and sent Abbie a quick text, at roughly eleven o'clock.

—Hello, beautiful. I'm still two hours away. Sorry I won't be home to see you tonight as expected, but we'll catch up tomorrow. Miss you so much. Love you. J xxxxx

She replied straight away.

— I'm sorry too. I wish you were here. Call for me in the morning? Miss you more. Love you. A xxxxx

I smiled and sent back:

— I wish I was there too. Now get some sleep. As I said to you last weekend, you're going to need it. J xxxxx

Her response made me laugh.

— God, I hope so. A xxxxx

We'd phoned each other every day during the week; Abbie calling me in the mornings, and me returning the favour when I got home from work each evening. And in between, we'd sent each other numerous texts, and quite often, they'd ended up with a teasing, suggestive tone to them, which always brought a smile to my face. I really had missed her and being apart – even though I was busy all the time – was far harder than I'd anticipated.

I called at the pub for her the next morning, as planned, greeting her with the longest, deepest, most passionate kiss we'd ever shared, and we spent the day together, both longing for the evening, when her father would be busy, and we could sneak upstairs to her room, and take that kiss a stage further. We both knew that our longed for sleepless weekend was a pipe-dream, because we didn't have the luxury of having somewhere we could be together for that length of time, but a few hours alone in Abbie's room was enough, and we knew it. When I got there,

I almost ripped her clothes from her, my desperation to feel her soft skin, to touch her and taste her, overwhelming me. Joining us together again was sublime; feeling her, seeing her come apart and hearing her whisper her love for me was almost too much, and for a moment, I couldn't even speak, until I found my voice again, and told her how much I loved her. Then I put my words into actions, showing her, for a second time that being apart for an entire week had its compensations.

Afterwards, as she lay in my arms, she told me that, with the deadline looming for her confirming her living accommodation at uni, she'd decided she was going to take a place on the campus at Falmouth.

"You're not here anymore, so it's not the same... and I feel like a change will do me good," she said, sounding sad.

I pulled her into my arms. "I'm sorry I'm not here, but I think you'll have a great time. You'll enjoy being with all those other arty people."

She smiled at me, her nose wrinkling. "Arty people?"

"Yes... you know what I mean."

She nestled into me. "Yes, I do."

"What will you do after the first year?" I asked and she shrugged.

"I don't know. I'll worry about that when I get there."

It hurt that she sounded so despondent and resigned, so I shifted down the bed slightly and kissed her, hoping that might help.

We couldn't sleep together, so unfortunately, at just before eleven, I had to return to my mother's for the night, but on Sunday morning, Abbie came over and we took advantage of that hour of peace while my mother was at church. I'd wondered if my mother might try and spite us by not going, by staying at home and making it impossible for us to be together. But she didn't. In fact, she barely spoke to me and didn't mention Abbie at all, leaving for church on time as usual. In her absence, I made love to Abbie more slowly and tenderly than ever before, savouring every sight, sound and taste, knowing we'd have to part again in just a few short hours.

"I hate that you have to leave so soon," Abbie whispered into my neck as I held her, getting my breath back.

"So do I."

"But you're enjoying the work, aren't you?"

I'd told her how much I liked it over the phone during one of our evening conversations. "Yes."

"And the people you work with… what are they like?"

I shifted down the bed, turning onto my side to face her.

"Why do you ask?"

"Because I'm interested." Her eyes widened and I knew in an instant what was behind her question and that I had to give her the reassurance she needed.

"They're okay," I replied. "But if you're worried, you don't need to be."

"You're not tempted?" she asked, revealing her fear openly.

"Never." I moved closer to her, wrapping my leg around hers. "I don't even look. Why would I? I love you." I pulled her into me. "You own me. I'm yours, remember?"

She smiled. "And I'm yours."

Saying goodbye was still hard, but not perhaps as difficult as the first time, being as she knew I'd be back. And so did I.

The following week was more busy at work. The book launch was looming, the stress levels were rising; for those who flourished under it, I suppose it must have been heaven. For the rest of us, it was a nightmare.

By Friday, I was tired, but there was less traffic on the roads and I got down to Porthgowan just before midnight.

I spent another spectacular weekend with Abbie, trying to ignore the tiredness, and the frustration that our time was limited to just a little more than twenty-four hours, snatching a few brief moments to be alone, whenever circumstances permitted. The contrast with our perfect summer seemed almost too great to contemplate.

By Wednesday of the following week, the awful truth had dawned on me, and it was with a heavy heart that I called Abbie when I got home that night, at just before eight. Luckily, Uncle Tim was out and I had the flat to myself, so I sat on my bed and didn't worry about whispering.

"Hi," Abbie answered quickly as usual, her voice caressing my skin, even from hundreds of miles away.

"Hello."

"What's wrong?"

I sighed. There was no point in beating about the bush. She could obviously tell from my voice that something was bothering me. "I've got bad news," I said.

"About the weekend?"

How did she know? "Yes. I won't be able to make it." I said it before she guessed. It seemed fairer that way.

"Why?" She'd gone much quieter now and I pressed the phone to my ear so I could hear her.

"It's this book launch. They've set it for Monday – which is a really stupid day to hold it, if you ask me – and that means we're going to have to work the weekend."

There was a pause. "Promise you're not lying to me." Her voice cracked.

"Of course I'm not lying."

"Promise this isn't an excuse."

"Abbie… I promise it's not an excuse. Please believe me." I heard her let out a sob, although she tried to stifle it. "Don't cry."

"I'm sorry," she said. "I just miss you when you're not here."

"I miss you too. All the time. And I promise I'll come home next weekend."

"Promise?"

"Cross my heart."

The launch went well and when we got into work on Tuesday, everyone was full of congratulations for our success. Charles Tatnell was back from his trip abroad and came into our office to tell us how well we'd done, and when he'd gone, Stacey was beaming from ear to ear, puffed up with self importance, as though she'd handled the whole thing herself, completely unaided.

The thing I hadn't allowed for, because I had no experience of such matters, was that after the launch, there would be even more work than before. The phones didn't stop ringing, with people wanting to interview the author, wanting revised press releases, wanting copies of the book for reviews and to arrange signings and talks. On top of all of that, there were another two launches coming up as well, not for celebrities this time, but for best-selling authors. Put bluntly, it was a madhouse and Elena went through even more boxes of tissues than she had during the previous two weeks, despite telling anyone who'd listen, how much she loved the stress of the job.

We worked until gone nine every evening, so I don't know why it came as such a shock to me when I looked up at the clock on Friday evening, just as I was putting on my jacket, and saw that it was already nine-twenty. It was far too late to start the drive to Cornwall, but despite the disappointment, I reasoned to myself that I could still go down in the morning. If I left early, I'd get there by lunchtime. It wasn't ideal, but it was better than nothing.

I got back to Uncle Tim's flat at about a quarter to ten and called Abbie straight away.

"Where are you?" she asked, after we'd said hello to each other.

"I'm still at home."

"Home…?" she queried.

"Well, Uncle Tim's." I realised my slip of the tongue. "You know what I mean."

"Why are you still there?"

"Because I've only just finished work."

"Again?" She knew I'd been working late all week, because I'd had to call her from the office in the evenings, knowing I'd be too late home to catch her before she went to bed.

"Yes." I couldn't help yawning as I settled down on the bed. "But I'll drive down tomorrow. I promise."

"You promised last weekend."

"I know, but…"

"Oh, what's the point, Josh," she whispered and I felt my skin tingle, fear washing over me, as I sat up again.

"What do you mean?" I heard her whimper, then sob. "Please don't," I begged. "Please don't cry."

"I—I cant do this," she muttered.

"Can't do what?"

"The long distance thing," she said and I felt the walls of my heart crash in, crushing the breath out of me. "I hate it. I hate everything about it. It's breaking me, Josh, and it's only going to get worse when I'm at uni."

"No, it's not," I said, clutching at straws, desperate to keep hold of her, even though I could feel her slipping away from me with every word. "You've decided to live on campus for the first year at least, so that means we can be together even more than we are now."

"How?"

"Because I'll be able to spend the night with you."

"But I'll be in halls," she wailed. "You won't be allowed to."

Why hadn't I thought of that? *Because you've been too busy thinking about yourself and your career, that's why.* "Can't you sneak me in?" I asked.

"At one o'clock in the morning?" she said. "How would I do that? And anyway, you're not listening."

"Yes I am." I wasn't just listening; I was hearing every word. They were etched on my heart – or at least on the pieces of it that were fracturing inside me.

"No you're not," she persevered. "I can't do this. I've been trying so hard to hide it from you, to put a brave face on it, but I can't be yours, and never see you; I can't look forward to being with you all week, and then keep being disappointed."

"It's one week, Abbie. When have I let you down before?"

"It's two weeks," she said, raising her voice slightly. "You didn't come back last weekend either, remember?"

"I couldn't help that. And anyway, I'm not saying I won't come this week, I'm just saying I can't come until tomorrow, that's all."

"I know." She breathed deeply, calming. "And I know I'm being selfish, but that's the problem."

"What is?"

"I need more. I told you, didn't I? You created a monster."

"You're not a monster."

There was a silence that stretched between us. I didn't want to be the one to break it, so I waited until eventually Abbie spoke, and pierced my heart a little bit more. "I need someone who can be with me, Josh, and that's not you. Not any more."

"How can you say that?"

"Because it's true. You belong in London, chasing your dreams."

"No. I belong with you." She sobbed and I longed to hold her. "Don't do this, Abbie," I begged. "I'll come back… I'll give up my job…"

"No!" I startled at the vehemence in her voice. "No, Josh. I don't want you to do that."

"You… you mean you don't want me?" I whispered, unable to speak any louder for fear my voice would crack.

"I mean, I don't want you to give up your dreams for me. I don't want to be responsible for that, and I don't want you to have to choose. I won't make you do that. Surely you can see… living like this… it's too hard."

"And you think it'll be easier if we break up?"

"At least I won't have to be disappointed anymore."

That hurt. That really hurt. "I didn't realise I was such a disappointment to you." I couldn't help but say it.

"You're not. I'm sorry. That came out wrong." She sighed again. "Can't you see, what I'm saying, though… it's for the best."

"How can that be? We love each other; how can it be for the best for us to be apart?"

"We're already apart, Josh. We're just pretending we're still together."

"I'm not."

There was another silence; an even longer one this time, and then I heard her say, "I'm sorry."

"Don't be." I wanted to remind her that friends – especially best friends – never have to say 'sorry', but I couldn't get the words out.

"But I am," I heard her whisper. "I'm so sorry." And then the phone went dead in my hand as my heart finally shattered in my chest and I let out a wild howl of despair that started in the pit of my stomach and filled the room, filled the whole apartment, the tears tumbling down my cheeks as I thought about a life without Abbie, and let the pain consume me.

Chapter Five

Abbie

My course at uni was everything I'd dreamed it would be, and more.

It gave me the freedom to be an individual, both in my art, and in myself, and I learned so much. I drew, I sketched, I painted. I gained new techniques, as well as enhancing my existing ones, honing my skills. My tutors praised my abilities and helped me improve, pointing me in new directions, showing me different paths to follow, encouraging my every step.

Every night I'd fall into bed in the halls of residence, in my simple room, with a single bed, wardrobe and desk, and recall a day well spent.

And then I'd remember Josh.

I'd wonder where he was, and what he was doing, whether he was happy again yet. I knew he hadn't been happy when I'd ended our phone call, and our relationship. I could hear it in his voice. I could hear the heartbreak. It matched my own. But I knew, with an absolute certainty, that the life he wanted wasn't compatible with mine. Not any more. And he knew it too.

I think I'd known that when he came and told me he was going for the interview. I think that was the moment I knew he'd leave, and that living apart from him was more than I could cope with. I didn't say anything, of course. I supported him. I told him to go... because I loved him and I wanted him to be happy, even though I knew it would be the end of us. All the rest was just playing for time.

I was astounded that he offered to give it up and come back to me, and I'll admit that a part of me was tempted to say 'yes... yes, please', but I couldn't let him do that. I couldn't let him sacrifice everything he'd ever wanted... for me. If I'd let him do that... if I'd let him make that choice between me and his career, his life in London, then it would have driven a wedge between us, and although we would always have loved each other, nothing would ever have been the same again. I would always have felt guilty and he would always have felt cheated. It was better not to go there... for both of us.

I won't deny though that in those few weeks between me ending our relationship and me leaving Porthgowan to go to university, I used to sit on the beach and daydream that Josh would appear in front of me, kneel down and tell me he'd ignored my wishes, and he'd come home for me anyway; that he couldn't live without me, and that I meant more to him than anything. I would jump up into his arms and he'd hold me and kiss me, wildly, frantically, and tell me that he'd never leave me again. It never happened, of course. But then why would it? Why would he do that? I'd hurt him. Badly. I'd given him no reason to come back, no hope for reconciliation. I'd ended it between us, pushing him away in a vain, stupid attempt to control the pain of missing him. And in the end, I only missed him more.

I'd thought that not seeing him from one week to the next was too hard. But cutting him out of my life was so much worse. The problem was, by the time I realised that, it was too late.

My first year at Falmouth went by in a whirl of new experiences, some of which helped to drown out the pain of losing Josh.

Even so, I sometimes used to wake myself up at night crying, grateful that I had a room to myself and there was no-one to witness my tears... my self-inflicted heartbreak.

I made a friend though. Her name was Bethan Thomas. She was shorter than me, although not by much, and had light blonde hair, and pale blue eyes, a high-pitched giggle, and a fanatical love for chocolate... and she came from Cardiff. She was studying Fine Art, like me, and towards the end of our first year, we decided we'd try and find a flat together for our second and third years. In reality, I could have gone home and commuted from the village; Porthgowan was only an hour away, after all. It had taken me ages to decide what I was going to do – whether I was going to stay at home, or live in Falmouth. Josh and I had discussed it endlessly, batting my alternatives back and forth. But in the end, him moving to London was the deciding factor. Looking back, I suppose that was probably because I knew we couldn't survive him leaving and I couldn't bear to be in the village any longer than was strictly necessary – not without him. At the time though, I just told myself that I'd always wanted to get that 'university' experience, and that it was the right thing to do.

As my first year drew to a close, I knew I still wasn't ready to go home yet. Not permanently, anyway. I knew I would one day. I knew the sea and the sky would call me back, and that I'd go. And that I'd probably never want to leave again. But at that moment, I needed to be somewhere else for a while longer. The memories were still too raw.

In the meantime though, I had to get through the holidays and so, it was with a hesitant, wary heart that I packed up my things and loaded them into Dad's car on that warm June morning, gave Bethan a hug and set off back to Porthgowan for the long summer break. We'd already found a flat, not far from the main campus, and had paid a deposit – which Dad had helped me with – so we knew we had somewhere to move into when we came back in the autumn. Bethan waved me goodbye and turned away, going back into the halls to finish her own packing, and I faced the front of the car, and the reality of going home… of those familiar sights and sounds; the beach, the sea, the massive sky, the walks, the waves crashing on the shore… everything that had long since made Porthgowan my home. Only now I'd be seeing them, feeling them and hearing them without Josh.

I'd spent a few weeks there without him before starting at uni, after I'd broken our hearts, but I'd been in too much pain to notice anything around me then. I'd also been home at Christmas, of course, but had managed to stay indoors for most of the short break, avoiding the beach and all of our other familiar haunts – helped greatly by some truly appalling weather – and focusing on spending the holiday with Dad and catching up with the changes he'd made to the pub, which included redecorating my bedroom. He'd done it in a neutral, light yellow colour, covering over the purple that had long since replaced the pale pink of my childhood and he presented it to me as a surprise – a kind of 'ta-da' moment – and I flung my arms around his neck, grateful that he'd put so much thought and effort into it, and in doing so, had eradicated a lot of the memories of Josh. He hadn't done it for that reason, but it made it easier, somehow.

Even as we drove back on that bright, sunny Saturday morning, I couldn't help wondering if Josh might return at some point during the summer. His firm would allow him holidays, and although his relationship with his mother had never been good, I thought there was a chance he might come home. I let the idea run about my head for a moment, contemplating how I'd react if I saw him; imagining the moment and how I'd feel. My body still ached for him, I knew that much, and I didn't think that seeing him would ease that at all. Touching him, on the other hand…

I shook my head, bringing myself back to reality, and the stark realisation that nearly ten long months had passed since I'd broken us. Ten months… I felt the tears welling in my eyes, appreciating the length of time, and the fact that he hadn't once been in contact during that whole time; not with anyone. Not his mother, not Simon… and not me. Of course he hadn't. He had a new life now; it was the life he'd always wanted, and he'd have found someone else to share it with, and to share himself with, of that I had no doubt. He was in London, after all: a city filled with temptations. Perhaps he'd go on holiday with his new girlfriend – abroad, maybe, to somewhere exotic, somewhere romantic.

I looked out of the side window and tried to wipe away my tears without Dad noticing; tried to erase the images that were invading my head… images of Josh and a faceless, nameless woman walking hand in hand along a white, sandy beach staring out across a perfect azure sea, the two of them having a candlelit dinner, feeding each other and toasting their happiness, then lying naked on a silk-lined bed, him whispering his love for her as he joined their bodies together.

*****

Josh didn't come back. But Simon did.

He'd changed a little since the last time I'd seen him. His blond hair was a shade darker, presumably because he wasn't spending so much time in the sun; he seemed a little taller, although not as tall as Josh, and he'd filled out somewhat – no longer the skinny kid he'd been when we were growing up.

It had been a while since we'd spent any time together and to begin with, things between us were awkward, consisting of nodded heads and stilted 'hellos' whenever we passed each other. Our friendship had waned over the last few years, partly because Simon had been working at the camp site and hadn't really had time for us, but also because Josh and I had been so wrapped up in each other. I felt a bit guilty about that.

The other problem, of course, was Andrew.

Simon knew nothing of what had happened – well, unless Andrew had told him, which I doubted – but that didn't stop me from feeling uneasy around him. What if I ran into Andrew?

I'd been at home for nearly a month and was sitting on the beach sketching, when Simon appeared by my side, quite unexpectedly.

"Why are you sitting here?" he said, stringing a sentence together for the first time as he plonked himself down on the rug next to me. I turned and looked at him, my confusion presumably obvious, because he continued, "You always used to sit on the other side of the cove."

"Oh." I understood what he meant now. I'd deliberately chosen to sit as far as possible from the spot Josh and I used to occupy, just to try and suppress some of the memories. "I felt like a different view," I said. "I can't keep drawing the same things."

He nodded his head and looked out at the horizon.

"I always used to wonder about that," he said. "I used to think it was odd that you'd sketch the same view over and over."

I didn't feel like telling him that it wasn't the view I used to come to the beach for; it was the company. "How's uni?" I asked instead. He was at Plymouth – the same university Josh had intended going to – studying law.

"It's great," he replied, smiling for the first time. He had a nice smile. It touched his blue eyes and made his nose crinkle.

"Do you want to go into law then?" It seemed odd that, although I'd known him since I was seven years old, I didn't know the answer to that question, but I didn't.

"Yes." He turned to face me. "Unlike my layabout brother, I want to make something of my life." He'd mentioned Andrew, even if not by name, and I felt the tension rise inside me. "You heard he lost his job?" he continued, unaware of my discomfort.

"No."

He nodded. "Yeah. He got the sack. He's working in a supermarket warehouse now." He picked up a handful of sand and let it run through his fingers. "With a role model like that, you can see why I have ambitions to do better."

"Yes," I replied, just for something to say.

"The atmosphere at home is pretty toxic when he's around," he added, almost to himself, and I wondered if he'd forgotten I was there, until he turned to look at me again. "But luckily, apart from coming back to sleep every so often, he doesn't put in too many appearances."

"I see." I'd wondered about Andrew's absence from the village; now I had an explanation of sorts.

"That doesn't stop Mum and Dad from arguing about him though." He sighed. "Honestly, I think the best thing I can do is to qualify, get a job, and move out."

"You want to leave the village?"

He shrugged. "I'm not that attached to it," he said. "Obviously if I had a reason to stay, I would…" His voice faded and he looked at me, with an odd, uncertain expression in his eyes, before turning away again and focusing on the horizon.

I picked up my pencil and started to shade in the cliffs, wondering what that had been about.

Over the course of the next couple of months, Simon and I met more often, sometimes for a drink in the pub, sometimes on the beach, and occasionally we'd go for a walk, or a drive somewhere. He'd usually give me the choice of where we went, and I'd always make a point of selecting a destination as far away as possible from the places I used to go with Josh.

I found him easy to talk to, but then we did tend to stick to safe subjects, and the summer passed quickly.

It was near the end of the holidays, one windy Saturday in the middle of September, and we were sheltering in the chilly beer garden, reminiscing about our childhood, when he suddenly turned to me, a serious expression on his face.

"Can I ask you something?" he said.

"Yes." I looked up at him, surprised by the intensity in his eyes.

"Will you be my girlfriend?" His voice had dropped to a whisper and he seemed shy about asking.

I hesitated, thinking of Josh, even though it had been over a year since I'd even heard his voice, let alone seen him, or touched him.

"I know you and Josh ended badly," Simon murmured, still staring at me, and I wondered how he knew that, being as he hadn't really been around at the time. "And if you're not ready yet, I will understand." He paused, then added, "But I'll look after you, I promise," and I gulped down my tears.

Josh had promised that too, and it wasn't that he hadn't kept his word. It was that I hadn't let him. Would things be any different with Simon? And, perhaps more importantly, if I said 'yes', would my feelings for Josh come between us?

"C—Can I think about it?" I asked.

"Sure." He turned away again, but not before I'd noticed that same uncertain look in his eyes, and then he got up and helped me to my feet, holding my hand as we walked back into the pub.

A few days later, we both returned to Uni. Simon was driving himself back to Plymouth that lunchtime, but Dad was taking me early, so he could get back and open up the pub. Simon and I said goodbye outside The Lobster Pot, as Dad finished loading my things into the car. I still hadn't given him my answer and we both knew it, although Simon was polite enough not to bring it up.

"Call me?" he said, sounding a little nervous, almost desperate. "Let me know you've arrived safely."

"Of course."

He leant down and kissed my cheek and then pulled back as my dad gave an artificial cough, letting us know he was waiting.

"I'll see you soon," Simon added and then let go of my hands, stepping away from the car as I climbed in, and waved goodbye.

As we reached the main road and Dad had to stop the car to wait for a passing tractor, he turned to me. "Are you sure about that?" he said.

"What?"

"Simon."

"Why shouldn't I be?" I wondered if he knew something I didn't, but he shrugged and pulled out of the turning.

"No reason."

I wanted to tell him that I hadn't made a decision about Simon yet; that I wasn't sure about anything, but as I opened my mouth to speak, he said, "So, are you looking forward to having your own place?"

I turned to him, the moment lost. "Yes," I replied. "Yes, I am." It was true. Bethan and I had stayed in close contact over the holidays, planning the things we needed to buy and dividing the cost between us. The flat was already furnished, so we only really had to worry about cooking equipment, bedding and personal items, but it felt exciting, nonetheless. My own flat…

My room was large, with a double bed, a big wardrobe, chest of drawers and dressing table, which I was going to use as a desk. The walls were painted cream – as they were in every room in the flat – and the window looked out across some playing fields. It was warm and welcoming. The kitchen was small, but big enough for the two of us, and the living room had a comfortable sofa, coffee table, and a television, mounted on the wall. It was the most basic room in the house and Bethan and I decided we'd look out for a cheap table and chairs – there was space for one and neither of us really liked eating off of our laps.

We settled in quickly, unpacking our things and then, as a treat, ordered in a pizza. We were both tired and didn't feel like tackling the kitchen on our first night, especially as I was such a shocking cook.

My phone beeped, a couple of minutes after the pizza arrived and, wiping my fingers on a piece of kitchen towel, I checked the screen, seeing that I had a message. My heart always leapt whenever this happened, wondering if it might be Josh, but it wasn't. It was Simon, and I realised I'd forgotten to call him.

— Are you okay? Your dad got back before I left home, but I still haven't heard from you. Can I call you? Simon.

I replied at once, feeling guilty.

— Sorry. I got bogged down with unpacking. Just having dinner. I'll call you in half an hour. Abbie.

I did call, and he answered on the first ring, sounding pleased to hear from me. I apologised again for not calling him, which he said was 'fine', and he asked for my address, in case he ever needed it. I thought it was an odd request, but gave it to him anyway, and we spent fifteen minutes or so chatting before tiredness got the better of me and I ended the call, had a shower, and went to bed.

The next morning, Bethan and I both had lectures, but I got back to the flat before she did, and had only been there a few minutes when the doorbell sounded, making me jump out of my skin. Scolding myself for being so nervous, I opened the door, to find a huge basket of white roses, hiding a diminutive young woman. She handed them to me with a smile and asked for a signature on her clipboard, which I gave, despite my confusion, before she said goodbye and I closed the door, taking the flowers with me into the living room and setting them down on the coffee table. I pulled out the card from the envelope, which was attached to a long stick in the centre of the arrangement, and read the note printed on it:

'Welcome to your new home.

Love, Simon'

I had to smile. It was such a sweet thing to do, and I called him straight away. He didn't answer, so I left a message thanking him, and he called back later on, telling me he'd been in a lecture himself, and had turned his phone off.

"Thank you for the flowers," I repeated, even though I'd already said that in my message.

"Do you like them?" he asked.

"Yes. They're beautiful."

"Good." I could hear the smile in his voice, but I couldn't think what to say next.

"How's it going?" I asked. "How's the house?" I knew he'd moved into a four bedroomed house, with a few friends.

"Noisy," he replied, although I thought he was still smiling. "How's the flat?"

"It's lovely," I said. "I mean, it's modern, obviously, but other than that, it's lovely."

"What's wrong with modern?" he asked.

"Nothing, I suppose. I've just always preferred old houses."

He chuckled – well, it was a short of half-laugh, anyway. "You wouldn't say that if you lived in our house," he said. "The window in my bedroom has a howling gale coming through it. I'm dreading the winter."

"Oh dear."

"I'm sure I'll cope," he said, and I believed him. Simon seemed like someone who would cope – no matter what.

That weekend, after we'd been to the supermarket and stocked up properly, I decided to tackle the laundry while Bethan cleaned the bathroom, which was right by the front door. It was she, therefore, who answered the doorbell when it rang, and called me, telling me there was someone to see me.

I went through to the small hallway and my mouth fell open, as I saw Simon standing on the doorstep, looking very smart, in jeans, a formal shirt and a jacket.

"Are you busy?" he asked, smiling.

"I'm just doing the laundry."

"Can it wait?"

"Yes, it can," Bethan said, before I could answer, handing me my coat from the peg behind the door. I still had my shoes on from our earlier shopping trip, and she virtually pushed me out of the door, grinning.

"W—What are you doing here?" I said to Simon, as we walked towards the stairs.

"I came to see you." He held the door open, letting me pass into the stairwell ahead of him.

"Oh." I looked up at him, and he took my hand, leading me down the stairs and out into the small car park at the front of the building. His Vauxhall Astra was parked in one of the visitor's bays, and we walked over and got in, before he turned to me.

"I thought I'd take you to lunch."

I smiled at him, and he started the car, reversing out of the bay.

Lunch was lovely – at a country pub a few miles away. It was followed by a long walk, before he took me to dinner, at an Italian restaurant in the centre of town.

Afterwards, he drove me back to the flat and, once I'd climbed out of the car, he came around and stood in front of me.

"I know you haven't given me an answer yet," he said quietly, looking down into my eyes in the bold street light. "But I'll wait."

I saw the kindness, the hope, the friendship, in his face and smiled up at him. "You don't have to," I replied.

"I don't?" He looked confused now.

"No. My answer's yes. I'll be your girlfriend." As I said the word, it sounded strange, but I didn't have time to reflect, before he swept me up into his arms, twirling me around, and then he lowered me again, and bent to kiss me.

His lips were soft, his tongue insistent and I responded to his touch. But there was no heat, no passion, no fireworks. He pulled back, and brushed his thumb across my bottom lip.

"Can I come back next weekend?" he asked.

I nodded my head and he kissed me again.

He came back every weekend from then on.

After about six weeks, he asked if he could stay the night, rather than driving back to Plymouth late on a Saturday. He offered to sleep on the sofa and I agreed. As much as I was enjoying his company, I wasn't ready to share my bed with him, and he accepted that.

During the holidays, we went home together, with Simon picking me up from Falmouth on his way back, and we spent Christmas curled up on the sofa, watching old re-runs of TV shows, and then the long summer days walking, holding hands and occasionally talking about the future. Simon wanted to start working for a small local firm, commuting from the village, and build his way up from there. He smiled and told me he no longer had any ambitions to leave; he'd found his 'reason' to stay. He kissed me as he said that and I presumed that meant I was the reason and felt relieved. At least he wasn't going to abandon me too.

It was the middle of November, in our third year. Simon and I had been together for just over a year by then and I was working hard on my final pieces, while he'd been given a reading week, which basically meant he didn't have any lectures and was supposed to be spending the time studying independently, revising and getting ready for his exams, which were just a few short months away. He could have stayed in Plymouth, or gone home to Porthgowan, but he didn't. He came to see me instead.

Bethan had a new boyfriend at the time – a fellow art student by the name of Marcus, who she was madly in love with, and at some point during the previous week, they'd finally gone to bed together. Bethan wasn't one for sharing things like that – thank goodness – but the fact that Marcus had come out of her bedroom at seven in the morning, just as I was warming the teapot for my first cup of tea of the day, and that he was wearing the same clothes he'd had on the night before, was a reasonably large clue. He'd looked at me rather sheepishly and muttered something about 'going home to change', before disappearing out of the front door. Since then, he'd either stayed over at our flat, or Bethan had gone to his place, which was a few streets away, and on the night that Simon arrived, that was where she was.

"So, we have the place to ourselves?" Simon asked, when I explained Bethan's absence.

"Yes." I wondered what he had in mind, but he smiled at me and put his arm around my shoulders, pulling me back into the sofa with him.

"Shall we order in a pizza and watch a movie?" he suggested, and I nodded my head in agreement.

The movie was halfway through, and the pizza was nothing more than a few crusts in the bottom of the box, when Simon turned and kissed me, his tongue entering my mouth. I responded and felt his hands start to wander from their usual position on my back, around to my front, cupping my breasts through my thick shirt. He groaned and deepened the kiss, changing his position and pushing me down into the sofa a little more, and then a little more still, until I was lying and he was on top of me, breathing hard, his erection pressing into my hip.

I felt the ache return; the longing to be myself, to let go, to scream out my pleasure, and parted my legs so he could lie between them. He broke the kiss and knelt up, gazing down at me.

Without a word, he stood, then moved slightly and, grabbing my legs, he twisted me around, so my feet were on the floor, my bottom on the edge of the sofa. He knelt and reached out, undoing the button of my jeans and pulling down the zip.

"Lift your hips," he said, his voice lower than usual.

I did as he said and he pulled down my jeans, and my knickers at the same time, leaving them around my ankles. Then he leant forward and I remembered my first time with Josh, when he'd done this too, in exactly this position, his eyes locked with mine, kissing and licking me intimately until I came apart, thrashing wildly as he drove me onwards into that perfect insanity… I shook my head. I had to stop it. I couldn't think about Josh while I was with Simon. That wasn't fair. So, I focused on Simon as he pushed a finger inside me, then added a second, moving them around a little. I parted my legs, shifting forward to give him entrance, longing for that sweet, tortuous pleasure, but he pulled away again and I heard his zip, felt him move closer, and then the intrusion as he entered me. He didn't say a word still, but when I looked up, even in the dim light from the television, I could see his eyes were closed, his expression one of pure rapture as he started to move, his rhythm becoming faster and faster, harder and harder, a grunt emitting from his throat with every stroke, until he suddenly pulled out and spurted warm liquid all over my stomach, panting, his head rolling forward.

"God," he murmured. "You're amazing. So tight… so wet, so… so amazing."

I lay there, feeling the gelatinous fluid already cooling on my skin. "Um… could you get me a towel?" I whispered.

He focused properly and smiled. "Sure. Sorry." He stood and pulled up his jeans, tucking himself in, and wandered in the direction of the bathroom, returning a few moments later and handing me the guest towel. I took it and wiped the sticky mess from my stomach as he sat beside me, looking down.

"Sorry about that," he said, smiling. "I didn't bring any condoms with me. I hadn't expected you to say 'yes'." He leant over and kissed me, and I wondered, in that case, why he hadn't waited, why he hadn't been more responsible, and whether I had, in fact, said 'yes'. I hadn't said 'no', and I knew I could have done if I'd wanted to, but I didn't remember saying 'yes' either.

"You don't need to worry," I said, automatically. "I'm on the pill."

He sat back, grabbed the TV remote and turned the sound down. "Excuse me? Did you just say you're on the pill?"

"Yes."

"Um… Exactly how many men have you slept with?"

I felt myself bridle and struggled to my feet, bending and pulling up my briefs and jeans, fastening them and looking down at him. "Just Josh," I said. "But I don't know what that's got to do with it. Girls go on the pill for all kinds of reasons, you know. It's not just about sex." Obviously it had been in my case, but I still found his assumption a bit insulting.

He stood too now. "I'm sorry," he said, apologising yet again, but with a lot more emotion in his voice this time. He'd made a mistake – a big one – and he knew it. "Forgive me?" I hesitated and then nodded and he kissed me deeply, before sitting us both back down. "You really were amazing," he said, turning the sound back up on the TV, and settling down, his arm around my shoulder.

I wasn't sure how to reply to that. I couldn't say he'd been amazing too, because that would have been a lie. So I said nothing and we watched the end of the movie in silence.

When he turned off the TV, Simon stood and took my hand, pulling me to my feet. "Coming to bed?" he said and I looked up at him. He'd made the assumption that having sex meant we were going to share a bed.

"Um…" I wasn't sure how to say I wasn't ready for that. I'd never spent a whole night with Josh, and while I would have loved to do so with him, I felt like I needed a little longer to get used to the idea of sleeping with someone else.

"What's wrong?" he asked, interrupting my thoughts. "Surely you don't still have a problem sleeping with me… not after we've made love?" A smile formed on his lips and he leant closer, whispering, "And anyway, I might want to do all that again…"

He didn't wait for an answer, but led me through to my room, where he undressed me and then himself, and we got into bed together.

"Don't you want to know how many women I've slept with?" he asked, pulling up the duvet.

I didn't, not particularly, but he seemed to want to tell me, so I turned to him and raised my eyebrows. "Okay," I said, with a certain amount of trepidation.

"You're the third," he replied and I slowly nodded my head, feeling relieved. Part of me had expected him to say I was the first, and I wasn't sure I wanted that responsibility. "The other two were years ago," he added, when I didn't say anything. "But that's because I've wanted you for such a long time."

"Please tell me you used contraception when you were with them?" I said, ignoring his compliment and focusing on practicalities, and he put his arms around me, pulling me close to him.

"Of course I did. Tonight was… well, it was completely unplanned and spontaneous." He hesitated, then kissed me gently. "And I'm sorry… about what I said…" He didn't need to elaborate. We both knew what he was talking about.

"It's okay."

He smiled, then rolled me onto my back, nestling between my legs, his arousal obvious. "So," he said, "I take it that you being on the pill means I can come inside you?"

I nodded my head and he smiled, raising himself above me.

This time, he didn't pull out, and he groaned even louder when he climaxed, before rolling over onto his back.

"I can't believe how good you feel," he said and then hugged me tight in his arms. "I love you, Abbie," he murmured into my hair and I stilled. He loved me? My head was on his chest and I could tell he'd stopped breathing. He was waiting for an answer, waiting for me to say it back.

"Me too," I replied and he turned, so we were facing each other.

"You've made me so happy," he whispered and kissed me deeply.

He fell asleep quickly after that, his arms still around me, and I lay there for a while studying his face. He was an attractive man, and he was kind, even if he did sometimes say the wrong thing. He was quick to apologise when he did mess up, and he made me feel safe, and wanted. I may not have been in love with him – not in the same way I'd been in love with Josh; not in that breathless, heady, passionate, consuming way – but I cared about him. And fireworks weren't for everyone, were they? Perhaps a love like the one I'd shared with Josh wasn't everything it was cracked up to be. Maybe it had burned too bright, and would have eventually fizzled out and died from sheer exhaustion. I snuggled into Simon and he moaned in his sleep, holding me tighter and making me smile. This was better, wasn't it? After all, Simon was reliable, and faithful; he'd never leave me. He'd stay with me, by my side, protecting me always, keeping me safe. Yes, this was much better; this was right. I knew that now. The kind of relationship I could have with Simon was more secure… more permanent. More 'me'.

I fell asleep, utterly convinced in my decision… and dreamt of Josh.

*****

We finished uni, spending our intervening weekends together at my flat, while we both studied hard during the week. I learned to drive in my final year, although Simon still insisted on coming to see me, rather than me driving to Plymouth. Whenever I asked why that was, he'd just say, "I like it this way." And then he'd kiss me.

We both gained good degrees and attended each other's graduation ceremonies as proud boyfriend and girlfriend. I met some of his friends then, for the first time, and Simon seemed keen to show me off, keeping his arm around me all the time.

After that, we settled back into our lives in Porthgowan. As soon as we'd finished at uni, Simon had moved back in with his parents, and I with my father at the pub. Simon already had a job lined up, working for a small firm of solicitors in Helston, and it didn't take me long to find work either, taking on a job as a freelance illustrator for a children's book publisher in Exeter. I worked from home, using a drawing board set up in my bedroom, and I liked it that way. I was disciplined about my working hours, but I found it easier to be creative in a comfortable and familiar environment than I think I would have done if I was somewhere I didn't know.

Because we were both living at home again, sex became quite difficult, as we had nowhere to go. We still spent a lot of time together, just on the beach and around the village, holding hands and kissing and, to be honest, I was fine with that. I wasn't that bothered about the lack of sex, but Simon was, and he resolved the issue one summer's evening, taking me to a remote area after dark in his car and moving us to the back seat, where he lay back, undid his jeans and suggested I 'go on top'. I did, and I tried really hard to enjoy it – or at least give the impression of enjoying it. The problem was, it wasn't romantic. It wasn't even exciting. It was awkward, slightly embarrassing sex in the cramped back seat of a car. It was tricky working out where to put my legs and trying not to bump my head on the roof every time I moved. Simon seemed to find it quite exciting though, and climaxed quickly, telling me how 'fantastic' I'd been as I struggled to pull up my knickers.

I think it was on the drive home that I first began to wonder if I'd ever really enjoy sex again. But, even as the thought crossed my mind and images flashed before my closed eyes of Josh and I writhing together on his bed, our bodies glistening, filmed with sweat, our kisses drowning out our mutual cries of ecstasy, I dismissed it and convinced myself that I was being unreasonable. Simon and I weren't able to spend that much time together. We were still getting used to each other, and I reminded myself that everyone was different, and that making comparisons with Josh was unfair. I felt sure that, if I could just be patient, Simon would eventually re-awaken the monster that I knew still lurked inside me, desperate to be let loose again. I just needed to give it time.

We'd been at home for a few months, and I was working on my second project for the book publisher, which I was thoroughly enjoying – a story about the adventures of two lost teddy bears, going hunting for their parents – when Simon appeared at my door. My dad had let him in just before opening the pub and he'd come straight on up, without announcing himself, which was almost unheard of.

"What's wrong?" I took one look at him and knew something was.

He stood in the doorway, staring at me. "It's Andrew."

I felt my skin shiver at the mention of his name. Would that feeling never go away? "What about him?" Had Andrew found out about Simon and me? Had he decided to tell him what had happened between us all those years ago, and maybe add a few embellishments to cause trouble? How was I going to prove my innocence? How could I...

"He's dead."

Instinctively, my thoughts and fears forgotten, I stood up from my drawing board, and went over to Simon. "Dead?"

He nodded, gazing at me, or rather through me. "Yes." Tears were welling in his eyes and I took his hand, leading him to my bed and sitting down with him, on the edge of it. "My dad called me at work this afternoon," he said, the emotion audible in his voice. "He told me Andrew had been in a car accident with a couple of his friends. He wasn't driving, but they were all over the alcohol limit... the... the car rounded a bend on the wrong side of the road and ploughed into an oncoming vehicle. Two people in the other car were killed too." His voice cracked and a tear fell down his cheek. I'd never seen him cry before and I put my arms around him, wanting to help, or at least to comfort. "Andrew was in the front passenger seat," he continued. "He took the brunt of the collision…"

"Don't talk," I whispered. He was clearly finding it hard and I held him like that for ages, feeling the pain pouring off of him, until he eventually pulled back from me.

"I never even liked him that much," he said, shaking his head. "But I didn't wish him dead."

"I know." I tried to sound understanding, even though I felt nothing, other than shock at the suddenness of it.

"Maybe I should have tried harder," he added. "To like him… you know?"

I shook my head. "Don't blame yourself," I said. "And don't feel bad."

He looked at me and leant in, kissing me briefly. "Thank you," he murmured.

"What for?"

"Being here… listening to me, helping. It means a lot."

The look in his eyes told me the truth behind that statement, and I think that was the first moment I felt anything akin to love for him. It didn't matter that it was born out of pity. What mattered was that he needed me, and I was there for him.

Months turned into years, with very little change – other than the fact that, a short while after the funeral, Simon's parents had an extension built, converting part of it into a sort of bedsit for Simon. It still formed part of their house, but it gave us a lot more freedom to come and go, and it was certainly more cosy in his bed than in the back of his car and, while we still only really saw each other at weekends, and I never stayed a whole night with him, the time we did spend together was more relaxed than it had been. I felt more comfortable with him than I had before and slowly reached the conclusion that 'comfortable' was a good place to be.

On my twenty-fourth birthday, Simon finished work early and collected me from the pub, taking me to dinner in a very exclusive restaurant in Falmouth, with soft lighting and gentle music playing in the background.

We talked and held hands, sampling each other's dishes and enjoying the romance of it, because it was romantic, and, when the waiter took away our main courses, Simon stood, putting his serviette down on the table. I assumed he was going to the toilet and took a sip of my wine, before looking up and realising he was still standing beside me. I tilted my head, feeling uncertain, just as he dropped to one knee, and my uncertainty vanished when he pulled a small box from his jacket pocket.

"You know I love you, Abbie," he said. "And you know I'll always take care of you. Please… please… say you'll marry me?" He opened the box, to reveal a beautiful solitaire diamond, set in white gold, and I gazed at it, before looking into his eyes and seeing the love within them. The room had fallen silent with anticipation, each of the diners awaiting my response, just like Simon.

"Yes," I whispered and he stood, lifting me into his arms as the restaurant exploded in spontaneous applause.

"I'll do everything I can to make you happy," he murmured into my ear and I leant back, looking at him again, noticing a shadow pass behind his eyes. And I wondered if he knew…

We were married the following summer.

I didn't want a big, fussy wedding, so the ceremony was held at the registry office in Helston, and everyone came, including my mother, who Simon had persuaded me to contact several months beforehand. I hadn't spoken to her for nine years, even though she and Dad had officially divorced about a year after Mum left, and our initial telephone conversations were very stilted and difficult.

Simon drove me up to Padstow a couple of months before the wedding, because he didn't want our first meeting to be on the day itself, and I think he felt that, if we really didn't get on, it would at least give one or other of us time to back out. She'd changed a bit, put on some weight and dyed her hair a darker shade, but she was pleased to see me. Devin was there too, although Tara was away, travelling in Australia, evidently.

When we went home, I told Dad about the visit and he listened, and then got up and said, if I wanted to invite Devin as well, he was okay with that. I gave it some thought and then called Mum and issued the invitation. She seemed really happy.

I wore a simple off-white shift dress and carried a bouquet of wild flowers. Simon wore a dark blue suit, and as we said our vows, I resolved that it didn't matter if Simon didn't make my heart soar. It didn't matter if my body didn't ache with need for him. He loved me; he cared for me and he'd always be there for me. And, in my own way, I loved him too.

We honeymooned in the south of France, in a beautiful villa, at the end of a long driveway, with a large secluded garden and a private pool. It was perfect. I honestly couldn't have asked for more. We ate local delicacies, drank excellent wines, discovered the town market, held hands on long walks, skinny-dipped at midnight, kissed in the moonlight, and made love under the stars. The stars didn't burst – at least not for me –but that didn't matter. We also talked. We talked a lot. And in one of our lengthy discussions, we agreed that we both wanted to have children – although I wondered why we hadn't talked about it before we'd got married, being as it was such an important decision.

"There's no need to rush though," Simon said, looking into my eyes. "We're still young."

I agreed with him. "And there's a lot of work to do on the house," I added.

We'd bought a small cottage in the village just a few weeks before the wedding, in West Street, which was one of the turnings off of The Street, that led up into the hills above Porthgowan. There were only around a dozen or so houses up there, dotted along the lane, and like its counterpart, East Street, on the other side of the village, it was quieter, set back, away from the tourists. We were both looking forward to moving in on our return from France, and deciding on colours and fabrics for our first home. Babies could wait.

We decorated the house. I say 'we', but what I really mean is that I did it. Simon didn't like my ideas, telling me they were outdated. I didn't like his, because he wanted to rip the heart out of our beautiful old house. And so, within days of returning from our perfect honeymoon, we argued for the first time as a married couple, and what had started as a mild disagreement about differing tastes, became a slanging match, in which I only just held back from telling him that Josh would never have spoken to me like that, would never have treated me – or my opinions – with such distain. It was true. Simon's tone was dismissive and superior, his body language arrogant, his words bordering on vulgar as his temper rose. In all the years that I'd known him, I'd never seen anything like that from Josh, and I felt certain that he was incapable of such behaviour. I refrained from making comparisons, however, bit my tongue, and took refuge in our bedroom while Simon stormed out into the back garden. After an hour, he came to me and held me, apologising – because he was always quick to apologise – and I said sorry too, and then he said I could do whatever I wanted with the house.

"You've got better taste than me anyway," he murmured and kissed me, rolling me onto my back on the bed and undoing my jeans.

Make-up sex was different – very fast, hard and more intense, perhaps – but it wasn't worth the argument, and I made a mental note to myself as I showered afterwards, to avoid any kind of disagreement in the future, if at all possible. I didn't like the conflict, or the way it made me feel.

By the time I'd finished, the house was exactly how I wanted it. The living and dining room, both had plain white walls, which accentuated the original beams and stone fireplaces, and I'd used beautiful floral fabrics and antique furniture to complete the picture. In the kitchen and bathroom, however, I'd compromised and used more modern fittings – a slight concession to Simon's need to update things. Upstairs, in our bedroom, I'd stuck to tradition, painting the walls a very, very pale grey – so pale, it was almost white – with the curtains and soft furnishings in different shades of blue. The spare room, which doubled as my office, was more functional, allowing space for my drawing board and storage, and as I completed each area of the house, Simon smiled and said he approved. Whether he really did or not, I don't know, but he said it anyway, and I was grateful.

A few years went by before he changed jobs, moving to a much larger firm in Falmouth, and getting a big pay rise into the bargain, as well as the promise of a future partnership if he played his cards right. It was what he'd always wanted and he marvelled at his good fortune, being as he'd only just turned twenty-eight.

The only problem with his new job was that the hours were longer, and so was his commute, being nearly double what it had been before. He had to be out of the house by six in the morning, and often didn't return before eight at night. And when he did, he was exhausted. Not only that, but his firm belonged to a local Sunday league football team and Simon had decided to join them.

"It'll be good for my career," he reasoned, when we went into Helston to buy his boots.

The games usually took place on alternate Sunday mornings, during the winter months, so by Sunday afternoons, he was generally to be found asleep in an armchair.

After six months of that, commuting back and forth, he decided he'd had enough.

"Look at this," he said to me one Friday evening when he got in from work. I was dishing up the curry I'd just cooked, and paused, spoon mid-air, to look at the piece of paper he'd thrust under my nose. It was the details for a house in Falmouth.

"What about it?"

"I thought we could go and look at it tomorrow," he said, stepping back slightly and staring down at the particulars himself now.

"Why?" I wasn't being deliberately stupid. I genuinely didn't understand what he was saying.

"To buy it, of course." He sounded impatient.

"Buy it?"

I put down the pan I was holding, resting the spoon on the side, and turned to face him. He kept hold of the piece of paper, but pushed his fingers back through his thick dark blond hair. "I can't keep doing this commute," he said. "I'm exhausted, and I don't feel like we have a life together anymore." He moved closer. "I barely see you."

"But I like living here." He stared at me, his eyes darkening and I could feel the argument brewing. Even so, I wasn't just going to back down. "Can't you cut your hours or something? Maybe you could work from home?" I knew of other people who did that. Me, for one.

He scoffed. "Don't be ridiculous, Abbie. I want to make partner before I'm thirty-five. They're not going to take me seriously if I ask to cut my hours, are they?"

"I know, but…"

"I've never stopped you from doing anything you wanted," he said, sounding hurt all of a sudden. "I've never questioned any of your motives or decisions. Why are you standing in my way?"

"I'm not."

His eyes were locked with mine, and it was me who looked away first, lowering mine to the piece of paper in his hand and taking it from him. "Let's see it," I murmured, feeling the life drain from me as I read the description.

The house was a box. Well, it was a series of boxes within a larger box, surrounded by roads and roads of identical boxes. It had no personality, no style, no character.

It did have four bedrooms, one with an ensuite, two receptions, and a utility room off of the big kitchen. There was a garage and a hard-standing, which Simon assured me was 'perfect', being as we now had two cars, and there were two small patches of grass; one at the front and one at the back.

"It's ideal," he said, repeating his praise over and over, as we looked around the tiny blank rear garden, and I tried hard not to make comparisons with the beautiful wild flower and herb beds that I'd taken the last couple of years to cultivate back in Porthgowan. "There's just enough space out here for you to do your gardening."

There was, providing I didn't want to do anything else, like sit outside in the mornings, drinking my tea, or hang out the washing.

"Don't you love it?" He looked down into my eyes, his hands resting on my hips. I didn't hate it, so I nodded my head, rather than have an argument in front of the estate agent, and Simon put in an offer there and then.

It took me a while to settle in. Simon managed it almost straight away, but I found it harder. I think one of the problems was that Simon insisted on buying new furniture, saying our old things didn't fit properly. He didn't throw anything away, but stored it in the loft, and let me use some of it in my 'studio' – which was really the second biggest bedroom, at the back of the house. In that anonymous box, however, I felt as though I'd lost my identity, and I struggled to find it again.

It wasn't long after our second Christmas there, when Simon came home from work one evening, arriving at about seven-thirty, as usual. It hadn't escaped my notice that, despite our move, which was supposed to enable him to spend more time at home, he still left the house by six, and rarely returned before seven, but was often later than that. I sometimes sat in my studio by myself and wondered why we'd bothered to move at all.

"I've been thinking," he said, after he'd kissed me and put his briefcase down by the kitchen door, opening the oven to check what was cooking.

"Yes?" I was standing at the sink and turned to face him, wondering what was coming next.

"We're quite settled here now, don't you think?" He went over to the kitchen table, where I'd laid our places and put out a bowl of salad. He helped himself to a slice of green pepper and munched on it, looking over at me.

"I suppose."

"I'm doing well at work," he continued between mouthfuls, "and… well, you're going to be thirty on your next birthday."

I needed reminding about that little milestone, which was only six short months away. "What's your point?" I asked, drying my hands on the tea towel.

"I think it's time we started a family, don't you?"

His suggestion had been fairly typical; matter of fact, and mechanical, but I was thrilled, nonetheless, and showed my appreciation by throwing myself into his arms and kissing him, before we adjourned to the living room for twenty minutes, deciding that the lasagne could wait. Afterwards, while we ate, we discussed the idea further, going into practicalities, such as finances and work, as well as wondering to ourselves what it would be like to be parents. It was a good evening – one of the best in ages – and as I lay in bed that night listening to the sound of Simon's breathing while he slept, I mentally started to look forward to the next stage of my life: motherhood.

I imagined fulfilment and satisfaction, warmth and comfort, as I pictured myself cradling an infant, loving it, nurturing it, while Simon cared for us both. Because he would. I knew that.

I stopped taking the pill, and we started 'trying', and I have to say, it was actually quite good fun to begin with. We didn't worry too much about timings or anything. We just had a lot of sex, and because there was a purpose to it, it almost seemed enjoyable. Sometimes I even felt a spark of something like the passion I'd felt with Josh… usually right before Simon climaxed and rolled off of me, panting hard and grinning about a 'job well done', which made us both laugh. At least for a while.

The months went by though, and each time my period started, my disappointment grew. I'd tell Simon the bad news, hoping for support and comfort, but invariably, he'd smile and tell me, "Well, there's always next month." As I stared at him, wondering how he could be so insensitive, I even started to wonder whether he was enjoying the 'trying' so much, he didn't really want the end result.

Over the years, certainly since Simon had started his job in Falmouth, we'd settled into a routine of having sex on Tuesday and Thursday nights, plus Saturdays, if Simon wasn't playing football on Sunday morning, and Sunday evenings when he was – his afternoon sleep having rejuvenated him.

But when we started trying for a baby, the routine changed, and we had sex as often as we could, sometimes twice a day, if Simon wasn't too tired. After eighteen months of that; eighteen months of shattered hopes, I changed the routine again. In my desperation, I resorted to thermometers and charts, and a strict timetable, and when the moment was right, I'd text Simon. Obviously, he might be in the middle of something, or with a client, or just plain busy, but if he could, he'd give up his lunch break and come home. If not, I'd be waiting when he walked in the door. To say it was mechanical was an understatement, and I knew that, as the months progressed, any pleasure Simon might have once gained from our intimate liaisons had been lost to my regimented obsession.

We kept that up for about six months, until one evening, after a begging mid-morning text message from me, asking him to come home 'now', which he'd answered with a perfunctory 'I can't', Simon walked in the door, a good hour later than usual, and as I approached, he held up his hand.

"Stop," he said.

"What?"

"I can't keep doing this." His face bore a pained expression.

"Can't keep doing what?"

"This." He almost shouted and I stepped away from him. "I can't keep fucking you to order, Abbie. Do you know what this feels like?" Of course I did. I'd been fucking him to order since the very first time. I didn't say that. I stared at him instead, in shock. "I know how much you want a baby," he said, softening his voice. "But this is no way to live. We don't have sex for pleasure anymore." *Did we ever?* "I feel like I'm just a performing sperm bank."

"W—What are you saying?" I heard the emotion in my voice.

He moved closer and pulled me into his arms. "I'm saying we need to take a break from this."

"You want to stop trying?" How could this be happening? My body clock was ticking louder than Big Ben… and he wanted to stop trying?

"For a while," he reasoned and I pulled away from him. "Don't," he said as I walked to the other side of the room.

"Don't what?"

"Don't be like that."

"Do you have any idea what you're doing to me?" I yelled, feeling the tears fall down my cheeks and not even bothering to try and stop them.

"Yes." His voice was quiet, restrained. "I know this is hurting you."

"And you promised you'd never do that."

He sighed. "I know. And I'm not saying we'll give up for good... I'm just saying I need a break. I need some normality."

"*You* need?" I shouted.

He stepped closer. "You want me for three or four days of the month, Abbie. The rest of the time, it's like I don't exist."

"That's not true. We still have sex in between."

"Not like we used to."

I couldn't deny what he was saying. It was true that, in between my fertile days, I would often make excuses not to have sex, reasoning to myself that we should save up his sperm for when they were really needed. It was a ludicrous argument, but I wasn't being logical at the time.

We stared at each other for a long, long while, and then I moved closer, walking past him. "Have it your own way," I mumbled bitterly. "I can't make want me, can I?" I ran up the stairs.

"For Christ's sake, Abbie," he called after me, but he didn't follow and I lay on the bed for hours, until sleep finally claimed me.

I remained awake long enough to hear Simon come upstairs though. He didn't come to our room, but I heard him go into the guest bedroom instead, and close the door behind him.

The next morning, when I woke from my fitful sleep, he'd already left for work.

I felt emotionally bruised and it took me a while to heal as I tried to reconcile myself to the very real prospect of a life without children.

In the meantime, Simon threw himself into his work, coming home even later than ever in the following weeks – presumably to avoid me, although we'd started talking again within a few days of our shattering argument, even if just to be practical. He moved back into our bed as well and sometimes that was the only way I knew he'd been home at night – the indent his head had left in the pillow.

He made no attempt to have sex with me though, or even to kiss me, or touch me, and his supposed hopes to get back to 'normality', came to nothing. Literally, nothing.

As for me, I lost myself in work. I'd always been really busy, which was gratifying, but I took on a new client, in the form of a fiction publisher, who employed me as a freelance cover artist. It was different and kept me occupied, which was a good thing. It meant I had less time to think.

I still felt empty though… unfulfilled. I couldn't accept the fact that I might never be a mother, and in my desperation, I had an idea. It came to me one night while I was lying in bed by myself, being as Simon had called to say he was working late and that I shouldn't wait up for him. The next day, I even did some tentative research before I started work, and it soon became clear this was something I was going to have to discuss with Simon, because it was going to be expensive and difficult, and we were both going to have to be committed to it… but to my mind, the prize was worth it. Well worth it.

Despite my impatience, I waited until the Saturday evening before I said anything, because I wanted to be able to talk without work getting in the way. It would have been coming up for the end of June by then, many months since our argument and since we'd stopped having sex – or 'trying' as I suppose it had become to us – and literally a few weeks before my thirty-second birthday, which for some reason had taken on a greater significance in my illogical brain.

"Can we talk?" I asked, having made us a coffee and brought it into the lounge after we'd finished dinner.

He looked up at me as I sat beside him, putting the cups down on the table in front of us.

"Sure," he said, although he didn't sound too certain.

"I don't want to argue."

"Neither do I."

I smiled across at him and he smiled back. "I wanted to talk to you about having a baby." He closed his eyes and I heard him sigh. "And before you tell me you don't want to…"

"I never said I didn't want to," he interrupted.

I specifically remembered, during our argument, him saying that having a baby was something *I'd* wanted, rather than something *we'd* wanted, but I really didn't want another fight, so I backed down.

"Okay, you didn't say that, but can you hear me out?" He paused for a worrying moment, and then nodded. "I've been thinking about whether we could try IVF," I said, spilling the words out quickly before I lost my nerve.

"IVF?" He was surprised.

"Yes."

He twisted in his seat to look at me, his head tilting to one side. "We don't even know if one of us has a fertility problem, and you want to have IVF? You do know how invasive it is, don't you?"

"I've done some research, yes."

"And you didn't think it was mechanical enough before?"

I stared at him, incredulous, angry, heartbroken. "Are you going to deny me this as well?" It certainly sounded like he was.

He paused. "No." His voice was quiet, thoughtful. "I'm not saying that. I just don't see the need to rush into it."

I swallowed down my emotions, trying to be reasonable. He was trying too, so it was the least I could do. "We wouldn't be rushing into anything. I'm just asking you to give it some thought… to maybe come and see the doctor with me…"

He hesitated and then let out a long breath. "Let me think about it," he said.

"That's all I'm asking."

"Okay."

"Thank you," I whispered.

"Christ, Abbie. You don't have to thank me."

I sidled closer to him and rested my head on his chest for the first time in months, listening to his heartbeat as he slowly put his arm around me. "I do," I murmured. "I know I made it miserable for you."

He didn't reply and after a few minutes, I looked up at him. He was staring down at me, our eyes locked, and I leant up, gently brushing my lips across his. He groaned, and for a moment, I thought he was going to pull away, but then his tongue darted into my mouth, and his hands were everywhere, literally all over me, frenzied. He pushed me down onto the sofa, lifted my skirt and pushed my knickers to one side, entering me before I'd even realised he'd undone his jeans. It was hard and fast and although I didn't climax, it was probably the most satisfying sex I'd ever had with Simon. He grunted loudly as he filled me, his body spasming and shaking above me... and then he opened his eyes and I saw a brief flicker of pain, before he pulled out of me and stood up.

"I'm sorry," he murmured, running his fingers through his hair and then awkwardly tucking himself back into his jeans, like a teenager who'd been caught out by his parents – or hers, probably. "I shouldn't have done that."

"Why not?" I smiled up at him. "We are married, you know. It is allowed."

He gazed down at me. "I know. I know." He sat down at the end of the sofa and put his head in his hands, a picture of despair. "It's not that."

"What's wrong, Simon?" I asked, sitting up and moving closer to him.

"I'm sorry," he whispered again, still not looking at me.

"What for?"

Now he turned to face me again and the look in his eyes took my breath away. "For the way I've treated you over the last few months. I'm sorry for all of it. For everything."

I felt like we'd turned a corner after that evening. He'd agreed to think about the IVF, and we'd broken down the barriers that had kept us apart for so long. His apology for what had happened between us, for the way he'd behaved, had been so heartfelt, that it made me realise it wasn't just me who was in pain, and that we needed to work together to rebuild our relationship. After all the heartache, I felt as though we had something to hope for.

We didn't have sex again for the next couple of weeks, but Simon was exceptionally busy at work, and I was trying to come up with ideas for a historical romance novel cover, which, according to the brief, couldn't look 'too old fashioned' – which was a challenge in its own right.

I suppose it was probably just over two weeks later that it happened.

I was on the phone to the children's book publisher, agreeing a deadline. They'd given me the brief at the beginning of June, and we'd previously agreed that I could have until the middle of September to complete it. However, the editor was now telling me the deadline would have to move to August the thirtieth. It wasn't an enormous project, and it wasn't impossible to do, but it was the principle of the thing as far as I was concerned.

I flicked back through my diary, still using a paper one, which I kept on my desk in my studio.

"You're cutting two weeks out of the schedule, Miranda," I said, checking the dates. "Actually, it's nearer to three, because you may have briefed me in our meeting on the 6th, but you didn't actually send the text and characterisations down until following week." I flicked back and forth in my diary again, to check I wasn't telling fibs, and noticed the black cross next to the tenth of June; the date of my last period. While she carried on talking, telling me about the production issues they'd encountered – not that I cared – I quickly leafed through my diary, counting on four weeks, my mind racing when I had to add another three days, to get get to today's date.

I was three days late… and because I'd been so busy, I hadn't even noticed. Okay, so it was only three days, but…

"I'll do it," I interrupted her.

"Sorry?" She sounded surprised.

"I said, I'll do it."

"For August thirtieth? You're sure."

"Positive."

"Thanks, Abbie," she gushed. "You're a lifesaver."

I made the right noises and hung up the call, running down the stairs and grabbing my handbag from the kitchen. I positively sprinted to the car, my hand shaking as I let myself in and sat behind the wheel, taking a deep breath. I needed to calm down. Three days didn't mean anything.

The chemists was busy, but I waited in turn, the pregnancy test clasped in my hand, and when it was time to pay, the assistant rang it up without even looking at me and took the ten pound note I handed her. Didn't she have any idea how momentous a thing this was? Didn't she realise that the contents of that box were possibly going to change my life – forever?

I raced back home and sat at the kitchen table, carefully reading the instructions. As I was three days late, it said I could take the test there and then, although it promised a greater degree of accuracy if I waited until the morning. Sod accuracy. I couldn't wait that long. In any case, there were two tests in the box, so if it looked even vaguely positive, I could always do it again first thing, couldn't I? Just to be sure… and besides, I needed to pee anyway.

I went into the downstairs cloakroom and, with the leaflet balanced on the edge of the sink, followed the instructions, holding the stick awkwardly between my legs, while keeping the fingers of my other hand crossed.

I had to wait three minutes – the longest three minutes of my life – and I left the stick on the shelf at the back of the sink while I paced the hall floor, checking my watch every few seconds, until the time was up and I took a breath, going back into the cloakroom and picking up the stick, my eyes closed tight, fear overwhelming me.

I opened my eyes slowly and blinked. There was a line. There was definitely a line – and it wasn't even very faint. It was clearly visible. I picked up the leaflet, my hand shaking again, and double checked what the line meant. 'You're pregnant' the leaflet said and I looked up at my own reflection in the mirror.

"You're pregnant," I said to myself, and burst into tears.

I didn't bother to dry my eyes, or to clear up the mess in the bathroom. I went straight up into the studio, where I'd left my phone, and dialled Simon's mobile. He answered on the fourth ring, just as I was beginning to think I'd get his message service.

"Abbie?" he said, sounding flustered.

"Yes. I'm sorry to bother you."

"What's wrong?" he asked.

"Nothing." I replied, smiling. "Absolutely nothing."

There was a pause. "Then why have you called me?"

"Because… because I'm pregnant."

"You're what?" he almost shouted.

"I'm pregnant."

"Pregnant? How?"

I laughed. "Haven't you worked that out yet… at your age?"

"That's not what I mean, Abbie." He sounded serious, impatient.

"We had sex a few weeks ago, remember?" I said, wishing I didn't have to explain it to him, wishing he could just be happy, like I was.

"Wait a second," he said and I heard muffled voices and then a door closing, before he came back on the line. "Sorry."

"No, I'm sorry. I didn't realise you weren't alone. You should have said."

"It wasn't a client," he explained. "A—Are you sure about this? I mean, we only had sex once."

"I know. But I worked out earlier that I was three days late, so I went to the chemists and bought a test. I've literally just done it… and it's positive."

"Definitely? No mistakes?"

"No. It's something like ninety-eight percent accurate." I paused and then voiced the thought that was now running through my head, that maybe he'd changed his mind since we'd stopped actually trying to have a baby. "Are you disappointed?"

"O—Of course I'm not."

"Then why don't you sound very pleased?"

"I'm sorry," he said, sounding genuinely contrite now. "I am pleased. Really I am. It's just such a shock. After all those months…"

It would have been so much nicer if he could have said 'surprise', rather than 'shock', but I didn't say anything, except, "I know."

"I mean, we tried for so long, and then you fall pregnant, after just one time?"

"It's incredible, isn't it?"

I heard a knocking on his door. "Hang on," he said and there were more muffled voices. "I'm going to have to go," he said, talking to me again. "Something's come up."

"That's okay. I just wanted to tell you."

"We'll talk about it later," he said and I felt a shadow pass over me.

"Talk about it?"

"Well… celebrate. You know what I mean."

I wasn't entirely sure that I did, but I was too happy to care.

I spent the day floating on air, delighting in my new status as mother-to-be, although every so often I found myself wondering, posing internal questions… what was morning sickness like? When should we tell people the news? Did labour hurt as much as everyone said? Should I breast feed? Should I give up work? The questions rolling around my head seemed endless and I felt like I was six again, being faced with the life-changing decision my parents had presented me with over a plate of spaghetti. Only now there was no-one there to tell me not to worry, and that everything would be okay. At least not until Simon came home, anyway.

He walked in the door a little earlier than usual that night, and I knew right away that something was wrong.

"Simon?" I said, getting up from the sofa.

"We need to talk." He looked weary… older, even.

I stood in front of him. "You don't want to have a baby anymore, do you?" I said, re-voicing my fear from earlier. "You've changed your mind."

He shook his head. "It's not that," he said.

"Then what is it?"

He sighed. "It's just that… well, it seems a bit convenient."

"Excuse me? Convenient? We went through hell to get here, Simon. How can you say it was convenient?"

"That's my whole point," he replied, walking away from me, and then turning back, a dark expression on his face. "We tried for months and months, and nothing happened… and then we stopped having sex… and then after just one time, you get pregnant. Don't you find that a bit strange?"

I stared at him. "What are you suggesting?"

"I'm not suggesting anything."

"Well, it sounds to me like you are."

He looked away, then down at his feet, before taking a breath and raising his eyes to mine again. "Is it mine?" he asked outright.

My whole body trembled, my stomach churned, and my heart pounded in my chest. "How dare you?" I yelled. "How dare you say that?" Tears poured down my cheeks and he took a step closer. I could see the change in him already, the realisation that he'd messed up properly this time. But the damage was done. The words were out there and I held my hands up to him. "Don't even think about coming near me, you bastard. Trying to get pregnant was torture…"

"Thanks," he interrupted sarcastically. "I didn't realise making love with me was such a hardship."

"I didn't mean it like that, and you know it. I meant that being disappointed every month was hard to take."

"I know it was."

"But finding out today that I actually was pregnant… it made all of it seem worthwhile. Even your rejection."

"I didn't reject you, Abbie."

"Yes, you did. And now you're accusing me of… of having an affair?"

"I'm sorry."

"Yes, well, 'sorry' isn't good enough, Simon. Not this time."

I stormed past him and ran up the stairs, slamming our bedroom door behind me and grabbing a suitcase from the top of the wardrobe. Without even thinking, I threw clothes into it randomly; jumpers, jeans, dresses, underwear, paying scant attention to whether they were suitable for the warm weather, then added some toiletries and zipped it up, lifting it and lugging it to the top of the stairs. Simon was standing at the bottom, his phone in his hand, looking up at me.

"You're leaving?" His face paled and he put one foot on the bottom step, replacing his phone in his pocket, his call evidently forgotten.

"Yes. I'm going to my dad's."

He started to climb, coming to a stop in front of me, one step down, our faces level. "Don't do this," he said. "Please. I beg you. Don't leave me."

"How can I stay, knowing that's what you think of me?" Tears started to fall again, and he reached out, brushing them away.

"I don't."

"Then why say it?"

"I don't know. Because I'm stupid… because I don't deserve you. I don't, Abbie. You're far too good for me." I'd never heard him speak like that before. He was usually so confident. "I'm sorry," he said. "And I know that's not good enough, but please… please stay. Let me make it up to you."

"How? How can you make that up to me?"

He bent and moved my case to one side, then sat us both down on the top step, holding my hand tight in his. "Honestly?" he said. "I don't know. But I don't want to lose you…" I looked into his eyes and saw the tears forming. "Stay," he whispered, his voice cracking. "Please."

"If I stay, Simon," I said, weakening in the face of his raw emotion, "things need to change."

"I know." He sighed and closed his eyes for a moment. "We haven't been right for ages, have we?"

"No."

"And that's been my fault," he said. I opened my mouth to disagree, because we'd both been to blame really, but he continued, "Give me another chance," his voice pleading. "I'll make it right again. I promise." He shifted slightly and moved his hand, resting it on my belly. "For all of us…"

I burst into tears and he pulled me into his arms, holding onto me.

"I'm so, so sorry, Abbie," he whispered. "I'll never do anything to hurt you again."

I wanted so much to believe in the future I was growing inside me, that I let myself believe in him.

Simon worked hard at making it right again.

He cut his hours right back, ensuring he was home by seven, or seven-thirty at the latest, helping around the house and making sure I got plenty of rest.

For the first few weeks, there was a tense, sometimes difficult atmosphere between us. I think we were both treading on eggshells, scared of saying the wrong thing, and therefore not saying much at all. But slowly, and steadily, we rebuilt our relationship, learning to talk to each other, without fear or barriers, reminding ourselves whenever it got tough, that we had something worth fighting for now: the child we couldn't wait to meet.

I can honestly say that, once we'd settled down, our marriage had never been stronger, or better. We went for the first scan together and Simon held my hand, binding us in more ways than one. We were given a due date of March sixteenth, and told everything was progressing perfectly, and that night, Simon instigated sex for the first time since he'd made me pregnant, all those weeks before. Strangely, although I still got no physical pleasure from it, I found I'd missed him and, as he climaxed inside me, his eyes closed tight, I held onto him, bound by his fulfilment.

At eighteen weeks, we had the second scan and, when asked, we said 'yes' we wanted to know the baby's sex. It wasn't something we'd discussed before, but I looked at Simon and he nodded, so I did too, and then smiled my delight when the sonographer announced, "It's a girl."

Simon seemed a little subdued and I asked if he'd wanted a boy.

"No," he said, squeezing my hand and leaning over to kiss my forehead. "As long as it's healthy, I really don't mind."

I thought it was odd that he still referred to our daughter as 'it', but I didn't say anything, and we took home the grainy black and white images, to cherish.

That night, as we lay in bed, Simon revealed that the reason he'd thought we should find out the baby's sex was entirely practical. We could buy the appropriate clothes and decorate the nursery in the 'right' colours. I had to smile at his obedience to convention, but that didn't stop me from coming home the following week, after a shopping trip, my bags filled with beautiful dresses and pink baby grows, adorned with lambs and kittens. When Simon smiled indulgently, I couldn't help but smile back.

We decorated the nursery together, selecting a very pale pink paint, and on the wall opposite the window, where we'd decided to place the cot, I designed a mural. It was an intricate woodland scene, with trees and wild flowers, butterflies, and brightly coloured birds, and fairies, with gossamer wings. I kept it a secret from Simon, forbidding him to enter the room until I'd completed it, and when I did, I took him upstairs, the door closed, and made him shut his eyes, taking him into the room and turning him to face my masterpiece.

"Open your eyes," I said, feeling nervous for the first time. He'd never really shown much interest in my art, or my work, and I wasn't sure how he'd react now I'd placed it before him.

He stood in silence for ages, then he walked up to it, examining the detail closely, and finally turned back to me.

"You really painted this?" he said, coming to stand before me.

"Yes."

He suddenly leant down and kissed me, his tongue demanding mine with an urgency I hadn't felt from him in years, and when he pulled back again a short while later, his eyes were filled with love – and something else I couldn't read.

"You're incredible," he whispered.

And then he took me to bed.

By my thirty-sixth week, we'd chosen a name.

Molly.

It had taken us a while, but Molly was the only name we could both agree on. As for a second name? There wasn't a hope of that. Simon wasn't overly keen for her to have one anyway. He hated his middle name, which was Alexander, and although I quite liked it, and also my own, which was Mia, we'd had enough trouble choosing one, so we both decided that was enough, and thanked our lucky stars that at least we'd thought of something.

It was Friday, the twenty-seventh of February, just a little over two weeks before my due date, and I had my thirty-eight week ante-natal appointment with my midwife, booked for nine o'clock. Simon wasn't coming with me, but had agreed to drop me at the hospital, because I too closely resembled a beached whale to get behind the wheel of my own car.

"Why don't we got out for dinner tonight?" he suggested as he pulled into the hospital entrance.

"That sounds lovely."

We hadn't been out for a while and it seemed like a good idea to make the most of our chances before the baby arrived and claimed all of our time – at least for a while, anyway.

"I'll book us a table," he said, smiling as he leant over and kissed me briefly before I climbed out of the car. "Call me later and tell me how it goes?"

"Of course." I leant back into the car to pick up my bag, feeling a slight twinge in my side and wincing.

"Are you alright?" he asked.

"I'm fine. I just need to remember not to bend down so quickly."

He nodded. "Take care," he said and we waved to each other as he drove off.

I rested my hand on the side of my bump, right where the pain had been. "Only a little bit longer," I whispered. "I'm sure you can hang on…"

I'd talked to Molly all the way through the pregnancy, telling her about my day, about all the things we'd do together once she was born, me and her, and her father. I'd cradled her while I sat or walked around the house, my hands resting on the growing bump, occasionally feeling her kick or nudge me, and chuckling to myself when she did, wondering if she was excited at the prospect of coming out into the big wide world and meeting us, or whether she was actually telling me to be quiet… she was trying to sleep in there, after all.

Mine was the first appointment of the day and my midwife, Jess, greeted me with a cheery smile.

"You're looking well," she said as I sat down.

"I'm feeling well."

"That's good to hear." She settled at her desk and asked a few questions. Was I sleeping okay? Were there any problems? Any issues I needed to talk about? Had the baby been moving regularly?

"Um…" I suddenly felt myself chill. "Come to think of it, she hasn't moved that much in the last couple of days. Not as much as usual."

Jess looked up from my notes, and then smiled. "Don't worry," she said soothingly. "Molly's quite a big girl, and sometimes there just isn't enough space in there for her to wriggle around."

I felt reassured as Jess went over to the couch, pulling out a length of blue paper from the roll at the end and laying it flat. "Come and lie down over here," she said. "We'll do your measurements and then have a listen to the heartbeat, just to set your mind at rest."

I did as she said, staring at the baby growth charts on the wall while she ran a tape measure over the bump.

"Well," she said, going back over to the desk to check my notes, "there hasn't been much change in the last two weeks, but that's nothing to worry about."

She came back again, bringing the heart monitor with her. I'd had this done before, so knew what to expect as she rested the end of the device against my expanded stomach, moving it around.

She adjusted the position several times, then fiddled with the controls on the monitor itself.

"Damn thing," she said eventually. "This one plays up sometimes. I'll just pop next door and borrow Jane's." She smiled. "Don't go anywhere, will you?"

"As if I could get up from here without help," I joked, even though I was starting to feel uneasy.

Jess returned a few minutes later, bringing another midwife with her. Her name badge said 'Jane' and underneath, it said 'Senior Midwife'. I started to feel more than uneasy. Jess had said she was going to borrow Jane's monitor, not bring Jane herself.

Jane took over, going through the same performance as Jess, but with a new monitor, and a deafening silence filled the room, lengthening and lengthening, until Jane moved back and Jess stepped forward again, pulling down my jumper and putting her hand on my shoulder.

"I'm so sorry, Abbie," she said. "There's no heartbeat."

"No!" I heard myself scream. "No! No! No!"

I clutched the bump – Molly… my baby girl – holding her to me, even as Jess's arm came around me, offering a crumb of comfort.

"We'll call your husband," Jane said from behind her and I nodded. "He can be here when we do the scan."

"Scan?" I queried, through my cascading tears.

"Yes," Jess said. "We have to do an ultrasound, to confirm… death." She whispered the word and I felt the pain lance though me, tearing me apart, body, heart, and soul.

Everything became a blur.

Simon arrived, his face pale, and stood beside me, holding my hand, while a distressed-looking sonographer carried out the ultrasound. There was a doctor present, and Jess was there too, the whole time, standing at the end of the bed, when the doctor broke the news to us, confirming that Molly had died.

"How?" Simon asked, his voice breaking.

The doctor shook his head. "It's impossible to say." He sounded calm and compassionate.

"W—What happens now?" I whispered and everyone turned to me.

"We'll give you some medication," Jess said and I looked at her, her friendly face giving me solace in the tempest of emotions. "That will induce labour."

"She has to give birth?" Simon seemed incredulous, but I didn't know what else he'd expected.

"Yes." The doctor spoke again. "I'm sorry."

I was given the tablets and told to go home; labour would start sometime in the next forty-eight hours and there was no point in me sitting at the hospital waiting for it. Part of me wanted to stay there, because I felt safer, watched over. But when we got back to the house, I felt grateful for the time we had, those few hours to just sit together and hold onto each other, by ourselves. Simon called his parents, my father and my mother, and told them. They all offered to come, but he said 'no'. We wanted to be alone. They understood and respected that, even though they must have felt the pain of it themselves.

The contractions started on the Saturday afternoon and although Simon wanted to go straight back to the hospital, I wanted to wait a little longer – partly to be sure, but also to postpone the inevitable, I think. By six o'clock, there was no delaying, and Simon ran upstairs and grabbed my hospital bag from the bedroom. I'd packed it a week or so beforehand, just in case. He came back down, and helped me up from the sofa, and out to the front door.

"Wait!" I held onto his arm.

"What?"

"The bag… it's still got Molly's things in it; her baby grow, nappies… I can't…"

"Shit," he muttered under his breath, and ran back upstairs again, taking the bag with him, and returning a few minutes later. "Sorry," he muttered, "I should've thought."

I looked up at him. "So should I."

Labour was painful. Every bit as bad as I'd expected; only worse, because I didn't have the joy of our baby to look forward to at the end of all that agony.

They offered me an epidural, but I refused. I knew I wasn't going to feel any other part of Molly's life, so I was damn well going to feel this. And besides, there was nothing on earth that could hurt me as much as the pain of losing her.

Jess was with me the whole time, supporting me and comforting me, and when Molly was finally born in the early hours of Sunday morning, she took her away for the briefest of moments, and then returned her to us, wrapped in a pink blanket, a little bonnet on her head.

"Take as long as you need," Jess said, just before she left.

I wanted to ask if I could have the rest of my life, but I knew that was impossible.

We stayed with Molly for the whole day.
We held her, talked to her, cried over her.

With Jess's help, we bathed her and dressed her in a pink baby grow, which the hospital provided.

When the time came to leave, I couldn't walk away and leave my baby girl there in that room by herself, so Jess took her from me. I don't know where they went, but at least I didn't feel as though I'd abandoned her... not entirely. I wept and wept, and then just as Simon and I were packing up my things, Jess returned, bringing the pink baby grow with her, along with a small box.

"She'll get cold," I murmured, illogically, looking down at the tiny folded garment.

"No. She's wearing another one now... identical to this."

I took it and held it to my nose and smelled my daughter in its fibres, sitting back on the bed and sobbing harder still.

Simon finished packing, taking the leaflets Jess offered and putting the unopened box in my holdall, while I clutched the baby grow and hugged Jess goodbye. I had no words and neither did she. We didn't need them.

The journey home was silent, and when we got back to our empty house, Simon put me to bed.

"Try and get some sleep," he murmured, then he left the door ajar and went downstairs. Through my own tears, I heard him crying, but I didn't have the strength to go to him.

Simon took over everything.

He phoned our parents, his work, my clients, and told them the news; repeating the same thing over and over and over, until it became meaningless. Except it wasn't meaningless. It would never be meaningless, because Molly meant everything.

My mother arrived, quite unexpectedly, by herself, the very next day, and although I wasn't sure I wanted her there to start with, she proved invaluable; going with Simon to register the birth, and the death, and helping to organise the funeral, which we held ten days later, in Porthgowan. I told Simon I wanted Molly to see the sky and smell the sea, and while he looked at me as though I was mad, he didn't argue.

My mother went back home a few days after the funeral, and Simon took another week off work, using it to dismantle the nursery. We both knew there would be no more babies, even then. At my request, he repainted the room, covering the mural with the most neutral and bland of magnolias. He installed a double bed, although no-one ever slept in there. In fact, we barely opened the door again.

After that, he went back to work. He had to. He had clients, responsibilities, and I understood that. I dwelt in a world of silent pain, drifting, lost and lifeless.

One day, about a month after Molly's death, I decided to open the box Jess had handed me, and inside I found a set of baby footprints – Molly's – the blanket she'd been wrapped in, the bonnet she'd worn, a lock of her brown hair, and a card from the charity who'd put it all together, telling me this was a memory box. There was a phone number and a website address.

I didn't feel like talking, but I went online. I read about other couples who'd lost their babies, other women who felt the same things I was feeling, and while I wasn't ready to put that into words yet, I found comfort in the knowledge that I wasn't alone.

When Simon came home that evening, I showed him the website, and the contents of the box.

"It's a bit morbid, isn't it?" he said, rifling through it.

"No." I straightened the blanket where he'd messed it up, adding the folded pink baby grow and closing the lid again.

He looked at me and shrugged. "Well, if it helps," he murmured and got up, going through to the kitchen.

I suppose that's when I should have known. Or at least when I should have seen the signs. Perhaps if we'd tried harder then, things would have worked out differently. But we didn't. We were both too lost, and there was no way back.

I went back to work a couple of months later, looking to fill my days with something other than thoughts of what should have been.

My clients were embarrassed, not knowing what to say to me, and I found myself comforting them.

"It's fine," I said. "Please don't worry."

And they relaxed and started briefing me on jobs.

In a way, that was a relief. It gave me something to do and I lost myself in work, ignoring the pain, ignoring my life… and ignoring Simon.

He'd already started working longer hours again, coming home most nights after I'd already gone to bed. At the weekends, I kept myself occupied in the garden, and Simon took up golf. I knew that was to escape the house – and me – despite his protests that it was 'good for work'. I didn't blame him. I didn't blame anyone. It was what it was.

We muddled along like that, barely exchanging half a dozen words in a week, for months and months. At some point – I can't remember when – I started driving down to Porthgowan two or three times a week. I probably should have been working, but I missed Molly so much it hurt. That's rather odd, when you think about it, because how can you miss what you've never had? But that was how I felt, so I got into my car and took the hour's journey to my childhood home, to be with my child.

Simon and I made the journey together on Molly's birthday – I refused to refer to it as the anniversary of her death – going down to the village for the day, where we stood at her graveside, laying wild flowers beneath the marble headstone, and then going to sit on the beach. For the first time ever, I was able to be there and not think of Josh.

It was strange… I'd always thought that nothing could hurt me more than losing him. I'd thought that nothing could break me more than the pain of losing his love.

I was so wrong.

Spring turned into summer and Simon seemed to stay out even more. When he wasn't at the office, he was at the golf course, the longer hours of daylight allowing him to improve his handicap, or whatever it was called. I took even less interest in his golfing habits than I did in his work, and thus I was surprised when I was tending to the garden one Sunday afternoon in early August, nearly eighteen months after Molly's birth, and I heard him calling my name.

I turned and saw him standing in the doorway to the kitchen, leaning against the frame.

"Can we talk?" he said.

I didn't answer, but got to my feet and followed him into the house.

He didn't stop in the kitchen, but went through to the living room, sitting down on the sofa and waiting. I sat beside him and looked up into his face. His eyes were sad and I knew this was it…

"I'm sorry," he said simply.

"I know."

He held up his hand. "Let me finish." I sat back a little. "I'm sorry," he repeated. "There's no easy way to put this, so I'm just going to say it… There's someone else."

Although I hadn't really expected him to say that, I wasn't surprised.

"I see," I said, because I couldn't think what else to say.

"Did you hear what I said?" He seemed confused by my response.

"Yes. There's someone else."

He nodded slowly. "I know it's selfish of me and I fully expect you to hate me…"

"I don't. I don't hate you. H——How long has it been going on for?" I asked, intrigued now.

"A while." He suddenly looked guilty, more guilty than before, and within my own mind, the pieces of the jigsaw started to fit into place.

"Since before Molly?" I asked and his eyes darted to mine.

"Yes."

"When you came to me and said you didn't want me anymore?"

"I never said that." He sounded exasperated.

"Okay… when you said you were fed up with fucking me to order then."

He sighed. "Sort of."

"What does that mean?"

"Haley and I were thrown together, working on a case…"

"You work with her?"

"Yes. But to start off with, we were just friends. I'll admit I was attracted to her, but I resisted. Things weren't right between you and I, but I still loved you, and we were trying to get pregnant at the time…

but then after we argued, and then we stopped trying… after we stopped having sex altogether, Haley and I…" He blushed and he didn't need to finish his sentence.

"So, your late nights at the office…"

He shook his head. "I was with Haley. And I gave up the Sunday football as well, so I could be with her." He looked at me, guilt written all over his face. "I'm sorry."

I swallowed hard before asking my next question. "Did it carry on all the way through my pregnancy?"

"No." He answered straight away and I believed him. "When you called to tell me you were pregnant, Mark from accounting was in my office. He obviously heard what we were talking about and left to give us some privacy, but he must've gone straight to Haley and told her…"

"Your colleagues know about you… and her?" I queried, interrupting him, and feeling stupid.

"Mark does, and a couple of the others." He had the decency to look sheepish.

"So was it Haley who came in at the end of our call?" I asked, remembering how he'd cut our conversation short.

"Yes." A shadow crossed his face, like he was remembering the scene. "I had to tell her what had happened. She was… she was devastated. I—I'd told her – quite legitimately at the time – that you and I weren't having sex anymore. We weren't. Apart from that one time…"

"No…" I murmured.

"After she'd stopped crying, Haley got angry, demanding to know how often I'd slept with you since I'd been seeing her. It took me ages to calm her down, and then I explained that it had only been the once and that I felt bad about it."

I remembered his reaction at the time, how he'd said he was sorry for everything and that he shouldn't have done that, and I realised that he hadn't been apologising for the reason I'd thought, after all. It hadn't had anything to do with me, or our marriage, or our past mistakes – not in the way I'd imagined. I'd heard what I wanted to hear, and missed the blindingly obvious. "You felt bad for cheating on your mistress… with your wife?"

He blushed and looked away, and there was a moment's silence while we both absorbed the irony of that.

"What happened once you'd explained?" I asked.

"She said, if it had only been the once, how could I be sure the baby was mine?"

Tears formed in my eyes and, even as I tried to blink them away, they fell. Simon reached out for my hands, but I pushed him away. "Don't," I snapped and he sat back. "You listened to her… to her lies?"

"No." He shook his head.

"Yes, you bloody well did. You came back here and accused me of having an affair. Even though you were the one who was cheating."

"I know. I've always regretted that and maybe she did sow a seed of doubt in my head, but I should never have said those things to you. It was unforgivable."

"Did you regret it?" I asked.

"I've just said I did." He turned to me, looking confused.

"Not that. I mean, did you regret getting me pregnant. The fact that it forced you to give up Haley…"

"I didn't regret the pregnancy, no." The truth in his voice was unmistakable. "But telling Haley was tough; giving her up was really hard. I don't know if I was in love with her then. I know I was still in love with you, though, in spite of everything that had gone wrong between us. But I knew I'd hurt her and I felt awful about it." He took a deep breath. "That night, after you told me you were pregnant, after we fought and you went upstairs, I called her and told her that it was definitely over between her and I, that I couldn't keep betraying you. She cried and begged me not to leave her. She told me she loved me. She said she'd wait for me… she was really pleading with me. I—I felt like I was in an impossible situation, that I had no way out and I was going to end up hurting either you or her, even though I didn't want to do either. But deep down, I knew I had to stand by you and our child, and in the end I just had to hang up on her…" He looked at me, his eyes locking onto mine. "It was then that I saw you at the top of the stairs with your suitcase."

"Why did you fight so hard to make me stay?" I asked, remembering his words, his tears, his pleas. "Surely, if I'd left, you could just have gone back to Haley?"

He shook his head. "No. Things may not have been great between us for a while, Abbie, and I might have been having an affair, but as I just said, I did still love you. I really did, despite appearances to the contrary, and I genuinely did want to make it work for us. I wasn't staying with you out of duty, or pity, or loyalty. It honestly was out of love… for you and for Molly."

A few more tears fell at the mention of her name, but I brushed them away and he turned to face me, taking my hands in his. This time, I let him.

"I regretted what I'd done. I knew I was largely to blame for how things were between us because, even though you didn't know it, I'd let another woman come between us, but I hoped I could work hard enough to make it right again… to build a life for us as a family. And I did. I think it was working. I think we were happier than we'd ever been… until we weren't a family anymore." His voice cracked and I felt his emotion. Then he cleared his throat and sat back a little, although he kept hold of my hands. "I think we both knew we weren't strong enough to survive Molly's death, didn't we?"

I looked up at him, but I didn't reply. I didn't need to.

"After Molly," he continued, "I needed someone. Just someone I could be with, and be myself; someone I could talk to without having to analyse every word before I said it. The whole office knew what had happened, and one day a month or so after Molly's death, Haley came to me. We talked… well, I talked. She listened. She was there for me."

"And I wasn't," I whispered.

He moved closer again. "This isn't your fault, Abbie," he said firmly. "Is it anyone's?"

"Mine, I guess." I shook my head and he sighed. "I'm not proud of what I've done," he said slowly. "And I don't think I'll ever really forgive myself for it, but as Haley and I spent more time together, I fell in love with her."

"And out of love with me?" He didn't answer, but we both knew it was the truth. "The golf wasn't real either, was it?"

"No. I hate golf."

I almost smiled at that. Almost.

"I—Is she younger than me?" I was thirty-four then – just – but on most days I felt at least ten years older.

"A couple of years… But this isn't an early mid-life crisis, Abbie. She's not a twenty-two year old bimbo. She's a thirty-one year old paralegal."

I nodded my head. "She… she's not pregnant, is she? Is that why you're telling me this now?" I could hear the panic rising in my voice as I spoke and he shifted closer to me, so we were touching.

"No." His voice was achingly gentle. "It's nothing like that. I just don't want to live like this anymore. The lies are killing me. And I think we both deserve better than this. You certainly do."

We sat for a long while, just holding hands, until eventually he moved away again.

"I've got a friend," he said, rather randomly. "He's a good divorce lawyer."

"Divorce…" The word sounded strange on my lips.

"Yes. There's no point in prolonging the agony, is there?"

I shook my head. "I suppose I'd better find myself a solicitor as well," I murmured.

"No… that's not what I meant. The friend of mine, I'll send you his details. He'll handle everything for you. And I'll get him to send me the bill."

"No." I shook my head. "You don't have to do that."

He stared into my eyes. "Yes, I do." He sat back and looked around the room. "I assume you'd rather sell the house and split the proceeds?"

"Well, I don't want to stay here, if that's what you're asking."

He smiled. "I didn't think you would. You never really liked this place, did you?"

I frowned, looking over at him. "No, but if you knew that, why did you insist on moving here?"

He sighed and ran his fingers through is hair. "To get you away from Porthgowan… and from your memories."

My skin tingled. "Memories?"

"Of Josh." He took a deep breath. "He was always there, wasn't he? I mean, I know you tried your best to hide it, but when you didn't think anyone was looking, the sadness in your eyes was… well, it was heartbreaking. I thought, if I got you away from there, you might find a way to fall in love with me. I just used work as an excuse…"

His voice faded and I reached over and touched his arm. "I did love you, Simon."

He smiled. "You're not listening. I know you loved me. But I wanted you to be *in love* with me. There's a difference. You know that, just as well as I do. Because you were in love with Josh… and if you're being completely honest, you still are. You always have been. I knew that all along."

"You knew?" I couldn't see any point in denying it after what he'd just said.

"Of course." He smiled. "And if I'm being completely honest, I probably never should have asked you to marry me… but the thing was, I was so in love with you, Abbie, and I thought that was enough."

"I'm sorry," I murmured and he moved along the sofa, putting his arms around me, pulling my head down against his chest.

"Don't be. Like I said, I knew how you felt. It was my choice." I wondered if he was going to add 'my mistake', but he didn't.

He held me like that for hours. Day turned to night, and still he held on. I cried and he comforted me, and then in the morning, just as dawn was breaking, he went upstairs and packed a bag.

When he came back down, I met him in the hallway.

"I'm truly sorry," he said and I reached up, putting my fingers over his lips.

"Friends never have to say sorry," I whispered, through my tears.

He looked at me for a moment, then nodded his head, bent down and kissed my cheek… and left.

The divorce was very amicable.

To make things easy, I stayed on at the box in Falmouth while things were dealt with and, as promised, Simon paid all the legal fees and his friend, a man named Ryan Harrison, explained the whole process and took care of everything for me.

Within six months of our conversation, our marriage was all but over, and we'd exchanged contracts on the house, agreeing to split the significant proceeds fifty-fifty. I'd made plans to move back to Porthgowan, back in with my father to start with, although I'd viewed a cottage I really liked, on East Street, a little further up from where Tara and her father had lived, and had put in an offer, which had yet to be accepted. I really wanted it to go through. It was called 'Hope Cottage', and to me that seemed like a good omen… something I could cling to.

We divided up the furniture and belongings over a weekend, with Simon keeping most of the modern things he'd chosen to buy when we moved in, and me retaining all the antiques and older pieces I'd always wanted.

When it came to the memory box, I called him into our bedroom and asked him what he wanted to do.

"You keep it," he said, coming and sitting on the bed beside me, as I clutched it on my lap.

"That doesn't seem fair. She was your daughter too."

He placed his hand over mine and I turned to look at him. "I know," he said softly. "But I can't take a single part of her from you. I couldn't live with myself if I did that." He let go of me and tapped the lid of the box. "You keep it."

He stood up and looked back down at me. "Thank you," I whispered.

"I know you're moving back to Porthgowan," he said, going over to the door. "But I hope you won't mind if I come down there to see her every so often."

"Of course I won't."

"I'll come by myself," he added.

I shook my head. "You don't have to. Haley's part of your life now, and that makes her part of Molly's." I put the box down and went over to him. "It's okay... really."

"Thank you for saying that," he murmured. "I appreciate it."

We looked at each other for a moment, and then he moved away, going back downstairs.

We said goodbye on the doorstep, although I don't think either of us really knew what to say. We'd been married for nine years. We'd shared a lot. We'd shared Molly, for one thing, and that meant that walking away from each other – even though the love was long gone – was always going to be hard.

It was.

I moved back to Porthgowan in the middle of February, just a couple of weeks before Molly's second birthday. Dad closed The Lobster Pot for the day, and hired a van, coming to help me move my things, and we stored a lot of it in one of the pub outbuildings until I was ready to move out again. Looking around my old bedroom that night, I wondered how I'd ended up back there... back at the beginning again. But then Dad came in and handed me a cup of tea, silently giving me a hug at the same time, and it didn't seem quite so bad, after all. Not quite.

By that stage, my offer on Hope Cottage had been accepted and the sale was proceeding quickly. With luck, I hoped to be in by Easter, which was in the middle of April, and in the meantime, I set up my drawing board in my old room and got on with working, just to keep busy.

On Molly's birthday, Dad came with me to the graveyard.

"You're not going by yourself," he said when I mentioned it at breakfast. "And anyway, I often walk up there to see her." His voice dropped. "When we're not busy..."

"You do?" I had no idea.

"Yes. I just go and make sure she's okay... you know."

We wandered up to the church later on in the afternoon. We didn't see Simon, although there were some fresh flowers on her grave, so I guessed he must have been there earlier in the day.

"You alright?" Dad said as I stood up, having placed my posy of wild flowers in the vase beside Simon's white roses.

I nodded, although I couldn't speak.

It didn't get any easier.

I wasn't sure it ever would.

I managed to move in to Hope Cottage the week before Easter, with Dad's help yet again.

The place had been lived in by the same man for more than sixty years – a man by the name of Fred Callaway – and had lain empty for almost twelve months after his death at the age of ninety-three, while his two nephews argued over what to do with it. As a result, when I bought it, the house was in dire need of attention. I didn't mind that though. I was actually looking forward to it. I needed something to work on; a project to keep me occupied and stop me from thinking.

And so, over the next few months, in between commissions from my clients, and visits to Molly, I scrubbed and cleaned, painted and polished, until by the autumn, as the nights were drawing in again, the cottage was exactly how I wanted it.

The walls were white, the fabrics bold and patterned, but still feminine, the floors stripped, the rugs thick and cosy, and logs crackled and burned in the open fireplace. The furniture consisted in part of the antiques I'd kept from the cottage I'd shared with Simon. The old oak table and chairs fitted perfectly into the large kitchen-dining room, alongside the Rayburn I'd had installed, which not only provided me with a cooker, but also hot water and heating throughout the cottage. A stripped wooden work surface, quarry-tiled floor, and floral fabrics completed the look. In the living room, I bought a new sofa, its cushions soft and deep, and placed the two gnarled antique side tables at either end, the small lamps on top giving off a soft glow.

I toyed for a while with moving the downstairs bathroom into the box room upstairs, but it would have meant a huge amount of work, so

I decided against it, and installed a shower cubicle and replacement roll top bath instead, keeping the box room as it was and just decorating it with white paint until I could decide what I wanted to do with it. In the guest room, after painting and hanging curtains, I purchased a new bed and some basic furniture. My mother and I were still talking fairly regularly, and there was always a chance she might decide to come and stay… maybe.

For my own bedroom, I bought a beautiful wooden sleigh bed and new, deep mattress, complimenting them with an antique pine chest of drawers and wardrobe that I found in Helston.

My favourite room in the house, however, was the attic, which I converted into a studio. It was a large space, covering the whole surface area of the cottage, and I installed my drawing board, a plan chest and a small sofa, which still left plenty of room for shelves and storage. Best of all, there was a window that looked out towards the bay, and beyond, to the ocean.

And it was from there that I started to slowly rebuild my life… one day at a time.

Chapter Six

Josh

I didn't go home.

I wanted to. Obviously. That's why I'd offered to give up everything I had in London and go back to her. But Abbie told me not to – quite forcefully. So I didn't.

That doesn't mean I didn't think about it though. I thought about it all the time. I pictured myself jumping into my car, racing down to Porthgowan, finding her on the beach, or at the pub, and begging her, pleading with her, not to let me go. But every time I pictured that scene, I also pictured her rejecting me. Again.

Maybe that was my old insecurities coming through; maybe I didn't feel worthy of her… maybe I never had. Maybe I knew I'd let her down too much for her to want to try again. Maybe it was the way she'd told me not to, that hurt tone in her voice. Whatever it was, she'd made it very clear she didn't want me, so begging her wasn't going to help. It was only going to hurt more. Because being rejected a second time had to be worse, didn't it? That said, at the time, I didn't think anything could feel worse than the utter desolation of trying to live without Abbie. The pain was surprisingly raw, surprisingly physical.

I had nothing else to do to fill the void in my life, so I worked. I worked hard. I even got a promotion, when Elena left about eighteen months or so after I started at TBC, and moved to America to be with a boyfriend I didn't even know she had. And then, a while later, Stacey handed in her resignation, and Charles called me into his office, asking me if I'd consider taking her place. I was stunned by his offer, and I think it must have showed.

"Don't look so shocked," he said, smiling across the desk at me. "Obviously I could advertise the position, but I'd rather promote from within, if I can. It keeps the continuity going. And while I know you're young, the clients really like you. You're dedicated; you're good at what you do; and you've got a calm head, unlike a lot of others in this business."

I couldn't argue with his last statement. My life was filled with people who insisted on turning a drama into a crisis, at every opportunity.

I accepted his offer, naturally. I'd have been mad not to, and three new members of staff started within the month. There was Jared, an eighteen year old, much like I'd been when I first arrived, keen to learn, and willing to do anything I asked of him. Then there was Paige, a graduate from Manchester, rather loud and bossy, but good at getting things done. And finally, there was Natasha. At twenty-one, she was the same age as me, and had worked in another London agency for a short while. She came with her own ideas, but I couldn't fault her work ethic. The fact that she flirted incessantly was a problem, but it wasn't something I couldn't handle – mainly because I wasn't interested – and after a couple of months, she got the message and moved on to Ant. Poor guy…

And then, just as I was settling in to my new role, feeling like maybe I was starting to get my life back on track, I got the phone call.

My mother rarely telephoned; I think I'd heard from her two, maybe three times since leaving Porthgowan, but on that particular Saturday, at the end of June, I could tell, just from the tone of her voice, that she'd called for a reason.

"Have you heard the news?" she asked, after the usual 'hellos' and enquiries about Uncle Tim, who was away in California at the time.

"What news?"

There was a pause. "About Abbie…" My hands started to shake and I sat down on the edge of the couch, wondering what was coming next.

"What about her?"

"Her and Simon Trelawny. I had a feeling last summer that there was something going on, although I didn't see that much of them, so I couldn't be sure, and I didn't like to ask his mother outright, but they've been back from university for a couple of weeks now… and although they're both working, whenever they're together, they're literally all over each other. And I mean, *all over each other*." She made a point of stressing her last few words.

I didn't reply. My voice didn't work.

"Are you still there?"

I made a noise, mumbled something incoherent.

"It was always going to happen," she said.

Was it?

I managed to tell her there was someone at the door, and hung up, letting the phone drop to the floor and burying my head in my hands as I cried my eyes out for the second time in my adult life, my head filled with images of Abbie and Simon 'all over each other'.

It was later that afternoon that I discovered that mixing scotch, gin and vodka – even if they're not in the same glass – isn't a good idea, especially if you don't want to throw up over your uncle's thick pile carpets.

I woke up the next morning, in a pool of my own vomit, feeling like I'd died, and I wishing I had. Even as I groaned my way around the flat, I felt grateful that Uncle Tim was away. It at least gave me time to get the carpets professionally cleaned and to replace the alcohol I'd consumed, and the glasses I'd broken when I'd fallen into his drinks cabinet and then onto to the floor, too drunk to stand.

As I looked around the flat a couple of days later, making sure I'd cleaned everything thoroughly, and feeling a little more like a human being again, I vowed never to repeat that mistake. Next time my heart shattered, I'd stick to just one type of drink… and I wouldn't stop until I reached oblivion.

I thought the best thing for me to do was to focus on work, servicing the dozen or so publishers who were now our regular clients, and making sure my department ran like a well-oiled engine.

That Christmas, there was the usual office party. Clients, magazine editors and general hangers-on were invited too, and it was there that I met Caroline. She worked for a sports magazine, which meant she had nothing to do with my department, and we soon hit it off. She was pretty, blonde, and unlike a lot of the people there, she wasn't either drunk, or giggly – or both. We sat in a corner and talked, and at the end of the evening, she suggested we should share a cab home. She lived in a flat in Bayswater, and while my knowledge of London was still fairly limited, she assured me it made sense.

As the taxi pulled up outside her apartment building, she turned to me and whispered, "My flat-mate's staying with her boyfriend tonight… would you like to come up?"

She seemed embarrassed to be asking and I felt that I'd kind of intimated something might happen, just by agreeing we could share the cab, so it would have been rude to say 'no'.

I nodded, said, "Okay," and then I paid the driver and followed her up to her flat, which was on the first floor.

It was small, but then I was used to a six-bedroom mansion flat, so almost anywhere else was going to be small by comparison, and I'd no sooner closed the door, before I turned, and she leant up and kissed me, her tongue darting into my shocked, open mouth.

"I've been dying to do that all night," she sighed, breaking the kiss, then immediately starting a second one, her fingers twisting into my hair, her breasts heaving against my chest.

Her embarrassment, if that was what it had been, was a thing of the past, as she groaned and writhed against me, making her wishes obvious.

"Do you want to come through to the bedroom?" she breathed, leaning back and looking up at me.

"Um…" I didn't know. Did I?

"It's this way."

She led me down the hallway and through a door, into her bedroom, although I couldn't see it very clearly, and she didn't bother to put the lights on. Instead, she turned and pulled my jacket from my shoulders, undoing my shirt as well and letting them both drop to the floor, before she knelt in front of me, unfastening my jeans, her hand delving inside. I had a fairly good idea what she had in mind, and I wasn't going there. Abbie had done that and it was far too intimate an act for me to consider with anyone else… So I grabbed hold of her and picked her up, dropping her on the bed behind her. She squealed in delight, giggling, before kneeling up, undoing the side zip of her short dress and pulling it off over her head, revealing that she was wearing just a thong and lace topped stockings beneath it… and nothing else. She removed her thong, but left on her stockings and high heeled black shoes, before lying back on the bed.

I'd watched her every move, but was still not completely aroused, and was then forced to admit, "I don't have a condom," trying hard to disguise my relief that we could, maybe, limit ourselves to fooling around, rather than having sex. I wasn't sure I was ready for that… not with someone who wasn't Abbie. And it seemed my body agreed with me. Caroline had other ideas though, and she sat up, rolling her eyes as she reached into the bedside cabinet and pulled out a box, handing it to me, before lying back down again, her legs parted.

Now I had a problem. Caroline definitely had expectations, but my body was less than willing to go along with them… so, as I turned and removed my jeans and trunks, I closed my eyes, remembering all those times I'd been with Abbie, the way she felt beneath me, her perfect naked body against mine. That was all it took, and as I turned back to Caroline, rolling the condom over my erection, she leant up on her elbows, watching me.

"Oh God…" she whispered. "That's just beautiful…"

I crawled up over her body, trying to distance myself from what I was about to do. It was just sex, after all… She parted her legs even wider, giving me access and I pushed inside her easily, hearing her gentle groan, seeing the smile forming on her lips as she hissed out a, "Yes…" her hips grinding up into mine, greedily. I started to move, and after a few hesitant attempts to match each other's rhythm, we got there, and she lowered her right hand between us, rubbing herself, and coming twice – very loudly – before I finally managed to reach my own climax, almost overwhelmed with guilt. I'd cheated on Abbie – at least that was how it felt to me. I made my excuses, pulling out of Caroline and asking directions to her bathroom, scared I might actually break down in front of her. Once locked in the bathroom, I stared at myself in the mirror, holding back the tears – just – and wondered what Abbie would think of me, and how long it would take before I'd stop loathing myself.

When I came back into the bedroom, Caroline was sitting on the edge of the bed, wrapped up in a bath robe and seemed embarrassed again, so I got dressed. We exchanged phone numbers, saying we'd call, but I never heard from her again… and I never called her either. I had no desire to repeat that experience.

I don't know why she didn't contact me.

Maybe she guessed my heart wasn't in it.

The years went by, and out of sheer loneliness, I think, I had a few more dates. Not many, but a few. That's probably because I didn't go actively looking for anyone, but was occasionally 'picked up', so to speak, in either a bar, a coffee shop, or once, on the underground. It was never the other way around. We'd see each other for drinks, or sometimes dinner and if we got on well, we'd maybe arrange to meet up again. I even tried having sex with two of them – on more than one occasion, much to my surprise, being as they both requested repeat performances – and I found it easier to get aroused each time. I didn't consider myself to be in a 'relationship' with any of them though, and I don't think they did with me either. Nothing lasted. I didn't want it to. I just didn't seem to be built that way anymore. Besides everything else, that feeling of guilt never went away. It was ever-present, like a dark shadow that haunted my life…

By the time I was twenty-four, I worked out that, other than Abbie, I'd had sex with three women, less than half a dozen times in total, and that since I'd been with her, I'd never once felt fulfilled, or even contented. Not once.

Not only did I not go home, but I didn't move out of Uncle Tim's flat either, although he did tell me to stop calling him 'Uncle' all the time. We got on well. We enjoyed each other's company and we'd grown used to living together; not that he was there very often, and the size of the place made it possible for us both be there at the same time and be ignorant of the fact, if we chose to.

With six bedrooms, it was more than big enough for both of us, even if Tim had converted one of them into a study, and another into a gym, which I made daily use of, and had done since my arrival. There were two spacious reception rooms, both with televisions and stereo systems, and a large kitchen-breakfast room, as well as a more formal dining area, although I wasn't aware of that ever being used. Between the hours that we both worked, and his trips abroad, we could sometimes go for days, or even weeks without seeing each other.

My hours were often unpredictable, so I'm sure my mother didn't expect me to still be at work when she called me one evening in July. I was working on a launch that was due the following weekend, and although everyone else had gone home already, I wanted to make sure we hadn't forgotten anything.

When my phone rang, I checked the screen and, seeing it who it was, thought about leaving it for the voicemail to collect. However, my inbuilt sense of duty towards my mother got the better of me and, on the fourth ring, I answered.

"Josh Brewer," I said.

"You don't need to answer the phone to me like that," she said, sounding huffy. "I'm sure you knew it was me."

"Hello, Mother."

"Where are you?" she said. "You sound very echoey."

"I'm at work."

"At this hour?"

"It's only nine o'clock, but yes."

I wished she'd just get to the point and let me get on. "I thought I'd call and update you on the latest news," she said and I sat back in my chair, recalling the last time she'd called with 'news' and how badly that had ended.

"Yes?"

"Abbie and Simon have announced their engagement," she said, and I thought I heard a note of triumph to her tone. "They've set the date for the first Saturday in July, next year…" Her voice faded into the background, although I'm fairly sure she was still talking.

I hung up, regardless and, without thinking, went around the office, switching off lights, checking computers were powered down, and pushing in chairs. I was on auto-pilot, my world in tatters, yet again.

I made my way home, riding on the underground, unaware of everything around me, and letting myself into the flat, without even really remembering the journey at all.

I dropped my jacket in the hallway and went straight through to the main living room and over to the cabinet where Tim kept the drinks, opening it and grabbing the half-empty bottle of vodka, along with a new, unopened one, before going into my bedroom, and straight through to the wet room. I'd promised myself I wasn't going to stop until I'd reached oblivion, so this was going to get messy.

I sat down on the floor, propped up against the wall, and opened the bottle, drinking directly from it, closing my eyes and letting myself picture them together… her fingers in his hair, her lips on his, then her kneeling down slowly before him, her mouth open, poised… him buried inside her, her long legs wrapped around his hips as she writhed and screamed in ecstasy. I heard my own sob and opened my eyes again, my cheeks wet with tears as I listened to the sound of a key turning in the front door lock.

"Josh?"

Tim was home.

"Josh?" he repeated when I didn't answer. "I know you're here, because your jacket's on the bloody floor." I waited. "And why is the drinks cabinet open?" His voice was more distant now, but that made sense if he was in the living room. A longer silence followed and then he appeared in the doorway. "What the hell happened to you?" He sounded concerned and surprised at the same time.

"Abbie," I whispered.

"Abbie?"

"Yes."

"Who's Abbie?"

"You don't remember her?"

He raised his eyebrows. "Should I?"

"She was my girlfriend, when I lived at home… in Porthgowan. You met her once. Well, you saw her once. The day you came down to buy me the car?" I reminded him. He stared at me for a moment, his face darkening.

"Oh yes?" he said, coming further into the room. "What's happened? What's she done?"

"She hasn't done anything," I explained. "Well, she has, but not in the way you probably mean."

"You're not making much sense," he said, looking down at the bottles beside me. "How much have you had?"

"Nowhere near enough. She's… she's getting married," I said, my heart aching as I said the words.

"Oh," he replied. "Who to?"

"A friend of mine."

"Ouch." He attempted a smile, but then stopped when he saw my face. "You… you care about her, don't you?" he whispered, seemingly taken aback.

"Yes. Of course I do. I'm in love with her."

"You're in love with her?" His voice had dropped to a whisper. "But I thought she broke things off with you when you moved up here."

"She did… well, she did a few weeks afterwards. She couldn't handle the long distance thing." I hadn't explained it to him at the time. I'd just told him I wouldn't be going home anymore, because Abbie and I were over. Talking about it had been too much for me back then.

"Why not?" he asked. "I mean, why couldn't she do the long distance thing?"

"Because she wanted someone who would be there for her. A man, who'd put her first. Not an idiotic, selfish boy, who was always putting his career ahead of everything else, and who couldn't even guarantee to get back to her for one day a week. It hurt like hell, but I didn't blame her for doing what she did. I still don't."

He stared at me. "Because you're still in love with her?"

"Yes."

"And what about her?"

I paused, trying to swallow the lump in my throat. "Well..." I managed eventually. "I guess she's over me now – otherwise she wouldn't be marrying Simon. But when we were together, she loved me as much as I loved her."

"She did?"

I looked up at him. "Thanks for that."

He held up his hands. "Sorry. I didn't mean it like that." He paused. "I just meant... well, how did you know?" I remembered then that he was single; that I'd never seen him with a woman, or even heard him speak of one. Maybe he really didn't know.

"That she loved me?" I queried, just to be sure we were talking about the same thing, and he nodded. "She told me... and she showed me, every day we were together. But in any case, I just knew. I never doubted her love for me. Not once. Not even when she was breaking up with me. She broke her own heart, as well as mine when she did that."

His brow furrowed. "I don't understand... if you love her so much, then why haven't you gone back to her? It's been six years. You've had plenty of time to..."

"I offered," I interrupted. "At the time, I said I'd give all this up, leave my job and go back to her, but she told me not to."

"Why?"

"Because she was more sensible than I was. She worked out that if I'd gone back, I'd have ended up resenting it all in the end. I can't ever imagine not loving her, but I'd have resented the life we'd have had to live. She knew that, so she made the decision for me, because she knew our lives were incompatible and it had to be done, and I wasn't strong enough to do it myself. *That's* how much she loved me." It was the first time I'd admitted that, even to myself, and it felt strange to say the words aloud and realise the truth behind them. It had taken me years to work it out... too many years. And, even though I would still have gone back to her right there and then, even though I would have swallowed down all my insecurities and all my fears of rejection, jumped into my car and raced back to the village, and lived whatever life she'd wanted, if it meant we could have been together, I knew I'd left it too late. She'd moved on.

Tim leant back against the wall behind him, and then slid down it, crouching. "And yet she's marrying this other man?"

I nodded. "Things change, I guess. Well, for Abbie, anyway."

"But not for you?"

I shook my head and reached for the bottle again. "No. Like I said, I'll always love her. Always. But I suppose I'm just going to have to find a way to get used to the idea that she really isn't mine anymore." God, that hurt to say.

He let his head rock forward for a minute while I took a long sip of vodka, and then he stood and came over to me, holding out his hand. I looked up at him. "If you're going to get drunk, don't do it by yourself, on the bathroom floor," he said. "Do it with your uncle… in the comfort of an armchair. And use a bloody glass."

Abbie's wedding day came and went.

Uncle Tim spent the day with me. We didn't do much. We just hung around at the flat, but he was there, watching me I presumed, either to ensure I didn't drink myself to death, or to stop me from taking off for Porthgowan to make a dramatic entrance in the middle of the wedding ceremony, by declaring my undying love for the bride in front of the entire congregation. I had thought about it, even though I hadn't said anything to Tim, but the idea of ruining Abbie's day was too much for me. I knew her. I knew she wouldn't have given herself – or promised herself – to Simon, if she didn't love him. And no matter how much that hurt, I had to try and come to terms with it.

It took months – well, more than a year actually – but eventually, it got a little easier to breathe again. I stopped seeing a grey darkness everywhere, and I started to think about making some changes to my life; the first and most important of which was to leave TBC.

I felt as though the last couple of years of my employment there had become stale. I wasn't growing anymore; wasn't learning anything new. I wasn't developing. And I knew that if I wanted to get on with my life and build something for myself, I needed to develop. I needed a fresh start.

I lined up a couple of interviews with other agencies. They were both much smaller, and younger than TBC – but then that applied to almost every agency in town. They were looking to grow, and that gave me encouragement. I quite liked the idea of being part of something that was evolving, blossoming… changing.

I told everyone at work that I had some family commitments on the days of the interviews – it wasn't like I ever took much time off, so no-one minded – and I started to prepare myself, ready to wow them with my credentials.

The day before the first interview, I came home from work, feeling almost optimistic for the first time in years as I let myself into the flat. It was early November, and the lights were on in the hall and living room, directly ahead of me, although the bedroom areas to my left and right were both dimmed. Tim was obviously home.

"I'm back," I called, but there was no reply. In fact the place seemed eerily quiet and I wondered if he'd gone out and left the lights on by mistake.

I put my keys in the bowl on the hall table and went through to the living room, hearing the sound of running water.

"Tim?" I called, going through to the kitchen and the obvious source of the noise.

He was still nowhere to be seen, although the tap was running into the empty sink in the island unit. I leant over and turned it off, and caught sight of a denim clad leg, lying on the floor.

"Tim!" I ran around the unit, but I knew before I even knelt down, that he was dead. His staring eyes, bluish lips and whitened face were enough to tell me. "Oh God…" I mumbled.

Beside him, right next to his clutched hand, there lay a kitchen knife, and on the other side, there was a half-peeled onion. I knew better than to touch anything, and pulled my phone from my pocket, dialling 999.

The police arrived, together with an ambulance and Tim was declared dead. His body was removed once the police were happy no foul play was involved – which took all of about ten minutes to establish.

The paramedic said it looked like he'd had a massive heart attack, but the police informed me that the coroner would probably order a post mortem to confirm that. I gave a statement, detailing my own movements, recollecting – just in passing, really – that Tim always peeled onions under a running tap, because he thought it stopped his eyes from watering, and then everyone left, with expressions of condolence and sympathy.

The flat seemed silent and empty without him. He may not have been there all the time, and I might have been very used to my own company, but the thought that he'd never walk through the door again, was a strange one.

I didn't know what to do, so I decided to go to bed, even though it wasn't that late and I hadn't eaten. I wasn't hungry and the thought of cooking in the kitchen where he'd just died was enough to make my stomach churn. Even as I went through to my bedroom though, I realised there was one thing more I had to do. There was one call that had to be made.

"Yes?" I knew, straight away, that I'd woken her up.

"It's me," I said.

"Do you know what time it is?" she replied.

"Yes." My mother had always gone to bed early, so her mood didn't surprise me in the slightest. "I'm sorry, but I had to call you."

"What on earth for? And why couldn't it have waited until the morning?"

"Tim's dead." I blurted out the words, partly in anger at her attitude, and partly because I had no idea how else I was going to say it anyway.

There was a silence on the end of the phone. "Dead?" she repeated.

"Yes. I'm sorry." He was her brother and, as far as I was aware, her only relative apart from me.

"How?" she asked.

"He had a heart attack."

There was an odd noise, and then she said, "Well, I suppose it's not that surprising, not when you think how he lived."

"Mother!" I was shocked. Tim's lifestyle didn't immediately indicate he was a prime candidate for a heart attack. He exercised, ate healthily, didn't smoke... okay, so he drank a fair bit, but who didn't? Her words just showed me that she didn't know him very well, and that she was as callous and hard as I'd always known her to be.

"Oh, don't try and sound so shocked," she continued unabated. "You know exactly what Tim was, and don't try and pretend otherwise."

"I've got no idea what you're talking about." I genuinely didn't, and what's more, I didn't care. "I'm just calling to let you know your brother's died."

"When's the funeral?" she asked.

"I have no idea. I only discovered his body a few hours ago. And I think there's going to have to be a post mortem yet."

"Why?"

"Because it was a sudden, unexplained death, that's why."

"Well, let me know when you arrange it for... the funeral, that is. And try to give me a little bit of notice, so I can sort out some cover for the Post Office." There was a short silence. "What about his will?" she said.

"What about it?"

"Where is it?" she huffed, as though she thought I should understand what she meant without explanation. "What's being done about it?"

"I don't know. Tim was quite meticulous about things like that. I should imagine it's with his solicitor."

"Well, you'll need to contact them on my behalf," she said. "Make sure they're doing everything properly and not frittering away his money. You know what solicitors are like..." I remembered her 'expectations' and felt my skin crawl at her openly mercenary attitude.

"Fine," I replied and hung up.

The next morning, I cancelled my interview, explaining the situation to them. There were things to organise, people to see, phone calls to make. They were kind, sympathetic, and offered to re-schedule a date for me after the funeral. Being as I had no idea when that would be, I told them I'd get back to them. And then I arranged to take some time off work, speaking to Charles Tatnell in person, being as I knew he and Tim had been friends. He was devastated by the news and I heard the crack in his voice before he hung up, feeling relieved it hadn't been a face-to-face conversation – for both of our sakes.

Then I went through Tim's desk, feeling intrusive in doing so. He kept a paper diary and address book, thank goodness, because his computer was password protected. I discovered he had a full list of appointments for the following few days, so I called them up and cancelled, explaining the situation. Everyone was shocked and wanted to be kept informed of the funeral plans. After that, I arranged for an announcement to be placed in The Times. I knew he was quite an influential person in the city and it seemed like the best way to let people know, being as I couldn't possibly go through his entire address book. I found the name and number for Tim's solicitor though, and called him. His name was Brian Hall and his secretary informed me he was in a meeting and would call me back when he was available. She made it sound like that might be sometime never, but my phone rang within the hour.

"I'm the executor of your uncle's will," he explained, once I'd given him the details of what had happened, and he'd recovered himself, seemingly as upset as Charles Tatnell had been – indeed, as everyone had been, on hearing the news.

"I see." I didn't. I had no idea what being an executor of someone's will entailed.

"I have certain duties to perform," he said, as though he perhaps understood my ignorance, without me having to tell him. "Your uncle's will is very explicit in its instructions pertaining to his funeral." I was surprised by that, but not as surprised as I was by his next sentence: "The first of those being that I should take over all of the arrangements."

"All of them?"

"Yes. Your uncle was very insistent about that."

I felt a little hurt. "He didn't want me involved?"

There was a moment's silence. "He didn't mean it as an insult to you," Mr Hall said, showing his understanding of my feelings. "He just didn't want you to be troubled by it."

"But it's no trouble," I reasoned.

"Hmm… he told me you'd say that. But the thing is, dealing with the coroner's office, and with the post mortem and everything, it could get complicated, and time-consuming."

"I see." I still didn't mind, but Mr Hall seemed determined and as the executor of Tim's will, I assumed I couldn't argue with him. "You will keep me informed of everything though, right?"

"Of course I will. And I should probably point out now," he added, "that your uncle left very specific directives about the reading of his will."

"Do people do that? Formally read wills, I mean?"

"Sometimes." He paused. "He… he wanted it to be read after the funeral, at my offices, and he wanted you and your mother to be present."

I nodded my head, even though I knew Mr Hall couldn't see me. "And when do I need to move out of the flat?" I asked. It had dawned on me, while I was waiting for Mr Hall to return my call, that I'd have to; that the apartment would probably be sold, and that I'd need to find somewhere else to live, but I had no idea as to the timing of such things.

"Don't worry about that for now," Mr Hall replied. "We can discuss all of that at a later date."

"The thing is," I reasoned, "I do rather need to know. I'm not as well off as my uncle was, and although I earn a decent salary, I doubt I'll be able to afford central London prices, so I'd just like to know how long I've got, so I can start planning. I'm sure you understand…" I hoped he did, anyway.

"Of course, Mr Brewer. But as I say, there really is nothing to worry about. We can discuss all of that when you come to my office for the reading of the will."

"And in the meantime, I just stay here?"

"Yes," he replied, simply.

"And what about the bills? The electricity, water and so forth?" I knew they'd have to be paid, but as to who the suppliers were, I had no idea.

"Don't worry," he said soothingly. "I'll take care of everything. And I'll keep you posted about any developments."

I thanked him and we ended the call, but I felt at a bit of a loose end after that. My role in Uncle Tim's funeral arrangements had been usurped, and there was little point in looking for somewhere new to live yet, so after a couple of days mooching around the flat, I went back to work.

The funeral was held in the second week of December, once the post-mortem had been done, showing that no further action was required; Tim really had just died of a heart attack, exactly as the paramedic had said.

My mother came up from Porthgowan on the train the day before and I met her at Paddington, straight from work.

I hadn't seen her for a little over eight years, but she hadn't changed in the slightest.

We didn't kiss. We didn't even hug. Instead, she stood on the platform and looked me up and down. "You wear those clothes to work, do you?"

"Yes."

She narrowed her eyes. "And you don't feel the need to shave anymore?"

"The stubble is intentional," I said under my breath, bending and taking her bag from her hand. It actually took quite a bit of work to keep my facial hair at the right length, but it didn't seem as though she appreciated that, so I didn't waste my time explaining.

We settled into the taxi and she turned, staring at me.

"Simon wears a suit to work every day."

Fantastic. We hadn't even got to the flat, and she was already talking about Simon. How long before she mentioned Abbie's name?

"That's nice," I replied.

"I see him driving out of the village most days," she continued, my sarcasm going over her head. "He's got a very expensive looking car. A Mercedes, I think."

"Well, bully for Simon."

"He's—"

"Do you want to eat at the flat, or go out?" I interrupted. I didn't want to hear anything more about Simon, or what he had. I knew exactly what the had. He had Abbie and, as far as I was concerned, that meant he had the only thing any sane man could ever want or need in his life.

"Out," she said decisively. "I'm too tired to cook."

"I wasn't suggesting you did the cooking. I was going to cook for us."

She chuckled and stared at me. "You? Cook?"

"Yes. Do you think I've been living on take aways ever since I left home?"

She clasped her hands together. "Well, this I've got to see…"

I cooked a simple stir-fry, leaving out the chillies, and making sure to tone down any of the usual spices I might have normally added. I'd developed a taste for more exotic foods since my arrival in London, but on this occasion, I knew they wouldn't go down well. Despite that, she moaned all the way through, although she still ate most of it, and then announced she was tired and going to bed. I showed her to the guest room and heaved a sigh of relief that at least she was only staying for two days.

The funeral itself was a very well attended and surprisingly jolly affair, the wake being held in a bar not far from the flat. Tim had left instructions that no black was to be worn, and despite the grey chill in the air, it was a colourful, cheerful and remarkably upbeat afternoon – although my mother, being a law unto herself, ignored Tim's wishes and wore a black coat and hat, with a matching scowl, like a spectre at the feast.

Charles was there, and we spoke briefly. I introduced him to my mother, who grunted her greeting and looked impatient to move away. I mouthed my apology behind her back, and he shook his head in understanding.

Everyone departed by four o'clock, and we climbed into a taxi with Mr Hall, who turned out to be younger than I'd expected, at around forty. He was tall and slim, and was wearing a pale grey suit, white shirt and the brightest polka dot tie I'd ever seen. Whether that was his usual apparel, or something he'd chosen to wear specifically for the funeral, I had no idea, but we sat in silence during the short journey to his offices.

Once there, he offered tea, which I accepted and my mother declined. Her eagerness to hurry the proceedings along was embarrassing.

The tea was brought in, and once poured, Mr Hall settled back in his chair, holding up a folded document.

"I'm sure you're both aware that Mr Brewer was a very wealthy man," he began. "His testamentary dispositions are, however, quite straightforward."

He raised his eyes and looked from me to my mother, before taking a sip of tea and continuing, "Mr Brewer came to me over a year ago now, and asked me to draw up a new will for him." I was aware of my mother shifting in her seat, but focused on Mr Hall. "Although it's not a complicated document, I won't bore you by reading it in full. I will simply tell you the main points of interest – well the only point of interest really." I nodded my head and waited. "In his new will, he leaves his entire estate, including his properties in London, Malibu and Chamonix, to his nephew, Joshua Brewer."

There was a moment's silence, and then I heard the scream, right before I felt my mother's hand make contact with my cheek. She was standing before me, her face like thunder, wailing loudly, even as I still struggled to take in what was happening.

"Miss Brewer!" Mr Hall moved quickly – more quickly than I would have given him credit for – and stood between us. "That will do!"

"I want to know what's been going on," she said, moving away, but raising her voice. "What's he done?" She turned and pointed at me.

"I haven't done anything." I assumed she was accusing me of exerting some kind of influence over Tim, persuading him to leave me his fortune… a fortune I hadn't even known existed until a few moments ago.

"Really?" she hissed, stepping closer again. I was ready for her this time and sat forward, refusing to stand and create a real drama.

"Yes, really."

She shook her head, hostility pouring off of her. "Tim was gay!" she shouted.

I almost gasped in surprise. How on earth had he kept that hidden from me, considering we'd lived in the same flat for so many years? "So what?" I replied instinctively.

"So, I ask again… what have you done?"

I stared at her for a moment. Was she saying what I thought she was saying? Judging from the look on her face, it seemed so.

"If you're suggesting there was anything between myself and Tim, other than that he was my uncle and I was his nephew, then you need to get your head out of the gutter."

"Do I?" She turned to Mr Hall, who was still standing by his desk. "Can I contest this… this travesty?"

He shrugged and leant back on his desk, staring at her. "You can. But you'd need a reason. You'd need to prove that either your brother wasn't of sound mind when he made the will, or that it wasn't properly drawn up, or that he didn't fully understand the content of the document, or that he came under undue influence from the beneficiary, or that the will was in some way fraudulent, or that it had been drafted in a negligent or ambiguous manner." He counted off his points on his fingers. "And I'm afraid, I'd have to advise you that you can do none of those." He sighed and stood again. "You are of course at liberty to take independent legal advice, at your own expense…" He left his words hanging and went to sit down again.

Defeated, she turned to face me again. "You bastard."

I smiled, and then laughed and she tilted her head in confusion. "For once, your insult is entirely accurate, Mother. I am, indeed, a bastard, being as I have no idea who my father is. But whose fault is that?"

She glared at me, her face reddening with anger and shame, and then, without another word, stormed out of the office, catching her bag on the door handle and humiliating herself further by having to twist around and unhook it.

She left the door open and I got up, walking over and closing it quietly before turning back to Mr Hall.

"I do apologise," I said, sitting down again.

He held up his hand. "No need," he replied. "Your uncle did warn me she'd react like that, when he changed his will."

I looked across the desk at him, as he reached into a file and pulled out an envelope. "Why did he do that?"

"What? Warn me, or change his will?"

"Change his will."

He smiled. "It's all in here." He tapped the envelope with the backs of his fingers. "He left instructions that I was to give you this… and that you should read it on your own, in your flat." *My flat?* Of course… it was mine now. That explained Mr Hall's attitude to me staying on there, and his reassurance that I shouldn't worry about moving out or paying the bills. I owned it, even if he hadn't been at liberty to tell me at the time.

He leant across, handing me the envelope and I got to my feet, feeling that our business was concluded – at least for now. "There was one other thing," he added and I paused, looking down at him.

"Yes?"

"Your uncle said to make yourself comfortable before you read that… and to use a bloody glass. He said that would make sense to you."

I sighed, nodding and started to feel slightly nervous about what lay ahead.

When I got back to the flat, my mother was nowhere to be seen. I checked the guest room and found her small suitcase had gone, so I assumed she'd got the concierge to let her in and had promptly taken herself back to Porthgowan in a fit of pique. I wasn't sorry. I didn't relish the prospect of another confrontation with her.

Going through to the living room, I sat in an armchair, turning on the lamp beside me, even though the rest of the room was in darkness. I didn't pour myself a drink – in a glass, or otherwise. I had a feeling I was going to need a clear head for reading whatever was in the envelope. Drinking could come later… if necessary.

I tore open the envelope and let it fall to the floor as I unfolded the sheets of handwritten paper inside and started reading.

My Dear Joshua, the letter began, and I smiled at Tim's use of my full name.

If you're reading this, then I have to assume I'm dead. I rather hope that by now, you're old and married, with a few children, perhaps, because that means you'll have found happiness, and I'll have lived to a ripe old age myself, and will have been able to spoil my great nephews and nieces to distraction. But if you're still young, and still heartbroken, then I'm sorry… for both of us.

The fact that this letter has found its way into your hands means you'll know by now I've left you my money. All of it. You weren't aware of that, or of how much I was worth, in the same way that you lived in ignorance of my sexual preferences. In case you still don't know, I'll tell you now… I was gay. I was never a promiscuous man. I had a few lovers over the years, and knew great happiness with all of them, and while you and I may have lived together, I never had to try very hard to hide my lifestyle from you, although if you'd ever guessed, or asked, I'd have told you whatever you wanted to know. But you didn't. You respected my privacy. You let me live my life, and you lived yours. And I was grateful for that. In the same way as I was grateful for your company over the years. You were an admirable companion and a good friend.

The changes I made to my will, however, had nothing to do with my gratitude to you. They had everything to do with the reason we found ourselves living together in the first place, and the one regret in my life.

This is going to be hard for you to read, and before you do, I want to apologise, and to say that, when I did what I did, I honestly believed I was acting in your best interests. The fact that I was wrong about that, has remained a lasting sorrow to me.

I'll begin by telling you that it had always been my intention to try and give you a head start in business. Through my own work, over the years, I'd formed many acquaintances – some of whom had significant influence – and I wanted to give you the opportunity to get ahead in your chosen profession, when the time came. I'd expected you to go to university, and then that you and I would sit down at some point and discuss your future.

However, my plans were changed when I received a telephone call from your mother near the end of the summer after you finished your A-levels. She explained that your relationship with your girlfriend had become more serious than she'd realised, and told me of her fears for your future. I revealed to her that I'd already seen you with Abbie, and that you seemed happy together, but she said Abbie was manipulative, and a 'good for nothing whore with a reputation to match'.

I felt my grip tighten on the pages, creasing them slightly, but forced myself to read on.

I apologise if that language offends you. It is offensive. I know that. But I'm just repeating what she said. She told me it had come to her attention that your relationship with Abbie had become intimate, and that she fully expected Abbie to turn up on the doorstep at any moment, announcing she was pregnant, claiming the child to be yours – even though it probably wouldn't be – with the aim of trapping you into a marriage you didn't want, and ruining your future. Again, those are your mother's words, albeit slightly paraphrased.

She was crying down the phone at me, and begged me to help, to find some way of getting you away from the clutches of this girl. Your mother was very convincing and, to my shame, I believed her. I wanted to help, so I did the only thing I could. I moved my plans forward. I went to see Charles Tatnell at his home that very afternoon. He said he'd interview you for his new department, as a favour to me. And then I came down and saw you.

You know the rest. You were offered the job, and you moved to London. Your relationship with Abbie didn't last the test of separation, and I felt vindicated in my decision when she broke it off with you, especially as you progressed further and further in your career.

I continued to feel I'd done the right thing, until that evening when I came home and discovered you in your bathroom, so obviously upset.

When you told me your news, that you'd heard Abbie was going to be married, and it became clear that was the reason for your despair, I started to have doubts about what I'd done. You explained to me how you felt about her… and that she'd felt the same about you, and I realised your version of the relationship didn't ring true with your mother's, and I knew then that I had to find out for myself what had really happened.

So, I made some discreet enquiries. I spoke to some of the people she'd been at university with, and a couple of her lecturers as well, and I found out that, rather than being the money-grubbing prostitute your mother had painted her to be, Abbie was in fact a shy, unassuming, but hard-working, talented and honest young woman, who was well thought of by everyone who knew her. She was, in reality, the complete opposite of everything my sister had portrayed her to be, and it came as no surprise to me when I later established that it was Mary who had told you of Abbie's engagement and impending marriage.

I contemplated approaching Abbie myself, and telling her what had gone on, or coming to you and explaining it, in the hope that you could put things right between the two of you. But I decided it was too late by then. Too much time had passed; Abbie had committed herself to another man, and it wasn't fair to cause further heartache to the two of them, or to you, merely to assuage my guilty conscience. So, I stayed silent. If that was wrong, I apologise – again.

I don't claim to understand your mother's reasons, but she'd manipulated you – and Abbie – and had made me a party to her schemes, causing me to lie to you and hurt you, and I cannot forgive her for that, any more than I can forgive myself for believing in her so easily.

I'd always known that Mary had ideas of inheriting from me, so I decided to hurt her in the only way I could. I changed my will, cutting her out and leaving everything to you, Josh.

I know this in no way makes up for everything else you have lost and I know you'd rather have Abbie and the years you could have had together, and a long and happy future with her, than any amount of money. But this is the best I can do.

I hope you will find a way to forgive me, because I truly am sorry, and I hope that you've found happiness by the time you read this. If not, then I pray you will, one day. You deserve it.

Thank you, again, for your friendship.
With love,
Tim

I held the letter for what seemed like hours, the words flowing over me, their meaning sinking in. My own mother… she'd broken us up; she'd broken our hearts and she alone had ruined my life. I'd always known she didn't love me, not like a mother should. But this…? It was too much to take in. The pain, the agony, the emptiness of all those years had been because of her.

Tim was right. The money didn't mean a damn thing, not when compared to losing Abbie; the torture of living without her, and the years we'd missed out on, the future we'd never have… Nothing else mattered. Nothing.

He was right about something else too, though. We couldn't go back. Abbie had found a way to move on and, although I knew I was a long way from doing that myself, that didn't give me the right to trample over her happiness. It wouldn't bring mine back.

I knew there and then that I'd never forgive my mother. Ever.

As for Tim? That was easy.

He'd been manipulated too, and I didn't like the idea that he'd died with regrets, feeling guilty over something my mother had done.

I got to my feet and went over to the drinks cabinet, taking out a bottle of vodka, and pouring a good measure of it into a highball tumbler.

"Friends never have to say sorry," I whispered to the empty room, as I raised my glass to him.

I had a lot of decisions to make. My future had changed overnight and the first thing I did was something I'd been thinking about for a while… I resigned from my job.

Discovering that I hadn't been given my initial post on merit made the whole thing seem like a farce to me, and while I may have worked hard and earned my promotions, I didn't feel that I belonged at TBC anymore. Charles said he was sorry to see me go, and that the door would always be open if I wanted to return, which was nice of him. I didn't tell him that I knew about his role in Tim's plan. Instead I reminded myself that I'd learned a lot from him, and we parted as friends. I was pleased about that at least.

And then I booked myself a ticket to Malibu, deciding to check out Uncle Tim's beachside home there. Well, it was now *my* beachside home there, I supposed.

As it turned out, I didn't particularly like it. The house was fine, although it was very modern, with lots of glass and chrome and leather, but the beach was nothing like Porthgowan, and I felt like I didn't belong there.

After a few calls to Brian Hall, I decided to sell the house, and only then discovered that things don't work quite the same in the US as they do in England. Brian was fantastic about it all, and took over everything, dealing with the American estate agents and lawyers and leaving me free to travel to Chamonix.

Tim's chalet there was huge, and set on the outskirts of the town, at the end of a quiet lane. Built over three floors, it was – like most of the houses nearby – wood clad, and had spacious rooms, which Tim had furnished in a more homely style than the Notting Hill flat. I chose to keep it, and spent Christmas and New Year there, being as I had nothing to rush home for. I couldn't ski, but I started taking lessons and by the time I arrived back in London at the beginning of January, I was at least able to remain upright while moving in a vaguely forwards direction. It seemed like an achievement.

The decision to keep the Notting Hill apartment was an easy one. I'd grown used to living there, for one thing, and I liked the area.

Uncle Tim's fortune was considerably larger than I imagined my mother had probably anticipated, even after the payment of death duties, and a few days after the sale of the Malibu house had gone through, Brian transferred an eye-watering sum into my personal bank account.

I was a multi-millionaire.

And I felt like the loneliest man in the world.

I called the company AIM PR.

Starting my own business felt like the logical progression. I'd wanted to build something, to create something – so why not do that for myself, instead of someone else?

A lot of people liked the name and said it was a good idea, that it was progressive and forward-thinking, although I never told anyone the real reason I'd chosen it. Abbie's middle name was Mia… all I did was to spell it backwards.

The first thing I did after registering the company, on a cold early March day, four months after Tim's death, was to contact Ant. He'd left TBC a couple of years beforehand, but we'd stayed in touch and I knew he was bored working in his new place. He jumped at the chance of joining me, and together we looked at offices in Covent Garden, Soho and Bayswater, settling on the Covent Garden premises in the end, simply because we liked the feel of them. They were set over two floors, above a florists, and were open plan, with large windows front and back.

Ant took on the task of recruitment, weeding out the wheat from the chaff, while I made myself responsible for finding our first clients and, sticking to what I knew, I began with publishing houses.

I had meeting after meeting, made presentation after presentation, wined, dined and talked myself to death, and by the end of our second month, we had two clients: a small independent fiction publishers, run by a woman called Gretchen, who worked from home – a very nice home in Chiswick; and a non-fiction outfit, owned by an older man, called Steven, whose office was the most disorganised place I'd ever set foot in. He was literally surrounded by manuscripts and books, with an ancient computer and a black cat sitting on his desk. It was like something out of the ark. But we got on well, and I liked him.

In the meantime, Ant had been carrying out the initial interviews, discarding anyone who he knew wouldn't fit – which basically meant anyone who was too stress-oriented – and I stepped in at the end, and between us, we selected three full-time members of staff: Carl, who was very much the office junior, keen and eager to please; Robyn, from Nottingham, who had moved to London to be near her boyfriend, was quite shy, but had worked for a small PR company in her home town for eighteen months and showed promise; and Cathy, who'd been in PR for years, before stopping to have kids, and was looking to make a return to the business now that they'd flown the nest. Along with Janice, our part-time book-keeper, she was keen to mother us all, and often arrived at the office bearing coffee and pastries, or better still, her homemade brownies.

The hours were long, the schedules occasionally punishing, but everyone pulled together and, within a few short years, we'd built the business beyond even my wildest dreams.

The only thing missing from my life was someone with whom I could share my small triumphs and moments of success.

Cathy noticed this more than anyone and would occasionally try and set me up with one or other of her younger, single, female friends. I had a couple of dates, just to please her, but I was careful never to sleep with any of them, because I knew I'd feel guilty still, and also because there was no chance of anything coming of it, and I didn't want Cathy to think badly of me. Abbie was still on my mind the whole time, no matter how hard I tried to forget about her, and I found that if I concentrated really hard, I could still remember how she felt, her lips on mine, the softness of her skin, her scent, the taste of her, the sounds she made when she came apart beneath me. It may have been torture to think of her, but I did it sometimes, on purpose, just to remember how good it had been; that I'd had someone that perfect once upon a time, and she hadn't been a dream.

Every so often, usually at night when I was in the flat by myself, I'd think about calling Robert, just to catch up. Well, and to find out how Abbie really was. I never did of course, even though I'd transferred the pub's number to every phone I'd owned ever since I'd left Porthgowan all those years ago. I'd deleted Abbie's number after she got engaged to Simon, just in case I ever got tempted to call and tell her I was still in love with her. Abbie was Simon's. She wasn't mine anymore. One day, I might even get used to that… one day.

The years went by.

The company grew and when we celebrated AIM's fifth anniversary on a Monday evening in early March, there were ten of us around the table I'd reserved, at a very expensive restaurant. We were doing well. We were doing fantastically well and we toasted our success before we left to go home, looking forward to the next five years… and more.

The flat was warm, which was just as well, because it was freezing outside. A cold northerly wind was blowing and, although it was officially spring – the first of the month having passed the previous day – it felt like it might snow.

I didn't really feel like sitting up and was about to go to bed, when I noticed the light flashing on the phone. I rarely received calls at home, because most people rang my mobile, but I went over and picked up the handset, dialling the answering service to see who'd called.

My heart sank as the automated message relayed the number and I realised, it was my mother.

I'd changed my mobile number a few days after Tim's funeral, to ensure she couldn't contact me again, but it hadn't dawned on me to do likewise with the phone at the flat. To my knowledge, she'd never used it. Until that day.

I stood, leaning against the wall, and waited.

"It's me, Josh," she said, her voice sounding monotone, disinterested. "I know you don't want to hear from me, but I thought you'd want to know…" There was a long enough pause for me to wonder if the voicemail had cut her off, but then I heard her again. "It's about Abbie's baby." I nearly dropped the phone. Abbie had a baby? Of course she did… she'd always wanted to. I remembered that. I closed my eyes and struggled not to think about that time, all those years ago, when she'd told me that she wanted us to have a baby together… 'one day'. *If only*. I deliberately stopped the daydream and forced myself to listen as my mother's voice droned on, "Of course, you didn't know she was pregnant, did you?" she said, as though we were having a conversation. "Well, a lot of people around here didn't, considering she and Simon moved to Falmouth quite a while back now, but I heard it from Doctor Trelawny himself." She was rabbiting on, and not getting to the point, although I sensed it was coming. "Anyway, she was pregnant… and she had the baby yesterday. It… it was stillborn."

I heard the click, and then the automated voice, asking if I wanted to repeat the message.

"No!" I yelled, hurling the phone across the room, smashing it against the wall opposite me. "No…" I sank to my knees, the ache building in my chest, until it overflowed, and tears began pouring down my cheeks. "No…" I kept saying the word, over and over, trying to make it untrue. "No, Abbie… No…" I sat back on my heels and looked up at the ceiling, seeing through it and the flats above to the starlit sky. "Please, God… why? Why Abbie?"

How was she going to bear it? How much pain must she be in? Too much… that was for sure.

I realised, of course, that my mother had only called to tell me, because she wanted to inflict as much damage as possible, not just because she'd always enjoyed doing so, but also in revenge for me inheriting Tim's money. She knew I loved Abbie. She knew it would hurt me to hear about her baby. And she wanted to be the bearer of the worst news.

What she didn't appreciate, was that, no matter how much it hurt me, I didn't care. I didn't give a damn about myself, because this time it wasn't about me. It was about Abbie. And it was about Simon. I hadn't thought about him for years; not really. But I thought about him that night. I thought about how I'd feel in his shoes, about the agony of losing a child they'd prepared to meet and grown to love, and had presumably waited for, considering they'd been married for over seven years by that stage... I thought about how he'd have to hide that pain from Abbie, to be strong for her, to cope for both of them, when Abbie's world must be falling apart. I hoped he had someone he could talk to... a friend to turn to, and for the first time in years, I wished I could be there for him. I wished I could be that friend.

I wished I could be there for Abbie too. I wished I could take her pain away. I'd have born it myself, if I could, but I couldn't.

I couldn't do anything.

Except cry, and wish, and hope that they'd come through it.

Both of them.

Another year went by.

Another anniversary.

I thought about Abbie. And Simon too.

The last year must have brought them closer together. I couldn't imagine going through what they'd gone through and not building a stronger bond... I couldn't imagine not falling even more deeply in love with Abbie, allied in grief and pain, but holding onto each other to try and get beyond it.

I didn't feel like celebrating the company's birthday, so I let the day pass and got on with work as usual, and at the weekend, I went out with a few friends for drinks.

I called them 'friends', but they weren't really. They weren't the sort of friends who, if you were in trouble, you could pick up the phone, and they'd be there, no questions asked. I didn't have any friends like that, not any more. Of course, I'd had one once, in Abbie, but that was a long time ago.

These were people I'd met over the years, who liked hanging out with me, because I had money. I wasn't under any illusions about that. I didn't spend that much time with them, but every so often, I got fed up with my own company, and my memories, and I'd meet up with them.

This was one such occasion, and I knew that night that a group of them had arranged to get together at an exclusive bar in Mayfair.

Ordinarily, I'd have gone by tube, but I'd just bought myself a new car and I felt like driving. Besides, it would give me an excuse not to drink… and not to stay too long.

It turned out that her name was Lauren. But I didn't know that when we bumped into each other as we were both trying to get in through the front door of the bar. After one of those awkward moments, when you're not really sure what to do, whether to step back, or move forward, I just held the large glass door open for her and she thanked me, with a sweet smile, and then we made our way over to the same group of people, being as it transpired we were there to meet mutual acquaintances. After one of them had made the introductions, and in spite of our inauspicious meeting, we ended up spending the whole evening together.

I liked the fact that she wasn't impressed by my money. It had become an issue over the last few years, to the point where I'd stopped dating altogether. But Lauren had seen me climbing out of my new Aston Martin – which did tend to scream 'wealth' – and she wasn't even remotely interested. In fact, as we started talking, I realised she didn't fit in with that crowd of so-called 'friends' any more than I did.

She worked in the marketing department of a well-known cancer charity, so it felt like we had something vaguely in common in terms of our professions, and if I'm being honest, she was easy on the eye, as well as being interesting to talk to. She had dirty blonde hair, big brown eyes and full lips and, as the evening progressed, I surprised myself by wondering whether her hair might not be the only thing about her that was 'dirty'.

I wasn't disappointed. She had a filthy laugh, which I discovered when it became clear that we shared the same sense of humour.

We'd been there for a couple of hours when I noticed her glass was empty – for the second time that evening.

"Can I get you another?" I suggested, nodding towards it.

She looked me in the eye. "You could," she said. "Or… or we could go back to your place?"

I swallowed down my astonishment, and tried to look like I took women back to my place all the time – well, not *all* the time, but I at least tried to look as though that wasn't the very first time. "You want to?"

She smiled, biting her bottom lip, and nodded her head.

We didn't say goodbye to anyone, but I grasped her hand and led her out of the bar, taking her to my car, opening the passenger door and lowering her into the seat.

"Thank you," she said, twisting around and getting comfortable.

I closed the door, walking around to the other side, trying not to think about Abbie, trying not to have second thoughts, and trying to think positive. I could do this… couldn't I?

I drove us back to my place. We talked about the weather, which I guess was to hide our nerves, being as we both knew we weren't going to my flat to have a lengthy discussion on the unusual behaviour of the jet stream, and why it was so abnormally warm for early March.

When I let us into the flat, Lauren stopped for a moment, and looked around.

"You live here?" she said, open mouthed.

"Yes."

"Wow," she breathed, as I led her into the living room, flicking on the lights. "This is beautiful."

After Tim's death, I'd had the whole place refurbished. I'd done it partly to try and eradicate the memories… not of him, but of all the times I'd got drunk here, trying to forget Abbie. It hadn't worked though. She was still everywhere I looked.

"Thanks," I said. "Can I get you a drink?"

"No, I'm fine." She looked up at me and took a step closer, and then leant up and kissed me. It was strange. Even as her lips brushed against mine, it dawned on me that I never did seem to be able to make the first move, not since Sara Towers had kissed me, all those years ago, not with anyone but Abbie. Not once. Even so, as Lauren's tongue demanded entry, I actually found myself responding to her, putting my arms around her and pulling her onto me, letting her feel my growing erection against her hip. She moaned, her hands coming up around my neck, her breasts hard against my chest.

We undressed each other, taking it in turns, the pace increasing with every item of clothing we discarded, until she knelt before me, naked, holding my erection in her hands. I didn't object when she leant forward, removed one hand, and placed her mouth around me… that is, until I felt the actual contact of her lips, and the swirling of her tongue, and the memories came flooding back. I closed my eyes to banish them, but all I could see was Abbie.

"Stop," I said and she did, looking up at me and smiling, I guess assuming that I was finding her actions too exciting. I didn't have the heart to disillusion her and I smiled down, then raised her to her feet and walked her backwards to the wide leather sofa, laying her down and positioning myself between her legs.

"Um… hold on just a second," she said, placing her hand on my chest, and I sat back up, looking down at her. "Condom?"

She said it like a question and I felt such an idiot for forgetting, and then an even greater fool when I had to admit, "I don't have any."

That wasn't strictly true. I had the remains of a box in my bedside table. I'd learned my lesson from my less than happy experience with Caroline, and bought some, making sure I had one in my wallet, 'just in case'. But it had been so long, both the contents of the box, and the 'just in case' one in my wallet were all well and truly out of date.

"Don't worry," she said. "I've got some in my bag."

Although the whole scene was starting to feel like déjà vu, I moved out of the way, letting Lauren get up and walk over to her bag, which she'd left on the chair. I knelt and watched her while she delved inside, taking in her hourglass figure and long, tanned legs. The hair at the apex of her thighs had been shaved into a neat vertical line, which made me wonder why she didn't just shave it off altogether. Then I smiled, remembering Abbie and how perfect she'd looked, recalling her shyness, when she'd revealed that she'd shaved herself, on our 'special' evening, and how incredible she'd felt and tasted, how soft and delicate her skin was… Lauren looked up at that moment, her lips twitching upwards, and I felt guilty then. I'd been smiling and looking directly at her, but my mind had been filled with images of Abbie, and that seemed unfair – even to me.

"I always carry a couple with me, just to be on the safe side," she said, waving a condom in the air, before coming back over, her large breasts swaying with each step. "I'm on the pill," she added, "but you can't be too careful, can you, especially not when you first meet someone?"

"No." Evidently not.

She handed me the condom while she lay back down again and I put it on. It all felt a little mechanical after that, but she seemed appreciative, climaxing loudly right before I did.

I sat back, pulling off the condom and dumping it on the floor for the time being, then turned, sitting properly, leaning against the back of the sofa, and glancing down at her, trying not to think. She smiled up at me, before sitting herself, unashamedly naked and flushed, still breathing hard.

"That was really lovely," she sighed. I didn't reply, because I was struggling with the feelings of guilt. Even then, so many years later, they were still there. Ever present. She rested her hand on my thigh, looking at me closely. "Has it been a very long time?" she asked softly.

I took a deep breath, locking down my emotions and focusing on Lauren. "You could say that," I confessed.

"I wondered," she mused, smiling again.

"You did?" What had I done to give myself away?

Her smile turned into a grin and her eyes twinkled. "Yes… I mean, I haven't been with that many men, but I've never known one who looked like *that* immediately after he'd had sex with me." She glanced down at me and I followed her gaze to my still surprisingly hard erection. "So I guessed it had been a while."

I wasn't sure what to say to that, but I didn't need to worry, as Lauren locked her eyes with mine, bit her lip and whispered, "I'm sorry, but that's just too damn tempting," as she knelt up and sat astride me. She let out a long sigh as she lowered herself down, and I did my best to concentrate, to focus on what she was doing, and not to think about Abbie. *Some hope.*

She didn't stay the night, and I was relieved about that. Despite my advancing years, I'd never slept with anyone before, not even Abbie; although she had occasionally fallen asleep on me, which I used to love, and I could still remember the feeling of her soft, warm body against mine, her head cradled, her breathing, even and gentle.

"I've got an early meeting tomorrow morning," Lauren explained, getting to her feet and starting to get dressed. "I'll need to get home."

I stood, pulling on my jeans, just to be decent.

She fastened her bra and was shrugging on her blouse when she looked over at me. "I've had a lovely time," she said, sounding shy, in spite of the fact that she'd just instigated sex with me – twice. "D—Do you want to maybe do something next weekend?"

"Okay. I'll call you."

She frowned slightly. "Don't say that if you're not actually going to do it."

"I will do it," I said and reached into my back pocket, where my phone had remained, despite my jeans having been dropped to the floor earlier on. "Here," I said, unlocking it and handing it to her. "Put your number on there. Then you can't accuse me of 'accidentally on purpose' entering it incorrectly."

She took the phone, but continued to stare at me. "If you want to just write this off as a one night stand, then I'm okay with that," she said, sounding kind of sad now. "I'm not one of those clingy women, who can't let go."

"I know. And I will call you. Well, I will if you put your number on my phone."

She hesitated for just a moment longer, and then tapped on the screen of my phone, before handing it back to me. I checked, to make sure she'd actually saved it properly, which she had, under 'Lauren' in my contacts.

"Do you want mine?" I asked.

"No. I'll leave it up to you."

"I don't mind giving it to you, if you'd rather call me."

She shook her head, doing up the buttons on her blouse and for a moment I wondered if all women were this difficult. Abbie never had been – not that I remembered anyway. Or maybe I just didn't mind with her.

Lauren finished dressing and I pulled on my shirt, feeling awkward standing there, bare-chested. When she was ready to go, she picked up her bag and looked at me.

"I meant what I said. I really did have a lovely time with you this evening. Thank you." I felt guilty then. She didn't have to thank me.

"I will call," I reiterated, because I felt like she needed to hear that.

"Okay." She smiled now and leant up, kissing my cheek.

I showed her to the door and said goodnight. We didn't kiss again and I didn't mention calling her any more, even though I knew I would. And that wasn't because she'd made me feel guilty about it, but because I actually did want to see her again. I wasn't under the impression that we were going to stay together for any great length of time, but I'd enjoyed her company. She was fun to be with, the sex had been good – not great, but good – and I didn't mind the idea of doing the whole thing again, maybe a few times. I wasn't going to lead her on into thinking there could ever be anything more between us than a few dates and some good sex, because there couldn't. Not for me.

I went back into the living room and sat down on the sofa, leaning back and looking up at the ceiling. I'd had a nice time with Lauren, probably the nicest time I'd had with any woman since Abbie, and yet it still wasn't enough. Looking back, I think that was the moment when I finally accepted it. There was no point in looking for someone else to share my life with – not permanently. Not any more. It was a waste of time. Because there was never going to be anyone else for me. It was always going to be Abbie.

Part Two

Chapter Seven

Abbie

I've just finished my latest assignment for Little Bonnet Books. I've been working for them ever since I left university and for the best part, I really enjoy it. Illustrating children's books is creative and fun – although in the last few years I've found it harder sometimes, but I suppose that's only to be expected.

I've packaged everything up and sent it back to Miranda, the editor in chief, and now it's time to clear up my studio.

I love this space and always have done, ever since I moved in here after my divorce from Simon. The colour scheme is pale blue and yellow, although you'd never know it at the moment, because every surface, including the walls, is covered with paper. It can get like that during a big project because I have a tendency to scatter discarded ideas and half-finished drawings, unwilling to throw them away in case I change my mind and want to refer back to them. Some get piled on the stripped pine floorboards, others on the painted wooden work surfaces, and some I stick to the pale yellow walls, which are dotted with drawing pin holes from previous commissions.

I stack up the papers and put them away in the enormous plan chest that takes up one end of the studio space. I won't throw them away until Miranda and the author confirm they're completely happy with everything... just in case.

Then I clear away my paints, cleaning my brushes and, as I'm doing so, I notice that a few of them are getting a bit tatty. I should probably order some more, being as I'm going straight into my next commission. It's not one I'm looking forward to – a sci-fi cover for a fiction book – but that's no excuse for painting it with shabby brushes. My iPad is downstairs, so I'll order some new brushes when I get down there.

I stretch my arms high above my head, my fists clenched tight, feeling the muscles pull, gratefully. I've been sitting for hours and I need to do something different. But then, it is tea time – and although it's not really 'different', it is a welcome break.

I go down the narrow staircase through the door at the bottom and along the landing, past my own bedroom and the guest room and then down again to the ground floor, through the living room, the fireplace empty as it's mid-June, and brilliantly sunny, and then into the kitchen, the back door wide open, the sounds of birdsong and gulls cawing filtering into the cottage.

Filling the kettle with fresh water, I put it on to boil on the Rayburn, and then sit at the table, picking up my iPad, and going to a browser. I've saved my art supplier into my bookmarks and I go straight to their site and put three new sable brushes to the basket, adding express delivery and paying for them with my debit card. They'll be here tomorrow, probably in the afternoon, if past experience is anything to go by.

The kettle's nearly boiled, so I get up and prepare the teapot, rinsing it out and waiting, drumming my fingernails on the wooden work surface until the water is ready and then warming the pot, swirling it around and discarding the water, before adding two spoons of fresh tealeaves from the china caddy that lives on the shelf by the sink. Filling the pot from the kettle, I give it a quick twirl with a teaspoon, and I put the lid on, opening the cupboard beside the Rayburn and getting out my favourite cup and a plate, onto which I put two homemade cinnamon and raisin cookies. I've developed a very sweet tooth in the last couple of years and, if I didn't restrict myself to two, I know I'd eat the whole batch.

Leaving the tea to brew for five minutes, I pour it out, adding a splash of milk, and then take it and my cookies out into the back garden, placing them on the slightly rickety table, which could really do with a fresh coat of varnish, or paint. Perhaps I'll try and do that at the weekend... if the weather holds. And if the cloudless blue sky is anything to go by, I think it might.

I sit, munching a cookie and taking occasional sips of tea, looking around my garden, the flowerbeds on two sides, filled with wild blossoms, and the small vegetable patch at the end, where I grow the things I like to eat... soft fruits and salad greens, tomatoes, peppers, onions, garlic, and pots of herbs.

I snap out of my daydream and check my watch. It's three-thirty. What's wrong with me? I need to hurry and finish my tea, and then get back to work.

I like to keep to a schedule, you see. I've become a creature of habit since I moved in here. I find it helps.

I wake early, usually between six and six-thirty and, after my shower, I throw on a pair of jeans and a top and come downstairs, going straight out of the front door, walking slowly down the hill to the end of the road, and then turning right, up to the church. I spend around half an hour with Molly, checking she's alright, straightening her flowers, making a mental note to bring fresh ones the next day, if necessary, telling her about the squirrels, the butterflies and bumble bees who share my early mornings – except in winter, when I feel the solitude more profoundly. It's so much better than when I lived in Falmouth and could only come a few times a week. Now I'm back in Porthgowan, I have to see her every day, so she knows I'm here. Even so, I don't go later in the day. The church gets busier then, and I like the time to myself. I also like to think that, although Simon doesn't visit as much as he used to, if he wants to come and see her, he can do so without worrying about running into me.

When I've said goodbye to Molly, I come back home and make myself a bowl of porridge, to which I add nuts, seeds and some fresh fruit – which today was raspberries, not freshly picked from the garden yet, because it's too early in the season, but bought from the supermarket just outside Helston. They were still nice though. Surprisingly sweet. When it's warm, like it is at the moment, I sit outside in the garden and eat my breakfast, drinking a cup of fruit tea. That's a habit I got into when I was pregnant and I haven't wanted to kick it – not completely, anyway. At the moment, I've got a taste for a lemon and ginger infusion, but it varies, depending on my mood, and the weather, as much as anything. I head upstairs to work by eight-thirty, stopping off at my bedroom on warmer days to change into something cooler to wear, being as it can get stuffy in the attic room, even with the window open. And then I focus on whatever the latest project might be. I've developed a tendency to forget lunch and plough straight on through to mid-afternoon, like I did today, supported only by glasses of water, to which I add a slice of lemon.

At three o'clock, I'll come downstairs and make a cup of tea – proper tea this time, made in a pot and left to brew for no less than five minutes, served with a drop of milk and either a homemade cookie, or two, or a slice of my favourite indulgence: chocolate cake. Then at three-thirty, or just after, I'll return to work, continuing until early evening, when I'll switch everything off, close the attic window and come back down, to make myself a simple meal. I'm not a great meat eater anymore, but I like chicken and fish, usually served with salads or vegetables – from the garden, if possible.

After dinner, I might do some research on whatever my latest commission is, or go for a walk down to the beach. Sometimes I call in to see Dad at The Lobster Pot, but only if the bar isn't too busy, and I'll have a glass of wine with him. He knows what subjects are safe; what to ask and what not to. Sometimes Stephanie is there too, working behind the bar. She's been living in the village for about a year now, and working at The Lobster Pot for a few months, and she and Dad have just started seeing each other. He thinks I don't know, but I'm not blind; I can see the way he looks at her. And besides, it's impossible to keep anything quiet in this village. I know Dad found it hard to date after Mum left. To start with, I think he was nervous about trusting someone else, after what Mum had done, but then he ran into more practical difficulties. He was working every night in the pub, and had little spare time to meet anyone. Stephanie's arrival has been a godsend. Not only does she help out in the bar, but she's put the smile back on his face.

Later on in the evening, I'll read for a while. I stopped watching television ages ago. It can be unpredictable. Upsetting scenes can creep up on you without warning and I don't need that.

At the weekends, I try not to work, not unless I really have to. Instead, I spend my Saturday mornings going food shopping and baking, and in the afternoons, I'll do the laundry. Sundays are spent on housework and ironing.

It's a routine I've honed and developed, and it works. It stops me thinking.

Regardless of what day it is, I'm always in bed by eleven. And that's when I let myself cry… usually until I fall asleep.

I drink down the rest of my tea and take my cup and plate back into the kitchen, putting them in the slimline dishwasher, before going back up to the studio.

Hazel at Constantine Publishers has sent me through the brief for the latest commission, and I sit at my drawing board and start to read it through, feeling my shoulders drop. If there's one genre I hate, it's sci-fi and I always struggle to think of something creative for the covers, no matter how exciting she makes the novel sound.

A child squeals and giggles outside the window and I startle, my skin tingling and tears forming in my eyes, even though I try to bite them back.

Even now, over four years on, the sight of a pregnant woman, the sound of a baby crying, a child laughing… or sometimes even just talking… is too much.

"Damn," I mutter under my breath, wiping the tears with the back of my hand and putting away the briefing notes again. I'll look at them tomorrow. I can't sit up here and torture myself any longer.

Even though I know there's a risk of seeing a child, or a baby, I know exactly where I need to be, and I run down the stairs, grabbing a cardigan from my bedroom, and then down again, and into the kitchen, shutting the back door and locking it, before picking up my keys from the hook by the front door and going out, slamming it closed behind me.

My cottage opens right onto the lane and I step out, walking down the hill, and turn at the bottom of the road, into The Street, where I come face-to-face with Doctor Max Harvey and his young wife. They moved here shortly before my return, when Simon's parents decided to leave the village.

"Good afternoon," he says, his kindly brown eyes gazing down at me.

"Hello," I manage to say, before moving quickly on.

They're both nice enough people, but I'm not in the mood for conversation.

When I heard that Simon's parents were moving, I felt a bit offended that they didn't want to stay near their granddaughter, but now I'm back, I'm actually relieved that they're gone. It means I don't have to face them, or discuss Molly with them, and I don't have to worry if I need to see a GP. Doctor Harvey has my medical records, so he knows about Molly, but there's no connection between us. It makes it simpler – for both of us.

I continue on my way, heading towards the beach, past the pottery and the post office, and I'm just about to enter the car park, when I startle and glance up as a few noisy teenagers come out of the coffee shop, where the art gallery used to be, next to The Lobster Pot, fooling around on the pavement outside.

The coffee shop has changed hands twice since it opened, but has always been popular, with locals and tourists alike. I know Dad toyed with the idea of getting a longer license a few years ago, so he could stay open all day, but then realised he'd probably put the coffee shop out of business and decided against it. He said he wouldn't have felt right about it… but that's my dad for you.

Because it's only just gone four, and Dad never got that all-day licence, the pub is closed. I always think it looks a little forlorn when it's not open, but I don't suppose it does really. That's probably just me.

The beach isn't as busy as I'd feared it might be, although there are a couple of young women sunbathing, and I make my way around to the right, laying my cardigan down on a low rock and sitting on it, staring out to sea.

This side of the beach has become familiar to me over the last few years. It's not the place I used to sit in when I was a child, when I was growing up… when Josh was a part of my life, when the beach was our second home and we had our own particular spot, where we sat, sunbathed, talked, and grew up together; where he asked me to be his, and where I said 'yes', where we lay together, holding hands, just staring into each other's eyes, where he fed me strawberries, kissing me gently between each bite, where he whispered tender words of love and where I dreamed of a future that was never to be.

I could stay there for hours with him, doing all of that, or doing nothing at all. Either way, it didn't matter, as long as he was with me.

They were happy days.

I lie back, squinting up at the sky and cover my eyes with my arm, wondering how different might my life have been, if we'd somehow stayed together…

Would he have wanted me to move to London with him? *Probably. It was the best place for his career, after all.*

Would I have done it? *I don't know. I suppose if he'd been with me, I might have considered it. I'd have been older by then, at the end of my degree, I imagine, because he would have wanted me to finish that before making the suggestion. I know he would. So, I'd have been less of a child and more of a woman… not so scared.*

Would we have married? *I think so. I hope so. Well, if he'd have asked, I would have said 'yes'. In a heartbeat.*

Would we have had children? *I can't answer that.*

Would we have been happy? *Without a doubt.*

I never had a day with Josh – not even an hour – when I was anything but happy. Until I broke us.

I sit up sharply.

I have to stop thinking like that. It doesn't help to dwell on what might have been. It just hurts. And besides, I'm sure Josh has been better off without me holding him back.

I hope he's been happy. I always wanted him to be happy, more than anything.

I get to my feet and pick up my cardigan.

I can't be here. The echo of distant happiness is too real. And I don't deserve to feel happiness; not even in my memories.

Chapter Eight

Josh

It's been a week now since I signed on the dotted line.

I thought AIM was my life, but it seems it wasn't and when it came down to it, selling the business was an easy decision. I enjoyed it while it lasted, but after eighteen years in PR, it was starting to wear a little thin. And, although I hate to admit it, the stress was starting to get to me.

I'd built up a profitable, successful business, but there was always the pressure to achieve more, to do better. And that was getting harder and harder to accomplish. After nearly a decade, my small company, with a handful of employees, who I'd come to regard almost as family, had morphed into something I barely recognised, with more than twenty members of staff. It wasn't what I wanted anymore, and it made sense to get out, before I lost sight of it altogether.

So I quit while I was ahead, and sold the business, having first obtained a guarantee that all of the employees would be able to keep their jobs, and that the new owners couldn't use the name 'AIM' any longer. It meant too much to me to just let it go.

The board of the company who bought me out were happy to oblige. They wanted to retain our offices – which by that stage were much larger, even if they were still in Covent Garden – and run what had been 'AIM' as a separate branch of their own operation. I recommended they put Ant in charge of it, and although they wanted to bring in someone of their own as well, they agreed. He was thrilled, and more grateful than he needed to have been.

Saying goodbye to everyone was hard; especially the guys who'd been there since the beginning. We didn't have a big party, just a quick farewell. Cathy gave me a long hug and made me promise to stay in touch. I will. I really will. But first I need to get my head together.

Although the last few years have been incredibly busy in all kinds of ways, on a completely personal level, they've also been even more lonely than ever, and I think that was one of the reasons behind my decision to sell AIM. I've finally recognised the need to make some changes.

To start with, in the first couple of days after walking away from the business, I thought about going over to Chamonix for a few weeks. It's June, so I knew there wouldn't be any skiing when I got there, and although I've never been in the summer before, I wondered about maybe just going there to walk in the mountains for a change. But, when I really thought about it, imagining myself in that too familiar place, I realised it wasn't what I needed.

So, I went online and checked out a few destinations I'd always talked about visiting, but had never found the time to see through. I almost pressed the 'book now' button on a villa in the Bahamas, but hesitated for so long, the page timed-out, and I saw that as a sign that maybe I wasn't meant to go there after all. I spent hours scrolling through hotels in Thailand, but couldn't decide on one. New Zealand seemed attractive, but the weather in June didn't look great, with forecasts saying to expect anything from fine cool sunny days, to snow.

After a few days of that, and of lounging around the flat, my mood getting lower and lower with every passing hour, I managed to work out where I'd been going wrong. I'd been looking in the wrong place.

I didn't need to explore somewhere new.

I needed to go home.

I needed to see that huge expanse of sky, feel the sun on my face and the wind in my hair; to walk on the beach and sit on the shore... and think.

Obviously, I realised I can't stay in Porthgowan... I mean, going to my mother's is out of the question, and unless there have been some really drastic changes in my absence, there isn't anywhere else to stay, so I've decided to find somewhere nearby, and then do the same as every other tourist, and drive down into the village, soaking up the atmosphere and the scenery, before leaving again at the end of the day.

I haven't made any exact plans. I haven't even booked myself a hotel. I've just spent a couple of days tying up loose ends in London, seeing the people I needed to see, and checking to make sure that Abbie and Simon haven't moved back to the village for some reason. Although I'd found it hard to take in anything of my mother's phone call, when she'd informed me so callously of what had happened to Abbie's baby, I did recall her saying that Simon and Abbie had moved to Falmouth, and I just needed to be sure that they were still there – or elsewhere. Anywhere but Porthgowan. I couldn't bring myself to search for Abbie online, scared that I might find a profile picture from a social media site, or something that would rake up too many memories. So, I looked up Simon's details instead, and found he's still working in Falmouth, listed on his firm's website as a junior partner. That didn't surprise me, and I didn't bother to look further. I just finished packing and getting myself ready to leave. It's not like I'm going away for good – I can't do that. But a few weeks' break, or maybe a month or two, over the summer, is just what I need to clear my head and hopefully make a fresh start.

I've spent the last eighteen years trying to forget Abbie, trying to live without her, and I've failed miserably. I know I'll never have anyone permanent in my life again... not like Abbie. But if I'm going to stand any chance of happiness, I need to stop torturing myself over what might have been. I need to try and put her in the past.

And then I need to leave her there.

The journey down has been easier than I thought, but then it's a Tuesday, not a weekend. And it's not the holiday season yet, so there was always bound to be less traffic.

As I pull off the main road and into the village, I slow right down, wondering what the villagers are going to make of my car. In my experience, the sight of an Aston Martin isn't a regular occurrence in the village, but this is my only car, and my one extravagance since Tim died and I inherited his fortune. Okay, so I have a chalet in France, but I didn't buy that, it came with the inheritance. And I know I have a lovely flat in Notting Hill, but that has little to do with me. That was Tim's investment, not mine. My bank balance may be ludicrously healthy, but that's only because I don't have much to spend it on – well, not really.

It's late afternoon, gone five o'clock, when I pull up in the car park by the sea, one of only four vehicles. I get out of the car, surprised by how warm it is, having grown accustomed to the air conditioning on the journey, and I stretch my arms above my head, before looking around the village behind me, careful to ignore the post office, where I know my mother will be serving behind the counter for the next half hour or so, until she closes for the day. The general store hasn't changed much, other than the addition of a more modern sign, and the chemists and gift store look essentially the same. The pub is closed, which brings a wry smile to my face. Robert obviously stuck to his guns and didn't extend his licensing hours, despite my advice all those years ago. And next door to the The Lobster Pot, the coffee shop is still there, although the name has changed to 'The Coffee Hut'.

I know exactly where I want to go though, and locking the car, I pocket my keys and head onto the beach, glad I went out and bought some shorts before I left London, and wishing I was wearing them now, the sun is so hot.

There are a couple of twenty-something women making their way up the beach, dressed in skimpy bikinis, heading for two towels, and a couple of large bags, which they've abandoned during their swim. They giggle, catching my eye and whispering to each other, but I look away, feeling self-conscious, and walk along the beach to my 'spot' – well, 'our spot', being as this was the place I used to sit with Abbie.

I didn't bring a rug, but the sand is dry and I sit on it, feeling the heat, and gazing out to sea, grateful for the breeze coming off the shore.

Despite the passage of time, the pain is still incredibly raw, the memories still so fresh... and I'm relieved she's not here. Now I'm back, I know that seeing her with Simon would be too much for me.

I lie down, resting against the rocks behind me, and remember the time I asked her to 'be mine', just a few feet from where I am now; I recall the feeling of her lips on mine, the touch of her tongue and her delicate fingers... the sweet torture of waiting for her, and the bliss... the sheer breathless fulfilment, when the wait was over. I can still feel her, even now. I can still taste her and hear her too, her voice, her moans, her cries, like an echo on the wind.

My arms may be empty, my heart might ache, but my senses have locked her inside; because she belongs in me.

The breeze picks up, a gust catching my hair, and I sit up, checking my watch, and discover that it's just gone six o'clock already. I glance around, seeing that the pub is open, then I pause for a minute, wondering whether I should go over. I'd like to see Robert again, and I could do with a drink, if I'm being honest. And I can't avoid either him or the pub for the whole duration of my stay, so it's probably best to get it over with, before he hears that I'm back and wonders why I'm avoiding him.

Getting to my feet, I wander over towards the gap in the sea wall, noticing that the women who were giggling at me earlier have gone. I didn't even notice.

My eyes take a moment to adjust from the bright sunlight to the darker interior of the pub and when they do, I can see that there are a few people already sitting at tables, although I don't recognise any of them, and I wander over to the bar, where a woman I also don't know is serving. She's probably in her mid-forties, attractive, with long brown hair, and a voluptuous figure.

"What can I get you?" she asks, with a Devonian accent, giving me a broad smile.

I quickly check out the wine list, written on a chalk board above the bar. "A glass of Merlot, please."

She turns, taking down a glass from the shelf, and starts pouring, just as a familiar voice rings out from the passageway that leads to the kitchen area. "Sorry, Stephanie… Sean just wanted a word…"

Robert enters the bar, and I notice immediately that his hair is greyed, not just at the temples, but all over. He's gained some weight too, but not an excessive amount, and there are a few wrinkles around his eyes… but then I suppose none of that is surprising. It's been eighteen years, after all. The man is nearly sixty. He stands, completely still, the polished counter between us, and stares at me for a couple of seconds, before a grin forms on his face. "Well, what have we got here?" he says. "The wanderer returns… at last." And then he moves to his left and opens the hatch in the bar, coming around, and pulling me into a surprisingly firm hug. He slaps me hard on the back a couple of times, before stepping away and looking up into my face. "God, it's good to see you, Josh."

"It's good to see you too, Robert." I hadn't been expecting such a warm welcome and I think it must show on my face.

"You look surprised," he says as the woman I now know to be called Stephanie hands me my glass of wine and I reach into my back pocket for my wallet. He halts me, his hand on my arm. "That's on the house."

"You don't have to do that."

"I know, but I want to." He looks around, then turns to Stephanie, giving her a smile. "You can manage for a while, can't you?"

She nods her head and moves along the bar, while Robert leads me to a table in the furthest corner of the pub, away from everyone else, where we sit, and he looks over at me. "So? Why the surprised expression on your face just now?"

I shrug my shoulders. "I wasn't sure what kind of welcome I'd get," I explain.

"Why?" He frowns slightly.

"After what happened… between Abbie and me."

He takes a breath. "That was half a lifetime ago. And anyway it was Abbie who made that decision, not you."

"Yes, because I went to London and left her behind."

He tilts his head, but doesn't reply, and I take a large sip of wine.

"So," he says, filling the short silence, "what have you been doing for the last couple of decades?"

It sounds such a long time when he says it like that, but then I suppose it is.

"Working," I reply. "I started my own PR agency."

He raises his eyebrows, looking impressed. "Really?"

"Yes. I inherited a small fortune from my uncle…"

"I know. Actually, the whole village knows. Your mother didn't hold back in telling everyone how you'd cheated her out of her inheritance."

"I'm sure she didn't." That news doesn't surprise me in the slightest, although I can't hide my disappointment that things don't change.

He shakes his head. "No-one believed her, not about the cheating part, anyway," he says, a smile forming again and I have to smile back. "So, you started your own business, did you?"

"Yes. Tim's money helped, obviously, and it was… successful."

"Was?" he queries.

"Yes. I've just sold it."

"Oh?"

"I felt like a fresh challenge."

"And you thought you'd come back here for that, did you?"

"Well, no. I thought I'd come back here to… to recharge my batteries." I can't think of another way of putting it.

He stares at me for a moment, then says cryptically, "Well, go on then…"

"Go on then, what?"

"Ask me. You know you want to. You know that's why you came in here in the first place."

"Who says I didn't come in here for a glass of wine?"

"Because you can afford to buy much better wines than I serve."

"Your Merlot isn't bad," I reply, taking another sip.

He doesn't respond but continues to stare at me. We both know he's right – and not just about the wine.

"How are they?" I ask eventually, giving in to my curiosity.

"They?" he queries, evidently confused.

"Abbie and Simon." Saying their names together, out loud, for the first time in years is harder than I thought it would be and I look down at the table between us until the silence stretches uncomfortably and I'm forced to look up, to find him frowning.

"You didn't know?"

"Know what?"

"About the divorce."

I feel like I'm weightless, floating, looking down on myself, unable to comprehend the unreality of the situation his words have just placed me in.

"D—Divorce?" I stammer, managing to utter the single word.

"Yes. It was about two years ago now, I suppose."

"They got divorced?" I don't know why I'm repeating that, but I feel the need to make sure, because this changes everything... literally everything.

"Yes." He nods his head. "And I'm going to assume, if you didn't know about that, then you also didn't know that Abbie's here."

I stand, almost knocking my chair over. "Here?" I look around the pub, wondering where she is, whether she's going to appear from the back kitchen, just as her father did a few minutes ago, and how I'll react to seeing her. The few customers sitting at tables and standing at the bar, are staring at me, and Robert leans forward, pulling on my arm, until I sit back down again, in a daze.

"Not here as in 'here', but here in the village. She bought Fred Callaway's place."

"On East Street?"

"Yes."

My head is spinning. "Why?" I murmur, as thoughts whizz around my brain and my anger rises, unchecked.

"Why did she buy the house?" he asks. "She wanted a fresh start and she liked the old place, even if it was falling down."

"No... I don't mean that. I mean, why didn't my mother tell me?"

"Why would she?" He seems puzzled.

"She told me everything else." I finish my drink in one gulp. "She told me when Abbie started seeing Simon; when they got engaged… She even told me about their baby."

Robert sits back, letting out a long sigh. "Oh God… That was awful," he murmurs. "The most awful thing imaginable."

"I know."

We sit for a moment, and then he leans forward again. "And Mary told you all of that?"

"Yes. She made a point of calling me, each time something happened."

"But she didn't tell you about the divorce, or that Abbie moved back here?"

"No." I twirl my empty glass between my fingers. "I suppose she hated me enough to want to hurt me, but she couldn't risk telling me that. After all, the last thing she would have wanted was for me to move back here."

"Would you have done?" he asks. "If you'd known?"

"Yes." *In a heartbeat.*

He nods his head. "Well, you're back here now… so I suppose the question is, what are you going to do about it?"

"That rather depends on Abbie, doesn't it?"

"How do you mean?"

"Well, two years is a long time… I mean, if she's happy by herself, or if she's got someone else in her life, then I'm not going to do anything. I don't want to make things hard for her. So, if that's the case, then I'll… I'll just ask you not to tell her I've been here, and I'll go back to my car and drive out of here again… And I won't come back…" I let my voice fade.

"She's hasn't got anyone else," Robert says quickly. "And as for being happy…"

"What?" I sit forward, sensing his hesitation. "Tell me."

"She puts on a half-decent show of it," he replies, sadness filling his eyes. "but when she thinks no-one's looking, you can see the pain still. I'm not sure that'll ever go away."

My chest fills with an aching sorrow, at the thought of Abbie hurting.

"Can I stay?" I blurt out, shocking myself. I have no idea what I'm going to do, or how I'm going to make this work… I just know that I can't leave. Not now.

He smiles. "Well, I'm not going to stop you."

"No, I mean, can I stay here?" I sit forward, lowering my voice. "I'd planned on finding a hotel outside the village, but… well, now I know Abbie's back, and that she's not happy, I—I can't go anywhere." His face is serious now and he nods his head, just once. "I know you don't rent out rooms, and I'll pay whatever you ask…"

"You bloody well won't," he interrupts firmly. "I'm not taking your money."

"Oh really?" I smile at him. "Well, either you take something for rent, or I'll just have to start washing up again."

He grins and we both get up, him putting his arm around my shoulder. "Now, there's an offer I can't refuse."

I go out to the car and fetch my bags while Robert pours me another glass of wine. When I return, he's talking quietly to Stephanie, and the way they look at each other and step apart, makes me wonder if there's more to their relationship than meets the eye. Dumping my bags in the corner of the bar for now, I sit down on a stool and start looking at the menu, which has changed beyond recognition since I was last here.

"I still can't quite believe you're back," Robert murmurs, standing before me and pushing a refilled wine glass in my direction.

"Well… believe it." I look up from the menu. "Although if me staying here is going to cause you problems, you only have to say."

"Problems?" he queries and I glance at Stephanie.

"I don't want to get in the way." I smile across at him and he takes a moment to realise my meaning, a blush creeping up his face when he does.

"Stephanie doesn't live here," he says, his embarrassment obvious. "We've only been seeing each other for a couple of months."

"And?"

"And I like her." He lowers his voice, the corners of his lips twitching upwards. "But her last relationship ended badly, and we're not rushing into anything."

I nod my head. "And you're sure it's okay for me to be here?"

"I'm absolutely positive. You coming back is the best thing that's happened in years."

I take a sip of wine and look around the bar, hoping with all my heart that Abbie's going to feel the same.

Chapter Nine

Abbie

It's another beautiful day, with a clear blue sky, not a cloud in sight, and the sun beating down, despite the fact that it's only seven-thirty.

Molly's grave is set under an old oak tree in the churchyard, and I sat there this morning, enjoying the shade, arranging the fresh flowers I'd picked from the garden, and telling her about my walk last night, which I took behind the house, up onto the cliff-tops to watch the sunset. It was beautiful up there, the wind catching in my hair, the sun falling slowly into the clear, calm sea.

I only walked that way because, my afternoon trip to the beach had made me realise that I need to stop going there for a while, because all I seem to do when I'm there is think about Josh, and looking back, thinking about him, just reminds me of my past mistakes.

My porridge made, topped with the remaining raspberries, I sit outside letting my tea cool, and try to take my mind off of the main task of the day; coming up with some design ideas for this sci-fi cover.

I've been dreading it ever since I glanced at the paperwork yesterday afternoon and, even though I have a full brief, together with some suggestions the author has put forward, I've got no idea where to start. It doesn't help that the author's proposals seem at first glance to be a bit disjointed, and I'm not sure how I'm going to incorporate everything he wants into one design.

When I've eaten my porridge, I take my tea cup, sipping from it as I wander slowly around the garden, dead-heading a few early roses, and pulling up a couple of weeds, before returning to the table and picking up my empty bowl, depositing it and my cup in the dishwasher, and going upstairs to the studio.

Normally, at the beginning of a new project, I feel energised, but I just can't raise the enthusiasm today, so it's with a heavy heart that I sit down at my drawing board and start reading through the brief.

By tea-time, I'm feeling a little better. I've worked through lunch, as usual, and I've come up with three initial designs, and although I'll present them all to Hazel, I'm going to do so with the recommendation that only one really works alongside the unbelievably long title of the novel. The other two are going to look very cluttered indeed. But then, based on the author's ideas, I think he might like 'cluttered'. I think it might suit him.

Taking a break, and feeling a little more optimistic about the whole project, I go downstairs and through to the kitchen, filling the kettle and putting it on the Rayburn to boil, before preparing the teapot.

I'm just adding the second spoonful of tealeaves, when there's a knocking at the front door, and I recall my order of paintbrushes is due for delivery. Luckily, I didn't need them to do the initial designs, which are just rough drawings, and I go through to the front door, pulling it open with a smile.

The man before me is wearing grey cargo shorts and a white t-shirt and he's looking away from the house, to a spot further down the road, but as I open the door fully, he turns back and our eyes meet… and I know…

My mouth dries, my head spins and I feel my legs start to buckle beneath me, just as he steps forward and catches me.

"Whoa… Abbie?"

I grab his arms, holding on, and stare up at him. "You?"

"Yes. Me."

"You're here?"

"Yes." He smiles and I burst into tears. "Oh God… Come here," he whispers, putting his arms around me and walking me back into the house, kicking the door closed behind him.

"I'm sorry," I whisper into him as we stand in my living room. "I'm sorry."

"It's okay," he says, although I know he doesn't understand. He thinks I'm saying sorry for crying. He has no idea that I'm apologising for all the wasted years, all the hurt I caused. I shake my head, and feel him sigh, just before he leans back, looking down at me. "Remember?" he whispers. "Friends never have to say sorry." And with that, I start crying again. "Hush," he murmurs, holding me tighter. "Don't cry."

How can I not cry? How can I not, when all I can think about is what we lost.

Eventually, I manage to calm down and I lean back this time. "Why are you here?" I ask, between sniffles.

"Here in the village, or here in your very pretty living room?"

"Here in the village." It seems like a safer place to start.

"Because I wanted to take a few weeks out, to think things through. This seemed like a good place to do it."

I nod my head. "And here in my living room?"

"Because I wanted to see you," he says, like he's stating the obvious.

I stare into his deep brown eyes, still dark and intense, just how I remember them. They haven't changed at all, even though the rest of him has. His hair is shorter, but it suits him that way, as does the stubble. And I know it sounds odd, but he seems taller; I feel as though I'm having to crane my neck just a little further upwards to see him.

"I—I was just making some tea," I stutter. "Would you like to stay and have a cup?"

"I'd love to." He lets me go and I walk ahead of him into the kitchen, the teapot on the corner of the table, where I left it.

"You're still making tea in a pot then?" he says and I turn to see he's leaning against the door frame, a smile touching the corners of his lips. He folds his arms and I notice that his muscles seem more defined, more toned, before I look away and add another spoonful of tealeaves into the pot.

"Of course," I reply. "It tastes better this way."

He doesn't respond and I take the kettle from the Rayburn, then add the water to the pot, stirring it and putting on the lid, before preparing the tea tray, loading it with cups, the tea pot, milk in a jug, and a plate with a few cookies on it.

Once everything's ready, Josh steps forward and picks it up, before I even have the chance, and I look up at him. "Shall we go outside?" I suggest and he nods, letting me lead the way into the back garden.

"Wow," he says, depositing the tray on the table. "This is beautiful."

"Thank you." He wanders down the garden, taking in my modest patch of greenery. Exept it's not that green, because I grow wild flowers in various shades of pink, to place on Molly's grave.

"You did this yourself?" he asks, turning to face me, but continuing to walk backwards, his eyes fixed on mine.

"Yes."

He nods his head. "I'm impressed."

After a quick look around, he comes back and sits beside me, watching as I pour the tea, adding milk.

"You remembered," he murmurs, taking the cup as I hand it to him.

"Remembered what?"

"That I don't take sugar."

I nod my head, feeling a blush creep up my cheeks. *I remember everything.*

"I've always loved Henry's crockery," he says, taking a sip from his cup.

"Well, I know they say you should drink tea out of bone china, or porcelain, but I think it tastes just fine out of Henry's cups."

"So do I." He admires the handmade piece of pottery in his hand, turning it this way and that. "I love the fact that they're mis-matched." He places his cup next to mine. "They're part of a set, and yet they're not the same... I like that."

I smile. "Me too. When I needed to buy new china after I moved back here, I went straight round to Henry and bought everything in one go. He probably thought it was Christmas."

Josh laughs and I offer him the plate of cookies. He takes one and bites into it, a smile spreading over his face as he chews.

"Are these homemade?" he asks, swallowing at last.

"Yes."

"They're good." He takes another bite and I feel myself blush again, nibbling at my own cookie and staring at him, wondering that Josh, of all people, is sitting in my garden, drinking tea.

"I—I heard about your divorce." He stammers slightly, looking at the space between us. "I'm sorry things didn't work out for you and Simon."

I shake my head. "D—Do you mind if we don't talk about it?" I'm not sure what to say to him, how to explain it, and anyway, I'm scared that, if we start, I won't be able to stop, and I'll end up telling him about Molly, and I'm not ready for that.

"Sorry," he says. "I didn't mean to upset you."

"It's fine," I reply quickly, because I don't want him to feel guilty, not when none of this is his fault. "Are… are you married?" I don't think he is, because I doubt his mother would have kept quiet about it, but I suppose he could have got married and not told her. Their relationship is distant enough…

"No." He doesn't elaborate and I wonder for a moment if he's like me; if maybe he's too damaged by his past to talk about it. I hope not. I hope he found happiness somewhere along the way. The alternative doesn't bear thinking about.

"Are you still working in London?" I ask, desperate to change the subject.

"Sort of." He takes another bite of his cookie, and watches me closely, then continues, "I started my own PR agency about ten years ago."

"Really? Congratulations."

"Thank you."

"So, why did you say 'sort of' just now?" I ask.

"Because I've just sold the company. That's why I came back here. It's what I meant earlier when you asked why I was here and I said I needed to think things through… well, kind of, anyway. I—I felt the need to make some changes in my life."

I'm not sure what he means by that and I feel as though we're straying too close to personal territory again.

"Do you think you'll start another business?" I ask.

"Eventually, yes. I can't do nothing. I'm too easily bored." He sips his tea. "So, what have you been doing?" he asks.

I know he means professionally, and even if he doesn't, that's what I'm going to talk about, so I explain that I've freelanced, ever since leaving university, for two publishers.

"I much prefer illustrating children's books," I explain, coming to the end of my story. "Designing covers is hard work, especially when you don't like the genre, like the one I'm doing now."

"Which is?" he enquires.

"Sci-fi." I pull a face and he chuckles.

"Hmm. Not your thing, I wouldn't have thought."

"No."

He leans forward. "Do you work from home?"

"Yes."

"So… can I see what you're working on?"

"You want to?" I'm surprised, but maybe that's because Simon never took any interest in my work, and I've just become used to that.

"Of course."

He smiles and stands, and I get up, leading him back into the house and up the stairs, past the bedrooms and through the door that leads up again, into the attic studio.

"What a lovely room," he says, smiling and looking around, leaning forward and gazing at some of the illustrations I've stuck to the walls. "God, you're good," he breathes, leaning back again. "You always were."

"Thank you," I whisper, blushing, and then raise my voice. "Although you might change your mind when you see my latest creations.

He comes over to my drawing board and studies the three designs I've spent the morning working on.

"Why would you say that?" he says, looking down at me. "They're amazing."

"They're okay." I shrug and he turns, his eyes fixed on mine.

"Don't put yourself down."

I can feel the intensity of his gaze, and although it ought to make me uncomfortable, it doesn't. I need to change the subject again, though. Now.

"So, will you go back into PR?" I ask him.

"No."

"Really? But you always loved it. That was what you wanted most of all."

"No, not *most* of all, it wasn't," he replies and turns away, going over to the window. "Believe it or not, I'm thinking of going into publishing," he says eventually, answering my unasked question. "It's where I started off when I first got to London… doing PR and marketing for publishing houses. And most of my clients at AIM were publishers too."

"AIM? Was that what you called your company?" He nods his head. "It's a good name." I could never think of something like that.

He turns back, looking directly at me. "I think so," he whispers. "Especially when you spell it backwards." I think, just for a second. A.I.M… M.I.A… Oh my God…

"You named your company after me?" The words spill out of me.

"Of course."

"And then you sold it?" I'm trying not to read anything into that, although it's hard.

He lowers his eyes, his hands in his pockets. "Yes, but I kept the name. They weren't allowed to use it. That was part of the deal."

We stand for a moment, him gazing at the floor, me staring at him, and then he finally looks up. "We should probably go downstairs," he says softly.

I nod and lead the way back down the stairs and into the living room, where we come to a stop between the sofa and the front door. I wonder for a moment if he's about to leave, and I know I don't want him to. Not yet.

"How are things with your mother?" I ask. "I assume you're staying with her?"

He shakes his head. "No. No, I'm not. I haven't even seen her. And I don't intend to."

"Really?" I'm surprised, and I suppose it must show.

He lets out a long sigh, pushing his fingers back through his short, dark hair. "Her manipulations ruined my life."

"I know your relationship was difficult, but... how? I mean, what did she do?" His eyes lock with mine and I sense there's something he's not telling me. "Josh?"

He moves closer. "If I tell you something, will you promise not to hate me?"

"How could I hate you?" The words are out before I can stop them and he pauses, a smile twitching on his lips, before it fades again.

"Because she's my mother and what she did was... unforgivable." I lean against the back of the sofa, waiting. He sighs, blinks a few times, and then turns to me. "I had no idea about this at the time... obviously. I only found out when Uncle Tim died, because as well as his money, he left me a letter," he says, hesitantly. "In it, he explained how my leaving for London came about in the first place..." He paces the floor in front of me a couple of times.

"Josh... what are you saying? You left for London because you were offered a job; a dream job. It was the chance of a lifetime..."

"No, it wasn't. The dream job never really existed. My mother convinced Tim to arrange it all."

"Why?"

"To get me away from here... from you."

The lump in my throat threatens to choke me, but I blurt out, "From me? Why? What did I do?"

"You didn't do anything. I'm not going to tell you what she said about you to Tim, but she suggested you were going to try and trap me into marrying you, and she asked him to help prevent that from happening."

Tears well in my eyes. "H—How did she think I was going to trap you?" I ask, barely able to speak.

"Please don't make me tell you that," he replies. "I can't repeat her words." I can hear the emotion in his voice and nod my head. I think we both know what he's talking about, and I'm not sure I'm up to hearing it either. "Tim had always planned to try and give me some assistance in getting work," he continues, sounding a little stronger. "But he'd intended to wait until I'd finished at university. After my mother's intervention, he moved his plans forward and spoke to Charles Tatnell – his friend at TBC. Charles interviewed me and offered me the job."

"I—I don't understand," I murmur, trying to take it all in. "Why did your mother do it? Why did she want to hurt you... us... so much?"

"I don't know why she wanted to hurt you, but she hated me. She hated my very existence, and she wanted me out of her life." He steps closer. "I'm sorry, Abbie," he whispers. "She convinced Tim that you were manipulating me, but really it was her all along."

"S—She broke us up?" A single tear falls onto my cheek and Josh steps forward. We're almost touching and I can feel the heat from his body burning into mine. But just as he reaches forward to brush away my tear, the enormity of it washes over me. "No..." I step away and he pulls back, surprised by my outburst, I think. "No, she didn't. She didn't break us up. I did." I move around the sofa and sit on it, my head in my hands.

Before I've even had a chance to draw breath, I'm aware of Josh kneeling in front of me, then his hands on my wrists, pulling my arms away, and his finger beneath my chin, raising my face to his, the deep sadness easily visible in his eyes. "No," he says. "She's the one who forced us apart in the first place."

"And then I..."

"Don't," he interrupts. "Don't blame yourself for what happened. I never did."

"Do you blame her?" I ask him. "Now you know the truth?"

"I did. I don't anymore."

"You've forgiven her?" I'm surprised. As much as I hate myself for the hurt I caused to us, I'm not sure I'm capable of such leniency.

"No." He shakes his head. "I'll never forgive her for what she did to us, for all the pain that she put us through. But I don't think about her enough to blame her anymore." He moves closer. "Do you hate me?" he asks, his voice filled with fear.

"No. Of course I don't. You're not responsible for her actions."

"Then try not to hate her either."

I swallow down my tears. "Why? Why does it matter?"

"Because hate is an ugly thing, Abbie. And you're not ugly. You're beautiful."

I suck in a breath, taken aback by his compliment. Simon never called me beautiful. The last person who did, apart from my dad, was Josh… so many years ago. "I'm not sure I can forgive her," I murmur.

"Then don't. But don't let hate take root in your heart. It doesn't belong there."

We stare at each other for what seems like a long while, but eventually Josh leans back.

"I suppose I'd better let you get back to your spaceships," he says.

I doubt I'll be able to concentrate on them, but I smile up at him. "Hmm… I ought to try and get something more done today."

He gets to his feet and holds out his hand, and I take it, letting him pull me up, wiping my tears on the back of my other hand. I haven't cried this much during the day for years and, for a moment, I wonder if I'll have any tears left by tonight. But then I realise… of course I will.

We walk together to the door and I go to open it, before turning back. "So, if you're not staying with your mother, where are you staying? Or is this just a flying visit?"

He shakes his head. "No. Like I said earlier, I came down here to try and work out a few things." Oh yes, he did say that. He didn't say what the 'things' were though. "I hadn't expected you to be here…"

"You came back, even though you weren't expecting me to be here?" I query, and he hesitates before he says anything.

"I came back *because* I wasn't expecting you to be here."

I feel a little hurt by that, although I don't know why. "You didn't want to see me?"

He smiles. "Yes… and no."

"What do you mean by that?"

"The things I wanted to sort out in my head," he says, staring into my eyes, "they all related to you. I needed to come home so I could try and put some perspective on our relationship, and try to leave it in the past. Knowing you wouldn't be here made that possible, because… because the thought of seeing you with Simon was too much for me. I knew it was more than I could handle." I've stopped breathing, listening to his words, trying to understand their meaning. "I didn't know about the divorce, Abbie. I didn't know you were back here, on your own. Your dad told me last night when I arrived… and then I asked him if I could stay at the pub, rather than finding a hotel somewhere else, as I'd originally planned, because I knew that I had to see you again, and I knew I couldn't leave the village until I had."

"Why not?" I whisper, just about managing to draw breath enough to speak.

He sighs, moving closer. "Isn't it obvious?" I shake my head. "I'm still not over you."

Chapter Ten

Josh

I look down into her eyes, seeing a momentary sparkle, which is quickly replaced by confusion, pain, sadness… and then what looks like fear, and maybe anger.

"You can't say that." She steps back from the door, moving away. "You can't come in here and say that."

"Why not? It's true," I reason. "I'm not over you. I still…"

"No! Stop!" Her voice rings out. "Stop."

"Hey…" I step closer to her and reach out, but she holds her hands up, halting me. She looks like she's in agony. "Abbie?"

She shakes her head. "How can you do this?" She turns on me, her eyes alight. "How can you come back here after all this time and tell me about your mother, about what she did? And then tell me that you're… you're…"

"Not over you," I supply the words she obviously can't say, although all she does is stare at me for a moment.

"Eighteen years," she cries, finding her voice again. "Eighteen bloody years, Josh. Not a single word… not a phone call, not a text, nothing. And then you come back… and say *that*, of all things." She shakes her head. "I can't do this——"

"Don't say that to me," I interrupt, raising my voice above hers. "Don't you dare say that to me. Not again." She stops short, eyes wide, her words echoing between us, through the years. "The last time I heard those words, they broke my heart. It's… it's been in pieces ever since." I can hear the crack in my own voice as she raises her hand to her forehead, resting it there for a second, pushing it back through her hair, and glancing around the room, confused... lost.

"But... But can't you see, Josh?" she murmurs.

"No, I can't. What's wrong?"

She pauses and takes a deep breath. "Everything. It doesn't matter about what happened before, or how we feel now, I—I can't be..."

"You can't be what?"

"I can't let you... I can't let myself..."

She's not making sense, but as she blinks two tears fall onto her cheeks, and I reach out to her, just for her to step away again. "I'm sorry," I whisper, finally getting the message; finally seeing the pointlessness of the situation. As far as she's concerned, I waited too long. Too much time has passed for us. I'm too late. "I didn't mean to hurt you, Abbie... I never meant that. I—I'll go."

I turn to the door, opening it, and then feel her hand on my arm, the warmth of her body beside mine. "Don't. Please don't go. I'm the one who's sorry," she says through her tears.

"It's fine. Honestly." It isn't, but it won't help either of us if I tell her how it really feels to have the life crushed out of me again.

"Are you leaving? The village, I mean?" She sounds scared now, and I look down at her, bewildered.

"Do you want me to?"

"No." Her eyes are still filled with tears, her voice so choked and quiet, it's a struggle to hear her.

"If you want me to stay, then I'll stay." *I may not understand what's happening here, but please say 'yes'... please.*

She nods her head and I feel the relief wash over me. She wants me to stay, and that's all I need to know. "Are we still friends?" she asks.

I turn and cup her face with my hand, the softness of her skin against mine sending a warm pulse through my body. "Always."

I take a slow walk back to the pub, trying to put my thoughts in order. It's hard though, mainly because I'm feeling so confused still. She was hot and cold, up and down, happy and sad.

I pull her business card from my pocket, where I stashed it after sneaking it from the pile in her studio when she wasn't looking, and study the neat lettering. 'Abbie M. Fuller'. She's gone back to using her maiden name… I like that thought, and I'm also reminded of her reaction to me having named my company after her, and her very obvious discomfort at the idea that I'd then sell the business – and her name with it. As if I'd ever do that.

Telling her about Tim… about my mother, and what she did was awful. There were so many aspects that I couldn't explain properly. I couldn't tell her that my mother had called her a whore. I couldn't tell her that my mother had accused her of trying to trap me by getting pregnant. That would have been too cruel, although I'm pretty sure she knew what I was talking about, and I wonder now if I should have kept quiet about the whole thing. But that would have meant lying to her about my ruined relationship with my mother, and about where I'm staying, and why, and even if I've held some elements of Tim's letter back because I don't want to hurt her, I've never been able to lie to her.

"I should have planned it better," I mumble under my breath as I saunter back towards The Lobster Pot. I'm not sure how I think that would have been possible though, considering that I didn't even plan to go round there in the first place. I was walking on the beach, trying to work out what to do and how to approach Abbie, what to say to her and how she might react, when the urge to see her overwhelmed me and I just walked straight to her cottage, knocking on the door before I even knew what I was doing.

When I saw her, she took my breath away. The years have been good to her, and I smile to myself now, thinking about her shoulder-length chestnut hair, which shone in the sunlight, her beautiful lips, soft skin and, most of all, her amber eyes. I know Robert said she hides her sadness, but I could see it there, even when she smiled. And she did smile. Well, she did after she virtually collapsed into my arms, anyway.

To me, it feels like she's just the same person she was eighteen years ago, and yet she isn't. She's grown into herself. Perfectly.

I just wish now that I hadn't blurted out that dumb line about not being over her. It wasn't a 'line', it was the truth. But it wasn't what she needed to hear. That much was obvious. I also wish I could understand her reactions. After she yelled at me for not contacting her for eighteen years, I know I heard her say something about it not mattering how we feel. That suggests she feels something for me, as does the fact that she yelled at me in the first place, I suppose, because if she didn't care, she probably wouldn't have bothered. But then she repeated those words that have torn at my heart and eaten at my soul ever since she first said them, all those years ago: "I can't do this…"

I get back to the pub, surprised that it's a little after six o'clock already. I've been with Abbie for over two and a half hours, and yet it seems like it was just minutes. It always was like that for us though. Every time.

Robert's behind the bar, having just opened up, and he looks up as I walk in through the door. "Are you alright?" he asks, seemingly worried. I nod my head and make my way over to him. "You don't look it."

"Thanks."

He turns, bringing over a bottle of Merlot, and pours a glass, pushing it in front of me. "You've been to see Abbie then?" he guesses.

"Yes."

He nods. "How did it go?"

"Well, she didn't actually throw me out." Although now I come to think about it, she came close, I suppose.

"Why would she do that?" he asks. "The way things ended between you wasn't your fault. She broke up with you, remember? I know how badly she felt about it at the time, and I'm not sure she's ever really forgiven herself. She knows that what she did changed your life, and her own. And in her case, it wasn't for the better."

I stare at him, absorbing what he's just said. "It wasn't better for me either," I whisper. "But I don't think her reactions today had anything to do with how we broke up."

He sighs. "No, they probably didn't, but it's just another thing for her to beat herself up over."

"Why? I don't blame her. I never did. I told her that."

"That doesn't mean she won't blame herself." He reaches beneath the counter for a cloth, wiping down the bar, to avoid looking at me, I think. "Do you want me to mind my own business, or do you want some advice?" he says, rubbing hard at a non-existent mark on the polished oak surface.

"I'll take all the advice I can get," I reply and he stops what he's doing, his eyes searching mine for a moment. I presume he sees the truth behind my words, because he puts the cloth back and leans on the bar, moving closer, so he can lower his voice.

"Don't give up on her," he says. "She's been through hell over the last few years. She's still there really, and I have no idea how she keeps going. She gets by because she has a routine…"

"A routine?" I interrupt.

He nods. "Yes. She has a very regimented way of life. Every day follows the same pattern, starting with a visit to Molly's grave… at the churchyard."

"Molly's her daughter?"

"Yes."

"And she's buried here?"

"It's what Abbie wanted."

"Even though they lived in Falmouth?"

"Yes." He swallows and I sense he's finding it hard to talk. "She… she said she wanted Molly to see the sky and hear the sea."

I nod my head and let out a sigh. "It makes sense that Abbie would want that for her child."

He stares at me again, and then continues, "To start with, when she and Simon were still together, she'd drive down here by herself. I only knew she'd been because I'd wander up to the churchyard myself some days and I'd find wild flowers on the grave. Abbie always leaves wild flowers, you see… pink ones, especially for Molly. She and Simon sometimes came together too, but I reckon she came three or four times a week, by herself. Now… now she goes every morning, religiously, always before seven, before there are too many people around. She likes to have the place to herself, so she can talk to Molly."

"How do you know this?"

"Because for the first few weeks after she moved back, she was living here with me, waiting for the house purchase to go through, and I used to follow her up there and just stand by the gate, out of the way, making sure she was okay."

I don't need to close my eyes to picture him, standing by the covered church gates, silently watching over his little girl, as she sat by the grave of her own little girl, her heart broken.

"What's the rest of her routine?" I ask, sensing from his pained expression that he needs to change the subject – just slightly.

"Once she's finished at the church, she goes back home for breakfast and then she works until mid-afternoon," he replies, clearing his throat first. "Then she stops for a tea break."

"Not lunch?"

He shakes his head. "No. She doesn't bother with lunch." I make a mental note of that. "Then she works through until dinner time, and after she's eaten, she'll go for a walk, or maybe read. She stopped watching television and listening to the radio ages ago."

"She does that every day?" I can't disguise my surprise. "Even the weekends?"

"She tries not to work at weekends," he replies. "She still goes to see Molly, but she fills the rest of the time with housework and chores. She has to keep busy. All the time."

"So she can't think?" I suggest and a slight smile forms on his face as he nods.

"She needs to get her life back," he sighs. "And I think she knows that. I think she even wants it herself. She knows she's not happy." He picks up the wine bottle, topping up my glass, even though I've hardly drunk anything, and then fixes his eyes on mine. "The thing is, she feels guilty."

"What for?"

"For wanting it. For wanting to be happy."

"That's all wrong," I murmur, almost to myself.

"I know it is, but persuading her of that is going to be a very long, uphill struggle…" He pauses. "So the thing you're going to have to ask yourself is, do you want her back enough to deal with all of that?" I suck in a deep breath and slowly shake my head. He frowns and takes a step back.

"Don't look so disappointed. I'm not saying I don't want her back, Robert. I'm saying the precise opposite. I *need* her back. And that means I'll deal with her guilt and her tears, and her anger, and anything else she wants to throw at me…"

He sighs deeply and smiles. "Thank God for that. You had me worried then." I smile back at him. "It's going to be hard," he adds, his face falling, his voice more serious again. "And it's going to take time. She'll probably get angry with you. I wouldn't mind betting she'll blame you for things that aren't your fault, she'll argue with you for no reason, she'll maybe throw you out… or try to."

"She already has," I say and he tilts his head to one side.

"How come?"

"When I went to see her earlier," I explain. "I made the mistake of telling her I'm not over her… because I'm not. She… she didn't take it too well."

"What did she do?" he asks.

"She didn't really *do* anything. She asked me why I hadn't been in touch for eighteen years, even though she made it very clear to me eighteen years ago that I wasn't the man for her; even though she's been with Simon for quite a lot of that time, and for me to have contacted her, feeling the way I do, would have been wholly inappropriate… and then she said a whole load of stuff that didn't really make sense. It was just a lot of rambling, unfinished sentences, really, none of which added up to much, not in my head, anyway. But she was obviously upset… so I told her I'd leave, and then she asked me not to…" I look over at him.

"That'll be the guilt kicking in," he says, nodding slowly. "She'll have felt terrible for saying all those things to you."

"Well, it was very confusing at the time, but now you've explained things, it makes a bit more sense."

"She's still in hell," he says gently. "She's not thinking straight. To her, you represent happiness. You always did. So she's going to push against you, and the inner turmoil is going to be hard for her. She wants to be with you again… I'm sure of it. But dealing with the guilt over being happy is going to be hard for her, because she doesn't feel that she deserves it. If you really want her back, you're going to have to be patient with her, and give her time."

I get to my feet, picking up my wine glass. "I told you, Robert, I don't want her back… I *need* her back. I've got a chance at that, and I'm not going to give up. Ever."

I wake early, with a new sense of purpose. I didn't sleep very well, but I'm used to that, and besides, I had a lot on my mind. I kept replaying Robert's words in my head, especially the part where he said that I represent happiness to Abbie, and that she wants to be with me again. God, I hope that's true. Because there's nothing I want more than to be with her, and to try and make her happy again.

I leave the pub at six-thirty and make my way to the churchyard. I have no idea where Molly's grave is, so I stand well out of the way and wait, trying very hard not to imagine Abbie and Simon's wedding day here, an image forming in my head of them walking out of the church arm in arm, gazing into each other's eyes and smiling, as he leant down to kiss her… his bride. "That's the past," I mutter to myself, and I let the image fade.

Abbie appears at about twenty to seven, entering through the main gate, which creaks slightly as she closes it again, and then walks over to the old oak tree in the corner of the graveyard, bending and picking at something, and then sitting down, crossed-legged. I can see her lips moving, her face animated as she talks, although I can't hear what she's saying and I lean on the church wall for a few minutes, until I'm overwhelmed by the sense that I'm intruding into her time alone with her baby daughter, and I quietly slip away, through the small gate at the back of the churchyard and out onto the footpath.

I feel a little disappointed in myself. I'd intended to stay until she left, to stand guard, like Robert used to, but I can't escape the feeling that don't belong there. And I won't, not until Abbie chooses to tell me about her daughter, and decides whether or not to invite me into their lives.

I walk slowly, and a little dejectedly, back to the pub, where I join Robert for breakfast, telling him I've been out on the beach. I'm not sure if he believes me, but it doesn't matter.

"Got any plans for the day?" he asks as we clear away.

"Yes," I reply, even though I haven't actually decided what I'm going to do yet. I just know I have to do something.

He nods and smiles, understanding, I think. "Well, I'll let you get on with it…" he says, and leaves me to myself. I make a coffee and sit at the kitchen table, contemplating what to do next… and how Abbie might react this time.

"Strawberries?" she says, looking down at the small basket I'm carrying. "And cream?"

"Yes. Don't tell me you've gone off them?"

She shakes her head, the corners of her lips twitching upwards, and steps to one side, letting me enter the cottage.

I remembered, over my second cup of coffee, that strawberries were always Abbie's favourite fruit, and how I used to sometimes feed them to her, while we lay on the beach. I remembered that I also used to kiss her between each and every bite, the kisses becoming more and more intense, more and more urgent, as they were inclined to do, even when she didn't taste of strawberries… Obviously I don't expect to do that today – although it's a nice thought – but I decided it might be an ice-breaker, after the way things ended between us yesterday. So, I drove to the farm shop, about five miles outside of the village, and bought a basket of them… and some double cream. Because strawberries without cream is like roast beef without Yorkshire puddings, or apple pie without custard… or me without Abbie.

I follow her through to the kitchen, noticing that she's changed her clothes since this morning. When I saw her at the church, she had on jeans and a navy blue t-shirt, but now she's in a white sun dress, and I remember she was wearing something similar yesterday, when I called. I suppose it probably does get warm up in her attic though, and I marvel that, despite my nerves, and my subsequent confusion, I could have failed to notice how incredible she looks. Because she does.

"I'm not stopping you from working, am I?" I ask, even though I'm fairly sure I've timed my visit right. It's roughly the same time that I called yesterday, when she seemed to be making herself a cup of tea – which ties in with Robert's comment that she stops for a break mid-afternoon.

"No," she replies, turning as she enters the kitchen. "I've only just come downstairs. I was about to make a cup of tea to have with my cookie…" She eyes the strawberries.

"But you'd rather have these instead?" I hold the basket out to her and she smiles, taking it from me, although she seems slightly nervous and turns towards the Belfast sink to wash the fruit. I decide against getting too close, and resolving not to mention our conversation of yesterday, I offer to make the tea instead.

"I promise I'll use the pot," I comment and she turns.

"Yes, but will you warm it first?" she says, a smile touching her lips.

"If I must."

"Oh, you must." She tips the strawberries into a pale blue painted pottery colander, holding it under running water. "It makes all the difference."

"I'll take your word for that." I wait for her to finish at the sink, before filling the kettle. "Is that one of Henry's?" I ask, nodding to the colander, as she rests it on the draining board.

"Yes. It's not a standard design though. I asked him to make it for me, to match the rest of my china… and he did."

"It's lovely."

She smiles up at me, saying, "Yes, it is, isn't it?" then looks away again awkwardly.

"So, where's the tea pot?" I ask. "And the tea, for that matter… and, um… how do I boil your kettle?"

She giggles, and hearing that sound takes me back eighteen years in an instant.

"I'll show you," she says, and tells me how to use the hotplate of the Rayburn, before she starts hulling the strawberries, issuing instructions to ensure sure that I warm the pot and use the right amount of leaf tea.

We finish our preparations eventually and put everything onto a tray which I carry through to the garden, where we sit and eat the strawberries, dunking them into a bowl of double cream, and sipping perfectly made tea… which I have to admit does taste better made in a pot, even if I'm not convinced about the warming part yet.

"How are you getting on staying with Dad?" she asks out of the blue, wiping a drip of cream from her mouth, temporarily distracting me as her finger grazes across her lips.

"Fine," I reply eventually. I can hardly tell her that she's been a constant topic of conversation.

"Have you met Stephanie?"

"I wouldn't go so far as to say 'met', but I'm aware of her." I help myself to another strawberry. "Your dad seems happy with her."

"He does, doesn't he? And it's about time too. Mum left a lifetime ago…" Her voice fades and she looks down at her hands.

"Do you see your mum?" I ask, even though I'm aware this could be a difficult topic for her. She and her mum still weren't on speaking terms when I left Porthgowan.

"I don't see her that often, but we talk on the phone fairly frequently," she replies, with a hint of sadness. "Simon persuaded me to mend the fences before our wedding."

"That's good."

"Yes. She's a different person now."

"Better?" I ask.

"Yes, I think so. She's happier with Devin."

"Did they ever get married?"

She shakes her head. "No, but Tara did."

"Really?" For some reason, that surprises me. I'd never seen her as the settling down type. "When was that?"

"Last year. She married a restaurateur from Yorkshire."

"Yorkshire?" I smile at Abbie. "What was Tara doing in Yorkshire?"

"She didn't meet him there. They met on holiday in Vietnam, I think. Or it might have been Thailand. I can't remember. Tara travelled a lot…"

I nod my head. "That makes more sense. What was the wedding like? Incredibly flamboyant and over the top, if I know Tara"

"Judging from the photographs, it was quite lavish, but I—I didn't go myself." She falls silent and instead of asking her why she didn't go, because I don't need to, I offer her the strawberries. She takes another one and smiles at me, and I don't know why, but our silence and that simple gesture feel like a step forward.

We finish our tea and I check the time. It's almost four-thirty, and I don't want to outstay my welcome.

"I should go," I say getting to my feet. "You've got work to do."

She looks at her watch, her eyes widening. "Yes." She stands too, putting everything back onto the tray. "But thank you for the strawberries. They were delicious."

"My pleasure." I carry the tray back into the kitchen, leaving it on the table. "Would it be okay if I called round again tomorrow?" I ask.

"I'd like that," she whispers and then looks up, a blush spreading across her face. "I—I'll make a cake… if you want…" She seems shy, a little hesitant. She was never shy with me before though, and I make a mental note about that too, adding it to the list of things to bear in mind; to maybe try and do something about.

"You're offering me cake. Of course I want." I smile down at her and she escorts me through the house, opening the front door. "I'll see you tomorrow?"

She nods her head and I leave, turning back after a few yards. She's still standing at the door and I wave. She waves back and I smile. Today really felt like progress, but I know better than to read too much into it.

I set my alarm for six, just to be on the safe side, although I'm awake before that, and get up promptly, making sure I'm showered and dressed in time, leaving the pub at a quarter to seven, and timing my walk so that when I get to the church, Abbie is already sitting beside her daughter's grave. Her head is bent, but her lips are moving, as though she's having a conversation, or at least explaining something in depth. I stand out of sight, by the gate, and watch her for just a short while, and then turn, walking to her cottage. What I'm about to do is going to be hard – for me as well as for her. But I've thought it through and I know it's the right thing to do. It's the only thing to do.

I reach her house within a couple of minutes, noticing that it's called Hope Cottage. I probably knew that, and I should have seen the slate name plate beside the door on my previous visits, if I'd been paying attention to anything other than Abbie, that is. It seems like an appropriate name for her house. I'd like to think so, anyway, and I stand outside, leaning against the wall near to the front door, soaking up the early morning sunshine, and waiting… and waiting, until I hear footsteps approaching. They're light, but slow, and deliberate, and, as she comes into sight, walking up the hill, I focus on her hands, buried in the pockets of her stonewashed jeans, her slumped shoulders and bowed head, and I push myself off the wall, taking a couple of steps forward.

She glances up, noticing me and stops in her tracks, a few feet away, a puzzled expression on her face, her eyes locked with mine.

"Why…?" She falters and takes a breath, pulling her hands from her pockets. "Why are you here?"

I close the gap between us, and murmur, "So I can do this," and I pull her into my arms, holding onto her. She's stiff to start with, but then she relaxes into me and I feel her arms coming around my waist, her body shuddering against mine as she clings to me. I know she's crying, but I don't say anything. I don't do anything either. I just hold her, until she eventually calms and slowly leans back in my arms.

Her cheeks are tear-streaked, her eyes flooded, and she opens her mouth to speak, but I bring my hand up, placing my fingertips on her lips, and shake my head.

"You don't have to say anything," I whisper, moving my hand and letting my thumb brush against her cheek, wiping away her tears. "I know you're not ready yet. When you are, the words will come naturally. And when they do, I'll be here… waiting." She swallows hard and blinks, more tears falling, and I pull her back into my arms, holding her until she lets out a long sigh, and leans back again, looking up at me.

I release her, taking a half step back. "I'll see you this afternoon?"

She sniffles, seemingly puzzled now. "This afternoon?"

"You promised me cake, remember?"

Her lips twitch upwards. "Oh… yes."

I move away, out into the lane. "So… three o'clock?" She nods her head and I start walking away, turning back after just a few paces, although I continue to walk backwards. She's still standing there, staring after me and I call out, "It will be chocolate won't it?"

"What?" she asks.

"The cake."

"Yes."

"Good."

She smiles, just lightly and I smile back, our eyes locked for a second, and then I turn around, and make my way back down the hill.

My nostrils are accosted by the aromas of freshly baked chocolate cake the moment Abbie opens the door.

"That smells amazing," I remark as she lets me in.

"I love the smell of baking," she replies and leads me through the living room, just like she did yesterday. She's changed again, from her jeans and pale pink t-shirt, into a really pretty blue flared skirt that finishes just above her knees, and a matching top, which ends at her waist, tempting me to run my hands underneath, to caress her soft bare skin…

"Do you bake a lot?" I ask, distracting myself, even though I know she doesn't. It doesn't fit in with the routine Robert described to me, and I know that what she's doing today is a break from her accustomed habits.

"I usually do it at the weekends," she says, entering the kitchen and turning to face me. I notice that the tea is already laid out on the tray, alongside a magnificent looking chocolate cake. I don't comment on her making an exception to her rule. I don't want to embarrass her.

"Shall I carry this outside?" I suggest and she nods, holding the back door open as I pass through.

We sit, and she cuts the cake, giving me a slice, and taking one for herself, before pouring the tea. I take a bite, closing my eyes and savouring the rich, intense chocolate flavour.

"That's really good," I comment, as I finish chewing. "When did you learn to cook like that?"

"Well, not at uni, that's for sure," she replies, a slight twinkle in her eyes. "I was dreadful back then. Bethan – my flatmate – she used to joke that I could burn water."

"Oh dear." I'm reminded, as she mentions her flatmate, that there are elements of each other's lives that we know nothing about. For the last couple of days, I've been wrapped up in Abbie, and in the breathtaking, heart stopping wonder of seeing her again, but I can never truly forget that there I things I need to tell her about my life – when the time is right. And hopefully it won't be long before she's ready to tell me all of her story too.

"But then when I was with Simon, it just kind of clicked into place. Well, it was that, or we both starved…" She stops talking. "Sorry…" she murmurs, a blush suffusing up her cheeks. "Does it bother you? Me mentioning Simon, I mean?"

She said she didn't want to talk about him when I first came here on Wednesday, which didn't surprise me at all. But this… this feels like an acknowledgement; an acknowledgement that I might have a problem with it too, and that gives me a tinge of hope that she might just be willing to accept that I meant it when I said I'm not over her. And that feels like a real leap forward. Even so, I want her to be able to share everything with me, so no matter how hard it is, I'll deal with it.

"A little," I reply honestly, and those familiar furrows appear above her nose, making me smile as I recall how often I used to kiss them. "But let's face it, he was my friend too. And he was a huge part of your life for a very long time. He's going to come up in conversation and I want you to be able to talk to me without feeling awkward, so please… don't worry about it." She smiles at me, with something that looks like gratitude, but before she can open her mouth to say 'thank you', I continue, "So, I take it Simon couldn't cook?"

She shakes her head, her smile widening as I presume she's remembering something. "Oh no… he was shockingly bad. He even made me look good. And that was saying something." She takes a sip of tea. "So what about you?" she asks. "Can you cook?"

"Yes."

Her eyes narrow, although her lips are still curled up at the corners. "Somehow I'm not surprised."

"Well, I may have lived with Uncle Tim, but he wasn't about to start waiting on me. Actually he was hardly ever at home, so like you, I either learned to cook, or I starved. And anyway, Tim had a very impressive kitchen. It kind of made you want to cook, just so you could be in there."

"Did he like cooking too?" she asks.

"Yes. He was a great one for gadgets. As soon as something new came out, he'd be first in the queue to buy it, even if he only used it once." I shake my head, remembering some of the strange utensils and tools I threw out after his death. "I cleared the whole place out when he died, and then ripped the kitchen out too, and replaced it with something simpler. I might like to cook, but I don't see the need to over-complicate things."

She's staring at me, and the moment I stop talking, she blinks, as though she's suddenly aware of her gaze. "What… What's your flat like?" she asks.

"Huge," I reply.

"How huge?"

"Well, even when Tim was there, we could go for days without seeing each other, if we wanted to. I think that's why it worked out so well between us. We didn't step on each other's toes." I put down my plate. "I didn't even know he was gay until after he died."

"Really?" She's surprised by that.

"Don't tell me you knew?" I turn to face her properly, twisting in my chair.

"No, of course not. I'm just surprised you didn't notice, or work it out sooner."

I shrug my shoulders. "We kept ourselves to ourselves. It… it worked for both of us."

She lets her eyes drop to her lap, looking shy, or embarrassed again, although I'm not sure why, and I pick up my plate, taking another bite of cake. "This really is good. I'm going to have to find a gym nearby if I'm not careful."

"A gym?" She looks up, seemingly amused.

"Yes. Tim had one installed at the flat, in one of the bedrooms. I started using it pretty much as soon as I moved up there."

She nods her head. "I wondered…" she muses and then stops abruptly, blushing deeply.

"Wondered what?"

"Nothing… It's just that you look… different, that's all."

She's bright red now, and I'm trying very hard not to smile, biting my bottom lip in the effort. I'm not enjoying her awkwardness, but I am aware of the fact that her comment means she's been looking. And that feels good. It feels really good.

"Well, I'm going to look even more different if you keep feeding me chocolate cake," I reply, and hold out my plate for a second slice.

Chapter Eleven

Abbie

For the last couple of days, I've been on a roller coaster of emotions. Some good, and some not so much.

First, Josh appeared out of nowhere on Wednesday afternoon. After eighteen years of absence, eighteen years of total silence, there he was on my doorstep, large as life. That first visit seemed to be going okay – despite his shocking revelations about his mother's interference in our lives, which I'm still coming to terms with, and probably will be for a while – that is, until he admitted he's not over me. I still feel humiliated by my reaction to that. I was overwhelmed by the thought of all the lost years and everything that's happened in between. I was scared about what he might expect from me, and whether I can – or should – be that person again. But I shouldn't have taken it out on him. That wasn't fair. And then, when he said he was going to leave, I was overcome with fear. He sounded so sad, so dejected… and that was my fault. The thought of hurting him, of losing him for a second time, was too much. I had to make sure he wasn't going to leave Porthgowan for good. I needed to. But then, the guilt… Oh God, the guilt. It haunted me all through that evening and I cried so hard when I went to bed, engulfed with remorse for the brief moment of happiness I'd dared to snatch with him, even though I wanted it so much.

He came back yesterday, quite unexpectedly, and brought strawberries with him, which reminded me of happier times, and most especially how he used to feed them to me on the beach. I wondered if he'd remembered that too, and felt a little shy and embarrassed when he handed them over, but in the end, we had such a lovely time, sitting in the garden, just talking and eating them.

And then… he was waiting for me at the house this morning when I came back from visiting Molly. I have no idea how he knew to be there, or even how he knew what time I'd return. And I couldn't ask him either, because I can't talk about any of that yet, which he seemed to understand. But the point is, he was there, and he held me while I cried. And I let him, because it felt good to be held, especially by him.

And now, he's sitting here again, looking more handsome than ever, being more kind, more generous and more considerate than even I remember him being, and I thought I knew him inside out, better than anyone in the world. Or at least I did; once upon a time.

My emotions are reeling at the moment, veering between joy, and pure ecstatic happiness that he's actually here beside me once more, understanding, caring, listening… to ludicrous jealousy when he mentioned keeping himself to himself at the flat he shared with his uncle, and an image flitted through my head of him, behind closed doors, with countless women in his bed… and then on to the inevitable guilt that I shouldn't be doing any of this, that I'm not worthy of him, or the happiness he brings me… and finally to humiliation, when I made that stupid remark just now, about him looking 'different'. He does. He looks incredible, beautiful even, but did I really have to open my big mouth and say it out loud?

I dish him up a second slice of chocolate cake, passing the plate back to him.

"So, do you like living in London?" I ask, to alleviate at least some of my embarrassment.

"It's okay," he replies. "But I miss the sky."

I smile at him. "I know what you mean. I felt like that when we lived in Falmouth… Simon and I." I have to stop mentioning his name. I know Josh has said it's okay, but if I'm not careful, I might end up going further down that road than I'm ready for yet.

"Falmouth has plenty of sky," he argues, taking a bite of cake.

"Well, I know it's not London. I can still remember the tiny patch of sky I could see out of my bedroom window in Wandsworth, when we used to live there," I reply. "But even Falmouth isn't like it is here. It's not the same."

"Then why did you move there?" he asks. "Was it for Simon's work?"

So much for not mentioning his name… "Yes. We lived on a small estate there."

"An estate?" He pulls a face. "I wouldn't have thought you'd have liked that."

"I didn't… not really. But Simon did." He looks at me for a long moment, as though he's trying to work something out. "He thought it was more practical than the house we had on West Street." I point over to the other side of the village, in the direction of where our house used to be, and try not to think about Simon's real reason for moving us away from Porthgowan… so that I'd forget about Josh, and put my memories of him behind me.

"What was wrong with it?" he asks.

"What?"

"Your house on West Street," he replies. "They're all quite nice houses, aren't they? A bit like this one, if memory serves."

"Yes. But none of the rooms were square, there wasn't a garage like I've got here, the bathroom was downstairs – he particularly hated that, even though it's quite normal in old cottages like this." I remember some of the excuses he gave me at the time, the night after he'd put in the offer on the house in Falmouth and we were lying in bed talking it through. He was trying to make me feel better, to justify his decision… because at the time, only he knew the real reason for it, of course.

"So, he was looking for something convenient?" Josh suggests.

"Yes. And of course it was close to a really good school…" I stop, wishing I could bite back those words and feel a lump rising in my throat.

Josh puts his plate down on the table, dusting cake crumbs from his shorts. "Uncle Tim left me a couple of other properties, apart from the flat in Notting Hill," he remarks, changing the subject for me, to perfection.

"Oh?" I manage to say, through the lump.

He nods his head. "It certainly helped me to work out pretty quickly what I like… and what I don't."

"How do you mean?"

"Well, one of them was a beach house in Malibu," he says, smiling at me, his eyes fixing on mine, as though he understands I'm struggling at the moment, and he's just going to keep on talking until I'm okay again.

"Malibu?"

"Hmm… I went out there almost immediately after Tim died. I gave up my job first…"

"You did?"

"Yes. I'd been thinking about it for a while. I'd even arranged a few interviews… but discovering that I'd only really been employed by TBC because of my mother's plotting and Uncle Tim's influence, I didn't want to stay there a moment longer."

"That's not true at all." I find my voice again, but he tilts his head, like he doesn't believe a word I'm saying. "You got the job, because you deserved it. And you must be good at what you do…"

"How do you work that out?" This is the first glimpse I've had of his old lack of self-confidence; and I don't like it now, anymore than I used to.

"Because you managed to build a successful company, that's how."

"How do you know it was successful?"

"Because you sold it. Even I know that people don't generally buy failing companies. And they certainly don't adhere to the outgoing owner's demands… like not using the existing name…" I let my voice fade and he looks down at his hands.

"Well… maybe," he mutters.

I give him – and myself – a moment, and then sit forward slightly. "You were telling me about Malibu?"

He looks up, smiling. "Yes. I didn't like it."

"Oh? Why not?"

"I don't know. It just wasn't my cup of tea, I suppose. The house was really modern, and the beach was… too much."

"Too much?" I'm not sure what he means by that.

"It was too… big." He smiles.

"So what did you do?" I ask, intrigued.

"I sold it." He sighs, shaking his head. "It was a bit of a nightmare, but luckily Tim's solicitor took it over for me, because I didn't have a clue… not when it came to American estate agents and lawyers. And I took off for France."

"France?"

"Yes. Tim also left me a chalet in the Alps… at Chamonix."

"Did you sell that too?" I ask.

"No." He smiles again. "I really liked the chalet, and Chamonix. Apart from the mountains, which do occasionally get in the way, there's an uninterrupted view of the sky."

I chuckle. "So, do you go there much?"

"Yes. In the winter… I like to go skiing."

I laugh properly now. "You… you can ski?"

He looks affronted, but he's still smiling, so I know he's not really offended. "Yes. I was useless to start with, but I got the hang of it… eventually."

He looks down at his watch.

"I really ought to go," he says, and I feel a wave of disappointment crash over me, wishing I was brave enough to ask him to stay. "I'm keeping you from your work. Again."

We both get up, stacking the cups and plates onto the tray, which he carries indoors.

"Can I see you tomorrow?" he asks.

"Yes." I look up at him.

"As it's Saturday, can I take you out somewhere?" I hesitate, thinking about my routine, and the idea of breaking it for the first time in years. "I was thinking about a picnic," he adds.

"I'd love to," I reply, before my conscience gets the better of me.

We walk together through the house to the front door, where he stops, turning to face me.

"Are you okay?" he asks.

I nod my head, because I can't say 'yes'. Not yet.

And then I watch him walk away, waving when he turns back, halfway down the lane.

I go straight upstairs to my studio and struggle to concentrate on my illustration, forcing myself to focus. It's gone five o'clock already, and I don't want to have to work over the weekend, so I really need to get this finished.

A few minutes later, I hear the sound of a loud throaty engine passing through the village, up towards the main road. It's an unusual sound, distracting enough to make me stop drawing for a moment, but then I shake my head and put my mind to work.

"I wish you could have known him, Molly," I whisper, rubbing my fingers over the lettering on her gravestone. Of all the words engraved here, I think it's the date that bothers me the most, because there's only one. There's no birth date and death date, because they're the same. She never lived, except in my heart, that is. "You'd have loved him. And he'd have loved you." He would. I know it. And a tear falls onto my cheek. I rub it away angrily, because I never cry by Molly's grave. I hate showing her my tears… but the thought that they'll never know each other… it's too much, and I can't hold back the flood.

I get to my feet eventually, wishing I'd brought a tissue with me. I never do though. Because I never cry here. Well, not for a long time, anyway. Instead, I wipe away my tears on the backs of my hands.

"See you tomorrow, sweetheart," I murmur, and turn away, walking slowly out of the graveyard, and closing the creaking gate behind me, before making my way through the still quiet village, taking the turning into East Street and up the hill towards my house.

As usual, I keep my head down, my hands in my pockets, only looking up when I approach the cottage, to find Josh standing there, leaning against the wall, close to the front door, just like he was yesterday morning.

He looks at me, studying me closely, a frown settling on his face as he notices my swollen, puffy eyes perhaps, and then he pushes himself off the wall, walking towards me. Without saying a word, he envelopes me in his arms and I rest my head against his chest, letting the tears fall again as he strokes my hair.

How does he know? Has he guessed where I go in the mornings? He can't have done… and anyway, does it matter? He's here, and he's holding me and the relief is indescribable.

I pull back eventually, and he lets me, keeping his arms around me as I look up at him. I'm longing to ask why he's here. How he knows. But I daren't. I can't have that conversation with him yet.

"Okay?" he asks, his voice caressing my shattered nerves.

"Yes. Thank you."

He shakes his head and whispers, "Don't thank me," and then he lets me go. "I'll come back in a couple of hours," he says. "Will that give you enough time?"

"Yes. Shall I bring anything?"

"No… well, you could bring a sketch pad, if you want to."

I can't help smiling up at him. "Okay."

He moves away then, starting down the hill, and I stand, watching him, until he turns and waves. And I wave back.

Sure enough, just over two hours later, there's a knocking on my door, and I pull it open, to find Josh standing there, changed from jeans into shorts – navy blue ones today – and a white t-shirt. I'm wearing my pale yellow sun dress and, as he steps inside, letting me close the door behind him, he turns back to me. "You look lovely," he says quietly.

"Thank you." I can feel myself blushing.

"Are you ready to go?" he asks.

"Yes." I pick up my bag, checking I packed some spare pencils and that I've got my keys, and grab my sunhat from the chair by the window. "I am now."

"Good," he says, smiling, and opens the door again.

Parked outside is a very sleek, dark grey sports car, and as I follow Josh around the back of it, pausing while he opens the boot and I deposit my bag and hat inside, on top of a wicker picnic basket, I notice the badge says 'Aston Martin'. "This is yours?" I ask, looking up at him as we continue round and he opens the passenger door for me.

"No. I stole it to impress you." I tilt my head and raise my eyebrows, waiting. "Yes, it's mine," he admits eventually. "My one indulgence out of the money Tim left me."

"Well, I don't know very much about cars, but I know Aston Martins aren't cheap."

"No, they're not. But then Tim did leave me a scary amount of money."

"Scary?"

I sit down in the black leather seat, twisting around to face the front, and straighten my skirt.

"Yes. Eight and a half million is kind of scary." He closes the door and walks around to the driver's side, sitting beside me, then reaches over, his finger beneath my chin, and pushes it upwards, snapping my mouth closed. "See… I told you."

"Um… yes, you did." I can't stop staring at him.

"I'm still me," he whispers, looking worried now. "I haven't changed. I promise."

"I know."

He smiles. "You do?"

"Yes. I know you're still you." *Only better.*

"And the money?" he says, still sounding a little wary, despite his smile. "Does it worry you?"

I shrug my shoulders. "Does it worry you?"

"Sometimes, but only in so far as it can make people see me differently."

I shake my head. "Only people who don't know the real you, I'd have thought."

His eyes focus on mine, and I see something in them. Something familiar… from the past. "So that's almost no-one then," he says, starting the engine and selecting 'drive'. "Well, no-one but you."

And before I have the chance to reply, he puts his foot on the accelerator, and we shoot forwards, down the road to the junction, and out onto The Street.

"That noise," I breathe.

"I know. That's the best part." He grins over at me.

"No… I mean, I've heard it before. Last night after you left, I was working and I heard a car that sounded just like this, racing up through the village… even from my cottage."

"That would have been me," he says, looking a little sheepish.

"You? Where were you going in such a hurry?"

He purses his lips, like he's trying not to smile. "Well, I realised after I'd left you, that I'd invited you for a picnic, but that I didn't really have the means to see that through. So, I drove to Helston…"

"Helston? But the shops must have been closing by the time you got there."

"Not quite. I managed to get the hamper… and then I went on to the supermarket afterwards and bought the food." He glances over at me as we reach the junction that leads out onto the main road.

"We didn't need a hamper," I point out and he smiles properly this time.

"Yes, we did. I promised you a picnic… and that's what you're getting."

I shake my head, although I can feel myself smiling at him.

He's driven us to one of the old abandoned tin mines we used to come to when we were younger, about an hour's drive from the village. I haven't been here for years – well, not since Josh last brought me, anyway – but it's hardly changed at all. Josh has packed a rug, as well as the picnic and we find ourselves a shady spot, lying out on the rug and enjoying the peace and quiet.

"Enough sky for you?" Josh says, and I can hear the humour in his voice.

I shield my eyes from the sun and glance around. "Well, being as sky is all I can see, I'd have to say, yes."

"Do you know what I like?" he adds, as an afterthought.

"What?" I turn to him, to find he's looking at me.

"The silence. That's the other thing about London. You don't really notice it when you're there, but it's incredibly noisy. I don't think I've been anywhere truly silent since I left Porthgowan."

"I'd miss the silence, if I left," I remark and he sits up suddenly, looking down at me.

"You're not thinking of leaving are you?"

"No." I shake my head and sit up myself. "No. I'm not. I couldn't…" I let my voice fade again and he relaxes.

"Do you want to do some drawing?" he suggests, offering me my bag. I take it from him and delve inside, pulling out a small, A4 sized sketch pad, and a box of pencils.

"It's lovely just to be able to draw for myself," I muse, opening the pad and looking around at the scene before us; the lush, ripe fields, the abandoned mine shaft, and the forlorn buildings surrounding it, and the rugged cliff-tops, leading my eye out to the deep blue ocean beyond.

He reaches over, undoing the picnic hamper, and retrieves a paperback book. "You should do it more often," he says quietly, almost to himself.

"It's been so long, I've forgotten what it feels like to lose myself in drawing… just for pleasure," I confess, as he puts his book down again and I turn to face him, the sadness in his eyes tearing at my heart.

"Do you need to lose yourself?" he asks, edging a little closer.

"Yes."

"It won't always be like that," he whispers.

"Won't it?" A tear falls onto my cheek and he brushes it away with his thumb.

"No. One day you'll find yourself again."

I let myself lean into him, wishing I could hug him, just for saying that, and for believing it. Because he does… and when he says it, I can almost believe it too. Almost.

Josh has brought cold chicken and a selection of meats, various salads, some bread, and fruit, and we eat it from china plates, which are strapped inside the picnic basket, while I point out – trying not to smile – that I don't eat meat anymore. He's surprised and apologises for bringing it, even though I tell him repeatedly that the chicken is fine. And then he quizzes me about how I've managed to give up bacon, especially in sandwiches, because in his view, that's a human impossibility. I explain that the smell still drives me insane, but I manage to resist.

After lunch, I draw some more, while he reads his book, and then we pack everything away and go for a walk along the cliff tops. There's a lovely breeze and it's refreshing, blowing away the cobwebs.

As the sun begins to set, we start for home, stopping on the way at a small pub, where we have dinner… sea bass for me, and a steak for Josh. Before he places our order, he asks if I mind him eating meat and I tell him of course I don't. Why would I?

We've had a perfect day, without too many memories, or too much sadness. Instead, we've talked, we've laughed, we've occasionally just sat in silence, without feeling the need for conversation, and for the first time in a very very long time, I've felt at peace with myself. And that's all thanks to Josh.

By the time we drive back into Porthgowan, it's gone eleven, and Josh takes it slowly, so as not to wake the village with the throaty roar of the engine.

"Thank you for a lovely day," I say, looking at him as he turns the car around in the lane and pulls up outside my cottage. He twists in his seat, facing me, and without even thinking, I lean over and kiss his cheek, his stubble prickling gently against my skin. "Sorry," I mumble, embarrassed by my actions. "I—I shouldn't have…" I turn, eager to escape, but he grabs hold of my arm and pulls me back, gazing down at me.

"Don't say sorry to me," he says firmly. "That's the one word you never, ever have to say to me."

I shake my head. "After what I did? After breaking us up… breaking us both…"

"Yes. Friends never have to say sorry."

"Friends?" Is that what he wants? Even though he said he's not over me…

"Yes." He interrupts my train of thought. "You were my girlfriend. You were my lover…" I feel a warm glow spread through my body, remembering… "But more than anything, you were my best friend. Always."

I hesitate for a moment, wondering if I should lean in closer and kiss him properly. I know I'm sending him mixed messages. God knows, I'm sending myself mixed messages, and I can't expect him to understand what I want, when I'm struggling to work it out for myself. I know it was me who first suggested friendship, when he talked about leaving the village the other afternoon, but after being with him again, having spent time with him, knowing what I've missed out on all these years and discovering how kind and generous, how considerate and loving he still is, I know beyond a doubt, that Josh is my route back to happiness.

The only problem is, taking it.

Chapter Twelve

Josh

I stand, waiting outside her cottage again. If anything, today feels even hotter than yesterday, and that was warm enough. As I wait, I reflect on our parting last night, and I can't help smiling. Feeling her lips on my cheek was like spinning back through time. I was eighteen again, and Abbie was mine. The need for her was still there, just as sharp and strong as ever, and I wanted nothing more than to take her in my arms and kiss her. Except I couldn't. Because she isn't mine. Because, with her thanks for what was a simply perfect day, and then that kiss, and the muddled, bewildering apology that followed it, came the realisation that Abbie's still stuck somewhere in hell, and that she needs my help, my consideration and my patience. Love can follow… when she's ready to understand that, for me, it's always been there, and it's never changed.

I hear her footsteps and stand upright, starting my walk down the hill. She looks up as she approaches and I notice that she doesn't seem to have been crying today, unlike yesterday, when her eyes were swollen and red.

I still don't comment, and pull her into my arms, holding her until she's ready to pull back from me, looking up into my face.

"Have you eaten breakfast?" she asks.

"No, not yet."

"Do you want to have some porridge with me?"

"Porridge?" I ask, biting my lip. "Not bacon?"

"No… not bacon."

"I guess I can stomach porridge… as long as there's sugar in it."

She shakes her head. "How do you stay in such good shape?" A blush spreads up her face and she steps away, moving towards the house.

"I told you… I have my own personal gym."

"Not here, you don't."

"No. I'll have to start swimming again."

I suppose that's how I used to stay in shape when I was younger… although at the time I wasn't really aware of it. I thought of swimming as an excuse to look at Abbie in a bikini, which at the time seemed far more important than keeping fit.

"I haven't been swimming for years," she replies, closing the door behind us, as we enter the cool living room.

"Maybe we could go together later?" I suggest.

"I'm not sure…" She walks through the house to the kitchen and I follow, feeling nervous as she unlocks the back door and lets in a welcome, gentle breeze. Doesn't she want to spend time with me today? She turns on the threshold, looking up at me. "I sort of promised myself I'd mend my garden table and give it a coat of varnish."

"Well, I can help you with that, and maybe we can go swimming afterwards, if there's time?"

"You don't mind?" she asks, gazing up into my face, her eyes alight.

"No." God, I wish I could just pull her into my arms for no good reason, other than that I want to. But she's not ready for that. Not yet.

"Well, we could make a start after breakfast," she suggests. "Take a seat." She nods towards to the table. "I'll make us some porridge."

I do as I'm told and watch while she prepares our breakfast, trying not to think about all the mornings I've missed out on; all the years we could have been doing this. Together.

When it's ready, I carry the tray out to the garden and we sit… and I have to admit, Abbie makes really good porridge. It's really creamy and she's added nuts and seeds and some fresh strawberries that were left over from the basket I brought the other day. It didn't even need any sugar.

I notice that she drinks fruit tea with her breakfast, preparing it methodically – even though she makes me the normal version – and I don't ask why. I'm guessing it's just one of her habits. If it is, she'll tell me about it and the reason behind it, when she's ready.

Afterwards, Abbie clears away, while I inspect the table, establishing that the wonkiness is caused by loose screws, which are easily put right, and then we set about varnishing it.

Working together, it only takes a couple of hours and, once we're finished, we clear away the brushes, washing them in white spirits, before leaving them to dry in the sun. The table is going to need a second coat of varnish, but not until much later on today.

"Why don't we go to the pub for lunch?" I suggest as we sit down with a cup of tea in the kitchen. "And then we could go for a swim this afternoon?"

She looks at me doubtfully and I wonder if I've overstepped the mark in some way. Am I treading too hard on her routine with my size eleven shoes?

She runs her finger around the top of her cup, lowering her head. "What's wrong?" I ask her.

"Why are you doing this?" she says.

"Doing what?"

"Being so nice to me… helping me out… spending so much time with me."

"Because I want to."

She shakes her head. "But I don't understand. Why would you want to? I—I broke us. You should hate me… So, why are you being so kind?"

I move my chair closer to hers, as the first tear hits her cheek and am just about to put my arms around her when she holds up her hands, stopping me, and I lean back again.

"I tore us apart," she continues, through her tears. "I broke my own heart."

"And mine," I say, without thinking.

"Exactly," she replies. "So why are you doing this?"

I've already recognised her outburst for what it is. She's feeling guilty for her moments of happiness over the last few days. She's pushing me away. The thing is, this time, I get it. This time, I'm not going to let her. I'm not going anywhere.

"I told you," I say quietly, leaning closer, but not touching her. "I'm not over you. I don't want to be over you. Ever."

She lets out a loud sob and I pull her into my arms. She doesn't object and allows me to hold her while she weeps on my chest.

This isn't just about us. I know that much. It's not about her broken heart, or mine. It's about Molly, and Abbie's torment, the guilt and the pain… and the agony of trying to take the decision to let herself be helped back from hell.

It takes her ages to calm down, but when she does, she leans back in her seat, looking at me, her eyes awash with tears, her cheeks stained.

"I need a tissue," she says, sniffling.

"I'll get you one," I offer, going to stand, but she puts her hand on my arm.

"It's okay. I'll go. I need the bathroom anyway." The door is right behind her, and she gets to her feet, but as she turns to move away, I reach out and grab her hand, pulling her closer to me again.

"When you come back, can we talk?"

I notice the look of fear cross her eyes. "What about?" she whispers.

"I'd like to explain properly."

"Explain?"

"About why I'm doing this… what it all means…"

She pauses for a moment and then nods her head. And as she moves away, going through to the bathroom and closing the door, I hope I'm making the right decision here. I hope that by opening up to her – even if only in part for now – she might just be able to see that I'm serious and that my love for her has never diminished. Not even for one day, or one hour, have I loved her any less than I did that morning on the beach, when I was sixteen years old, when she talked about leaving the village with her mum and I first realised that she was my world. Entirely.

She comes back out of the bathroom, a handful of tissue clutched in her clenched fist, her eyes still swollen, but her cheeks dry.

"I look a mess," she murmurs, pushing her hair behind her ears.

"No, you don't."

She stands, staring at me, as though she doesn't believe me, but to me she looks beautiful. "Shall I make us some lunch?" she asks, screwing up the tissue a little more

She's putting off our conversation, and for the time being, I'm going to let her. We've got all day, as far as I'm concerned.

"If you want to."

"Well, I don't think I could face the pub."

That's understandable. "Okay. Do you want some help?"

"You can slice the mushrooms, if you want to."

"I think I can manage that."

She smiles, just lightly, and goes over to the fridge, pulling out a small box of mushrooms and bringing them back to me, with a chopping board and knife.

"I assume omelettes are okay?" she asks, turning towards the stove. I may have boiled a kettle of water on it the other day, but it looks complicated to me, even though Abbie seems at home with it.

"Omelettes are fine," I reassure her. She seems doubtful, about everything, at the moment, so I change the subject. "How do you cook on that?" I ask and she turns, noting the direction of my gaze.

"The Rayburn?" she clarifies, giving me a slight smile. "You get used to it."

"It looks nice." It does. It suits the kitchen perfectly.

"It's practical too. It provides the heating and hot water."

"Is that why it's on all the time, even in the summer?" I ask and she nods her head.

"Yes. Although obviously the radiators are switched off at the moment," she says, and then turns away, opening a cupboard, and taking out a small bowl… another one of Henry's by the looks of things. "I just need to go and pick some herbs. Are you okay for a minute?"

"I'm fine."

She seems to hesitate for a second, as though she wants to say something, but then goes out of the back door.

I start slicing the mushrooms, setting them to one side, wondering what she might have been about to say, hoping it wasn't anything negative.

"I'm sorry." Her voice makes me turn and I see her standing by the back door, the bowl in her hand, a few herbs hanging over its edge, and tears pouring down her cheeks again.

I stand and go to her, taking the bowl, which I place on the work surface, and pull her into my arms.

"Never say sorry," I whisper, my mouth right beside her ear.

She shudders slightly and leans back. "But you wanted to talk… and I've done everything to avoid it."

"I know." She frowns slightly. "And it wasn't that I wanted to talk. It's that we *need* to." She swallows and blinks back her tears. "And we will. After lunch."

She leans into me, her head on my chest and I hold her close, grateful she didn't pull away. Not only that, but she came to me. She didn't go quiet. She didn't hold it in. She came to me… and, God, that feels good.

I wasn't in any doubt that Abbie could cook – not having tasted her chocolate cake and her cookies – but her mushroom and herb omelette was incredible, and the dressing she made to go with the side salad, was perfect.

While we ate, we talked about food; about favourite dishes, the restaurants I've been to in London while entertaining clients, the foods we've both eaten abroad. As a result, I've discovered that Abbie and Simon honeymooned in the south of France. She didn't go into detail, other than to tell me about the most exquisite Bouillabaisse she'd eaten in a small restaurant they'd discovered in the next town to the place they were staying. Even so, it had sounded idyllic, and I wished it could have been me there with her, not Simon…

Once we're finished, Abbie clears the plates away, stacking them beside the sink and I get to my feet.

"Shall we sit in the living room?" I suggest. "It's probably cooler in there."

She nods her head and leads the way, sitting at one end of the sofa. I sit beside her, leaving a small gap between us, and turn to face her.

"I'm sorry," I say simply.

She tilts her head, looking confused. "What for?"

"All of it."

"But it wasn't your fault," she whispers. "It was mine."

"No. I should never have left you. I wish I hadn't."

"That's not true, Josh." She sits forward, angry I think, her voice raised. "You know it isn't. You wanted to work in PR. We both knew that, and we both knew London was the best place for you. We knew your career would take you away from here, and from me. And no matter how it came about, no matter how much your mother interfered, that offer was like a dream come true for you, so don't pretend it wasn't."

"I'm not," I reason, trying to stay composed.

"You worked for one of the biggest PR agencies," she continues, as though I haven't spoken. "You got to set up your business… you got what you wanted."

"What I wanted?" I say, raising my own voice slightly now. "I was too stupid to even know what I wanted."

"You wanted London… you wanted your career…" Her emotions are overwhelming her, and I know I have to rein in my own.

"Yes, I did," I reply, more calmly, taking a deep breath. "But I wanted you more…" I leave the sentence hanging and she stares at me, and then her expression softens, the storm abating, I think.

"If… If that's the case, then why didn't you come back?" she asks.

I can't help smiling. "There's nothing quite so contrary as a woman," I mutter and she gently slaps my arm. "Sorry," I add. "But I did offer, if you remember?" She nods her head, but doesn't reply. "And you told me not to… in no uncertain terms. That doesn't mean I didn't think about it though. I thought about it a lot. And every time

I contemplated jumping in my car and coming back here, I'd remember your words, and stop myself."

Tears form in her eyes and she looks down, so I place my finger beneath her chin and raise her face to mine. "I'm sorry," she murmurs, the fight gone from her now.

"Don't be."

"I hurt you."

"Yes." A tear falls onto her cheek and I wipe it away with my thumb. "I thought you didn't want me anymore. So I was hurt… and maybe a little bit angry too, if I'm honest." She swallows hard. "And then I found out you were with Simon…"

"But that was months later," she reasons. "Months and months. I didn't go straight from you to him."

"I know. Like I said, I was hurt, *and* I was stupid. It took me a long time to work all of this out."

She shakes her head slowly. "So… so, if you could go back, would you do things differently?" Her voice is enquiring, but almost pleading at the same time. She needs to know this, and I have to be truthful with her.

"If you're asking whether I'd still take the job, then the answer is 'yes', I would. But—"

She pulls away from me, her eyes betraying her renewed anger, then stands, her fists clenched at her sides. "Then you're lying. You didn't want me more than your career… You were better off without me, and you knew it…" Her voice fades and she looks around the room, like she wants an escape route.

I get to my feet and stand in front of her, capturing her face with my hands, grounding her, forcing her to look at me. "If you think that, you don't know me at all," I breathe, holding down the lump in my throat. Just. "I was in hell without you." I know she'll understand that, being as she's still there herself, and she looks into my eyes. "Will you let me finish what I was saying?" She nods her head, just once. "I'd still take the job, for the simple reason that, getting an offer like that blew me away. I never thought I was good enough for something like that – and as it turns out, I wasn't. It was all contrived and planned by other people. But at the time, I really believed in myself for the first time. And so did you. You encouraged me to go, and when Charles offered me the chance, I took it. I don't think I'd have known how to refuse it. But if I could turn back the clock, I'd change everything else. And I mean *everything*. I should have seen that you weren't happy with the way things were, I should have heard it in your voice, and I should have tried harder to make it work. I shouldn't have tried to keep commuting back here every week, not when I was working such long hours. It was too much… But I could have suggested that you come up to London and visit me sometimes, to take the pressure off."

"Me…?" she whispers, her eyes widening. "Come to London?"

"Yes. It would have made more sense, when you think about it. You could have caught the train up on Friday afternoons, and I could have met you at Paddington and you could have stayed with me at the flat… and then I could have put you on the train back here on Sundays. You were right, it was stupid of me to suggest I'd drive down here every weekend. It wasn't practical… It was exhausting, and my workload was bound to interfere, but we could have still stayed together, if I'd just thought it through a bit better."

"Or if I had…" she murmurs. "If I'd given us a chance, instead of—"

"So you'd have tried," I interrupt, "if I'd suggested it?"

She nods her head. "As long as you'd been there to meet me… to look after me."

"Of course I would have been." I move slightly closer to her, our bodies almost touching, her face still cupped in my hands.

She takes a long, stuttering breath, just about holding in her tears. "What… what about after university?" she asks. "I've often wondered… if… if we'd stayed together, would you have expected me to move to London permanently?"

"I wouldn't have *expected* you to do anything." I brush my thumbs against her cheeks. "I'd probably have asked you to, but if you really hadn't wanted…"

"I'd have come…" she whispers and I feel like my whole world just disintegrated. The last eighteen years of loneliness and pain flash before my eyes and I'm left wondering how different it could all have been… for me, but even more so for Abbie.

I swear under my breath. "We've both lost so much," I manage to say.

"I know, but at the time, I was just so scared. The thought of spending three years away from you, not knowing if I'd see you each weekend, not knowing what you were doing… it was too much for me to even think about."

"Well, I can promise you that I wasn't 'doing' anything, not in the way I think you mean. But I can understand how you felt. It wasn't enough, was it? If only I'd thought it through…"

"If only *we'd* thought it through," she interrupts.

"If only *I'd* thought it through…" I ignore her "… it didn't need to have happened. It didn't have to be about choices; it could – it *should* – have been about compromises. We'd both have made them. But when you're eighteen, three years feels like a lifetime, doesn't it? Of course, we both know it isn't now. I've had eighteen years of missing you… eighteen years alone. That's half my life. Half of yours."

She leans back, although I keep hold of her still. "I can't believe you've been alone for eighteen years," she says, looking at me suspiciously.

Now isn't the time to tell her about my life without her. Not in any detail, anyway. We need to work things out between ourselves first. "No," I reply. "I haven't been."

"Then why say it?" She looks hurt now.

"Because it is true… in a way." She tries to pull away from me, but I don't let her. "There have been other women," I admit and she blinks a couple of times. "A few… not many. But none of them mattered to me… not in the slightest. You're the only woman I've ever really wanted… ever really loved."

She stares up at me, our eyes lock, and then she shakes her head. "I —I don't deserve this. I don't deserve you."

"Yes, you do."

"No… I broke you. I broke us."

"Then let me put us back together again. We've already lost so much time, and I don't want to lose any more." Her eyes widen, her mouth opening slightly, and I move closer still, our bodies fused. "Please… I'm so in love with you, Abbie."

"B—But that can't be," she whispers, incredulous. "I—I lost your love."

I smile and shake my head. "No… you never lost my love. It was always yours; it always will be." She sucks in a breath. "I'm not going to rush you into anything, but I want you back. I want us back. And I'll do whatever it takes… I'll do whatever you need…" I stop talking, unable to say anything else, and I lean down, brushing my lips across hers. She opens to me and, within seconds, it's like we're eighteen all over again.

We break the kiss after a long, long time and lean back, breathless, although I keep a firm hold on her, in case the guilt I think she's probably feeling overwhelms her and she decides to bolt. She doesn't. Instead, she just stares at me.

"I know you don't think you deserve to be happy," I whisper, and she lowers her eyes slightly. "I also know there's been a lot of pain in your life, and this isn't going to be easy for you. I'm aware that there might be times when you'll find it so hard, you'll fight with me, you'll try to push me away, or you'll walk out on me yourself." She looks up at me again, surprised, I think, although she doesn't deny anything I've said, and I continue, "But I need you to know, that I'm going to take whatever you throw at me. You can shout and scream and call me every name under the sun, and I won't take it personally. You can go silent on me and I'll wait until you want to talk. You can cry as much as you need to, and I'll dry your tears and hold you until you feel like smiling again. If you walk out on me, I'll follow you, I'll stay right beside you, I'll make sure you're safe, and when you're ready, I'll bring you home. And if you push me away, I'll come back… and I'll keep coming back… until you work out that you *do* deserve to be happy. And that your happiness is all I care about. And that I love you far too much to ever lose you again."

Chapter Thirteen

Abbie

We didn't go for a swim.

We didn't do the second coat of varnish on the table.

We didn't even eat dinner.

We sat on the sofa. All evening. I cried, and Josh held me, on his lap, and wiped away my tears, just like he'd said he would.

We didn't talk. I'm not ready to yet, and he didn't push me to. He seems to understand, even though I haven't told him about Molly, how hard talking is for me, and I'm grateful for that.

By nine o'clock, I was exhausted and he said he thought he should go back to the pub and that I should go to bed. I couldn't disagree with him. I'd cried so much, I could barely keep my eyes open, and I accompanied him to the front door, where he kissed me again, more gently this time, and promised he'd see me tomorrow.

Closing the door behind him, I lean back against it, feeling a glow deep inside me that's been absent for eighteen years. Part of me wants to call him back, to ask him to stay. But I'm not ready for that yet either, and I push myself off the door, and go around the house, switching off lights and locking up, before climbing upstairs and going into my bedroom.

I undress slowly, putting on a pair of short pyjamas and, switching off the light, I settle down in bed, wide awake now. How is that even possible? I was literally falling asleep downstairs and now my mind is racing, filled with images of myself and Josh, kissing... his hands on me, touching, caressing... his tongue... I groan and turn over, trying not to remember how it used to be, even though it's impossible to forget, despite the eighteen year gap. Just a kiss is enough to remind me of what he could do...

After a couple of hours of torture, I get up and pull back the curtains, opening the window to its widest, looking down over the village. There are still one or two lights glowing in some of the houses, people making the most of the last moments of their Sunday, before the beginning of another working week.

I turn back to my bed, but I can't face getting into it, tossing and turning for a few hours, and instead I go upstairs and into the studio, opening the window to release the stuffiness and let in the nighttime breeze.

I flick on the desk lamp and gaze down at the illustration I've nearly completed. Hazel went with my suggestion, and chose the simplest design, allowing for the ludicrously long, eight word title of the book, and I've nearly completed it now. If I can get a couple of days of solid work on it, then I should get it done. A slight smile crosses my lips, as I wonder whether Josh will let me have a couple of days to work... or whether he's got other plans in mind.

That thought makes me wonder what he has got in mind. Obviously he said he'll see me tomorrow, which I assume means he'll be waiting when I get back from the church, but will he expect me to talk... to open up to him, like he did to me? I hope not, because I really don't think I can. He seemed to understand how hard I'm finding this – although I don't know how – but how far will his understanding stretch? And what does he want from me? Is he trying to recapture what we lost? Because if he is, I think he's going to be disappointed. That time has passed now...

I turn that thought over and over in my head, wondering if Josh and I can have a future together, when there's too much still unsaid about our pasts, until tears start to well in my eyes again.

"What does he want?" I whisper to myself.

My phone is beside my drawing board, plugged in and charging – well, probably fully charged now – and I switch it on, surprised to discover I have a message waiting for me. And that it's from Josh.

— *Thank you for giving me a second chance. I love you. See you tomorrow. Love Josh xx*

I have no idea how he got my number… but, 'a second chance'? Is that what this is?

I tap in the 'reply' box, noting that it's now nearly midnight and his message is timed at over an hour and a half ago, and start typing:

— *Thank you for your message. I have a question, and it won't wait, although I know you won't pick this up until the morning, but I need to know, are you trying to recapture the past? Is that what this is about? Abbie x*

I press send, even though I know I should re-read it. I know it's a rambling mess, but hopefully he'll understand it well enough to make sense of it, and I put my phone back down again, feeling a little more relaxed that at least I've asked the question. I've put my doubts out there, and I just have to wait until tomorrow for him to come back to me.

My phone beeps and I jump out of my skin, picking it up again slowly and focusing on the screen.

— *Why are you still awake? You were exhausted earlier. It's late and you should be asleep by now. And no, I'm not trying to recapture anything. This is about us. It's about who we are now. It's about loving you. Always. That's all. Josh xxx*

His reply brings tears to my eyes, but I can't hide my doubts and my fears.

— *I can't sleep. And I know it's late, but what if it's too late for us? What if there's nothing left? What if we lost it over the years, and we can't get it back again? Abbie x*

I know I sound desperate, but I can't help that. I feel desperate.

My phone rings and I check the display. The number isn't a familiar one, but I know who it is, and press the button to connect the call.

"Hello?"

"It's not too late for us." Josh's voice soothes my nerves, caresses my skin, and I almost feel my muscles unwind. Almost.

"Isn't it?"

"No. I know what this is, Abbie," he says quietly.

"What is it?"

"You're having doubts, feeling guilty... you're pushing me away."

"No, I'm not."

"Yes, you are. Maybe not consciously, but you're trying to find reasons not to be happy... for us not to work out."

I think for a moment. Maybe he's right... maybe that is what I'm doing. Trying to sabotage our relationship before it's even started; denying myself the happiness I feel I don't deserve.

"Am I right?" he asks.

"Maybe," I allow.

"Okay. So, remember what I told you earlier? If you push me away, I'm going to keep coming back." He pauses. "Do you want me to come over?"

Yes. "No." I want him to, but I'm also not sure I'd be able to let him leave again. And, like I said, I'm not ready for that, and it wouldn't be fair to lead him on.

"Are you sure? Because if you're having second thoughts about us..."

"I'm not."

"Good." I can hear the smile in his voice. "I'm sorry I said 'second chance' in my message. That was a bit thoughtless of me."

"No, it wasn't. It's just a turn of phrase."

"Yes, a turn of phrase that was bound to make you think I was looking to pick up where we left off... and we can't do that, can we?"

"No. We can't. Too much has happened."

"I know. Listen, if you want me to come over, I can be there in five minutes... no strings. No expectations. We can just talk." He pauses again. "And don't misunderstand that either. Don't for one second think that, because I'm happy just to talk, I don't want you. I do. I want you just as much as I did when I was eighteen, and it was all new to me. It still feels new to me, even now."

Oh God. I'm so tempted… "I know, but I should probably get some sleep," I murmur, despite the voice in my head, screaming at me to say 'yes'.

"Okay. As long as you're sure."

"I'm sure. I—I'll see you tomorrow?"

"I'll be there."

We're about to hang up, when a thought occurs to me. "Josh?"

"Yes?"

"How did you know my phone number?" I'm intrigued. I want to know. "Did my dad give it to you?" It's the only logical explanation.

"No."

"Then how?" I'm really puzzled now.

"Well… I have a confession. I—I stole a business card from your studio the other day."

I can't help smiling. He sounds so contrite. "Why did you do that?"

"So I could send you text messages… and call you in the early hours of the morning, if necessary, to tell you how much I love you." A gentle sigh escapes my lips. "Now, get some sleep," he adds and we really do end the call this time.

I wake, feeling more carefree than I have in years. Molly is still there, filling my head. She always will be. But Josh is there too, and because of that – because of him – I find myself smiling as I climb out of bed and head downstairs to the shower. I even hum a tune to myself while I'm washing my hair, unable to remember the last time I did that, and while I'm drying off, I wonder if he'll want to stay for breakfast again today, and whether I should maybe suggest that we get him some bacon from the store…

Sitting by Molly's grave, picking at the daisies that grow there, tell her about my conversation with Josh, tears pricking my eyes as I reveal the moment when he said he's in love with me.

"I'm in love with him too," I whisper to her. "I know I haven't said it yet, but that doesn't mean it's not true."

In my head, I hear her voice – the one I've invented for her – murmuring, "Tell him. Tell him, Mummy," and I blink away my tears.

"I will. I promise. I'll tell him everything." I get to my feet, kissing my fingers and touching them to the lettering of her name. "After breakfast."

I walk back, knowing that my conversation with Josh won't be easy, but that it has to be done. Obviously, telling him I'm in love with him won't be hard, but as for the rest… I don't know how he'll react to that. Still, there's only one way to find out.

There's more of a breeze today, and it catches my hair as I look up, stopping dead, my stomach churning.

He's not there.

My hair blows right across my face now, and I tuck it behind my ear. He said he'd see me today. Surely that meant he'd be here. Did I misunderstand that?

I carry on to the house, letting myself in, feeling despondent. I'd so looked forward to having breakfast with him, talking over the day, making plans… telling him I'm in love with him. And he's not even here.

I sit at the table, all thoughts of breakfast banished.

Where can he be?

I check my watch. It's just gone seven-fifteen, and I try to remember our phone call from last night, which we finished at just after twelve-thirty, and I wonder whether maybe he's overslept.

He hasn't done so on any other day, but maybe he's tired. Yesterday was an emotional day for him too. That'll be it… He's still asleep.

I get up and fill the kettle with water, putting it on to boil. I don't feel like eating anything, but I'll have a cup of lemon and ginger tea, and then think about working. I'm sure Josh will be over later…

The tea doesn't sit well in my stomach and I end up throwing half of it down the sink, feeling sick. I haven't felt like this since I was pregnant with Molly – but I know that's not the problem. It would be a biological impossibility.

A thought strikes me and, putting the cup on the draining board, I run up the stairs, all the way to the attic, grab my phone from beside my drawing board, where I left it last night, and check the screen, my heart falling when I see there are no messages, and no missed calls. I bite my bottom lip. Should I…? Why not?

I look up his number from last night, and connect a call to him, instinctively crossing my fingers, as I pace the floor, and then stop, as it goes straight to voicemail without even ringing, the automated voice asking me to leave a message. I hang up.

It's nearly eight o'clock now, and I know my dad will be up, just the same as I know I'm not going to be able to focus on work until I've seen Josh; until I can find out why he didn't come round this morning.

Pocketing my phone, I run back down the stairs and pick up my keys, then head out of the front door, pulling it closed behind me, and walk down into the village, keeping my head bowed to avoid seeing anyone. Luckily, it's still fairly quiet, although I pass the postman, who says, "Hello," to me.

I nod in reply and hurry on, arriving at The Lobster Pot and going around the back. The door is unlocked and I let myself in, calling out, "Dad?" as I walk inside.

"Up here," comes the reply and I make my way through to the stairs, climbing up, the smell of bacon meeting me half way, and I smile, half expecting to see Dad and Josh sitting at the kitchen table together, tucking into breakfast.

Dad greets me at the top of the stairs. "You're just in time," he says, smiling. "I was about to start the eggs."

"I've already eaten," I lie.

"Well, come and have a cup of tea with me, anyway." He walks back into the kitchen and I follow, sighing out my disappointment when I see that the room is empty. "You haven't come down to see me for ages." Dad goes over to the stove, turning the three rashers of bacon, and adding two eggs.

It's true. I haven't. "I've been busy."

He turns and looks at me, giving me a slightly odd look. "I know."

I sit at the table, running my fingertip along its edge. "I—Is Josh up yet?" I ask, feeling embarrassed.

Dad puts down the spatula he's been using and turns to me. "He's not here," he says, looking surprised. "I—I assumed he was with you."

"With me?"

He blushes slightly, two patches of red appearing on his cheeks. "I know the two of you have been seeing quite a lot of each other. I just presumed he'd... well, he'd spent the night with you."

"Why would you think that? He's staying here. He came back here last night."

"Did he? In that case, he must've come in the back way, while I was busy. And he's certainly not here now..." My skin turns to ice and a pain tears at my chest, but I swallow hard.

"What do you mean?"

"When I woke up this morning, I went downstairs to open the back door and bring in the milk, and I noticed his car was gone. So I came back up and knocked on his door. He didn't answer, so I let myself in, and his bed hadn't been slept in. All his things were gone." He turns off the hob and moves the frying pan aside. "Abbie?" he says, coming closer. "Is everything alright?"

I stand, holding my hands up. "Yes," I murmur, trying to smile, even though I can't. I'm not sure I'll ever smile again. "Everything's fine."

"It's not though, is it? What's happened?"

I shake my head. "Nothing." He stares at me, and I know he doesn't believe a word I'm saying. "I'm going home," I whisper, pushing the chair out of the way, desperate to escape.

I almost fall down the stairs, my dad's voice echoing in my head, my own footsteps drumming in my ears as I run back to my cottage... to my safe haven, slamming the door closed behind me and collapsing to the floor, pain surging through me, tears pouring down my cheeks, my own sobs ringing out and filling the empty space.

"How could you, Josh? How could you do this to me?"

It's the stiffness in my legs that finally makes me get up, even though the tears are still falling and the pain in the rest of my body is so intense I can't think straight.

I struggle to my feet and go to the sofa, lying back and staring at the ceiling. How could he lie like that? How could he say all those things, sound so sincere and look so genuine, knowing this was what he intended all along? I thought I knew him. I thought he'd never do anything to hurt me… but this? It's too much.

It has to be some sort of glorified revenge, doesn't it? He reeled me in with kind gestures and loving words, because he wanted to break my heart – as payback for all those years ago, when I broke his.

I can't stop sobbing, even though a part of me knows I should be grateful that at least he didn't take me to bed. At least he didn't make love to me again. He didn't remind me how good it can be, and then leave me. He stopped short of that, so maybe he does have a conscience after all, because that would have been so much worse.

My phone rings and I turn onto my side and reach into my back pocket, pulling it out, half expecting it to be my dad. It isn't. It's Josh. How dare he? Who does he think he is?

I decline the call, noticing that it's ten-thirty now, and put my phone down on the coffee table. It beeps twice, letting me know I have a message, but I turn to face the back of the sofa, and ignore it.

A while later, the phone rings once more, and I turn over. It's Josh again, so I switch the phone off this time.

I'm woken by a knocking on the door. I hadn't even realised I'd fallen asleep, and I jump at the sound, getting to my feet and feeling a frisson of fear tremble over my skin.

"Who's there?" I call out, raising my voice.

If it's Josh, he can go to hell.

"Dad." I hear the familiar voice and sigh out my relief, going over and opening the door.

"I've been knocking for ages," he says.

"Sorry. I fell asleep."

He nods. "What's wrong, Abbie?"

"Nothing."

"Then why aren't you answering your phone?" How does he know that? "Josh called me," he explains and I take a step back. "He's worried about you… and so am I."

"Well, you don't need to be," I reply. "I'm just not having a good day. I've been thinking… about Molly. Plus I've got a deadline looming and I wanted some peace and quiet, so I turned my phone off." I feel guilty for lying, and for using Molly as an excuse, but it works and his face softens as he steps forward and gives me a hug. I struggle to hold back my tears, feeling his arms come around me, but I manage it, and pull back after a minute or so.

"You need to call Josh," he says, looking down at me. "He said he's been trying to call you." *I know.* "He asked me to come and check that you're alright."

"Where is he then?" I ask.

"London. Something urgent came up, evidently."

"So urgent that he couldn't leave a note, or send me a message?"

Dad shrugs his shoulders. "I don't know. He sounded tired though. And worried. Mainly about you." He pauses. "You are okay, aren't you?"

"Yes, I'm fine." I'm not. I'm about as far from fine as I think I can get.

"I have to get back to open up the pub," he says, and I check my watch. It's almost five-forty-five. The whole day has nearly gone… nowhere. "Call Josh," he says, stepping back. "Talk to him."

I nod my head, even though I've got no intention of calling Josh, or talking to him. Ever again.

Dad gives me a wave and I close the door, leaning back against it for a moment, before going back to the sofa and sitting down. My phone is lying on the table in front of me, and I pick it up, turning it back on.

I've got nine missed calls. One is from Hazel at Constantine Publishers. The other eight are from Josh. There are four messages and I dial the answering service to pick them up, in case Hazel had anything important to say. She didn't, although she did leave a message, in her usual, shrill, panicking way, saying that she was calling to check that I hadn't forgotten the deadline for the cover illustration is this Friday, which means I'll need to send her the designs by overnight courier on Thursday. The other three messages are from Josh. I hesitate, wondering whether to just delete them, but decide against it, and listen to them instead.

"Abbie, it's me. I'm really sorry. I've been in London for an hour or so… actually it's probably nearer two. Sorry, the time's just gone nowhere. I saw you'd tried to call a couple of hours ago, but I was still on the motorway then and couldn't stop. Look, I—I umm… I got a call from a friend… well, a friend of a friend, and well… I can't explain it over the phone, but I've had to come back up here. I'll be home as soon as possible and I'll explain it all then. I love you. And I am sorry. Truly." He sounds sincere enough, but I still don't understand why he couldn't have just left me a note, or dropped by to tell me before leaving.

I delete that one, and listen to the next message, which came in about forty minutes after the first one.

"Um… your messages are going straight to voicemail now. I'm going to guess you've turned your phone off. That either means you're busy, or you're angry with me. If it's the former, then try not to work too hard, and remember to eat. If it's the latter, please don't be. I promise there's a good reason for all of this. I just… I just can't tell you over the phone. If I could, I would. I love you."

The third message only came in an hour ago.

"Abbie… you're scaring me. I'm going to call your dad and get him to check up on you. If you're cross with me, that's fine. I'll deal with that when I get back, but can you please just call me, or let your dad know you're okay. I told you, I love you too much to lose you."

I stare at the phone, the screen blurring through my tears. "Then why did you leave me again?" I whisper, and clutch the phone to my chest, sobbing out the pain.

I manage to get the book cover completed by Thursday lunchtime, and package it up, ready to send off to Hazel.

Over the last few days, I've had lots of time to think, and I've reached one major decision. I'm not going to do any more sci-fi covers. I composed a letter and printed it out, putting it in with the cover illustration, explaining to Hazel that I don't feel it's the best use of my skills, being as that type of cover is really not my forte. I doubt she'll see it my way, but I'm not sure I care.

I arrange for the courier and, once the parcel has been collected, I set about clearing up the studio again. I don't have another project to begin working on straight away, so I've decided to spend the next few days, starting tomorrow, giving the place a really good spring clean. Hopefully it'll stop me from thinking about Josh.

Who am I kidding?

I've thought of very little else all week. He called six times on Tuesday. I declined the calls, although I had to leave my phone switched on for work, but I did listen to his messages.

He said he'd spoken to my dad after he'd been here, and it seems I was right; Dad wasn't convinced that I was okay. Well, he wasn't convinced enough for Josh, anyway. He told me he was getting worried, and he wished he could come home, but he couldn't. Not yet.

He left another message early on Wednesday morning, in which he asked me to call him. He said he was going to be busy all day, but he'd leave his phone on, and would I please just call.

I didn't. And he obviously got the hint that I didn't want to talk to him, so he started sending text messages instead. The first one, which came late on Wednesday afternoon, made me cry:

— I get it. I really do. You're angry. I think you're probably beyond angry. And I deserve that. I'm just asking you to trust me. Can you do that? Please? I'll do whatever it takes to make this up to you. Just please, please trust me on this. I love you, Abbie. Josh xxx

The second one, which he sent a few hours later, just before bedtime, had almost the same effect, and I read it through blurry eyes.

— I'm sorry. I'll keep saying it every day for the rest of my life, as long as you forgive me for leaving you. I know I promised I'd be there for you. And I know I've let you down. Please believe me, there's only one thing in my life that could have made me do this to you, and when I get back, I will explain it to you. All of it. I love you. Josh xxx

I wondered if he was talking about a business matter, whether perhaps something had gone wrong with the deal to sell his company, which just made me feel worse, wondering if he'd put his financial dealings ahead of me… so this morning, when his latest message came in, I read it with some trepidation.

— I've got the hint, Abbie. You're not talking to me. You've made that clear. The thing is, I told you last Sunday, you can go as silent on me as you like, and I'll wait. And I'll keep on waiting. There's nothing more I can do here at the moment, so I'm coming home on Saturday. I'm not sure what time yet, but I'd like to see you, if that's okay. Even if you don't want to talk, can you at least listen to what I have to say? I'll call by your house when I get back. I know you probably hate me, but at least hear me out. I love you. Josh xxx

I know I have to hear his explanation, because apart from anything else, I want to know why he left like he did, but that doesn't mean I'm not dreading seeing him again, and I spend Friday cleaning the studio, like my life depends on it.

I work through my usual tea break – I haven't bothered with it this week; I've hardly bothered to eat at all, really – and make it to four o'clock, before stopping and surveying my handiwork, feeling rather pleased with how organised and tidy the place looks.

I've got two more shelves to straighten, and am just about to make a start when my phone rings. I check the display, wondering if it's Josh, telling me he won't be home tomorrow… letting me down again. It isn't. It's Hazel.

"Hello?" I answer promptly.

"Abbie," she says, sounding rather abrupt and I start to panic that I've made a mess of the cover in some way. "I've received your letter."

I sit down at my drawing board. "Yes?"

"I don't think you quite understand how this works." Her voice is so patronising. She's one of those 'women in business', who think that if they shout loudly enough about being female, people will assume they're better at their job, than a dozen others – of both sexes – who do the same thing more quietly and efficiently. She drives me insane. "You can't cherry pick the things you want to work on."

"I'm not suggesting I can," I reply, rubbing my temples with my thumb and fingertips. Talking to Hazel always gives me a headache – and today is no exception.

"You seem to be, reading your letter."

"No. I'm just saying that it doesn't make sense for me to work on things that I'm not suited to. Surely you're better off finding someone who can illustrate those covers with more enthusiasm than I can." A thought occurs, and I take a breath, but not a long enough one for her to interrupt. "And anyway, I don't have a contract with you. You pay me on a job-by-job basis, so I *can* pick and choose, if I want to."

"You're not painting the Mona Lisa, dear," she says sarcastically. "They're just book covers."

"I know."

"Then why all the fuss? We all have to do things we don't enjoy sometimes."

"No, we don't. Well, I don't. And if you insist on sending me things I don't want to do, then I'll refuse to take any work at all."

I'm starting to shake with nerves, but I hold firm.

"There's no need to over-react," she blusters, back-tracking.

"Do you know what? I think there is." I'm getting my second wind now. "I've had enough. You pay a pittance, and you take forever to settle my invoices. So, don't bother sending me anything else to work on. I'll submit my bill for the work I've just done… and you've got seven days to pay it, or I'll start proceedings in the small claims court."

I don't bother waiting for her to reply, but hang up the call, my hands trembling still.

I hate getting angry. It's not something I do very often. But for once, I feel that it was justified.

Bloody woman…

I've decided today to get back to my usual Saturday routine. So, after I get home from visiting Molly, I have some breakfast and then drive to the supermarket at Helston to do a big shop. It's been a couple of weeks since I've done one, due to the distraction of having Josh around, and I've relied on the local store for what I've needed, but it's good to stock up again. When I get back, I make a pot of tea and unpack everything, and then do some baking, making a batch of cookies and a therapeutic chocolate cake. I say 'therapeutic' because I've added chocolate chunks, which I picked up at the supermarket, into the batter, and if all goes well, they should end up as lovely lumps of chocolate in the middle of the cake. Either that, or they'll just fall to the bottom in a molten mess. Either way, it's still chocolate, so who cares?

Once it's baked, cooled and put safely into a tin, so I'm not tempted to just sit and eat it, I go upstairs and strip all the sheets off of my bed, putting on clean ones, before going into the guest room and removing all the bedding in there too. No-one ever sleeps in this room, but I still change the sheets every so often, even if only because they get dusty. I decide I'll remake the bed later, or maybe tomorrow. I'm too tired to make up another double bed right now.

The washing machine and tumble dryer are stacked, one on top of the other, in the small lobby between the kitchen and bathroom and I carry all the linen out there, putting both sheets in together and sorting all of the pillow cases into one pile, leaving the duvets separate. It may take a few washes doing it this way, but if I put it all in together, everything gets tangled and nothing gets properly cleaned.

I've just finished, when there's a knocking on the door and I wander through the house, pulling it open, my heart stopping as Josh looks down at me.

Despite my promise to myself that I'd listen to his explanation, the sight of him brings back the memories of this last week, and all the pain, and I instinctively try to slam the door shut, feeling it being pushed back against me as he holds up his hand.

"Don't," he says and I look up into his face.

God, he looks exhausted and my heart softens slightly. But only slightly.

Chapter Fourteen

Josh

I keep my hand up against the door, in case Abbie decides to try and slam it shut again.

"Please, just listen to what I have to say," I beg. Her eyes fix on mine, like she's trying to read them, to see inside me. She hesitates and then slowly nods her head, stepping back and folding her arms. She's not going to let me in, but that's okay with me.

"I know I've hurt you," I murmur, leaning against the door frame, so she can't shut the door on me again. "I know I shouldn't have just left like that, but something really did come up and I had to go."

"You couldn't even stop long enough to tell me about it, or to write me a note?" she says and I can hear the hurt in her voice. It cuts through me, like a knife, and I take a half step towards her. She takes one back.

"This wasn't the sort of thing I could tell you in a note, and I got the call at three in the morning. I had to get back to London straight away. It was important."

Her eyes flicker. "And I'm not?"

How could she think that after all the things I said to her? "Yes. Of course you are. You're everything. But this was something that couldn't wait." I push my fingers back through my hair. "Please, let me explain…"

"Why?" Her voice cracks. "Why should I?"

"Because I love you. I know I've hurt you, but please can you just listen to what I have to say? Please, Abbie?" I can hear the desperation in my own voice.

She shrugs her shoulders. "Okay then," she says, and I feel the relief wash over me. At least she's prepared to hear me out.

"Thank you. I suppose I should begin with telling you what happened on Sunday night… well, Monday morning. As I said, I—I got a message in the early hours… I still hadn't gone to bed by then because I was sitting up, thinking about us… or you, to be more precise. After we'd finished our call, I was just… I was just so damn happy, I couldn't sleep, so I sat up, looking out at the bay, remembering how we used to be, thinking about all the things we'd said to each other during the evening, wondering about the future. I knew we weren't all the way there yet, but it was a future I never thought we'd have…" I let my voice fade, but then remember the point at hand and continue, "Anyway, my phone beeped at about three in the morning, and I thought it might be you. I thought you might be texting to say you still couldn't sleep, or that you'd changed your mind and you wanted me to come over. But the message wasn't from you. It was from a woman I—"

"A woman?" Her eyes narrow.

"Yes. She's just a friend, I promise." I hold up my hands. "Well, she's not even that really. She's just a woman I sort of know."

"Is this the 'friend of a friend' you spoke about in your message?" she asks, speaking slowly and taking a slight step forward.

"So you did listen to my messages, then?" I can't help the slight smile that touches the corners of my lips.

"Yes," she admits.

I nod my head and sigh. "Yes. Tonya is the person I mentioned. She'd sent me a message, telling me that our… our mutual friend, who was a woman I dated for a while a few years ago, had been killed in a car accident."

I hear Abbie's gasp as her hand comes up, covering her mouth. "I'm so sorry," she says, moving even closer.

"Her name was Lauren," I explain, still trying to take in how any of this can have happened. "We weren't together for very long… just a couple of weeks, really." I look down at her.

"Is that all? Just a couple of weeks?"

"Yes. It turned out I wasn't very good at being with other people, for the simple reason that they weren't you." She frowns, then tilts her head to one side.

"If you were only together for such a short time, I don't…" She doesn't need to finish her sentence; I understand her confusion completely.

"You don't understand why Tonya contacted me, and why I had to go dashing back to London?" I ask and she nods. "It's a long story. But I promise, there is a good reason." I suck in a long breath, letting it out slowly, before I begin, "As I said, Lauren and I dated for a couple of weeks, but it didn't work out between us, and we split up and went our separate ways. Then a few weeks later, she sent me a text message, asking if we could meet up for a drink. I said 'no', because I thought she wanted us to get back together, and I didn't. She was really insistent though. She said it was important. So, I agreed, and I met her after work one evening." I move closer, because I don't know how she's going to react to the next part. "She… she told me she was pregnant. And that the baby was mine."

Abbie blinks twice, her eyes filling with tears. "Pregnant?" she whispers.

"Yes. Lauren made it very clear she didn't want me to propose. She knew, just as well as I did, that we weren't suited to each other…"

"Can I ask something?" Abbie interrupts.

"Of course."

"How did she get pregnant?" She blinks again a couple of times. "I mean… I know how, obviously, but you were always really responsible about things like that… so how did it happen?"

"It was an accident," I reply. "Lauren told me she was on the pill, but even so, the first time we… we used a condom, just to be on the safe side. But the second time…"

"You didn't?"

"No. The problem was that a few days before we even met, Lauren had suffered from a bout of food poisoning…"

Abbie nods. "So the pill didn't work?"

"No. Obviously we didn't know that at the time." I remember Lauren apologising, telling me she felt it was her fault; she should've realised it wouldn't work… "Anyway, these things happen. We talked it through and Lauren said she wanted to keep the baby. She was in her early thirties – a year or two younger than me – and she had a good job. She felt confident she could manage. She said she just wanted to let me know. She felt she owed me that, but she didn't want me to feel obliged to do anything." I shake my head, remembering the conversation. "She said she felt bad. She was the one who'd instigated it, really – the sex, I mean – and she was worried I'd think she was trying to trap me and my money. I didn't think that. She wasn't that kind of woman. And anyway, we were both responsible."

Abbie nods her head. "So what happened? Did you… feel obliged?" Her voice is barely audible.

"Of course I did. He's my son."

She gasps again. "Y—You have a son?"

"Yes." I nod my head, and I can't help but smile. "I told her I'd support them financially; that I'd pay for childcare if she wanted to carry on working, and I'd do anything else she wanted. She said I could be involved as much or as little as I wanted, and she wouldn't give me the role of a glorified uncle; she'd make it clear to our child, and to any partner she might have in the future, that I was the father. We… we stayed friends. Well, I suppose we became friends really. It was very civilised. I went to the scans and I was there at the birth." I move closer to her again, knowing that has to be hard to hear, and is bound to bring back memories for her.

"Do you still see him?"

"Yes. It was hard at first, because Lauren breast fed, but I'd take him for a few hours at a time, or I'd go to Lauren's apartment and see Ben there…"

"His name's Ben?" Abbie smiles.

"Yes. When he got a bit older, he'd come and stay with me. I think Lauren appreciated that. It meant she could get her life back a little, and get a decent night's sleep. She started dating again too, because she knew Ben was safe with me."

"Did you?" she asks.

"Date?" I clarify and she nods. "No. I haven't seen anyone in the last few years. Not since Lauren. And that wasn't because I was hung up on her, before you start wondering, but because I finally worked out that I was still too hung up on you to be of much use to anyone else." She nods her head slowly. "It worked okay for Lauren though… even if she didn't have much success with men. They tended to run a mile when they heard about Ben."

"So what happened last weekend?" Abbie asks, leaning against the doorframe herself now, our arms touching.

"Well, when I decided to come back to Porthgowan, I went to see her. I explained my decision, and that I wasn't running out on Ben, or my responsibilities, but that I had some things I needed to deal with. She… she asked if it was about a woman, and I said 'yes'." I look down at Abbie. "I told her about us. I hope you don't mind, but I thought she had the right to know why I needed the time to myself…"

"I don't mind," Abbie whispers.

"I explained what had happened between us, and how I felt, and she said I made more sense once she knew my story. She said she always thought I had unfinished business… I—I told her you wouldn't be in Porthgowan, but that I needed to come back here to work things out. She understood and said she and Ben would be there when I got back… and that if I did decide to stay here, we'd cope. We'd work something out." I shake my head. "She was a very understanding kind of woman."

"She sounds it."

"Anyway, she'd just started seeing a guy called Dan. They worked together and, for once, he wasn't fazed by Ben. They got along really well, and I think Lauren was kind of hopeful. But me leaving and coming down here gave her a problem: it meant they couldn't go out on their own so much. I was really apologetic about that, given that their relationship was so new, but she said it was fine. Her friend Tonya was due back in the country soon anyway." I stop speaking, realising I'm not explaining this properly. "Tonya's a model," I add. "She works abroad most of the time."

Abbie nods in understanding.

"So, last weekend, Tonya came back and on Sunday evening, Dan and Lauren went out for dinner, somewhere in north London. They… they were driving back, when a truck ran the lights and t-boned Dan's car." Abbie sucks in a breath. "Lauren was killed outright. Dan died the following day."

"Oh… my God." Abbie steps right in front of me. "I'm so sorry."

She said that earlier, but now I know she really means it. I can hear it in her voice and see it in her eyes. "Thanks," I whisper, looking down at her. "It's sad. I'm sad. For both of them. Dan was a nice guy. I may not have loved Lauren, but we were friends, and she was the mother of my son, so I cared about her. And I'm sorry that Ben won't grow up knowing her, and probably won't remember her, because she was a great mum."

A tear falls onto Abbie's cheek and she brushes it away. Part of me wonders if she's crying over Molly and what she missed out on herself, or whether she's crying for Lauren, and for Ben. It wouldn't surprise me if she was; her heart is like that. Either way, I wish I could hold her. The thing is, I can't. Not yet. I don't know where I stand with her.

"What's happening about Ben?" she asks, sniffling slightly. "Who's looking after him now?"

"I am." I decide to take a huge gamble and ask her, "Do you want to meet him?"

Her eyes widen in surprise, but she doesn't seem upset. "Meet him?"

"Yes. He's in the car." I've parked it right outside the door, immediately behind me and I walk around to the passenger side, looking back at her. "Don't panic. He was asleep when we got here, and I left the window open… I'm not completely irresponsible."

"I didn't think you were," she says, over the top of my car.

I open the door and lean in, unstrapping Ben from his car seat. "Come on, Champ… there's someone I want you to meet." He looks up at me, bleary eyed as I hoist him into my arms and grab Flopsy, his toy rabbit, without whom we daren't go anywhere, especially at the moment. Ordinarily, he'd struggle and try to get down, wanting to walk by himself, but the last few days have been strange for him, and he's become a little clingy, which isn't that surprising, in the circumstances.

Nudging the car door shut, I walk back around, keeping my eyes on Abbie, who's fixated with Ben. "This is Abbie," I say to him, unsure whether to add 'daddy's friend', or 'daddy's girlfriend' or to go for the absolute truth and say 'the love of daddy's life'. But I decide not to confuse him any more than he is already, and don't add anything – for now. Considering how quiet and withdrawn he's been since Lauren's death, he surprises me by smiling and leaning towards Abbie, and I guess that's proof, if it were needed, that he's my son… he's drawn to her, just like I am.

"Hi Ben," she says, stepping aside and letting us enter the house, before closing the door.

"Hello," he replies quietly, rubbing his eyes and yawning.

"Are you still tired?" Abbie asks and he shakes his head as she glances at me. "Have you had lunch?" she says, even though it's nearly three o'clock.

"Yes, we stopped on the way," I reply, and she looks at Ben again.

"In that case, would you like a biscuit and something to drink?"

He nods his head and I go to lower him to the floor, but he clings to my neck. "It's okay," I whisper, "I've got you." Abbie glances at me again, her brow furrowing. "He's just a bit unsure about things at the moment," I murmur and she nods her head, then reaches up and brushes her fingertips against his cheek.

"Let's find you something to eat, shall we?" she says, and turns, leading us into the kitchen.

I follow behind her, relieved that she at least heard me out, and that she seems to have taken to Ben so well, and he to her, even if she and I do still have a lot to talk about.

In the middle of the kitchen table, there's large cake tin and a batch of cookies, cooling on a wire rack.

Abbie pulls out the chair at the end of the table and I sit, with Ben on my lap. "What will he drink?" she asks me.

"Milk, or water… not juice. Lauren is… Lauren *was* really strict about that." I correct the tense, wondering how often I'm going to make that mistake.

"Okay." Abbie nods and crouches down beside us. "What would you like, Ben?" she asks. "Milk, or water?"

"Milk," he says, after a moment's hard thought, and Abbie gets up, going to the fridge.

"What do you say?" I turn to Ben and he looks up at me.

"Please?" he says.

"Good boy," I reply, smiling as Abbie pours a small glass of milk, before getting a plate from the cupboard, putting a cookie on it from the cooling rack and breaking it in half. She places the glass and plate in front of us and Ben leans forward to start eating, but I pull him back.

"And what do you say this time?"

"Tank you?" He looks at Abbie and she smiles.

"You're welcome," she says, and goes over to the stove, picking up the kettle and taking it to the sink to fill it with water, while Ben tucks into his cookie.

"Come and sit down," I say to Abbie as she turns away from the sink.

"I was just going to make some tea." She looks self conscious and shy again, like she did when I first came back.

"It can wait." I reach over and pull out the nearest chair. "Come and sit down."

She hesitates for a moment, and then puts the kettle down on the end of the table and comes over, sitting down beside us, her eyes fixed on Ben.

"Are you alright?" I ask her.

She glances back to me. "He's lovely, Josh," she replies, and I notice that she didn't answer my question.

"Yes, he is. I'm hardly unbiased, but I think he's perfect."

"What's going to happen to him?" she whispers, looking worried.

"He's my son. He's staying with me."

"For good?"

"Yes. He's been with me ever since I got up to London last Monday morning. Tonya kept him at Lauren's place and I drove straight there and picked him up. I've spent some of the last week talking things through with Lauren's dad. I'd never even met him before this happened, but he explained to me that he was really close to Lauren, especially since his wife – Lauren's mum – died a few years ago. All of this has obviously been really hard for him, and he's been struggling with a lot of it, especially as they haven't released the body yet, so he can't organise the funeral..."

"Why's that?" Abbie asks, looking intrigued.

"Because there has to be an inquest."

"How long will that take?"

"God knows. Richard – that's Lauren's dad – said he'll keep me posted, but there's so much red tape..." She nods her head and we both look down at Ben, who's nearly finished his cookie. "I know having Ben is going to mean adjusting my life," I say quietly, hugging him, "but I'm in a position to do that. And anyway, I *want* to do it. He belongs with me now. But I promised Richard and Tonya, before I came back here, that whatever happens, I'll make sure they see Ben regularly. I'm not going to cut them out. I think they were concerned I would... but I couldn't do that."

"Good." Her voice is soft, concerned.

"The thing is, I had to explain to them both that I didn't know exactly where we're going to be living."

She looks at me, that familiar furrow forming and I wish I could lean down and kiss it. "Why not?" she asks.

"Because that decision is yours."

"Mine?" she looks surprised.

"Yes. I had to come down here today, to explain things to you, but that doesn't necessarily mean we're going to stay."

"It doesn't?" I can definitely hear fear in her voice and, for the first time since she refused to take my calls last Monday, I let myself hope, just a little.

"No. You see, I need you to decide... If you think you can forgive me for leaving like I did on Monday, now that you know why I did so, and if you think we have a chance to be together, allowing for the fact that Ben is part of my life, and he's not going anywhere, then I'll work something out. I'll find a way to stay here, although I don't know how I'm going to do that yet. I can't really take Ben to the pub, and pretty much everything I own is still in London… but I'll find a way. I'll book us into a hotel for a few days, and then I'll rent us a house, or something. If you want me to. But, if you don't… if you're still too angry with me right now to forgive me, if you need time to think it through and work things out… well, then I'm going to wait for you, just like I said I would. I'm not letting you go, and I'm not giving up. And I'm not offering you the option of giving up either. Not ever. We're meant to be together, Abbie, and you know it, but if you need time to adjust, to come to terms with this and to forgive me for hurting you, then I'll give you that. The only thing is, that if that's what you decide, then I might have to do my waiting in London, because Ben needs some stability now and I can't just book us into a hotel indefinitely, not knowing how long you might take to let me back in. It wouldn't be fair on him… And I'm sorry if that sounds like I'm putting you second, but I'm not. I just have to think about Ben, and what's best for him, especially at the moment. So, if that's your decision, I'll take him back to London with me, and I'll miss you like hell… but I'll wait for you, and when you're ready to talk, I'll come home again."

"You want me to decide that?" she asks, looking up into my eyes.

"Yes."

"Right now?"

I smile down at her. "No. I can book us into a hotel for a few days, regardless. It'll be like a holiday for Ben. What we can't do is stay in a hotel for an unlimited time, without any end in sight, without any certainty to his life. That wouldn't be good for him."

"No," she says, thoughtfully. "No, it wouldn't." She glances at him as he nestles into me, Flopsy cuddled up in his arms, a smile forming on her lips, before she turns back to me and it fades, my hope fading with it. "Why didn't you tell me about him before Lauren died? We spent quite a lot of time together in those few days, and I would have thought informing me that you have a son is quite important."

I sigh, loudly. "It is. And I wasn't deliberately hiding him from you, or keeping secrets. But my visit here didn't turn out the way I'd planned.

As I've already explained, I wasn't expecting to find you here. I was thinking I'd spend a few weeks in Porthgowan, getting my head straight, and that then I'd go back to London and work out what I was going to do next with my life. Finding you here changed everything – well, and nothing, being as it really just confirmed that I've always loved you, and that trying to leave you in the past was a really dumb idea. But then it seemed important to try and work out what was happening between us before I brought Ben into the equation, for his sake as much as anything. I didn't want to introduce him into our relationship, when I wasn't sure that we even had one. And let's face it, you practically threw me out when I first came round…"

"But then you came back," she reasons, "and we talked… and things got better, didn't they?"

"Of course they did. You know they did. Everything was perfect… so perfect. And then last Sunday… after we talked, and we kissed and I told you how I feel about you, I started thinking that I needed to tell you about my past. It was one of the many things that was keeping me awake that night… one of the thoughts about our future. I—I knew I couldn't just announce it though. I couldn't just say to you, 'Oh, by the way, I've got a two and a half year old son, from a brief relationship I had a few years ago'. That would have been like rubbing salt into your very open wounds."

She sucks in a breath and puts her hands over her mouth – both of them this time – and I know I can't just sit here talking like this anymore, so I stand, holding Ben on one side, and take Abbie's hand, pulling it from her mouth and raising her to her feet, looking down at her.

"I know about Molly," I whisper and tears brim in her eyes. "I've always known."

"How?" she breathes.

"My mother called to tell me… the day after Molly was born."

She purses her lips, trying not to cry. "You said 'born'," she murmurs, wide-eyed now. "You didn't say 'died', even though she never lived."

"I know. Because that's how I think about her."

"And yet, you didn't say anything to me about her?" she says, tucking her hair behind her ear. "Not in all the time we spent together last week? Even when you were meeting me from the church?"

"No. I hoped you'd tell me about her one day… when you were ready to trust me."

She turns away, trying to hide her tears, I think. "I do trust you," she mumbles, and I step closer, so we're almost touching.

"In that case, will you please listen to what I have to say?"

I know I said I'd give her time to decide, but I need to know… for my sake, not Ben's. Thankfully, she nods her head.

"When Tonya called me last week, I had to put Ben first, because he's my son and he needed me. But because of your situation – because of Molly – I couldn't tell you about it. I couldn't tell you about him, and then just leave you here by yourself to deal with that. It wouldn't have been fair to you. I know I hurt you by leaving, but I'm fairly sure it would have hurt you more if you'd discovered that I have a son, after everything you've lost, and then I'd run out on you, to go and take care of my child. If I got that wrong, I will do whatever I have to, to make it right. I'm sorry that what I did hurt you and I promise I won't ever do that to you again. If you'll give me another chance, if you'll have me back, then I'll find a way to stay here. Permanently. I'm not sure how yet, but I'll find a way, and I promise you I will do whatever it takes to make you happy… Just tell me what you want me to do, Abbie… Do you want me to stay?"

She stares at me, her eyes searching mine, for a full minute; the longest minute of my life… and then she nods her head, as she starts to cry, and with my free arm, the one I'm not using to hold my son, I pull her close to me.

"I love you, Abbie," I whisper. "I love you so much."

I wish she'd say it back. God, how I wish she would. She doesn't. But I know she will… one day.

Chapter Fifteen

∽∾∾

Abbie

I pull back eventually, wiping my tears on the backs of my hands, to find that Josh is gazing into my eyes, and Ben is staring at me, looking confused. I'm not surprised. On top of everything else that's happened, he's now being confronted with a weeping woman.

"I'll finish making the tea," I murmur, glancing up at Josh, and he gives me an understanding nod of his head, before letting me go. I turn away, so Ben can't see my tear-stained face, and put the kettle on to boil, then fetch a couple of cups from the cupboard.

"Drink your milk, Champ," Josh says from behind me and I look back, to see him sitting down again and moving the glass of milk in front of Ben, who picks it up with both hands and takes a long sip.

I stare at the man before me; the man I thought I knew so well, as he sits at my table with his son, their two dark heads almost touching, picking up stray cookie crumbs from Ben's red t-shirt, and putting them on the plate. This is a new side to Josh; one I haven't seen before, for obvious reasons, and I turn away again, busying myself with the teapot for a moment, trying to take on board the revelations of the last half hour or so. Josh is a father. He has a truly beautiful son. And, while I'm still feeling a little bruised that he didn't tell me about Ben before the tragedy of Lauren's death, I do understand his reasons. Well, I do now that I know he was aware of Molly. He was aware of her all along… And I think I love him even more for letting me be myself when he first came back here; for not pushing me into talking about her, or sharing her; for not trying to force himself into our lives.

"Shall we go and find your toys?" Josh's voice breaks into my thoughts and I turn to find him looking down at Ben, who's now standing on the floor, holding his father's hand. That seems like a breakthrough, considering Ben wouldn't let Josh go when they first came in. Ben nods his head, and Josh looks over at me, getting to his feet. "We'll only be a minute."

"Okay."

He smiles, his eyes boring into mine for a second or two, before they turn and leave the room. On my own, I finish preparing the tea, trying hard not to think too much more about everything that's happened. Josh and I have a lot to talk about still, and overthinking isn't going to help.

"Let's put it down on here, shall we?" Josh says, coming back into the room, carrying a small wooden carry case in one hand, while Ben clasps the other, his toy rabbit still tucked under his arm. He settles Ben at the table and opens the case in front of him to reveal a wooden tool set, complete with pretend saw, spanners, and screwdrivers, along with several pieces of wood with holes in, and large, oversized screws, and nuts and bolts, which presumably have to be fitted and tightened accordingly. Without hesitating, Ben starts to take out various tools, and sets to 'work', and after a couple of minutes' supervising, Josh moves away, coming to stand beside to me, while still keeping an eye on his son.

"You didn't answer my question earlier," he says as he puts his arm around my waist, pulling me closer to him, and because I'm wearing my blue skirt and top, his fingers caress the bare skin just above my waistband, the gentle contact forcing me to suck in a sharp breath.

"W—What question?" I stutter.

"Are you alright?" he asks.

"I—I think so."

"What does that mean?" He looks down at me, concern etched on his face.

"Well, I'm not going to pretend this hasn't come as a bit of a surprise," I whisper, nodding at Ben.

"I know. I'm sorry."

"You don't have to be sorry. It's just going to take a bit of getting used to, that's all."

"Thank you," he whispers in my ear, his soft breath on my neck making my heart beat faster.

"What for?" I lean into him, just a little, nestling against his chest.

"For being prepared to get used to it; for giving me another chance. I know I let you down, and I meant what I said… I promise, I'll never do it again."

I twist slightly, looking up into his face. For a moment, I wonder if he's going to kiss me, and my nerves are so heightened that I wish he would, just to soothe me, to calm me, but right then, Ben drops a screwdriver on the floor, and with a slight sigh and a smile, Josh releases me, going over to pick it up, and replace it on the table. I notice that Ben's rabbit has fallen down too, on the other side, and go around to rescue him.

"Who's this?" I ask, handing back the soft, brown, fluffy toy, its ears disproportionately long, when compared to the rest of its body.

Ben glances up at me, cuddling the rabbit. "Lopsy," he says, rather sullenly.

"Lopsy?" I query and, after a second or two, he nods his head.

"He means 'Flopsy'," Josh says. "Named on account of his ludicrously long ears." Ben looks up at Josh and nods his head, and then tries to put the rabbit on his lap, so he can play with his tool kit again. All that happens though is that Flopsy falls to the floor. I retrieve him a second time, passing him back to Ben, and then an idea strikes me and I go into the living room and grab a few cushions from the sofa, where I notice there's a small canvas bag which Josh must have put there when he and Ben went out to the car earlier. I ignore it for now and return to the kitchen, bringing the cushions with me and putting them on the chair beside Ben, the one I was sitting on a few minutes ago.

"Why don't you put Flopsy on here?" I suggest. "Then he can see what you're doing, but he won't keep falling down."

"That's a good idea, isn't it, Champ?" Josh says, grinning at me, as Ben leans over and tries to settle Flopsy on the chair. He can't quite reach though, so I help him out, moving the chair around to the end of the table, literally right next to him, and once the rabbit is firmly seated, with a bird's eye view of the table, Ben seems happy to continue his woodworking.

"You're a genius," Josh whispers as we both move away.

"Not really." I pull out the chair at the other end of the table, sitting down, and Josh takes a seat to my right, moving closer to me, so our heads are almost touching as we lean forward. "Do you think he'll be alright?" I ask him, pouring out the tea.

"In the long term, you mean?" he queries, and I nod my head. "Yes, I do. I'm not saying it's going to be easy. I'm sure it'll take a while, and lots of love and attention, but he will be fine. I'll make sure of it." Josh puts his hand over mine and we sit for a moment. "Can I ask if that tin contains C.A.K.E?" he asks eventually, nodding towards the cake tin in the middle of the table.

"Yes… did you want some?"

"I'd better not."

I smile. "Why? Did you put on some weight the last time you were here?"

He grins. "Probably. But that's not the reason I'm saying 'no'."

"Oh? Have you gone off my cooking then?"

He shakes his head. "No. But if Ben sees C.A.K.E. he'll want some, especially if it's the same kind of C.A.K.E. that you made last time."

"Well, it is… but why on earth do you keep spelling it out like that?"

Josh smirks. "Because Ben has ears like radar when it comes to that word. And when it comes to that particular variety, I'm afraid there aren't enough wipes in the world to clear up the mess he gets into."

I giggle, because I can't help myself and Josh smiles at me. "I do like that sound," he says and lifts my hand to his lips, kissing my palm gently, his eyes fixed on mine. "And I do love you." He keeps staring for just a second longer, and I know he wants me to say it back. I want to as well, but I can't. Not yet.

He smiles and kisses my fingers, before letting go of my hand and reaching into his back pocket, pulling out his phone. "I suppose I'd better try and find us a hotel," he murmurs. "I'll start looking for a house tomorrow, but for the next few days, it's going to have to be a hotel…" His voice fades as he starts to scroll up and down on his phone. "I think we drove past a sign to a hotel, or a spa, or something, about five or six miles back," he says. "I can't remember the name… it certainly wasn't there when I used to live here…" He scrolls some more.

"You're actually going to stay in a hotel?"

He looks up at me, his thumb stilling over the phone screen. "Yes. Just until I can work out something else. Ideally, I'd like to find a house in the village, but that probably won't happen." He smiles and glances over at Ben. "I'd like for him to grow up here," he says wistfully, turning back to me. "We had a great childhood, didn't we – in spite of my mother."

"Stay," I say, on impulse, reaching out and placing my hand on his arm.

He puts his phone down and covers my hand with his. "I'm going to… *We're* going to. I just said. I'll find us somewhere as close as possible. I'll probably keep the apartment in London, at least for now, because we…"

"No, I mean stay here," I interrupt, sitting forward, desperate for him to stop talking and understand my meaning.

He does stop talking, but the look in his eyes tells me he doesn't really understand. "Here?" he whispers.

"Yes."

"With you?" His eyes widen and I can hear the emotion in his voice, and I know I have to make myself completely clear.

"Yes. But… but not in the same… I mean, I've got three bedrooms…" I'm getting flustered and I know I'm blushing. "Well, I've got two bedrooms and a box room, but that's more than big enough for a child's bed, and a small wardrobe or chest of drawers…" I'm rambling now. "And there's a guest room across the landing from my bedroom."

He smiles just slightly, nodding his head. "Can I ask you something?" he says.

"Yes."

"Are you offering us somewhere to stay, just as a temporary fix, until I can find us something else, because you're a kind person, and we're in need of help? Or would it be wrong, and really, really insensitive of me to read something else into this? Something more permanent?"

I suck in a deep breath, before answering, "I want to help you… obviously I do. What's happened to Ben, and to you, is awful, and I want to help however I can…"

"But?" he prompts, sitting forward, sensing I have more to say.

I take my courage in both of my hands. "But I want you back, Josh." He sighs, closing his eyes, just for a moment. When he opens them, I can see the depth of his love, and I know I have to be honest with him. "There are things we need to talk about. Actually, there are a lot of things we need to talk about, and we need to get to know each other again, and having you living in a hotel, or in a house in another village, miles down the road, isn't going to help with that. But it's going to take time for me to adjust… and I'm not ready to um…" I lower my voice, aware of Ben's presence in the room, even if he is preoccupied. "I'm not ready to sleep with you yet," I mumble under my breath.

Josh reaches over, cupping my cheek with his hand, caressing my skin with the side of his thumb. "You don't need to whisper," he says. "I'm pretty sure Ben doesn't get 'sleeping together' as a thing, so you're on safe ground with him." He shifts closer. "And with me."

"Why? Don't you get it either?" I lean in to his touch, trying not to smile and feeling grateful that, between us, we've lightened the moment.

He chuckles. "Oh, I get it," he replies. "Especially when it comes to you. But what I'm saying is, you're safe with me. There's no pressure to do anything. I'm just grateful you said 'yet' at the end of that sentence, that's all." He leans forward and kisses my forehead. "I love you, Abbie," he murmurs into me, his lips pressed against my skin. "And I'll wait for you… for as long as it takes. For as long as you need."

We've almost finished our tea, watching Ben play with his toolkit, and having a cookie each, before the first problem occurs to me.

"There's no bed," I say all of a sudden, reaching over and putting my hand on Josh's arm again.

"Sorry?" He turns to look at me.

"In the box room… there's no bed. There's no furniture at all, actually. I'm sorry. I don't know why I didn't think of it earlier."

He smiles. "What about your guest room? Is there a bed in there?"

"Yes."

"Then we'll be fine," he says. "I'll order some furniture for the box room, and Ben and I can sleep in the guest room, until it arrives." He gets up, going over to Ben. "Do you want to come and see your new bedroom?" he says.

Ben looks up at him, a broad grin on his face, and nods his head, taking Josh's offered hand, jumping down from the chair, and collecting Flopsy from his seat before tucking him under his arm.

Josh turns back to me. "Do you want to lead the way?" he suggests and I stand, taking them upstairs and into the box room, which the three of us almost fill.

Josh has carried Ben up the stairs and then put him down on the floor, crouching beside him. "What do you say about putting your bed along that wall?" he points to the wall by the window. "And then we can get you a cupboard for your clothes, and put it here." He points to the wall opposite, behind the door.

Ben nods his head. "Now?"

Josh chuckles. "Not today… maybe tomorrow, or the next day." Ben's face falls. "For now, you can sleep with Daddy… okay?"

"Shall I show you?" I offer and Ben looks at me, uncertainly.

"Come on." Josh stands, offering Ben his hand, which he takes and we go along the landing to the guest room. It's only when we get inside that I remember I haven't put on the clean sheets yet.

"I'll fetch some bedding," I say quickly, and leave the room again, going to the airing cupboard on the landing, pulling out a set of white bedding, and taking it back with me, hearing Ben's laughter and the odd squeal of delight as I approach. Inside, Josh is rolling around on the mattress with him and I stand, watching them, trying hard not to think about the lost chances, and choking back my tears.

Josh notices me suddenly and stops, giving Ben one last tickle before getting to his feet and lifting Ben into his arms, walking over to me. "Sorry," he murmurs. "We got carried away."

I shake my head. "Don't apologise." I move further into the room and dump the bedding on the chair by the window. "Why don't you go downstairs, and I'll join you when I've done this?"

"Because we can get this done a lot quicker if we do it together," Josh replies. "Just give me two minutes."

He leaves the room, still carrying Ben, returning a couple of minutes later, with the small canvas bag that I noticed on the sofa earlier, and going over to the corner of the room. He kneels down and puts Ben on the floor, opening the bag and pulling out some wooden trains and carriages, which he locks together, letting Ben push them along the carpet, with Flopsy by his side. Once he's happy, Josh comes over to me.

"Sorry about that," he says. "I didn't want him to get bored." He smiles. "I've got some track in the back of my car, but he can just play with the trains for now."

"How much did you manage to squeeze into your boot?" I ask him.

"More than I ever thought possible. In terms of toys, it was the tool kit, and the trains, plus there's a small wooden garage thing. I couldn't get anything else in; not if we were going to bring clothes too. I decided to bring his favourite toys from Lauren's place, so he'd have some continuity."

I smile at him, and then turn to pick up the bedding, but he puts his hands on my shoulders and twists me back around to face him. "Are you sure you're okay with this?" he asks.

"Okay with what?"

"With Ben… being here. I know it can't be easy for you…" His voice fades, but his eyes remain locked with mine.

I have to tell him the truth. "Honestly?" I whisper. "I don't know how I feel, except that he's been through a lot over the last few days, and I want to help."

Josh stares at me for just a moment longer, then nods his head, and goes around the other side of the bed. I throw him the sheet and, between us, we start tucking it in under the mattress.

"He doesn't realise what's happened yet," he says after a few minutes. "He just knows Lauren isn't here, and he doesn't understand why."

"He needs time," I say, picking up the pillows and throwing a couple over to him. "And he needs to feel safe and secure." I start pulling on a clean pillowcase. "He'll be safe here... I know he will..." I let my words taper out, looking up. Josh is staring at me, a pillow in one hand. "I—It's how I felt when I first came here."

"Like you needed somewhere safe?" he asks, lowering his voice a little.

"Yes." I drop the pillow and wrap my arms around myself. "I'd been to hell. I needed to find a way back." I look into his eyes. "I still do. That's why I came home." I look around the room. "This house felt like somewhere I could make myself better. One day."

He drops his own pillow now and walks back around the bed, pulling me into his arms. "I want to help," he whispers, echoing my words. "I want to make you feel safe, to make you better." He kisses me gently. "I want to bring you back from hell."

I lean into him and let him hold me for a while, until Ben's 'choo-choo' noises from the corner of the room make me chuckle, and Josh joins in, and then we get back to making up the bed.

Josh takes some rough measurements of the box room, and then we all go downstairs and back into the kitchen, and Josh sits with Ben on his lap, picking up his phone and going online, ordering the junior bed and wardrobe, letting Ben look at the pictures and point to the ones he likes the best. After that, he looks over at me.

"I'm sorry if we seem to be taking over your house, but would it be okay if I ordered a couple of stair gates?"

"Oh God... of course. I didn't think..." I mumble.

Josh smiles. "Why would you? It's not something most people have lying around their house, just in case a toddler they didn't know existed happens to turn up on their doorstep..."

"No, I suppose not." I pause for a moment. "Is there anything else?"

He shakes his head. "There's nothing I can think of at the moment." He glances around. "I'm sure things will come to us…" He smiles, his eyes shining.

"What?" I ask, wondering what he's thinking.

"Nothing," he replies, and then leans closer to me. "I just like talking about 'us', that's all."

I can feel myself blushing, even though I can't help smiling, just as Ben yawns expansively.

"I think someone's getting tired again," I say, nodding towards him. He leans into Josh's chest.

"I think you might be right. He didn't sleep as much as I expected on the way down here. Normally, when you put him in a car, he's out like a light, but he managed to stay awake until just this side of Truro." He smiles. "But that might have had something to do with the fact that I'd loaded up a couple of CDs of Disney sing-a-longs and nursery rhymes." I have to purse my lips to stop myself laughing.

"Disney sing-a-longs?" I repeat and he looks over at me.

"Yep. And I'm eternally grateful that there are no witnesses."

"Other than Ben," I remind him.

"I know, but he's on my side." I giggle and Josh leans back, looking down at Ben. "Before I get myself in any more trouble, do you want to come and help Daddy empty the car?" he suggests. "And then we can give you a bath?" Ben seems really enthusiastic about that and clambers down from Josh's lap. "Is that okay with you?" Josh asks, getting to his feet and looking down at me.

"Of course. You don't have to ask. Just make yourselves at home." Josh smiles at me gratefully, his eyes warm and loving. "I—I'll start on the dinner, shall I?" I add, as an afterthought, because it's just dawned on me that we'll need to eat.

"That would be great. Thank you."

"Um… what should I make?" I feel stupid for not knowing what a child of Ben's age will eat, and feel the blush rising up my cheeks.

"Do you have pasta?" Josh asks, taking Ben's hand in his.

"Yes. I've got spaghetti, or penne."

"If you make Ben spaghetti, he'll be your friend for life," he says, to my surprise.

"Isn't penne easier?" I ask. "Less messy?"

He shakes his head, "Cut-up spaghetti is a lot less messy than you'd think."

I nod, feeling slightly ignorant again, and they go out into the living room, leaving me to ponder the evening meal.

I decide on a tomato sauce, with some finely chopped vegetables, working on the theory that it's quick and, if the spaghetti needs to be cut up, then anything small should be okay. I grate some cheese to go on top, set the table for the three of us, putting out a glass of water for Ben, and opening a bottle of red wine for Josh and myself. I don't know about him, but after today, I could do with a glass... or two.

"Whatever you're making, it smells delicious." I turn at the sound of Josh's voice and see him standing in the doorway from the bathroom, carrying Ben in his arms, who's now wearing blue and grey striped short pyjamas, his hair slightly damp and combed neatly.

"Did you find everything you needed?" I ask.

"Yes, thanks," Josh replies, walking past me and back into the living room, returning a few moments later, carrying a booster seat and bib, while Ben struggles to get down. "Do you think he might be hungry?" Josh adds, smiling.

"I think it's possible." I smile back. "Do you want some help?"

"No, I'm fine, thanks," he replies, depositing the seat on the chair at the end of the table, where Ben sat earlier, before sitting Ben in it, and strapping him in.

"How did you fit that in your car?" I ask him.

"It went in the passenger footwell." He turns to face me, before fastening Ben's bib. "We had to utilise every available space."

"It sounds like it."

"Lopsy sit too," Ben says, distracting us and handing his toy to Josh, who sits the rabbit back on the chair that's still piled with cushions.

I turn back to the stove, giving the sauce one last stir, before picking up the pan of pasta and carrying it over to the sink.

"Here, let me do that," Josh offers.

"I'm fine."

He's beside me in an instant. "It's heavy…" He takes the pan from me. "Where do you want this?"

I put the colander in the sink and leave him to it, fetching the sauce and bringing it back to the sink, tipping the pasta into the pan and stirring the whole lot around.

"That really does smell good," Josh says, leaning over and sniffing.

I smile up at him. "I assumed bowls would be better?" I say, nodding to the dishes I've already set out on the work surface.

"Oh God, yes," he replies, and I dish up a helping of spaghetti, stopping when Josh tells me to, and leaving him to chop it up, while I continue to serve up the remainder for the two of us, keeping a little back, in case Ben should want a second helping.

Josh sprinkles some grated cheese over Ben's and places it in front of him as I bring over our bowls. Ben's dark brown eyes light up and he digs in enthusiastically, and I watch, enthralled as he gets in a huge, smiley mess.

We sit, and Josh pours the wine, raising his glass to mine. "Thank you," he says, looking into my eyes.

"What for?"

"You really need to ask?"

I shake my head and take a sip of wine, swallowing down the fruity, delicate liquid, and taking the bowl of cheese from Josh, our eyes connecting for a moment, before we start eating, and talking, and helping Ben occasionally, when he needs it. As I watch Josh wipe a big piece of spaghetti from Ben's chin, I swallow down my tears, reminding myself that I need to put my feelings to one side, that I need to help this poor young boy, but that I have to remember, Ben is not my child and we're not a family, even though, right now it feels like we could be.

Ben's nearly asleep by the time we've finished eating, so Josh takes him up to bed, staying with him for a while, and I use the time to clear up the kitchen, load the dishwasher, clean down the table and pour us both another glass of wine, moving into the sitting room by the time he comes back down, the wine on the coffee table, and me curled up in the corner of the sofa.

Josh flops down beside me, then twists in his seat, his arm along the back of the couch, turning to face me. "Did you really understand why I was thanking you at dinner?" he asks, and I feel his fingers brush against the back of my neck.

"Yes."

"Why was it then?"

"For letting you stay." I turn to look at him, and he shakes his head, sighing deeply.

"I'm grateful for that," he says, "but that wasn't why I said it."

"Oh?"

"No." He moves closer. "I said 'thank you' because you're giving me another chance… giving us another chance."

"You already thanked me for that earlier," I remind him.

"I know, but I'm not sure I can ever thank you enough. And anyway, I want to be sure…"

"What of?"

"That this is for real. I mean, you're not just doing this out of pity, or something, are you?"

"No. Obviously, I do feel sorry for Ben, and for you. What happened to Lauren is awful, and like I said earlier, I do want to help… but I promise, I'm not doing this out of pity." I hesitate for a moment, and then continue, "I understand now why you left in such a hurry, and why you didn't want to tell me about it over the phone. That would have been a difficult conversation for both of us, and I'm not sure I would have been able to handle it… hearing about Lauren and Ben, and that part of your life, if I hadn't been able to see you."

"See me?" He looks surprised.

"Yes. Seeing the love in your eyes and the smile on your face when you talk about Ben, it makes it easier…"

"Makes what easier?"

"The memories of last week. Knowing why you left… that you had something more important to do—"

"Not *more* important," he interrupts, sitting forward. "Just important. Ben's mother had just died. I had to get to him."

"I understand that. I really do."

"I'm not sure you do. You seem to think that you're not as important to me as Ben; and you are."

I swallow, trying not to let the lump that's building in my throat escape. "It… It's not that."

"Then what is it?" He moves his hand, cupping my face now. "Tell me."

"It hurt so much," I murmur, struggling to speak. "It hurt that you left right after we'd kissed… after all those things you'd said to me. I—I wondered whether you'd planned your departure… timed it like that, as some kind of revenge against me."

"Revenge?" He sits back, staring down at me. "What on earth for?"

"For breaking us up, all those years ago."

"Why would I do that? We talked through all that, Abbie. I told you, I don't blame you for what happened back then. It was my fault for letting you go." I don't agree with him, but I can't speak. "I love you so much," he whispers, moving close to me again, placing both of his hands on my cheeks now, looking deep into my eyes. "I would never intentionally hurt you…"

"I sort of worked that out," I manage to say, "when you started phoning so often."

"Then why didn't you take my calls?"

"Because I didn't understand your messages. I didn't understand at the time why you couldn't just tell me what the problem was. I didn't know what was going on and I—I felt rejected… like you didn't want me anymore."

"Oh God…" He leans in, kissing me gently on my lips, his touch soft and comforting. "I never meant for you to feel like that. I would never reject you." He sighs again, leaning back and looking down at me. "I ache for you – all the time. Literally every minute of the day. Just because I've suddenly become a full-time dad, in the saddest of circumstances, doesn't mean I'm not still a man, and that I don't still need you, and want you… so, so much."

He brushes his lips across mine once more and I hear myself moan, right before he pulls away again and I wonder about asking him not to.

"If I'm going to wait for you, I'd better stop that." He smiles down at me and reaches over, picking up my wine glass and handing it to me, before taking his own and clinking them together. "Thank you," he says again.

"You don't have to keep saying that."

"Yes, I do."

We both take a sip of wine, and I put my glass down first. "Does Ben ask about his mother?" I ask, breaking the charged atmosphere.

"He has done – just the once, so far." Josh puts down his own glass now and moves closer to me, putting his arm around me, which feels soothing. "We were at Richard's house, and I suppose it was natural that he'd ask about Lauren, because he's used to visiting his grandfather with her, not me."

"Yes, of course." I turn and look up at him. "What did you say to him?"

He frowns slightly. "I didn't get the chance to say anything. Richard distracted him with some cake and put the TV on."

"Oh. Was that wise?"

"Not in my view, no. But what could I say? The man had just lost his daughter, I could hardly start an argument with him about her son…"

I want to tell him that Ben's his son too, but I think he already knows that and I nestle back down against him, sensing his disappointment, or perhaps it's frustration – or both. "I assume he's being clingy with you because he's not used to being away from his mum for so long?" I decide to change the subject, just slightly.

"Yes. The longest he's stayed with me is four days, when Lauren had to go on a course, but he was only just over a year old then, so he probably doesn't remember it. At the moment, I imagine all the changes are confusing the hell out of him."

"Then we'll have to make sure he feels safe, and reassured and that you have the time and space to talk to him when he has questions," I muse, almost to myself, and Josh twists me around, holding me in his arms and looking deep into my eyes.

"I've always known that I love you," he murmurs, and kisses me very gently on my lips, "and I even know why I love you, although the reasons are too numerous to list… but if I was ever in any doubt, or if I needed another reason, I just have to listen to you, and it's right in front of me, staring me in the face."

I know it sounds pathetic, but by nine-thirty, Josh and I are yawning ourselves and, after we've cleared away and locked up, we head upstairs to bed.

We don't kiss again and our 'goodnight' outside my bedroom door is a little awkward. I suppose some tension between us is only to be expected though; after all, Josh has made it very clear that he still wants me, and although I'm still not ready, I have to admit that his kisses have got me thinking…

I change into my short pyjamas, climb into bed, switch off my light and turn over, thoughts of Molly coming into my head for the first time in hours, and the guilt washes over me. How could I have forgotten her so easily, just because Josh is back, and just because there's another child living here now? What does that say about me? I screw my eyes tight shut, trying not to cry, but a sob escapes my lips, followed by another, and another. How could I do such a thing? I roll over and bury my head in my pillow, weeping, and murmuring, "Sorry," over and over into the darkness.

The gentle knocking on my door startles me and I sit up, covering my mouth with my hand to stifle my own cries.

"Abbie? It's me." Josh's voice sounds from the other side of the door and I switch on my bedside lamp and clamber out of bed, wondering what I can have forgotten to give him, and go over to the door, pulling it open.

"Yes?" I whisper, knowing Ben will be asleep in the room opposite.

"I heard you crying," Josh says, stepping closer. "Can I… Can I do anything?"

I shake my head. "No. Thank you."

"What's wrong?" he asks.

"It's nothing."

"Abbie… it's not nothing."

"What I mean is, I often cry at night. You shouldn't worry about it. I'm sorry I disturbed you." I step back and go to close the door, feeling embarrassed, but he puts his hand up, resting it against the wooden panels.

"How many times?" he muses. "Never say sorry to me… and don't tell me not to worry. Not when you're crying." He takes a step into my bedroom. "Do you want a hug?"

I nod my head, because there's nothing I want more, and he puts his arms around me, pulling me close to him. I realise then that he's not wearing anything on his top half, although I don't really care, and I rest my head against his naked chest as he cradles me.

We stand like that for ages, until I eventually pull back, leaning away, and look up at him.

"I can sit with you until you go to sleep, if you want?" he offers.

"What about Ben?"

He smiles. "He's fast asleep. Do you want me to stay?"

"Would you?"

"Of course."

Without saying anything else, he takes my hand in his and leads me over to my own bed, pulling back the duvet for me to climb in. Once I'm lying down, with my head on the pillows, he covers me over and leans down, kissing my forehead.

"Sleep now," he whispers, and turns off the lamp, then sits beside me, stroking my hair for a while, resting his hand on my hip, and leaving it there. His touch is comfortable, like he belongs…

I wake up, hearing the sound of knocking on my door. My room is bathed in sunshine, peeping through the edges of my curtains and I glance around. Josh isn't here, but I know he was. I can remember his words and his touch. The knocking sounds again.

"Come in," I call, straightening the duvet to make sure I'm covered.

The door opens and I lower my eyes as Ben appears, poking his head around and smiling at me.

"Good morning," I say and he takes a step into the room, looking behind him, as the door opens wider and Josh comes in after him.

"Hello," he says. "We made tea."

I notice the cups he's balancing in one hand, and the glass of milk he's got in the other, and sit up slightly, smiling.

"Do you want to come up here?" I say to Ben, patting the bed, and he smiles, clambering up, climbing over me, Flopsy still tucked under his arm, and plonks himself down in the middle of the mattress. Josh puts the drinks down on my bedside table and sits halfway down the bed, close to Ben, with just my legs between them.

"You don't mind us coming in, do you?" he asks.

"Not when you're bringing me tea, no." I smile over at him.

"How did you sleep?" he asks.

"Very well."

He nods his head. "Good."

"Thank you," I murmur, trying not to blush. "For last night, I mean."

"You're welcome," he says. "Anytime."

Chapter Sixteen

Josh

Abbie gives me another smile, which just melts my heart even more. God, she's incredible. Not only has she taken Ben's existence in her stride, she's opened her home to us, and is willing to give me another chance, despite the fact that I hurt her so much. And I did hurt her; I know that now.

I realised last night, when I heard her crying, how hard she must be finding all of this. That's why I had to come and see her. I couldn't leave her in here by herself. And staying with her while she fell asleep, watching her eyes flutter closed, hearing that change in her breathing, was an honour... a privilege. I stayed and watched her for ages – a lot longer than was strictly necessarily – wondering how the hell I got so lucky.

Ben asks for his drink, but as I go to hand it to him, he crawls up the bed a little, surprising me by moving away from me for the first time since we got here – well, since Lauren's death actually – and settling down beside Abbie, leaning against her slightly, before reaching out for his drink.

Abbie glances up at me, but I don't know what to say. Yesterday, he seemed a little wary of her, which was understandable. He doesn't know her, and I'd just driven him hundreds of miles to a strange place. His confusion was only to be expected. But maybe I got that wrong. Maybe he was just tired, because looking at him now, it seems he's perfectly comfortable with her.

Abbie shifts slightly in the bed, putting an arm around Ben. He doesn't even hesitate, but nestles into her, his head resting against her as he continues to drink his milk. I feel a lump rising in my throat, and see the tears form in Abbie's eyes, knowing how difficult this has to be for her.

To distract her, I pass her her cup of tea and she looks at it and then smiles at me.

"You made me fruit tea?" she says, surprised, as she takes a sip.

"Well, I noticed that you seemed to drink it in the mornings," I reply, sipping my own, which is normal, and made in a pot, even though Abbie wasn't there to tell me to do it that way.

"Just for my first cup of the day," she explains. "It's something I did when I was pregnant and went off tea."

"You? You went off tea?"

She smiles. "I know it sounds unlikely, but it's true," she says. "And since then, I just prefer my first cup of the day to be fruit tea… I don't know why."

I shrug my shoulders. "Do you need a reason?"

"No." Her eyes sparkle at me and she takes another sip from her cup. "Shall we… shall we go for a picnic today?" she asks a little hesitantly, and Ben sits back, grinning and nodding his head quickly.

"I think someone is quite impressed with that idea," I observe.

"We could go to the beach, couldn't we?" Abbie suggests.

"Of course." Ben doesn't know what the beach is, so we may as well be discussing a trip to the moon, but he's excited now and jumps up, just about giving Abbie time to grab his half empty glass, before he starts to leap up and down on her bed.

"That'll do, Champ." I get up, putting down my cup and taking the drinks from Abbie, before I pull him back onto the bed again, noticing that Ben's actions have shifted the duvet to one side, revealing Abbie's skimpy pyjama top, and a very definite hint of what lies beneath. I wasn't unaware of her attire last night, or of how good she looked in it, but she was crying at the time, so my brain was otherwise occupied. Now though… I suck down a breath and struggle to control my reactions to her, especially as my toddler son is wriggling around on the bed, and I'm having to lean over her to restrain him.

"Shall I go and shower?" she says, ducking out from underneath me and getting to her feet.

"It might be wise," I reply, doing my best to avert my eyes. "I'll try and rein this one in and tone down the excitement levels."

Abbie giggles and I turn to look at her, in spite of myself. God, she looks good. It's odd, but I think she looks even better than she did eighteen years ago… and I never would have thought that possible. "Shall I get the breakfast ready for when you're finished?" I ask, grabbing Ben and lifting him into my arms, despite his wriggling. Abbie stops, her smile fading in an instant, and I know I've screwed up. "Sorry," I murmur and go straight to her, standing in front of her. "I should have thought." She shakes her head, but I know she can't talk, and I lean in to her, putting an arm around her waist and pulling her close to me. "Go and have a shower," I whisper in her ear. "Then go and do whatever you need to do… I'll make the breakfast while you're out."

She looks up at me, blinking a few times. "I'll only be gone for half an hour," she says softly.

I shake my head. "Take as long as you need. I'm not going anywhere."

I know porridge is Abbie's staple breakfast, but making it has never been my strong point, so I stick with toast, slicing some bread from a new loaf which I find in her pale blue painted bread bin, and setting out the butter, jams, some honey, and marmalade on the table, before making the tea, all the while keeping half an eye on Ben, who seems happy playing with his toy garage in the corner of the kitchen. Abbie has a toaster, thank goodness, so I don't have to try and work out the Rayburn – not yet, anyway – and I start toasting slices of bread, putting them on a plate when they're cooked, and then deciding to keep them warm in the bottom oven, which seems cooler than the top one. Abbie's been gone for nearly half an hour now, and I know that means she'll be back soon, and even though I'm not dressed yet and am only wearing my shorts, and Ben is still in his pyjamas, I take his hand and lead him outside.

"Come with me," I say, letting him bring a car and Flopsy with him.

I make sure to put the door on the latch, just in case Abbie didn't take her keys, and go to stand at the corner of the house, keeping hold of Ben's hand as we wait, just for a few minutes, until I hear the sound of Abbie's footsteps coming up the lane.

"Look who's here," I say to Ben and he turns, as Abbie approaches, her head bowed, and then pulls on my hand, wanting to go to her, which doesn't surprise me, being as I know I do. But I'm not letting him wander into the road by himself, not even on a quiet lane like this one, so I keep a firm grip on his hand, and we stroll slowly towards her.

She looks up and stops in her tracks, just like she did on that first morning, but then starts walking again, until we're facing each other, Ben standing between us.

She glances down at him, smiling, and then looks back at me. "You're not dressed," she says.

"No."

"And weren't you supposed to be making the breakfast?"

"Yes."

"So why are you out here?"

I take a step closer and whisper, "So I can do this…" and then I put my free arm around her, holding her tight for a few seconds, until I feel Ben tugging on my hand again, and lean back, looking down at him. "Sorry," I say and smile at Abbie, "Ben wants to join in." She's crying, but she nods her head and I bend down and lift Ben up, letting him join in our hug.

After a few minutes, Abbie pulls back and looks up at me, mouthing, "Thank you," as she wipes her tears on the backs of her hands.

I shake my head as we turn and start walking back towards the house, holding Abbie's hand, with Ben cradled in my other arm. "I'm sorry I wasn't here for you last week, and I know it's no consolation, but I thought about you every morning, wishing I could be."

She pushes open the front door and I put Ben down on the floor again, before standing and facing her. "I missed you when you weren't here," she whispers.

"I missed you too."

I lean down and gently brush my lips across hers, but Ben interrupts again, tapping my leg this time.

"Breakfast, Daddy," he says, looking grumpy.

"Okay… you're hungry. I get it." I glance at Abbie. "Sorry."

She attempts a smile, although I'm fairly sure I see a dark shadow cross her eyes, before she turns and we all go through to the kitchen together.

I apologise to Abbie for not attempting to make porridge, and she forgives me, smiling and evidently impressed that I worked out the bottom oven of the Rayburn is for warming.

"I didn't really," I point out. "I just guessed." I butter a slice of toast for Ben, cutting it into fingers and passing the plate to him. "You're going to have to give me some training on that thing." I nod to her stove.

"It's not that difficult."

"It looks it."

She pours the tea for both of us, then takes a sip before she leans back in her seat. "Can I ask you something?"

"Of course."

"Do you think Ben's bothered about us? I mean about us hugging… and kissing?"

"No," I reply. "Why would he be?"

"Well, if he's used to seeing you with Lauren, then he might be confused about seeing you with me."

I shake my head and lean forward, reaching across the table, offering my hand, which she eventually takes in hers. "Except he's not used to seeing me with Lauren. Not in that way. We didn't have that kind of relationship, Abbie. We didn't hug, or kiss, or anything like that. It was entirely platonic… well, it was after we'd split up, anyway." She nods her head.

"And you don't think that maybe we should stop the hugging and kissing… or cut back on it a little, so you can focus on him, and give him your full attention?" she suggests.

"No." I lean even closer, focusing on her eyes. "I'll give Ben all the reassurance he needs, but I won't stop hugging you, or kissing you. I can't. I need you too much."

She opens her mouth and, for a second, I wonder if she's going to say she needs me too, but then she bites her bottom lip and lowers her eyes. In a way I'm relieved. As much as I want her to tell me how she feels, I'd rather she did it when we're alone.

While Abbie starts preparing the picnic, Ben and I shower together. We often do this when he stays with me; it allows me to skip his bath, if I need to, and he thinks it's fun. He loves water – the more the merrier as far as he's concerned. Soap is a whole other thing, but we get there in the end, and once we're dry, I quickly get dressed, while Ben does his best to copy. He's mastered the art of most things now, as long as you give them to him the right way round. Back to front underwear has been known to lead to much hilarity and chasing around my flat, trying to put it right.

By the time we come back out of the bathroom, and into the kitchen, Abbie is already packing things into a cool bag, and Ben lets go of my hand and goes over to her to see what she's doing. The change in him since yesterday – well, since every other day following Lauren's death, actually – is astounding, but if there's one thing I've discovered about having a child, it's that you just have to go with it – whatever it is.

"Do you need any help?" I ask.

Abbie looks up. "No, I'm fine, thanks… Oh, there's some bottled water in the fridge… could you fetch that for me?"

I do as she asks, handing the bottles to her for her to pack away.

"I just need to run upstairs and get some towels, and my sunglasses. And some sunscreen," she says. "You can take the food and start walking to the beach if you want. I'll catch up with you."

I go and stand in front of her. "We'll wait."

"Sure?"

"Yes."

She smiles, and disappears, and Ben and I wander into the living room, where I left his baseball cap, which I pick up and dump on his head. He scowls at me, and I try not to laugh, because this is so much more like the Ben I know.

"If you want to go on the picnic, you're wearing the hat."

He yanks it off, throwing it to the floor, positively glaring at me now. *Fabulous.* I love him being more like his usual self, but I'm really not in the mood for a full-scale tantrum.

"Ben…" I try not to sound frustrated and I crouch down, picking up the hat, and put it back on his head again, just for him to repeat the process.

"Is something wrong?" I turn, looking up, and see Abbie standing at the bottom of the stairs. She's changed into her white sundress, and she's carrying a large canvas bag, and she looks breathtaking.

"No," I manage to say. "I'm just trying to persuade Ben that he needs to wear a hat, that's all."

"And you're not having much success?" She smiles, puts down the bag and comes closer, crouching down beside me and looking at Ben, who gives her a grin.

"None whatsoever," I reply and Abbie gets up again, picking up her own straw hat from one of the hooks behind the door, and coming back over. She crouches down once more, and puts it on her head. *Of course… why didn't I think of that?*

"I'm going to wear my hat," she says, turning her head one way, and then the other, smiling down at Ben. "Do you like it?" He nods his head and Abbie picks up Ben's cap from the floor, handing it to him. "Put yours on," she says, "let me see what you look like."

He plonks the hat on his head, all crooked, and Abbie straightens it for him. "Now, that's smart," she says, beaming, and he gives her another grin.

"Traitor," I whisper under my breath, and Abbie chuckles, and turns to me.

"Sorry," she murmurs as we both get to our feet, Ben putting his hand into Abbie's.

"I meant him, not you," I clarify quietly.

"I know. I just meant sorry for undermining you."

"You didn't." I turn to her, serious now. "I forgot… it's all about copying with him these days. I should have remembered that."

"Why?" She looks up at me. "You've got a hundred and one other things to remember at the moment. Don't beat yourself up over a hat."

I lean down and kiss her forehead. "Thank you for that," I whisper, and she smiles up at me.

When we arrive, the beach is quite deserted, even though it's a Sunday. Still, it's early, and I expect it'll get busier as the morning wears on. As we go through the gap in the sea wall, we pause, and then Abbie takes a step to her right, Ben going with her, being as they're still holding hands.

"Where are you off to?" I ask her.

"I usually sit over here…" She nods towards the base of the cliff.

"Since when?"

"Since you left," she murmurs, looking away, and I take a step closer to her.

"Since I left the first time? Eighteen years ago?" She nods her head. "You haven't sat in our spot, in all those years?"

"No."

I put down the canvas bag containing the towels, and let the cool bag drop from my shoulder onto the ground, then move in front of her, putting my hands on her waist, and pulling her in to me. "Then it's high time you did."

She's slightly resistant. "Why?"

I lean down. "Because I'm back… and that's our spot. And I'm damned if anyone else is going to sit there while we're on the beach."

She stares at me for a moment, and then her lips twitch up. "You're claiming ownership of that space, are you?"

"If I have to, yes." I move closer, so my lips are by her ear. "I've got too many good memories of it to let it go."

She pulls back and looks up at me, and then nods her head, turning and walking in the opposite direction. I pick up the bags and follow, only stopping when we get to our spot.

"We're going to need a parasol, or something," Abbie says, looking up at the sky. The sun is still quite low, but it's hot already.

I agree with her and crouch down in front of Ben. "Do you want to come to the shop with me?" I point over to the gift shop. He nods and lets go of Abbie's hand, taking mine instead and I stand again, looking at Abbie now. "We'll be back in a minute. I'll get him a bucket and spade while we're there."

She smiles. "Okay. See you in a minute."

Over in the gift shop, I let Ben choose a bright green bucket and two blue spades, while I find the largest parasol they have, and also pick up some beach mats and a football, from the display outside. We go inside to pay and then head back to Abbie.

"Great!" she says, smiling. "I was hoping you'd think of beach mats." She takes them from me and unrolls them, laying them out on the sand and setting out the towels, while I bury the opened parasol in the sand, as far down as I can, providing us with some shade. After that, Abbie smothers Ben in sunscreen, before he sits down beside me and, together, we fill his bucket with sand. We tip it upside down and tap it, pulling the bucket away to find our 'castle' beneath and Ben claps his hands in delight. We repeat the process a few times, with the same result, and I turn to see Abbie watching us, a smile on her face.

"You can join in, you know." I say to her.

"I know. But it's fun watching." Her eyes shift and she looks over my shoulder, smiling to start with, although it quickly falls and I turn, wondering what she's looking at, to see her father walking across the beach towards us, his face like thunder.

He's upon us before I can get to my feet. "You're back then," he scowls.

"Yes." He glances from me to Abbie, and then his eyes settle on Ben.

"Care to explain?" he says, focusing back on me again.

"Not like this, no." I stand and turn to Abbie. "Do you think you could take Ben for a paddle?" I ask, and she kneels up, pulling Ben's canvas shoes from his feet and kicking off her sandals.

"Come on, Ben," she says brightly. "Let's go and find the water, shall we?"

She gives her dad a beseeching look and, taking Ben's hand, leads him down towards the gently lapping waves. He glances back once, but sees I'm still here, and carries on with Abbie, feeling safe.

"I gave you a roof over your head," Robert says, once they're out of earshot, taking a step closer to me. "I trusted you."

"And I was grateful for that. But what is it you think I've done?"

"Well, you seem to have a child, so that means there's got to be a woman involved somehow." He glares. "Are you married? Is that why you ran out of here so suddenly last week? Was it an attack of guilty conscience?"

"No. Do you honestly think I'd do that to Abbie? And do you think she'd be here with me now, if I had?"

He looks down at the space between us and mumbles, "No, no she wouldn't." Then he raises his eyes to mine again, and I see they're still filled with disappointment, even if his anger has subsided. "So, you're divorced then? You kept that quiet."

"No, I didn't. I'm not divorced either." He narrows his eyes, confused. "Look, you can keep hurling accusations at me all morning, or you can let me explain. Which would you prefer?"

He folds his arms across his chest. "Go on then… explain."

I take a step back and look down at the sand. I can't think of an easy way to say this, so I just start talking. "Ben is my son," I say quietly. "He'll be three in November, and his mother and I would have been the first to admit that his conception was an accident. By the time Lauren found out she was pregnant, she and I had already split up, although we'd only been together for a few weeks."

"But you took responsibility for him?" he says, still sounding resentful.

"Naturally. He's my son." I push my fingers back through my hair. "I grew up without a father. Do you think I could have done that to my own child?" He stares at me, but doesn't reply, still clearly doubting my integrity, I suppose. "Ben used to come and stay with me every other weekend, and sometimes during the week as well, if Lauren needed him to…" I let my voice fade, looking down the beach, to where Ben is splashing in the shallows, Abbie holding onto his hand, glancing round at us occasionally.

"So what's happened? Did his mother call you last week? Is that why you took off so suddenly? Has she asked you to take him for a while? Is that why he's here?" He hits me with a barrage of questions, but I ignore most of them, turning back to him, and stick to what needs to be said.

"I got a message in the early hours of Monday morning to say that Lauren and her boyfriend had been killed in a car accident…"

His face pales and he mutters, "Oh my God… I'm sorry," and then he almost seems to crumple in front of me. "I shouldn't have said… I'm so sorry," he repeats.

"It's okay." I take a step forward and put my hand on his arm. "Don't worry about it. You weren't to know. But I'm sure you understand that, in that moment, Ben became my priority. I had to get to him… and I couldn't leave a message for Abbie, or wake you and tell you, and let you tell Abbie, or tell her over the phone. Knowing about Molly, like I did, breaking the news to her that I have a son was something I had to do myself, face-to-face, and I had to do it at a time when I could sit down and talk it through with her, not when I was about to dash off to London."

"No, I can see that," he murmurs.

"So, I went up there and dealt with everything… and then I came back here yesterday, and went straight to Abbie's."

"And you told her?"

"Yes."

"How did she take it?" Some of the colour has returned to his cheeks and he sounds concerned now, almost scared.

"She's been incredible," I tell him, truthfully. "She was hurt that I'd run out on her, and a bit confused that I hadn't mentioned Ben before…"

"Why didn't you?" he asks. "Why didn't you tell us… well, her."

"As I explained to Abbie, I hadn't expected to find her here, and I needed to work out what that meant… for Abbie and me. I had to know what was going to happen between us before I introduced Ben into our relationship. I was trying to be responsible, not secretive, and I was going to tell her, only Lauren was killed first."

He nods his head. "And she's really okay with it?"

"Yes. Once I explained everything, she agreed to give me another chance."

"So you're back?" He doesn't sound angry at all now.

"Yes."

"You… you came back yesterday?"

"Yes."

He frowns. "And where are you staying?"

"At Abbie's."

His eyes widen. "Is that wise… in the circumstances?"

I shrug my shoulders. "I don't know." I look down the beach at her. She's laughing now and I have to smile. "Once we'd talked everything through, I decided I'd find a hotel for me and Ben to stay in while I worked out where we could live. But Abbie asked us to stay. She's been so generous. She… she said Ben needed somewhere safe; she thought her place would give him that."

"But, with Molly… after what happened…" he murmurs a little incoherently. "She's still in so much pain…"

I turn back to him. "You think I don't know that? I know that she's your daughter and I understand that you're worried about her, but so am I… all the time. I can see how fragile she is – first hand, every hour of the day – and trust me, I'm watching her. I won't let anything happen to her."

He stares at me for a moment. "Promise me? One father to another?"

"I promise, Robert."

He pauses and then turns, looking to where Abbie and Ben are still paddling, Abbie lifting Ben over the incoming waves. "I'm sorry," he says quietly.

"What for?"

"For saying those things about you – for even thinking them. I should have known better."

I keep my eyes fixed on Abbie, hearing Ben's laughter drift towards us on the sea breeze. "I'll tell you the same thing I've been telling your daughter for almost as long as I've known her…"

"What's that?" he asks, although he still doesn't look at me.

"That friends never have to say sorry."

We wander down the beach and I haul Ben out of the water, his wet legs kicking against me, as I introduce him to Robert. Abbie seems wary of her father, but he hugs her and after a few minutes, we're all talking, as though our argument never happened. Ben struggles free of me and I let him, holding his hand while he kicks his feet in the water, and Abbie and I chat to Robert. He stays for a while and then makes his excuses; he needs to get ready to open the pub.

"Drop by whenever you like," he says, walking backwards up the beach.

"We will," I reply and I turn back to Abbie.

"What happened?" she whispers as he turns.

"We talked."

"I gathered that much. But I don't think I've ever seen my dad that angry."

"No… He thought I'd been messing you around, lying to you. Cheating."

"You explained to him?" she asks. "About Lauren?"

"Yes."

She looks down at Ben for a moment. "I'm sorry."

"What on earth are you sorry for?"

"He's my dad," she reasons.

"So? He's just concerned about you. I get that."

"But that doesn't give him the right to give you a hard time."

I turn to her, keeping hold of Ben's hand. "Yes it does. He cares about you. He thought I'd hurt you, and he wanted to protect you."

"Even if he was going about it the wrong way? None of this is your fault, He shouldn't have got angry with you."

"Don't worry about it; I can handle your dad."

She smiles. "Is there anything you can't handle?"

"Yes."

"What's that?"

"Losing you."

She doesn't reply, but she nestles into me and I put my arm around her as Ben leans down, splashing his hands in the water and giggling.

By the time we've eaten Abbie's picnic, of cold chicken, potato salad, bread rolls and raw vegetables, which she's cut into batons, specially for Ben, he's already beginning to tire.

"We'd better think about heading back," I tell her, kneeling up and starting to pack away. She looks up at me, seemingly confused. "The sun's too hot, and Ben's tired. If he's going to survive until dinner, he should probably have a nap," I explain.

"Of course. I should have realised." She stands, and I reach up for her hand.

"Why? Even I get confused by his sleeping habits, they change so often. He doesn't have a nap every day; only if he's been doing something tiring, like playing on the beach all morning, and trust me, if he's tired like he is now, it's better to let him sleep for half an hour, than have him being moody and horrible later, or to let him fall asleep at four o'clock and be bouncing off the walls this evening when we're exhausted and want to go to bed."

"You know so much," she whispers.

"No. I've *learned* so much. No one *knows* any of this. It's a learning curve, Abbie, all of it… so don't beat yourself up." I repeat her words from this morning and she smiles down at me, helping me to fold up the towels and pack away the picnic.

I carry Ben and the cool bag, which I sling over my shoulder, while Abbie manages the bag and the parasol, and we walk slowly back up through the village to Hope Cottage.

By the time we get there and Abbie lets us in, Ben is already half asleep, his head on my shoulder, Flopsy cradled in his arm.

"I'll take him upstairs," I whisper, and Abbie nods then removes the cool bag from me, taking it through to the kitchen, while I take Ben up to our room, putting him in the middle of the bed and opening the window, just an inch or two, making sure it's securely latched, before going back downstairs.

Abbie's in the kitchen, unloading the cool bag and I go and stand behind her, putting my arms around her waist and leaning down to kiss her neck.

"Half an hour of peace," I murmur, moving my lips down to her shoulder, which seems to make her shiver – with pleasure, I hope.

"Half an hour?" she queries, leaning back into me.

"Well, about that. It may be an hour… I'm working on the average. Like I say, it changes."

She sighs. "Would you like to make the tea?"

I smile to myself. I know what I'd rather do… but I said I'd wait. And I will. "Okay." I kiss her neck again and go over to the Rayburn, picking up the kettle as she puts a few things back into the fridge. "You'll have to give me your bank account details," I say, a thought occurring to me, as I cross to the sink.

"What on earth for?" she replies.

"So I can transfer some money to you." It seems obvious to me, and I go back to the Rayburn, putting the filled kettle on to boil, before turning back. She's facing me now, her arms folded across her chest and a frown on her face. Oh hell…

I walk over and stand in front of her. "Don't look so cross."

"Well, why do I need your money? I'm not charging you rent, if that's what you're thinking."

I smile down at her. "I know, although I'll pay rent if you need me to… and if you've got a mortgage on this place, I'll pay it off."

"Like hell you will." She steps back, bumping into the table behind her. "I don't have a mortgage, as it happens. I bought the cottage with the proceeds of the house I had with Simon… but…"

"But what?"

"I don't need your money." She's almost sulking now and I struggle not to smile.

"Stop being so stubborn." I place my hands on her waist and lift her into the table, parting her legs and standing between them, looking down into her fiery eyes. "I'm just trying to pay my way, that's all. You're putting a roof over our heads, and you're feeding us. And while Ben may only eat carbohydrates for the best part, I'm not cheap to keep. I can eat my own body weight in bacon alone…" Her lips almost twitch upwards, but she controls the smile, her anger still simmering, and I reach out and put my hands back on her waist. "I'm not trying to be a millionaire megalomaniac. It's not my style. I'm not trying to rule the world, Abbie – not even your world. I wouldn't know how to. I just don't want to eat you out of house and home, and more importantly, I don't want to outstay my welcome."

She tilts her head slightly and sighs, unfolding her arms at last and resting a hand on my chest, which feels fantastic. "You couldn't," she whispers.

"Which one? Eat you out of house and home, or outstay my welcome? Because, like I say, I can eat quite a lot."

She leans up slightly. "You couldn't outstay your welcome, Josh… not ever." I lean closer, our lips almost touching, but she mutters, "Excuse me," and ducks away, sliding off the table, twisting out of my arms and going through the door that leads to the bathroom, closing it behind her. I'm confused, but I'm also powerless to stop her, because she's taken my breath away. Again.

I know I can't follow her into the bathroom, so I wait, pacing the floor impatiently, just as my phone beeps in my back pocket, bringing me to my senses, and I pull it out, unlocking the screen. I've got a message from Tonya, with an attachment, which I open, a smile forming on my lips as I look down at a photograph of Ben, aged probably fifteen months or so, together with Lauren, snuggled up together in warm winter clothes, staring at the camera. I read the message below.

— *Hi Josh, Sorry I didn't get back to you earlier. I flew out to the States yesterday, so my timings are shot. It's no problem to send some pictures over. I love this one of the two of them, don't you? They look really happy. I miss her so much already. Hope Ben's okay and I can get to see him soon. Give him a big kiss from Aunty Tonya x*

I tap out a quick response, even as my phone beeps again, with another photograph being sent through.

— Thanks, Tonya. Wasn't sure where you were. Ben's doing fine. Keep me posted when you're back in the UK, and I'll arrange something. Josh.

I click on the next photograph and smile again. This one is of Ben and Lauren on a children's slide. He's around nine months old and she's holding him on her lap while sliding down, with a huge grin on his face.

It beeps again, and I check the screen, just as Abbie comes out of the bathroom. She looks a little flushed, but otherwise okay and, rather than be rude and keep looking at the pictures, I put my phone back in my pocket and turn to her, watching as she starts making the tea.

"Sorry," I say quietly. "I could have been doing that, couldn't I?"

"Don't worry."

The phone beeps yet again, but I ignore it and Abbie looks up at me, a strange expression now forming on her face, before she takes the teapot over to the stove and tips in a little boiling water from the kettle.

"Are you okay?" I ask her, wary of the signs that something's wrong.

"I'm fine," she says but I know she isn't, and go over, taking the teapot from her trembling hand, putting it down on the work surface, and turn her towards me.

"No, you're not. Tell me what's wrong. Why did you go into the bathroom just now?"

She stares at me. "Why do you think?"

"I don't know. That's why I'm asking. I was just about to kiss you, but I'm assuming you didn't want me to, that you were trying to get away from me."

She blushes. "No. That wasn't it at all. I just needed to pee."

I chuckle. "Sorry. I didn't realise." She shrugs her shoulders and I take a breath. "Okay, so if that's not the problem, then what is? Something's wrong Abbie…"

"Who are you getting so many messages from?" she blurts out, lowering her head, refusing to make eye contact with me. "Why did you just check your phone when I came out of the bathroom, and then put it away so quickly… and why are you ignoring it now?"

I reach around and take my phone from my pocket, unlocking it and handing it to her. "You can look for yourself, if you like. The messages are from Tonya."

"Tonya?" Her brow furrows as she takes the phone, glancing down at the screen.

"Yes. I sent her a text last night before I went to sleep, asking her if she could send me some pictures of Lauren and Ben together." She starts to scroll through my messages, her face clearing. "I've got photographs of Ben, but none of Lauren and I'd like to be able to show them to him one day. I know it could be ages before he's ready to understand, but I thought this might help at some point."

She looks up at me, tears welling in her eyes, and I put my arms around her.

"I'd like to take some of Ben and me too… and, if you're okay with it, I'd also like to take some of the three of us together?" Her eyes widen. "Even though Lauren's disappeared from his life, I want him to see that never for one second was he alone. I want him to know he always had people with him who cared." A tear falls, landing on her cheek and I bring my hand up, wiping it away. "I have no idea if I'm doing this right; but I hope I'm not getting it completely wrong."

"I think it's a lovely thing to do," she says and lets her head fall forward, resting it on my chest. I hold her there, stroking her hair, until she looks up again. "Lauren was very beautiful," she murmurs.

"Yes, she was." There's no point in denying it; she's seen the photographs. "But there's no-one like you… not as far as I'm concerned. There never has been."

"I'm sorry," she says, sniffling slightly.

"What for?"

"For doubting you. I—I thought you were getting text messages from another woman."

I smile down at her, brushing my thumb along her bottom lip. "I was… just not in the way that you thought. I'm not a cheat, Abbie. I never was."

"I know."

"So why would you think that?" There has to be a reason, but I'm not sure that it's got anything to do with me.

"It doesn't matter," she says. I want to tell her that it does, but she's obviously not in the mood for talking, so I lean down and kiss her instead, just gently. She moans into me and I pull back, before I get carried away. It would be so very easy with her. "I am sorry though," she says, and I rest my forehead against hers, feeling her breath on my skin.

"You're my best friend, Abbie; you know that, don't you?"

"Yes."

"Then stop saying sorry… especially when you haven't done anything wrong."

Chapter Seventeen

Abbie

Despite everything Josh said, I still felt guilty. I felt guilty all afternoon and evening.

How could I have doubted him? He's never done anything to make me doubt him, but I was so overwhelmed with jealousy, I couldn't help myself.

I know a lot of that comes from Simon's deceit – which, let's face it, I didn't really care about – but I missed the signs with him, even though they should have been obvious; and while I know that Josh isn't a cheat, I didn't think Simon was either.

We sit together after Ben's gone to bed, having a glass of wine, and discussing our plans for tomorrow.

"The bed and wardrobe will be delivered between nine and eleven in the morning," Josh says, "but I've realised there's a problem."

"There is?"

"Yes. I didn't order any bedding."

I roll my eyes. "Really?"

"I know… I'm an idiot."

I reach over and place my hand on his leg, just below the hemline of his shorts, his skin against mine, and he places his hand on top, which feels nice. "Stop giving yourself such a hard time. You've got a lot to think about at the moment."

"Yes. You mainly."

I smile up at him. "So, what did you have in mind?" I ask.

"I just said… you."

I chuckle and he pulls me in for a hug. "I meant, what do you want to do about the bedding?"

"Well, you've got to work, being as tomorrow is Monday…"

"No, I haven't," I interrupt. "I don't have anything on at the moment."

"Oh… I wish."

I lean back. "Are you going to stop that?"

"What?"

"Saying things like that?"

"Do you want me to?" he asks, and I can't say 'yes', because I don't… not really. He struggles not to smile. "If you've got nothing on tomorrow – work-wise – then after the bed's been delivered, we could go into Truro. I can take you and Ben out for lunch, and we can get whatever we need."

"Okay. I like the sound of that," I reply, taking a sip of wine as he nudges into me.

"Nowhere near as much as I like the sound of you with nothing on."

I choke on my wine and he has to take my glass, patting my back until I've calmed down again.

"Sorry about that," he says, not looking even remotely contrite.

"No you're not." I smile up at him.

He grins. "Okay, I'm not." We both laugh and he nudges into me again. "It's good to hear you laughing."

I stop and turn to face him. "It's not something I've done a lot of lately," I murmur.

"I know. That's why it's so special when you do."

He leans in and kisses me, his lips brushing over mine, his tongue seeking entrance, which I willingly grant, and we slowly lay back, our arms around each other, my fingers creeping up into his hair, his hands on my face and neck, our breathing matched. His kisses are deeply sensual and arousing, but there's no pressure to do anything else… other than enjoy each other.

I don't remember ever just sitting and kissing like this. In the past, there was always an element of thinking about what might come next, and maybe doing it, or trying to. But tonight, we literally just kiss. And when we finally stop, we're shrouded in twilight, its arrival unnoticed.

"It's dark," I say quietly, looking around.

"Yes."

"I didn't realise."

"No. Neither did I."

"I—I suppose we should go to bed. Today's been tiring and tomorrow sounds like it might be quite busy too."

Josh nods his head and kisses me gently again. "Do you want me to come and sit with you?"

"Sit with me?"

"Like last night. Until you go to sleep." He traces a line down my cheek with his fingertip. "I don't like the idea of you crying by yourself. So, if you're going to cry, I'd like to be there…"

"Well, I don't know that I am – going to cry, that is."

"But you usually do?" he guesses and I nod my head. "In that case, why don't you get ready for bed? I'll lock up and turn off the lights, and come up in a few minutes."

"You can get ready for bed first, if you want," I say, without thinking.

"Only if you're comfortable with that," he says, looking down at me, his eyes darkening visibly, even in the dim light, and I put my arms around him holding on.

"I'm so comfortable with you, it sometimes scares me."

"Why?" he asks, frowning slightly. "Why does it scare you?"

"B—Because when we're together, it seems so right, so perfect, that I honestly think I could close my eyes and make-believe that none of the things that happened in between ever took place… Except…"

"They did." He finishes my sentence. "And they hurt."

I nod my head, tears pricking at my eyes and he leans back, gazing at me.

"That doesn't mean you've forgotten them," he says, like he sees through me to the guilty secrets in my mind. "But it also doesn't mean you can't feel comfortable with me. And I promise, you have nothing to feel scared about." His breath whispers across my skin and I almost dare myself to believe him.

I wake to the sound of a gentle knocking on my door, and then a muttering from outside, before the handle twists and Ben appears, looking pleased with himself, to be followed by Josh.

He's found the tea tray, and as he comes in carrying it, he looks over at me, our eyes meeting. I know he's probably thinking about our kisses last night, and sitting in here with me for an hour or so, while I drifted off to sleep. I don't remember him leaving. I just remember how good it felt to fall asleep with him… and that I didn't cry. For the first time in over four years, I didn't cry myself to sleep.

"We brought tea," he says, putting the tray down on the end of the bed, and helping Ben to scramble up. I sit, puffing up my pillows and Ben clambers over, plonking himself next to me again.

He took me by surprise when he did this yesterday, and I'll admit I found it hard; the thoughts of 'what might have been' resounding through my head, but I couldn't help putting my arm around him. He's lost his mum – and he's so young. He's obviously used to having a woman featuring very large in his life and that's been taken from him, and although he clearly loves Josh, I think he's looking to the only other woman he can find at the moment for comfort. And I'll give that to him. I have to. For his sake.

And maybe for my own too.

He leans into me again and, just like yesterday, I put my arm around him, looking up at Josh, who's still standing at the end of the bed, staring at us. I hope he doesn't mind this; doesn't feel left out, or sidelined.

"Is this okay?" I murmur, asking the question, and nodding at Ben.

"It's perfect," he smiles and comes over, leaning across me to hand Ben his milk, then kissing me before he stands again and passes me my fruit tea, sitting down beside us. "We'll drink this and then you can have a shower, before you go out, and I'll have a big hug and some breakfast ready for when you get back."

"Are you sure?" I look up at him over the rim of my cup.

"About which part?" he asks, giving me a loving smile, that makes his eyes sparkle into mine.

"All of it."

"I'm positive."

I drink some of my tea, gazing at him, remembering the feeling of his lips on mine, and trying to fight the remorse over all the wasted years, and the inevitable guilt that follows. "I'll run the vacuum over the box room while you and Ben are showering," I say, desperate to stop my mind from wandering too far down the road of 'what might have been'. "It'll be easier to do it while the room's empty."

"Okay." He's still staring at me, his eyes softening, like he somehow understands that none of this is easy for me. "And then, once the bed's been delivered, we can go into Truro."

"Won't you need to build the furniture first?" I ask.

"No. It doesn't need building."

"It's not flat-packed then?"

He smiles. "No."

I try not to smile back, and take another sip of tea. "But you're not a millionaire megalomaniac…"

He shakes his head. "No… I'm just a man who has better things to do with his time than build flat-packed furniture."

"And who can afford to buy it ready-made?"

"That too."

He grins and, this time, I have to smile back.

We've been a bit more organised this morning, so I've been able to take a little longer in the shower, and I use the time to shave… intimately. It takes me a while, because… well, it's been a while, but when I'm finished, I have to admit, it feels really good. I'd forgotten how good it felt actually, but then as I say, it's been a while.

I know the reason why I've shaved, and staring into the mirror while I'm getting dressed, I'll even admit it to myself. The reason I've shaved is that, when we were together before, I really liked the way it felt when Josh made love to me like this. The skin there is so sensitive and, being shaved, it seemed to heighten the sensations, to make it all so much more intense... and I want that feel like that again. Maybe not today, or tomorrow, but soon.

Even so... even as I'm thinking about him, my body responding to the memories, the dark clouds start to gather in my mind... "I have to tell him," I whisper to myself.

I have to tell him the truth. It would be cruel not to. I meant to tell him before... before he went to London, but then he left. Now I really do have to tell him, though. It's only fair that he knows, before he gets in too deep.

I shake my head, feeling guilty, realising I've probably left it too late already. Will he hate me for keeping it from him? Will he leave me again? Oh God...

The furniture and stair gates arrive at just after ten, and although it takes some to-ing and fro-ing and a few choice words, the delivery men eventually get the bed and wardrobe up the stairs and installed in the box room.

Ben is excited beyond words and keeps bouncing on his bed, which is a cross between a cot and a bed, having a low wooden railing on both sides, to stop him falling, which seems like a good idea right now.

I can't help the lump in my throat, seeing a child's furniture in here, reminding me yet again, of all the things that 'might have been', even though Molly would have lived in the box in Falmouth, rather than here, if she'd lived at all, that is...

"Are you okay with this?" Josh says, coming over to me and putting his arm around my waist.

I nod up at him, because I can't speak and, as though he knows what's wrong, he just hugs me close and kisses the side of my head, not saying a word. Because he doesn't need to.

After a few minutes, he pulls away, giving me a watchful smile, and goes over to Ben, grabbing him from the bed. "Come on, Champ... let's get your shoes on. We're going shopping."

Ben doesn't seem too keen on the idea, until Josh points out that he'll get to choose his own bedding – and that he can't sleep in his new bed until he does – and then he cheers up and lets Josh put his shoes on, without arguing.

We gather up all the things we need, and make our way out to the car, whereupon Josh stops in his tracks.

"What's wrong?" I ask.

"My car," he replies, looking at it, and then at me.

"What about it? It's a lovely car."

"I know. But it's only got two seats."

"Oh. Of course." How could I have forgotten that? Well, presumably in the same way that Josh did.

"I've got a car," I point out. "It's in the garage."

I reach into my bag and pull out my keys, going over to the garage and opening it to reveal my small hatchback, which is coming up for its thirteenth birthday. Josh looks over at me. "Perfect," he says, winking, and he puts Ben down on the ground, telling him to stand still, while he opens his own car and gets out the child's seat. "We'll need to put this in the back," he says, bringing it over.

"Let me get the car out," I suggest. "It's a tight squeeze in the garage."

He stands back, holding Ben out of the way and I reverse the car onto the small space beside the house, and then get out so that I can watch over Ben while Josh puts the seat in the back. He struggles, pulling the front seat forward and clambering in, fighting with the seatbelt, and eventually getting back out again, sighing deeply.

"Are you going to get cross with me again, if I suggest that we buy you a new car?"

"Me? What about you… you're the one whose car only has two seats."

He picks Ben up and struggles back into my car, putting him into his seat and strapping him in place, before standing and pushing the passenger seat back into position.

"I know," he sighs. "And I'll deal with that too, but will you at least look at a new car with me?"

"I'll think about it," I concede, unwilling to admit that my car can be temperamental – annoyingly so.

"Well, that was easier than I thought it would be," he smiles, teasing me.

I hand him my keys. "That's because you haven't driven my car... yet."

He rolls his eyes and waits while I climb into the passenger seat, shutting the door after me.

When we get back from Truro, it's mid-afternoon. Ben slept all the way home and he's happy to lend a hand with getting his room organised. Well, he's happy to move his toys into the toy box that Josh bought, and which barely squeezed into the boot of my car. So, while he does that, I make up his bed and hang the curtains, and Josh fits the stair gate, talking to us while he works, I presume so that Ben knows he's there.

Once we're finished, we go down to the living room and Josh puts in the gate at the bottom of the stairs, while I prepare us some tea, making sure to bring some cookies back with me, which pleases Ben. Josh comes and sits beside me, getting out his phone.

"So," he says, taking a bite out of his cookie and keeping half an eye on Ben, who's playing with the building bricks Josh also bought him in Truro, "how would you feel about an Audi, or a Volkswagen?"

"We're talking about cars already, are we?"

"Yes." He turns to me. "As much as I love you, I really don't like your car. The gearbox is a nightmare." He grins at me and I do my best to scowl, whilst trying not to giggle.

"I did warn you."

"How long have you been driving that thing?" he says.

"Since the divorce. I had a leased car before that, but Simon made the payments... I couldn't afford to keep them going, so I bought 'that thing', as you call it, second hand, out of the proceeds of the house in Falmouth."

He gazes at me for a moment, and then looks back at his phone, going onto a browser and calling up a website, turning it towards me and showing me a picture of a very nice, very enormous looking Audi.

"It's lovely," I reply, "but I've never liked driving big cars… and that looks like it might be a bit on the large side for me."

He nods, not saying a word and changes the page, switching it back to me again. "How about that?"

"That's better… I think."

"Why don't I arrange a test drive for the weekend?" he suggests and, after a moment's pause, I agree.

"What are you going to do about your car?" I ask him. "Or are you going to keep it, and use the Audi when you need to?"

"The Audi – if that's what we buy – will be yours," he says, looking down at me again. "I've already got something in mind for myself."

"Oh yes?" I lean into him and he turns his phone back to me, revealing the Aston Martin website.

"An Aston Martin?" I frown up at him. "How does that help? You won't be any better off than you are now."

"Yes I will. They do make them with four seats, you know." He shrugs. "It may only work for a few more years, while Ben's still little, but I love Aston Martins, and they're my one bit of luxury…" His voice fades.

"So, have you actually ordered it yet?" I ask, smiling at him.

"No." He's grinning now. "But I've set the wheels in motion."

After dinner, Ben can't wait to go to bed and Josh takes him up, telling me he'll be down as soon as he'd got Ben settled and read him a story.

I clear up the kitchen, load the dishwasher and put the left-overs into the fridge, then carry our wine through to the living room, putting it on the table and sitting down on the sofa, feeling tired but contented. It's a novel sensation, but I like it.

When Josh comes down, he sits beside me, picking up his wine and taking a long drink, before replacing the glass and turning to me.

"What do you want to do tomorrow?" I ask him. "I've got to go to the supermarket at some point, but other than that, we can do whatever you want…"

He stares at me. "You can't keep doing this," he says.

"Doing what?" I wonder for a moment, if he's going to ask for my bank details again – being as I've just mentioned food shopping – whether he's noticed that I've managed to avoid giving them to him.

"Giving up so much of your time to be with us. You should be working, shouldn't you?"

I stare at him, my contentment vanishing in an instant, and I move away from him slightly, finding myself in the corner of the sofa. "Don't you want to spend time with me?" The words fall out of my mouth before I have time to filter them.

He's beside me in an instant, kneeling, his hands cupping my face, his eyes boring into mine. "Of course I do. I love being with you, and so does Ben. But I don't want you falling behind with your work, and then getting stressed over your deadlines. That's all I'm saying."

"Well, you don't need to worry," I reply, still feeling a little offended that he doesn't think I can manage my own time. "I don't have any deadlines at the moment."

"You don't?"

"No. I told you, I don't have any work on."

"I thought you meant just for today."

I shake my head. "I had an argument with one of my clients."

He smiles just slightly, sitting back a little. "Oh dear. What happened?"

"I finished the sci-fi cover," I explain. "You know? The one you saw when you were here before?" He nods his head. "But the thing is, I hated doing it. So I wrote to Hazel – she's the client – and I told her that I didn't want to do any more science fiction work for her."

"And?" he prompts.

"And she phoned me on Friday and said I couldn't cherry pick what I did or didn't do for her. I told her, in that case, I'd prefer not to work for her at all. Well, that was the upshot of it, anyway." I look up at him. "I probably shouldn't have done it, but I really didn't enjoy the work, and she was being a pain at the time."

"So you've got no work at all?"

"I've still got the children's publisher, and I expect they'll send me something soon. I rarely go more than a week or two without something coming in from them."

He nods. "Are you okay?" he asks, more seriously now. "Financially, I mean?"

"I'm fine. I've never been very expensive to keep." I smile up at him, remembering his comment about himself. "I don't have a mortgage and my bills here aren't that high… and if I do have a problem, Dad helps me out."

"Not any more, he doesn't," Josh says, almost like he's offended now.

I stare up at him. "Oh? I suppose you think that's your job now, do you?"

He nods, kneeling up again and leaning much closer to me. "Yes."

"Well, it isn't."

"Yes, it is." His voice drops a note or two. "I love you, Abbie Fuller. What's mine is yours. It always was, even when I had nothing to give you but myself."

I feel myself softening. "That's such a lovely thing to say."

"It's the truth." His eyes melt into mine and he closes the gap, kissing me deeply.

Chapter Eighteen

Josh

Pulling away from Abbie is getting harder and harder to do, especially when we seem to have got ourselves completely horizontal on her sofa, but I manage it eventually, and notice that it's dark outside again. Who'd have thought we could just kiss for hours? But this is becoming habit forming – and I can't think of a better habit to get into.

She's breathing quite hard and gazing up into my eyes, and I'm completely mesmerised by her; by the glow of her soft skin and by the sparkle in her eyes and by her slightly swollen bottom lip, which I've just been nipping at gently with my teeth, making her moan and sigh. I'm so tempted to suggest we take this upstairs, and I get the feeling that, if I did, she probably wouldn't say 'no'… and that's why I'm not going to suggest it. Because it has to come from her, not me. We both have to know that, when the time comes, there will be no regrets. None whatsoever.

And in the meantime, I'll wait.

"Bedtime?" I say, with a light note to my voice, letting her know there's nothing sexual in my suggestion.

"Probably. Ben may be excited about his furniture, and his new room, but I have no doubt he'll come and wake you early in the morning."

"He'll be in at six, I'm sure." I stand and hold out my hand to her, pulling her to her feet.

She looks up at me. "Can you sit with me?" she asks and I smile.

"Of course."

"Ten minutes?" she suggests, being as that was roughly how long it took us to get ready for bed last night.

"Ten minutes," I confirm, and she heads to the bathroom, leaning up and kissing my cheek first.

I go upstairs and check on Ben, who's fast asleep, looking angelic and perfect, and then go to my room and change into my shorts, before knocking on Abbie's bedroom door.

She tells me to come in, and I do, finding her lying down in bed already, and I go and sit beside her, stroking her hair. "Are you okay?" I ask.

She nods her head and snuggles down a little further. I wish I could get in there with her, and hold her properly, but she's not ready yet, so I sit, caressing her hair and her cheek.

"Can I talk to you?" she says, after a few minutes.

"Of course you can."

She turns onto her back, looking up at me, and lets out a long and slightly worrying sigh. "I—I need to tell you something," she says. "Well, ask you something, I suppose."

"Okay." I move closer to her and she looks up at me, her eyes locking with mine, their sadness almost overwhelming me. "What is it, Abbie?"

"I know we're… we're close," she says.

"Yes." That's a bit of an understatement, although I go along with it.

"But there's something I need to make clear. There's something you have to understand, before we can… before we can go any further." I nod my head, trying to restrain my fear. "I—I don't know if you remember us having a conversation when we were younger, about us having children together…?" She gazes up at me and I nod my head, wondering how should could ever think I might have forgotten a single word that passed between us. "The thing is," she adds, before I can say anything, "I can't. I can't do that again…" Her voice cracks and tears fall down her cheeks. I sit forward and pull her into my arms, holding her close to my chest.

"Shh… I already know," I tell her. "Deep down, I think I've known that since I came back."

She leans back. "You have?"

"Of course. I know you better than anybody."

"And… and you're okay with… with us not having a child together? Even though we said we would?"

I smile at her. "Abbie… as long as I have you, nothing else matters."

"Do you mean that?"

"I promise you. I swear to you, on Ben's life… I mean that. Every word of it."

"And you're not angry with me?"

I can feel myself frowning. "Why on earth would I be angry with you?"

"Because I didn't tell you sooner."

My frown fades and a smile forms on my lips. "It's not something we've really had a chance to discuss," I reason. "Not with everything that's been going on. And I understand that it's not an easy thing for you to talk about… so no, I'm not angry. I'm glad you've told me. Honestly. But as far as I'm concerned, it doesn't change a thing. Not a single thing."

She sighs and sinks into me, and I hold her tight.

I really am glad she told me that. Apart from the fact that it means she trusts me enough to open up to me, rather than bottling up her problems, it also means that, while she still may not have told me that she loves me, she does at least see us having a future together, a future that includes an honest, faithful, whole, and loving relationship – and that means the world to me. I meant what I said… I really have known all along that having another child would probably be too much for her, and while I suppose having a baby with Abbie is something I've always dreamed of, ever since she first mentioned it all those years ago, it's a dream I can live without… because I'm holding my dream-come-true in my arms. And that's all I need.

I wake with a start, and then smile, remembering my conversation with Abbie, and that she eventually fell asleep on me, and I lay her down on the pillows and watched her for a while, before coming in here, wishing I could have stayed with her and longing for the day when I will.

I let out a long sigh, turning over to face the curtains, the sunlight streaming in around their edges, brightening the room. Something feels wrong, although for a moment I can't work out what it is. And then I realise… It's *too* light.

And Ben's not here.

I shoot out of bed and quickly check the time on my phone.

"Shit!" It's gone seven. Where the hell is he? He's never slept beyond six fifteen before and, while I know his sleep habits are likely to change, he went to bed really early last night…

In a panic, I run from my room and into his, only to find his bed is empty, my heart leaping into my mouth, as I dash back onto the landing and check the stair gate. It's closed, thank God… but where can he be?

I'm just about to shout his name, when I hear giggling coming from Abbie's room and I go along the landing to find her door is slightly ajar. Pushing on it, I discover my son lying on Abbie's bed, while she's kneeling over him, her back to me, tickling him, as he rolls this way and that, trying to escape, chuckling and squealing with delight.

Unable to resist, I creep over, unobserved, going up behind Abbie and grab her around the waist. She yelps in surprise and I turn her, dropping her onto her back, beside Ben.

Seeing his chance, Ben clambers up and starts to tickle Abbie, not very effectively, so I kneel on the bed and join in, until she's giggling and screaming to be released, trying to scramble away.

I'm momentarily side-tracked by the sight of her, writhing on the bed beneath me, her head on the pillows, her back arched and her skimpy pyjamas riding up, all askew, but just then, she rolls away to the far side of the bed, in a bid for freedom, and shrieks as she almost falls off, so I reach out and haul her back, which makes Ben giggle even more.

Abbie sits up now, breathless and panting.

"You don't play fair," she accuses, looking up at me, all dishevelled, although she's smiling.

"Nope," I reply, sitting on the bed beside her, while Ben crawls between us. "Did I ever?"

She turns to face me. "Probably not," she whispers and then looks down, noticing for the first time that she's revealing more flesh than she probably realised. She flushes and tries to straighten her top, and I pull Ben onto my lap, so I can move closer to Abbie and lean into her.

"Hey, don't do that on my account," I murmur, as she looks up.

"I wasn't." Her reply takes me by surprise, but before I can respond, she continues, "There's a toddler in the room." She says the words with emphasis and nods at Ben, then tweaks his nose playfully.

"He's too young to care," I reply and Ben struggles free of me, clambering onto Abbie's lap instead and nestling into her. She puts her arms around him and lowers her head to his.

"We should probably apologise to Daddy, shouldn't we?" she says to him and he looks up. I wonder if she's going to say something about him having come into her instead of me. If she does, I'll just have to tell her – again – that I don't mind at all. I think this is pretty damn perfect actually.

"Why are you apologising?" I ask when she doesn't say anything.

"Because when Ben comes into you, you normally go and make us tea, but when he came into me this morning, we started talking… and that led to tickling… and…" Ben looks up at her, grinning.

"Well, you really don't need to apologise… for anything. I'm quite happy to do without tea, if it means mornings like this."

She smiles at me, and then turns away, seemingly feeling shy. "Oh God," she says, suddenly flustered, turning back again. "I didn't realise that was the time." I look at the clock on her bedside table and see it's gone seven-thirty already. "I—I…" she falters, tears welling in her eyes.

I take Ben from her lap. "Go. I'll deal with Ben."

She doesn't wait to be told twice, and leaps off of the bed, running from the room.

Ben looks at me, confused. "Abbie has something she'd got to do," I explain. I'm not sure he understands, but I get up, keeping hold of him, and carry him through to his bedroom, so we won't be in the way when Abbie comes back upstairs after her shower.

We're showered and dressed, and breakfast is keeping warm, by the time Abbie returns from the church. Ben is crouched down beside me, silently studying a butterfly that's perched itself on the rose bush that grows at the front of Abbie's cottage, and doesn't notice her approaching. I do though, and for the first time since we got back, she looks really down, walking up the hill, with her hands in her pockets and her head bowed low.

I wait for her to get to me and then take a single step forward, pulling her into my arms and letting her weep.

"I—I was having such a good time," she murmurs, and I know she feels guilty about this morning.

"Don't feel bad," I whisper and she sobs a little louder, burying her head in my chest. I hold onto her. "I'm here, whenever you want to talk about it," I say into her ear. "But please don't torture yourself. No-one wants that for you."

She calms eventually and we go inside to have breakfast, although she's quieter than usual. I watch her closely, noticing the shadows behind her eyes and wishing she'd talk to me and let me help her.

We've only just finished breakfast when Abbie's phone beeps. It's in the living room, so she goes to fetch it, coming back and reading something on the screen.

"Is something wrong?" I ask, seeing the expression on her face. She looks worried, and confused.

"No… well, not really." She looks up at me. "You remember I said I rarely go more than a couple of weeks without getting a job from the children's book publisher?" I nod my head, starting to clear away the breakfast things. "Well, they've just sent something in…"

"And?"

"And, looking at what they want, the deadline is going to be tight." She sighs, sitting down at the table. "It's not their fault. The author is quite well-known, and he's being a pain."

"In my experience with publishers, they often are," I say and she looks up smiling, although it quickly falls.

"It means I'm going to have to work," she says, looking sad.

"That's okay," I reply, going over and crouching down beside her. Ben comes too, not wanting to be left out, so I sit him up on my knee, and he pats Abbie on the thigh. She looks down at him, tears filling her eyes again as she ruffles his hair. "You can get on with your work," I tell her, "and Ben and I will amuse ourselves. I'll make us lunch, and you can join us?"

She nods, which surprises me, being as I know she didn't used to stop work in the middle of the day. "What about the shopping?" she says, biting her bottom lip, and blinking hard, seemingly overwhelmed with emotion, at even the smallest thing today. "I was going to go this morning. I did a big shop at the weekend, but…" She falls silent.

"But a couple of unexpected guests turned up and emptied your fridge?" I guess.

"I didn't say that. And you're not guests."

I sigh, smiling, simply because she just said that. "Why don't we go? Ben and I?"

"To the supermarket?" She seems surprised.

"Yes. I have been to one before…" I lean into her slightly. "Even millionaires have to eat, you know. And it hadn't escaped my notice that you've managed to avoid giving me your bank details, so this way, at least I'll get to pay for what we're eating."

She narrows her eyes at me and then rests her hand on my arm. "Thank you," she murmurs.

"Hey… you don't have to thank me." I lean back slightly and smile at her. "You haven't tasted my cooking yet."

She laughs and sniffles, just about holding back her tears.

The supermarket is fairly quiet, which is just as well, because Abbie's given me a lengthy list. She must know this place well though, because the items she's written down seem to be in roughly the right order, starting with the fruit and vegetables and working through meat – well, chicken and fish in Abbie's case – milk, yogurt and cheese, tinned and dried foods and on into household items, and finally drinks. We skip the pet food aisle, for obvious reasons, and while we manage to get everything on the list, we also throw in a few extras, just for the sheer hell of it, and I grab a couple of things I need.

Ben sits in the trolley all the way round, agreeing to my choices, even though he doesn't know what they are for the best part, and helping me count out things, like apples and bananas. It may take longer doing it that way, but it keeps him entertained for a while.

By the time we get back home to Abbie's, Ben's hungry, and it's nearly time for lunch, so I unpack the chilled and frozen things and leave the rest for later, before setting out the lunch. I'll admit, I cheated and bought some cold meats and cooked chicken, some bread, salads, and olives, and when I call Abbie down, she comes into the kitchen and looks at the food spread out on the table, before turning to me.

"This isn't really cooking," she says, smirking, and I'm glad to see she seems to have cheered up a little. She's also changed since this morning, into a pale pink skirt and a white top, that ends at her waist – rather like the blue one she was wearing the other day.

I hold my up hands, admitting my guilt. "No, it's not, but I knew Ben would be getting hungry by the time we got back… I'll cook tonight."

She sits down as I put Ben into his booster seat, helping him to some sliced bread and cutting him up some cold meat, before sitting opposite Abbie. "No, you won't," she replies, reaching over to take an olive, which she pops into her mouth, making me focus on her lips for a moment, as I remember, with great regret, that I haven't kissed her all day. That's something I need to rectify as soon as possible.

"I won't?" I concentrate on the conversation. "Why not? You'll have been working all day."

"I know." She smiles. "But I've got plans for tonight's dinner."

"You have? Are we going somewhere?"

"No, but I thought we'd cook something together… all three of us."

"All three of us?"

She nods. "I had an idea while I was writing out the shopping list," she says, taking some bread and cold chicken. "It's going to be messy, but I think Ben will enjoy it."

"If it's messy, I can guarantee he will."

I'm intrigued by what she's got in mind, but not so intrigued that I'm going to forget about kissing her, and once we've finished eating and I've started to clear away, I make good on that, pulling her up into my arms and letting my lips find hers.

I don't linger for as long as I'd like, mindful of Ben, but once I release her, she sighs deeply, looking up at me, leaving me wondering – yet again – if she wants more. I know I do, and for a moment or two, we just gaze at each other. Then Abbie smiles at me, her eyes sparkling, like she can read my mind. But then she always could, I think.

"I—I should get back up to work," she murmurs softly and I nod my head.

"If you must." She seems reluctant to go, but smiles and pulls back, going over to Ben and ruffling his hair once more. "Before you go," I say, calling her back, and she stops, turning to face me, "I thought I'd do some washing this afternoon. Can you just tell me how to work your machine?"

She smiles and comes over, taking me through to the lobby area between the kitchen and bathroom and giving me some basic instructions.

"Okay?" she asks, once she's shown me where the detergent is kept.

I pull her into my arms, my hands resting on the bare skin just above the waistband of her skirt, which feels delicate and soft to my touch. "Only if you are." She looks up at me, but doesn't answer. "Abbie? Are you okay?"

"I'm better than I was this morning," she replies quietly and I nod.

"If you need a hug, or you need to talk…" *Please God…* "or even if you just need me, you know where I am."

She lets her head rest on my chest. "I always need you," she whispers.

"I'm here." I hold her close, wishing I could do more.

Abbie goes back up to her studio and I take Ben upstairs to gather together our washing, coming back down with an armful, and him traipsing behind me. Once we've put the machine on, Ben settles down at the table to play with his toolkit for a while, and I finish clearing up the kitchen, and then take advantage of him being quiet for a minute or two, and send e-mails to Richard and Tonya, asking how they're likely to be fixed for the next couple of weekends. I'm going to have to go back to London to get some more clothes, my laptop, and a few other things, so we may as well try and tie up a visit with them while we're there, assuming they're available. Richard comes back straight away, telling me nothing's happened yet with the inquest, but that he's free for the next three weekends, and he can't wait to see Ben. Tonya doesn't respond, but I guess she's probably working, or maybe sleeping, being as she didn't say whereabouts in America she was, and I expect I'll hear back from her later.

I put down my phone and sit, watching Ben patiently playing with his toys, my mind drifting to Abbie, and how troubled she is. I know that's understandable. I get that what's happened to her is going to make her sensitive to just about everything, but I wish she'd just talk to me, tell me her story, in her own words, and how she really feels… because I'm pretty damn sure it would help her. I'm not for one second suggesting that I can make her problems go away; I know I can't. But I know can help her to smile again… and to feel less guilty for doing so.

I'm shocked out of my thoughts by Ben throwing his screwdriver across the room and then pushing his other tools across the table in an unusual display of temper.

"Hey…" I get to my feet and go over to him, crouching down beside him. "What's wrong?"

He won't look at me, staring at the table top instead, so I stand and lift him out of his booster seat and into my arms, despite his stiffness.

"Ben? Tell Daddy what's wrong."

"I want Mummy," he says sulkily. "Where's Mummy."

I sigh deeply. I knew he'd ask again at some point; it was inevitable, and I go through to the living room and sit down with him on the sofa, pulling him onto my lap and hugging him tight to my chest.

"Mummy's not here," I murmur softly, hoping I'm saying and doing the right thing, even though I don't have a clue what I should do for the best. "But she'll always love you, very much. And Daddy's here… and I love you too, and I'm never going to leave you." He looks up at me.

"Where's Abbie," he asks, and I wonder if he's scared that she's gone too, just like Lauren.

"She's just upstairs working, Champ. Why don't you come and play with Daddy for a while, and Abbie will be down later?"

He shakes his head, another tantrum building. "No. I want Abbie."

His bottom lip starts to tremble and, although I know I should probably hold out and find something to distract him, rather than giving in, he's been through so much, I can't help myself.

"Okay," I reply and get to my feet, lifting him with me and carrying him, as I walk up the stairs, negotiating the gates and then opening the door that leads up to the attic. "Abbie?" I call out, hoping she doesn't mind the interruption.

"Yes?"

"Can you spare a few minutes?"

"Of course." I hear footsteps above, and then she appears, descending the stairs, looking from me to Ben. "What's wrong?" she asks, clearly noticing his forlorn expression.

"A certain young man wants you… and, for once, I'm not talking about me," I reply.

She moves closer, reaching out and touching Ben's cheek. "Hey," she says, and he puts his arms up, leaning towards her. She glances at me, but he doesn't give her any choice and almost falls into her arms. She takes him, even though he's no lightweight these days, and holds him tight as he clings on, his head buried into her, while she looks up at me, confused.

"I'm sorry," I murmur and she shakes her head.

"What's wrong?" she repeats in a low whisper.

"He threw a bit of a tantrum downstairs, and then he asked about Lauren; about where she is." She nods, rubbing his back gently.

"What did you say to him?"

"That she's not here, but that she loves him very much. And that I do too, and that I won't leave him. It seemed like the right idea at the time, but…"

She stares at me, blinking rapidly, choked with her own emotions, and although I know I should be comforting them both, I hold back, letting her decide what to do; what she can give him, and what she needs from me. She swallows hard, and then sits down on the bottom stair, perching Ben on her lap.

"Your mummy loves you so much," she says softly, rocking him back and forth a little. "And just because she can't be with you, doesn't mean she's forgotten you." Her voice cracks and she takes a breath. "She never will."

She looks up at me, and I can see the pain in her face, knowing that she's not just thinking about Ben and Lauren, but about herself and Molly, and I crouch down in front of them, my hand resting along the side of her leg, just so she knows I'm there.

"Daddy loves you too," she adds, locking eyes with me. "He loves you *so* much. And so do I." I lower my head, struggling with my own feelings now. "We'll always be here for you and we'll keep you safe, Ben. I promise."

I look up again, and she's still staring at me, so I kneel, moving closer, and put my arms around both of them, just holding them tight to me, my heart overflowing with love for this incredible, beautiful, brave woman.

Ben shifts between us and I pull back, looking down at him. He seems a little more cheerful now and Abbie sits forward slightly.

"Shall we go downstairs and play in the garden?" she suggests, putting Ben down on the floor and getting to her feet, while keeping hold of his hand.

"What about your work?" I ask, standing with them.

"I'll do some later," she replies and we move towards the top of the main staircase, where Ben turns to me and raises his arms to be carried. I kiss his cheek as I lift him, grateful that he doesn't seem to object to me now – thanks to Abbie.

Outside, we find the ball that I bought at the beach and spend half an hour kicking it around, with Abbie helping Ben and him occasionally falling over on the soft grass and laughing, his mood altered beyond recognition.

After a while, Abbie suggests we stop for a drink and cookies, which Ben is never going to object to and, while I wash his hands, Abbie starts preparing the tea. We take it outside in the garden, bringing Ben's booster seat with us and, while we're eating, I turn to her, unable to hold back any longer.

"What you said upstairs… about loving Ben…"

"Yes?" She gazes at me, waiting.

"I take it you meant that?"

She nods. "I'd never lie to a child."

I shake my head, still reeling from everything that's happened in the last couple of weeks, but most especially from how lucky I feel right at this moment. "Thank you," I whisper and lean over, taking her hand in mine.

"What for?"

I raise her hand to my lips, kissing her palm. "Just… thank you."

After we've finished tea, we play again for a short while, and then Abbie announces that it's time to start getting dinner ready, and I recall she had something special planned, and that we're all supposed to be making it together.

Going into the kitchen, Abbie starts getting out bowls and dishes, explaining to Ben what she's doing. He takes an avid interest, staring up at her, seemingly as besotted as I am… although I know that's not possible.

"What are we making?" I ask, as Abbie puts a grater and a huge block of cheese down in front of me.

"Well, I thought we could try concocting our own pizzas." She moves around the table and helps Ben to kneel up on a chair, so he can reach the dishes in front of him, before leaning down and whispering, "And, being as Daddy's the one with the muscles, I think he should grate the cheese for us, don't you?" She looks up at me, her eyes alight, and I smile back, feeling happier than I thought possible. Not only has she just announced that she loves my son, but she's making a point of including him in everything, helping him to adjust, even though it's got to be hard for her… and then, just to make things even more perfect, she says things like that too?

I stand and watch for a while, as she goes over to the fridge and pulls out some diced ham, some cooked chicken, a box of mushrooms, a few olives that are left over from lunch, a pepper and an onion.

"You tip the ham, the chicken and the olives into bowls," she says to Ben, handing them to him, "and I'll just cut us up some vegetables."

She makes light work of the chopping, putting everything into individual bowls, and then fetching a jar of passata and a pack of pizza bases from the cupboard.

"I wondered what those were for," I say, as she opens the packet. "And now I know."

She smiles up at me. "They're for making a horrible mess."

"Yep… I think I got off lightly." I look down at Ben, who's still watching her keenly. "Rather you than me," I add, starting to grate the cheese, although I'm still watching them out of the corner of my eye, fascinated.

She shrugs and then pours the passata into the last remaining bowl, before laying out the pizza bases in front of Ben.

She hands him a spoon. "Put a dollop of the tomato sauce onto each pizza," she says and he smiles up at her, and does as she's said, only getting a few drops on the table. "Now, let's spread it out," Abbie suggests, helping Ben to coat the dough bases with rich tomato sauce until they're covered. "Now, what would you like on your pizza?" she asks.

He studies the bowls for a moment, and then says "Ham."

"Okay," Abbie replies. "You put some ham onto yours." She nudges one of the bases closer to him, and then looks up at me. "And what would Daddy like?"

I smile at her. "Daddy would like everything," I reply, gazing at her and after just a moment's pause, she smiles back, biting her bottom lip. God… that's sexy.

"Somehow I'm not surprised," she says, and then she drops some ham, chicken, chopped peppers, mushrooms and olives onto my pizza, sprinkling them evenly. She adds a few onion rings, before helping Ben to put some chicken on his, and then moves on to hers, which I notice is the same as mine – just without the ham. They're soon finished, and

I bring the cheese over, giving Ben a hand to spread it over his pizza, and then passing the dish to Abbie so she can finish off the other two.

"Was that fun?" I ask Ben, leaning down and helping myself to some of the chopped ham that's left in the bowl.

"Yes." He nods enthusiastically.

"Well, we're not finished yet," Abbie says, gathering up the empty bowls and putting them on the draining board. "Ben? Would you like to come outside with me?"

She picks up the colander from the work surface and holds out her hand to him. He jumps down and takes it and they wander off out of the back door.

I clean my hands, then go and stand just outside, watching as Abbie leads Ben down the garden to her small allotment, where she crouches beside him, picking a lettuce, tearing off one of the inner leaves and chewing it, letting Ben have a piece. He copies – as usual – and surprises me by not spitting it out. Abbie lets him pick another lettuce himself, pulling it from the ground, and then they move on, selecting a few other salad vegetables, some of which Abbie lets Ben try, before they return to me at the back door, where I take the colander from Abbie, and pull her into my arms.

"You're amazing… you know that, don't you?"

I feel her shake her head and know she can't talk, which is just as well, because it means she can't disagree with me.

"It's going to take me about twenty minutes to clear up, prepare the salad and cook the pizzas," she says, when I finally release her. "So, do you want to quickly bath Ben now?" She looks up at me.

I nod and hold out my hand to Ben. "Bath time," I say and he steps forward, then stops suddenly.

"Abbie do it," he says, turning back to her.

Abbie looks up at me. "He wants me to bath him?" she says, surprised.

"Looks like it." I grin at her. "I'll manage everything in here… you go and have fun."

She suddenly looks doubtful. "But I—I don't know what to do," she whispers and I can't help but love her even more.

"Okay. I'll come in there with you, at least to start with," I offer and she nods, relieved, leading the way through to the bathroom, Ben and I following behind.

While the water's running, I run upstairs to fetch Ben's pyjamas, like I usually do. And although I only intended to stay for ten minutes and then leave them to it, I end up watching them, leaning on the bathroom door frame, my arms folded, a smile etched on my face, and my heart swollen in my chest as my son splashes water all over the woman I love, giggling louder than I've ever heard him as she splashes him right back.

Once they're finished, Ben does at least accept that I'll have to dry and dress him, because Abbie needs to go upstairs and get dried off herself, and change her clothes.

"How come you don't usually get wet?" she asks, rubbing a towel over her hair. It's hard not to notice that her white top is now completely soaked, and that her lacy bra is clearly visible, as is the outline of her perfect breasts…

"I—I move faster," I manage to explain, struggling to control my voice, let alone the rest of my body, and she smiles, before turning away and going back into the kitchen and then upstairs to change. I let out a long sigh and focus on getting Ben dry, rather than letting my mind wander.

Abbie's already downstairs again when we come out of the bathroom, wearing her blue sundress, her hair a little damp still. She's cleared the table and put the pizzas in the oven, and is standing by the sink, washing the lettuce.

"I love you," I say out loud, unable to stop myself.

She smiles, shakes the water from her hands and comes over to me, leaning up and kissing me briefly. She still hasn't said it back of course, even though she's admitted to loving my son, and, until she's ready to say more, that's good enough for me.

Chapter Nineteen

Abbie

Over the course of this week, our routine has changed again, thanks to my work, and to Ben's sudden insecurity.

I don't know what brought that on, but it hit me hard. I think it hit Josh hard too, judging from the way he reacted, especially when I told Ben that I love him. I do. How could I not? But I'm not sure Josh was expecting to hear that, especially as I haven't told him that I'm in love with him yet. He must be so confused, and I know I should do something about that, but at the moment, as well as overcoming my own fears and insecurities, the problem is finding the time, because since Tuesday, since Ben's tantrum and his subsequent question, we've altered our days to fit around him, to focus on him and hopefully make him feel more secure.

I still go and see Molly first thing in the morning, and Josh and Ben are always waiting for me when I get back, which is good, because I need the comfort of Josh's arms at that point in the day, more than any other. Then, after breakfast, I get on with work, while Josh does something with Ben… that might be going shopping, or out for a walk, or doing things around the house; just something to keep him occupied. They're always back for lunch though, and I stop and join them. After that, we devote the rest of the day to Ben. We might go out somewhere, or bake cookies, like we did yesterday, or just play in the garden, or sit and read a book with him, but we make sure he's with us all the time, so he doesn't become anxious again. When he's gone to bed, I go back up to work, while Josh clears up the kitchen, and then he joins me in the studio, bringing a glass of wine for both of us, and he sits on the small sofa up there, reading a book and keeping me company while I draw. I miss our evenings on the sofa, kissing, but in a way, it feels just like it used to when we were younger, and we'd sit on the beach; him reading, me drawing... except, of course, we're not teenagers anymore.

Josh has just called up the stairs, telling me it's ten minutes until lunch and, today being Friday, I've got to decide whether I'm going to have to work over the weekend, or not. I've had quite a productive day so far and don't think I will, providing I can get in a few hours this evening. Still, I'll worry about that later. For now, it's time to go downstairs and spend the afternoon having fun.

"How's it going?" Josh asks as I go into the kitchen and Ben gets up from the floor, where he's playing with a couple of cars, coming over and raising his arms up to be lifted. I settle him on my hip and he nestles into me, his head on my shoulder.

"Not too bad," I reply.

The table is laid and there's a bowl of salad in the centre. "Any chance I can persuade you to have tonight off?" Josh says.

I tilt my head. "Only if I work on Sunday. Why?"

He sighs. "There are a couple of things I need to talk to you about, that's all."

"Should I be worried?" His tone of voice has me a little concerned, even though he's still smiling.

"No," he says, coming over and leaning down to kiss me, before he heads towards the back door. "Lunch isn't quite ready, so I'll just finish getting the washing in," he says.

Ben wants to go with Josh, so we follow him out into the garden, where Ben makes it clear he wants to be put down. I lower him, standing back up as he starts running around, and it's only then that I notice the washing hanging on the line is mine.

"Um... those are my clothes," I say, walking up to the washing line.

"I know." Josh turns to me and smiles. "I finished mine and Ben's, so I thought I do yours as well. You don't mind, do you?"

"No. Why would I?"

I turn, just then spying a few pairs of very brief knickers further down the line. I can feel myself blushing and wonder whether to rush down and remove them myself, but what would be the point? He's already seen them, he's already handled them, and I'd be making a fuss over nothing, really. He gets to them and unpegs them from the clothes line, turning back to me, a smile on his face.

"I like these," he murmurs under his breath, running his fingers over the fine lace, which makes my breath catch in my throat.

I smile up at him, noticing the fiery look in his eyes and knowing that we're both recalling all the times he used to touch me, and I can't help but think that nothing has been the same since... but that I really would like it to be.

We decide to spend our afternoon at the beach and we have a lovely time, going more appropriately dressed than we did on Sunday morning, with Ben and Josh in swimming shorts, with t-shirts on top, and me with my bikini underneath my dress. It's years since I've worn one and to start with I feel self-conscious, but looking after Ben soon takes my mind off my own feelings, and to be honest, the way Josh keeps looking at me is enough of a distraction in itself. By five o'clock, Ben is tiring, even though he won't admit it, and we have to almost drag him out of the water, drying him off and packing away. I wore a simple jersey dress and although my bikini is still wet, I put it on for the walk home, noticing the way Josh stares at me, which makes me blush and smile at the same time.

We begin the short walk back to the cottage, but just as we're coming out of the car park and going along the low wall, with Josh holding Ben in his arms, the post office door opens and Mary Brewer steps out. I hold my breath, knowing that Josh has managed to avoid seeing her since coming back to the village, and sense the rising tension in his body, close beside mine. She's stopped dead, staring at us – or more particularly, at Ben – and although we're still walking, Josh is now taking much slower, shorter steps.

"Leave me with the bags," he says quietly, "and take Ben home, will you?"

"You don't want me to stay?" I glance up at him and see the anxiety in his eyes, which are fixed on his mother.

"No." He looks down at me, his expression softening. "I don't think this will be pretty, and I don't want Ben here."

I nod my head and put down the beach bag and parasol that I'm carrying.

"Go with Abbie," Josh says to Ben, who luckily doesn't object and lets me take him.

"Try and stay calm," I whisper to Josh, as Ben clings to my neck, and without waiting around any longer, or taking a second look at Mary, we walk away up the hill.

We haven't got far – not more than a few yards beyond Henry's pottery – when Ben asks where his dad is.

"He'll be home soon," I reply. "He's just got to speak to someone."

Ben nods and nestles his head onto my shoulder, seemingly tired. I remember Josh saying though that it's a good idea to keep him awake now, because if he sleeps, he'll stay awake until really late, so I pick up the pace, despite the weight I'm carrying and get us home quickly, suggesting a bath straight away. Ben seems enthusiastic and I take him through the house, and straight into the bathroom, where I run some warm water and help him to undress, his damp clothes left in a pile on the floor for now.

I don't worry about changing myself yet, because I know how wet bath time can be, and I'm pleased about that, being as within a few minutes of Ben climbing into the tub, I'm soaked by his splashing. I don't mind though. He has such fun and hearing his giggles is worth every moment.

I suppose about ten minutes have elapsed when I hear the front door open, and then slam closed again.

"Abbie?" Josh's voice fills the house.

"In the bathroom," I call out in response, and within moments, he appears in the doorway behind us.

"Are you okay?" he asks.

"We're fine." I glance up at him, noting the darkness in his eyes, the tension around his mouth, and I want to go to him, to hold him and take away the pain that I can feel in him. "What happened?" I ask.

"She wanted to know why I'm back," he says quietly, coming and crouching down beside me, splashing Ben, who chuckles and splashes him back. "And she demanded to know who this one is." He's careful not to say Ben's name, so as not to attract his attention to our conversation.

"And what did you tell her?"

"The truth," he replies. "I told her I'm back here because I never stopped loving you, despite her interference." I suck in a breath and lean into him slightly, my head on his shoulder. "And I told her about Lauren and what happened."

"Can I assume from the look on your face that it didn't go well?"

He nods, then sighs. "She was singularly unsympathetic about Lauren and, among other things, she... she asked how many more children I've got scattered around the country..." His voice fades and he ruffles Ben's damp hair.

"My God," I whisper.

"In case you're wondering too," he says, seriously, his eyes still fixed on his son, "there aren't any others. Just Ben."

I reach out and touch Josh's arm, waiting for him to turn and look at me, and I see that old familiar sadness in his eyes again. "I know," I whisper. "I know you, Josh. I know you're not that kind of man."

"Well, evidently my mother doesn't," he retorts.

"Does it matter what she thinks?" I ask and he tilts his head to one side. "Don't let her get to you. She is what she is, and she's not going to change."

"I know," he murmurs, defeated. "I never thought she would, but seeing her again and hearing the way she speaks to me, it was..." He stops talking, seemingly beaten.

"Are you happy here?" I ask, turning slightly so I'm facing him.

He stills, then shakes the drips of water from his hand, wiping it dry on his t-shirt, before cupping my face gently and staring deep into my eyes. "You know I am," he whispers. "You know how happy you make me."

"And do you think your mother is happy?"

"No. I'm not sure she's ever been happy. I don't think she knows how to be," he says, shrugging his shoulders.

"Exactly," I reply. "And that's what you need to remember. Despite everything she's tried to do to you, you're the one who's come out better off. You're a beautiful man, Josh. Inside and out. You're an amazing father, and – more than anyone I know – you deserve to be happy."

He blinks rapidly a few times, although I can see tears welling in his eyes. "You're still doing it," he murmurs eventually.

"Still doing what?"

"Still getting me through. Still helping me... just like you always did."

"Because that's what best friends do."

"Oh, Abbie... you're so much more than my best friend." He leans forward, resting his forehead against mine and we sit for just a second, until Ben splashes us with water, soaking us, and we turn to see his cheeky little face grinning back at us, and both burst out laughing.

Once we're all dried and changed, we have an early dinner. Afterwards, Josh helps Ben down from the table and he comes over to me to say goodnight. I give him a hug, but he's very sleepy indeed and can barely keep his eyes open.

"Are you going to stay down here tonight?" Josh asks, taking Ben from me and lifting him into his arms.

"You want me to?" So much has happened since he first asked me about this at lunchtime, I feel as though my earlier fears about our conversation tonight have taken second place.

He nods. "I know it might mean you having to do some work on Sunday, but I really do need to talk to you."

"Okay." I feel like it's the least I can do after the confrontation Josh had with his mother. I don't think that's what he wants to talk about – not considering that he asked me to stay down here before he'd even met with her – but I can't abandon him now.

I set about clearing the table and tidying the kitchen, and despite my best endeavours, I try not to think about what he's got to tell me that's so important it can't wait. I mustn't second guess the situation and let my imagination run riot. I won't help.

"Leave that, and come and sit down." Josh's voice makes me jump and I turn around to see him standing in the kitchen doorway.

"That was quick."

"He was exhausted. We didn't even bother with a story," he admits, holding out his hand until I take it and let him lead me back into the living room, sitting us both down on the sofa, side by side, with him in the corner.

"Josh…"

"Yes?"

"Is there something wrong?" I have to ask. "I know at lunch you said I didn't need to worry, but…"

He puts his arms around me and turns us slightly, so I'm leaning back against his chest. "You don't," he says.

"Is this something to do with your mother?" I ask. "Do you want to talk about what happened?"

"No," he replies. "She's the last person I want to talk about. You were right about her. She's miserable and she hates to see anyone else being happy. I made it clear to her earlier that I don't want her involved with Ben, and I'm not going to let her interfere in my life, or in our lives ever again. I know I wasn't myself when I came back here this afternoon, and I know I needed you then more than ever, but I've had a couple of hours to think things through and to put some distance between us and her words." He holds me just a little tighter. "I shouldn't have let her get to me like that, but she was particularly vitriolic… and very personal."

"About me?" I guess.

"Yes," he admits. "And about Ben."

"And that makes it harder for you, doesn't it?"

"Yes. I suppose I can cope with her insults about me… I've had a lifetime of those, after all. But when she gets her claws into the people I love, I find it much more difficult."

"I know." I turn and look up at him. "But she doesn't need to have anything to do with us, Josh. Not if you don't want her to."

"I don't," he says fiercely.

"Good," I murmur, nestling into him again.

"Now," he says softly, stroking my hair. "Let's forget about my mother."

"Gladly," I reply.

"I wanted to talk to you about the weekend."

"The weekend?" I twist around properly, surprised by the change of subject, and look up at him. "I thought… I mean, aren't we going to test drive the car tomorrow? And then I'll be working for at least part of Sunday…"

"I'm not talking about this weekend, I'm talking about next weekend," he interrupts tightening his grip on me again.

"I didn't know we had plans for next weekend."

"I know. That's why I needed to talk to you."

"Why? What have you got in mind?"

He leans down and kisses my forehead. "Ben and I… well, we've got to go back to London," he says, and I pull away slightly, even though he tries to keep hold of me.

"London?" I can hear the crack in my voice, so I'm sure he must be able to as well.

"Yes, but don't get upset," he replies. "Listen to what I've got to say first." I swallow, and take a deep breath, nodding my head. "I've got to go back, because I didn't bring that many clothes," he explains. "I couldn't get everything into my car at the time, which is why I'm doing so much washing. Obviously I could just go out and buy a whole new wardrobe if I wanted to, although that seems incredibly wasteful to me, when I've got a dressing room full of clothes in London. And I could do with picking up some more of Ben's things as well, so he's got more toys down here. And I'd like to go to the Aston Martin dealership to see about organising my car."

"I see."

"And…" He pauses, making me wonder what's coming next. "And I've been in touch with Richard and Tonya, and they're both going to be free next Saturday afternoon, which means I could tie in a visit with them as well, so they can see Ben…" He lets his voice fade, then adds,

"The question is…" He pauses again, only this time, it seems like he's the one who's more nervous. "The question is, are you going to be able to come with us? We should have the Audi by then, and if not, I'll hire us a car, so transport won't be a problem, but I understand that I'm asking a lot of you." He's not kidding, and for a moment, I can't speak. "I know it's a huge step for you to be away from Molly," he says, before I have the chance to respond, and I swallow down my tears. "If it's too much…" He doesn't finish his sentence, and it takes me a moment to find my voice.

"It hasn't always been like this," I murmur. "I haven't always visited her every day. At the beginning, when I was still married to Simon and we were living in Falmouth, it wasn't possible for me to come down here all the time, no matter how much I wanted to. But I came as often as I could." I take a breath – just a short one. "So, I suppose that, as long as we can talk to Dad and make sure he visits Molly for me, so she's not on her own, and as long as you promise me faithfully that we won't be gone for more than a couple of days, then yes, I can come with you."

He smiles. "I promise we'll talk to your dad, and I promise it won't be for more than two days. We'll leave on Friday, after breakfast, and come back on Sunday, in time for you to go and see Molly in the evening. So, you'll only actually miss seeing her on Saturday. Is that okay?"

I nod my head, tilting it back to look up at him and he leans down and kisses me.

"Why do you want me to come?" I ask, once we break the kiss. I'm cradled in his arms now and it feels comfortable and relaxing.

"Because I don't like the idea of you being here by yourself, and because I promised I'd never leave you again," he says softly. "But I do have to take Ben back. I promised Richard and Tonya that I would."

"What will I do when you take Ben to see them?" I ask, my nerves returning all of a sudden. "I know I'm originally from London, but it's been thirty years since I've been there. I don't think…"

"You'll come with us," he says firmly.

"But surely, that'll be awkward, won't it? Especially with Lauren's father…"

"Why? He knows Lauren and I weren't together. He knows she died with her boyfriend. I've already explained to him who you are."

"You have?" I can't disguise my surprise and he smiles at me.

"Yes. When I told Richard I was coming back here and bringing Ben with me, I told him why. Obviously, I wasn't sure what the outcome would be, or whether you'd be able to forgive me, and I didn't give him huge amounts of detail, but I told him you were the only woman in the world for me."

"You actually said that?"

He nods his head, completely unembarrassed. "It's the truth. And while my relationship with Richard is still very new and quite tenuous, and certainly doesn't entitle him to know everything about me, I knew he wanted me to stay in London, so he could see Ben more often, and I needed to explain to him why I couldn't do that… Because I'd only just found you again and I certainly wasn't going to risk losing you."

I reach up and touch his cheek with my fingertips. "So, you won't leave me alone anywhere? When we're in London?" I ask, just to be sure.

"Of course I won't. This trip is really about Ben, but you're just as much of a priority for me, and I'll look after you. I promise."

I rest my head back on his chest. "Thank you," I whisper and he kisses the top of my head.

"There's one other thing I wanted to discuss with you," he says, after a slight pause, and I twist around again to face him.

"Oh yes?"

He takes a breath. "I don't like you working all these hours, Abbie. You're exhausted. You've been going off to sleep a lot quicker at night…" He's still been sitting with me each evening, after I've finished work, stroking my hair, whispering to me, making me feel safe enough to fall asleep.

"I know, but deadlines are deadlines, I'm afraid."

He nods. "I get that. But that's one of the things I've been thinking about when I've been watching you working and pretending to read each evening."

I wasn't aware he was pretending to read, and I stare up at him.

"I've been thinking about starting a new company," he says.

"And how is that going to help?" I ask. "If you're out at work all hours…"

He puts his fingers over my lips, silencing me.

"Because it wouldn't be like that," he says. "I will happily admit that I'm not cut out to do nothing, or to just take care of Ben. This last week has shown me that much. It's been fun spending time with him, and I love him to death, but I need to do something else, something productive. The thing is, I don't want it to take over my life again, not like it did before. More to the point, I don't *need* it to take over my life… because I want to have a life with you. So, I'm thinking about starting a publishing company, like I told you. I have a lot of contacts still, and I'd hire freelance editors and production people, rather than doing any of it myself. Essentially, I'd just oversee it really."

"From where?" I ask, feeling sceptical still.

"Here," he says. "If that's okay with you. Your attic space is huge and I'm sure, with a bit of re-modelling, we can both fit in there, and leave some space for Ben to play too."

"And I presume you'll want me to produce your covers, will you?"

He smiles. "No. I was sort of hoping you'd do a bit more than that."

"I thought you said you wanted me to work less hours, not more."

"I know… just hear me out, will you? I'd like you to be more than a freelance artist, and I'd like you to give up designing for other people too. We can work together, running the publishing company… sharing the load, side by side. I want us to be business partners, Abbie."

I stare at him, unable to speak for a moment. "But I don't know anything about publishing… not really."

"You know enough. You've worked in the industry for over fifteen years. You understand deadlines, and authors."

"And you want to do that from here?"

"Yes. I—I couldn't ask you to leave Porthgowan," he says, stammering slightly. "Molly's here, so I'd never ask you to go anywhere else." He stops talking for a moment, then adds, "I really think we can make it work, Abbie, and I think we can have a better life doing it. You can cut down your hours, and have a lot less stress. You can draw for fun again, and I can fit my days around you and Ben, and give him what he needs now, as well as doing something more fulfilling with my time… and then, when he starts school, we can adapt to that."

"We?"

"Yes. This is about us, Abbie. It's about building a future for us. Together. I'm not suggesting any of it would happen straight away. I need to give Ben a bit longer to get used to things as they are now, we'd have to refurbish your studio, and we won't be able to set the new business up in five minutes anyway; it's all going to take time. But, tell me you'll at least think about it."

I stare up at him, nodding my head and pondering over his idea. The thought of working with him is exciting – I love him, and I love being with him, and when I'm up in the attic in the evenings and he's sitting with me, I find his presence reassuring, so I don't see why we'd have a problem working together. The thought of cutting down on my hours and losing some of the stress in my life, spending more time with Josh and Ben, not having to worry about deadlines and money, is even better and I suck in a breath.

"I do often wonder if it's all too much," I remark. "Like this evening, when I had to decide whether I could afford the time to sit up and talk to you, even if it meant working on Sunday…"

"It shouldn't have to be like that," he murmurs. "It needn't be. Life isn't about stress…"

"I know. I sometimes used to ask myself if that was what caused Simon and I to have so much trouble conceiving," I murmur, without thinking.

"You had trouble?" he says, looking for clarification.

"Yes." Josh stares at me, his surprise obvious.

"I—I didn't know that," he says. "I assumed you'd just put it off… you know… waited for the time to be right."

"No," I reply and then realise that's not strictly true. "Well, we did, I suppose." And I rest my head on him again, letting him cradle me gently, knowing the time has come to talk… at last. "To start off with, when we first got married, Simon wanted us to have a bigger house, and for him to have a better job… with more money," I say quietly and he holds me tighter. "As a result of which, we'd been married for over four years by the time he said we should start trying."

"*He* said?" he queries and I nod my head.

"The timing was his decision. Only… it didn't work out as I'd expected," I explain. "I thought I'd just stop taking the pill, and get pregnant, like that." I snap my fingers together. "But that couldn't have been further from the reality."

"So what happened?"

I look up at him, raising my face, seeing his concern. "We tried… and we tried, but nothing happened. The disappointment every month was unbelievable, and I got so worked up… so stressed… and then after a couple of years, Simon came to me and said he wanted to stop trying." I manage a half laugh, remembering his words. "Actually, he said it was like fucking me to order, and he'd had enough."

"He said what?" I feel Josh grip me.

"I'm not repeating it," I say quietly. "But we argued. It was horrible. He said it wasn't any fun anymore." I shake my head. "I wanted to tell him it had never been much fun for me…"

"Excuse me?" Josh lets me go, sitting up and twisting me around, so we're facing each other, holding tightly to my shoulders, and looking into my eyes. "What did you just say?"

"That it had never been much fun for me," I reply. "Not with him. I didn't say that to Simon, of course, but I wanted to. I wanted to hurt him, like he'd hurt me."

He shakes his head. "But…but what happened to the monster?" he whispers and I feel tears welling in my eyes.

"The monster died years ago," I murmur, trying not to cry. "Eighteen years ago."

He lets out a long sigh and pulls me back into him again. "I'm sorry," he says gently and sits back, taking me with him, so I'm lying on top of him now. "Tell me, what happened, after Simon said that… Obviously something did."

I nod. "We didn't talk for a while. We didn't do anything for a while. But then I asked him if we could try IVF. He… he was shocked, but said he'd think about it, and I was so grateful, we ended up… you know…" I can't say the words, not to Josh, but I know he understands.

"And you got pregnant?" he asks, proving me right.

"Yes. It was just one of those things, I suppose. We'd stopped trying so hard, and it just happened. I was thrilled… I was beyond thrilled."

"And Simon?"

"Well, he found it hard to believe I'd got pregnant that easily after we'd been trying for so long… so he accused me of sleeping with someone else."

"What the fuck?" He stops talking suddenly. "Sorry," he says, because he rarely swears, although I don't blame him in this instance. It's how I wanted to react at the time. I still do sometimes, when I think about it.

"We really argued that time," I explain. "I even packed a bag and got ready to come home to Dad… but Simon persuaded me to stay. He said he'd make it up to me. He said was sorry. He was good at that."

"Was he good at meaning it?" Josh asks, sounding even angrier than he did when he was talking about his mother.

"Yes, I think so." I look up at him. "He wasn't a bad man, Josh." He frowns, like he doesn't believe me. "And he really was sorry about that. He did everything with me, all through the pregnancy… until…" My voice fades and I fall into silence. Josh doesn't prompt this time. He just holds me and waits until I'm ready. I take a few moments, sucking in a deep breath, before I start talking again. "I was thirty-eight weeks," I murmur quietly. "It was a routine check-up; nothing out of the ordinary… until they told me there was no heartbeat."

I sob silently, but I know he knows I'm crying, because he whispers, "Hush," his arms coming even tighter around me.

"One minute she was there, and the next she was gone."

I let my tears fall onto his chest, appreciating the physical comfort, the feeling of silent, unquestioning understanding and support; the things Simon didn't really give me at the time.

Josh waits until I'm ready to start talking again, until I'm able to explain that I had to give birth to Molly, and that they let us stay with her afterwards, for the whole day; that we could have had longer, if we'd wanted.

"They gave us a box," I add, through my tears.

"A box?" he queries, still holding me tight.

"Yes. W—Would you like to see it?" I lean up slightly, staring into his glistening eyes.

"Of course. If that's okay with you. I mean, as long as you're sure."

I pull away and clamber off of him, slowly getting to my feet. "It's upstairs," I explain, and he nods, and I can feel him watching me as I climb the stairs. In my bedroom, I open the wardrobe and reach inside to where Molly's box is stored, taking it out and carrying it carefully back down to the living room, where Josh is now sitting up. I take a seat beside him and he shifts forward as I open the lid, putting it on the table, and we peer inside.

"I—I don't open it very often these days," I murmur. "I find it too hard when I'm on my own."

I feel his arm come around me, as I start to take out the items inside, one by one, and show them to him. We don't speak, not until the end, when everything is gathered on his lap and he looks down at it. "It's beautiful," he whispers.

"It's called a memory box." I turn to him. "It's all I have…" My voice cracks and he moves closer.

"No, it's not, Abbie." He holds up the bonnet, handing it back to me to replace in the box. "You have your memories… your own memories of the time you carried her. I know they're not enough, but you do have them."

I manage to smile at him, because I can't deny the truth behind his words. Then slowly we replace the items in the box, making sure they're neat and tidy, before Josh puts the lid back on and pulls me down onto the sofa again, so we're lying along it, facing each other, his arms around me, hugging me close to him.

"Afterwards," I continue, getting back to the story, "we just got lost."

"You and Simon?" he asks and I nod.

"We stopped communicating… until months later, when he came and told me he was having an affair."

He startles, letting me go and leaning back, his eyes fixed on mine. "Abbie?" I nod my head. "Oh my God," he breathes. "I had no idea… I knew about your marriage, and about Molly, because my mother told me, and I found out about the divorce when I got down here, but no-one told me the reason."

"Well, that's because no-one knows. Not even Dad. Everyone thinks we fell apart because of Molly, which I suppose we did, really."

"But… he should have been there for you…" His arms come around me again, even though he seems to be in shock. "He should have been the one keeping you together, not thinking about himself."

"It wasn't really like that," I reason. "He'd been seeing the woman – Haley her name is – before I got pregnant."

His eyes widen. "But that just makes it so much worse, for crying out loud."

I put my hand on his cheek, trying to calm him. "No, Josh. You have to understand, I made it so boring between us… sex, I mean."

"*You* made it boring? Abbie, you've already admitted that it was no fun for you," he says, sounding more bitter than I think I ever felt.

"I know, but I made it too regimented. It was all about getting pregnant, about charts and temperatures."

"So?" he says. "That didn't give him the right to cheat."

I swallow my pride and confess, "I really was obsessed. I even used to text him in the middle of the day sometimes and tell him to come home… just because the timing was right."

"And did he?" Josh asks.

"At the beginning, yes, he'd come home during his lunch break, but as time went on, more often than not he'd tell me he was busy and I'd have to wait until the evening."

Josh shakes his head and leans forward, his face barely an inch from mine. "If that had been me, and you'd asked me to come home from work to make love to you, I'd have been there in an instant… in a heartbeat."

I stare at him, unable to breathe for a moment. "Well, of course, I didn't know he was seeing Haley at the time, so…" He sighs. "But when he told me… after Molly… it all made more sense."

"So you had no idea?" he asks.

"No. I didn't see it coming at all. Obviously I knew things weren't right between us, but…"

He brushes my cheek with the backs of his fingers. "So, is that why you went kind of weird on me when I was getting those text messages from Tonya?"

I let my eyes drop to his chin. "Yes." He waits and I add, "I'd missed all the signs with Simon, you see. I didn't want…"

"Abbie," he interrupts and I raise my eyes to his again. "You must know by now that I'd never cheat on you. I'd never do anything to hurt you."

I nod my head, because for a few moments, I can't speak.

"Were there text messages between Simon and Haley?" he asks.

"Not that I know of," I reply, finding my voice. "They spent a lot of time together at work, and their evenings too, and then Simon made excuses to be with her on Sundays as well. Looking back, they were pretty inseparable, I suppose, and I remember he said he'd felt really torn when I told him I was pregnant, but he did the right thing and stayed with me."

"No," Josh says, his fingers still caressing my cheek. "The right thing would have been not to cheat in the first place. And to love you properly, the way to deserve to be loved, to support you when you needed it, to be there for you all the time, without fail, and not to put his needs ahead of yours."

I nestle into him as he hugs me. "He stopped seeing her while I was pregnant," I explain, going on with my story, because I need to get to the end now. "And then, after Molly, he went back to her." I feel Josh's muscles stiffen, but he doesn't say anything and I continue, "He said it was because she understood him better than I did. He needed someone to talk to and she listened, evidently."

"And what about you?" he asks. "Who did you have to talk to? Who listened to you?"

"No-one," I reply simply, realising that fact for the first time perhaps.

"Exactly. That was his job, Abbie."

"I know, but to be fair, Simon and I had stopped listening to each other ages before Molly."

He shakes his head. "I presume he told you about his affair because he'd decided he wanted to be with her?" Josh says.

"Yes. He said he was in love with her, and not me."

"I assume he wasn't a complete idiot and that he had been in love with you once upon a time?" I lean back, startled by the anger in Josh's voice.

"Yes. But… but he knew it had been a mistake…"

"What? Loving you?" He looks confused now.

"No. Proposing to me," I explain through a deep sigh. "Simon told me that night, after he'd confessed to the affair, after he'd explained everything, that he'd always known I was still in love with you – even when he proposed." I feel the tension leave his body in an instant, one hand moving to the small of my back, pulling me closer to him. "He… he said he thought I'd learn to love him with time," I continue. "That was why he took me away from Porthgowan and moved us to Falmouth, in the hope that I'd forget you and fall in love with him." I shrug my shoulders. "It didn't work, and in the end, it was just incredibly sad, really… because we both knew…" I let my voice fade, seeing the sadness in his eyes. "Tell me it's been different for you, Josh," I whisper. "Tell me you've been happy."

He shakes his head and swallows hard. "But you must have been happy at times, surely? It can't all have been bad."

"I was happy when I was pregnant… at least until the end." I struggle to control my voice, then add, "As for the rest of the time, I suppose I'd say, I was contented. I'd made my decisions and I had to live with them, even if there was no pleasure, no satisfaction, no joy. I thought happiness was too much to hope for and maybe contentment was better. But I was wrong."

"Are you still in contact with him?" he asks, looking concerned, maybe even a little worried, I think.

I shake my head. "No. I was, for a while, but… but then about a year after our divorce, he and Haley got married."

"And that bothered you?" he whispers and I wrap my leg around him, to reassure him that it didn't. Not in the least.

"No… the marriage didn't bother me. It was the reason for the marriage…"

He shakes his head, closing his eyes. "She was pregnant?" he guesses.

"Yes. Simon drove down and told me. I suppose he thought I should hear it from him, rather than risk me seeing Haley with him in the graveyard, or somewhere in the village, on one of their visits to Molly, and discovering her pregnancy that way. He was trying to be considerate, I think."

He moves his hand from the small of my back to my cheek, caressing my skin with his fingertips. "Why didn't you say?"

"Because it's something I've just got used to keeping to myself," I explain. "Like everything else…"

"So, you and Simon don't talk anymore?" he asks.

"No. Since his marriage, we haven't been in contact at all. There hasn't been the need, and he doesn't come down to visit Molly as often as he used to. He even forgot her birthday this year…" My voice cracks completely and then fades.

"How do you know?"

"Because when he did used to come, he always brought white roses." I pause and look up at him. "I suppose the living become more important, don't they?" I mumble.

Josh shakes his head and whispers, "No," holding me closer still, making me feel safe, and loved, just like he always has done.

"I—I got it so wrong," I murmur into his chest. "I should never have accepted his proposal… not when…" My voice falters and he shifts slightly, raising my face to his and looking into my eyes.

"Why can't you say it?" he asks. "I've told you over and over that I love you, and I know you love me. Even if I couldn't see it in your eyes every time I look at you, you've already admitted it. You've just told me that one of the reasons your marriage failed was because you were still in love with me, so why can't you say the words? Why can't you tell me that you love me?"

I feel the tears start to fall. "Because… because it means admitting it's okay to be happy," I sob.

"But it is okay," he reasons. "No-one wants you to be miserable."

"I don't deserve it."

"Yes, you do." I stare up at him, seeing the longing and the love in his eyes. "Tell me, Abbie," he whispers. "Please… just let yourself say it."

I take a breath. "I—I do love you, Josh," I whisper, hearing his sigh. "I always did."

He leans in and kisses me, just briefly. "Don't feel guilty for saying that," he says, as though he can read my mind. "Or for meaning it. I want you to know that, whenever you're feeling doubtful, or sad, or helpless, you can talk to me. I will always listen and I will always understand."

"I know. That's what's so incredible about you."

"I just want to help," he adds. "I want to be here for you." He kisses me again. "I know I can't make the dark times go away, but I can hold you and help you through them. That's why I've sat with you at night, so you don't have to cry alone; and why I've waited for you every day when you come home from the church."

I look into his eyes, remembering his surprise appearance that first time. "Did you guess that was where Molly was buried, and what I was doing there… because your mother had told you about her?" I ask, feeling intrigued.

"No," he admits. "Your dad told me, and once I knew, I came and watched you."

"You did?" I'm surprised. "When was that?"

"Robert told me about it the day after I got here… after I got back from your house; and I came to the churchyard the following morning."

"But that wasn't the day you met me when I got home, was it?" I'm confused.

"No." He shakes his head. "I needed some time to think things through. And I needed to see you again. Our first meeting hadn't gone very well, if you remember?" I nod my head feeling embarrassed, as I recall nearly throwing him out of the house, just because he'd said he wasn't over me. "I knew that if I was going to help you, I had to get it right."

"You did," I whisper. "You got it very right."

"I hope so."

"But why didn't you come into the churchyard? You could have done. I wouldn't have minded."

He lowers his eyes. "For one thing, I know you married Simon there, so... well, if I'm being honest, it felt a bit awkward. And, more importantly, that's your place. Yours and Molly's. I wouldn't dream of intruding there."

I shake my head and cup his face with my hand until he focuses on me. "I didn't marry Simon there, Josh."

He stares at me, long and hard. "You didn't?"

"No. We were married at the registry office in Helston."

He smiles, a little half-heartedly. "It's a good thing I didn't come down here on your wedding day to try and stop the service then, isn't it?"

I sit back, a little stunned. "You were going to do that?"

"I considered it," he admits. "But then I thought you were in love with him. I thought you were happy, and I couldn't do anything to spoil that for you... Besides, it seems I'd have gone to the wrong place. I always thought you'd get married here. I always thought..." His voice fades.

"No," I muse, although I don't add anything else, and I know I don't need to. Josh doesn't need me to explain. He understands that there's only one person I could have married in Porthgowan... and it wasn't Simon.

He leans in and kisses me, and whispers, "I'm glad... although I still wouldn't intrude. Not there. As I say, that's your special place."

"Yes it is," I reply slowly. "But you wouldn't be intruding." He smiles and I let out a breath... a breath that I've been holding in for far too long. "Can you do something for me?" I ask and he nods his head.

"Of course."

"Can you come with me tomorrow? You and Ben… Can we go together to Molly's grave? All three of us?" I pause for a second. "I—I'd like to introduce you to my daughter."

He's struggling now, and he clears his throat, blinking a few times. "It would be my privilege to meet your daughter. I—I'll go with you whenever you need me to. And if you need to go alone sometimes, then that's fine too. I won't take it personally, and I'll still be here to hold you when you come home."

He shifts, so he's lying on his back and I'm on top of him. Then he puts his arms and his legs tightly around me, wrapping me up in him.

"Hold me," I whisper into his chest.

"I am."

"No… I mean keep holding me… Never stop. Never let me go."

Chapter Twenty

Josh

We lie for ages, our limbs entwined, our breathing matched, until eventually Abbie leans up, just slightly and looks down at me, her eyes still misted with tears.

"I've told you about my life," she whispers. "Can you tell me about yours?"

"You want me to?"

"Yes. I want to know what you've been doing for the last eighteen years... apart from working."

"Well, the answer to that is, not very much," I reply, turning us onto our sides again, and she smiles.

"You must have done something."

I shrug. "A few things... some of which I'm not very proud of."

She frowns. "Such as?"

"Such as almost destroying Tim's apartment," I confess and her frown deepens.

"How?"

I sigh. "I got very, very drunk. Ugly drunk."

"You?" She's surprised.

"Yes. It was a long, long time ago. My mother had called to tell me you were seeing Simon. I—I couldn't handle the thought of you with someone else." She tenses next to me, and I hold her tighter. "So, I decided to empty the contents of Tim's drinks cabinet into my stomach."

"Oh," she says simply.

"I pretty much trashed the place," I recall. "I threw up over his very expensive carpets… like I say, it was ugly."

"Was he angry?" she asks.

"Luckily he was away at the time, and I managed to get it all professionally cleaned before he returned, so he never actually knew."

"I'm sorry," she whispers, lowering her eyes, but I reach out, raising her face to mine.

"If you're going to say 'sorry' to everything I tell you, then I'm going to stop talking right now."

"Don't," she replies. "I want to know."

"Then stop apologising."

She pauses and then nods her head. "Did you get drunk much?" she asks.

"No. It only happened once more."

"When was that?"

"The night I found out you and Simon were engaged… courtesy of my mother, again. She called me at work that time."

"So you went out and got drunk?" she guesses.

"No, I went back to the flat and got drunk… well, I started to, anyway. But Uncle Tim came home and found me on the bathroom floor, crying my eyes out…" She changes position, pulling away from me, moving to the end of the sofa and sitting up.

"You cried?"

I sit up too. "Yes. It wasn't the first time, or the last."

She stares at me for just a moment, but then silently clambers onto my lap, her head bowed, and snuggles into my chest as I put my arms around her. I suppose this is the physical equivalent of saying 'sorry', and although she still doesn't have to, I don't mind at all.

"When was the first time?" she whispers.

"The night we broke up." She sighs and shakes her head slowly.

"And the last?"

"You mean apart from earlier this evening, in the bathroom, when I nearly lost it? And just now, when you asked me to come to the church with you to meet your daughter?" She nods and I pause, wondering how to tell her, but then decide to just say it. "It was when my mother called to tell me about Molly. I—I couldn't even imagine what you were going through, but just thinking about how much you'd lost… well, it broke me."

She leans back and looks up into my eyes, her own filled with tears. "What did I do to you?" she murmurs.

"You didn't," I reply quickly. "It wasn't you. It was me. Don't you remember… we used to lie on the beach, and in my bed, and on the sofa at your dad's place, and I used to promise you I'd never leave you? For heaven's sake, I told you I'd never leave you the first time I made love to you. Don't you remember that?"

"Yes." She nods her head.

"Well, I broke that promise. I left you. So whatever happened to me is not your fault, and it's nothing compared with what you've been through."

"But you were so hurt," she whispers.

"Yes, I was. But I'm not anymore." I pull her in close again. "I'll never break another promise to you, Abbie. And I'll never risk losing you again either. I've tried a life without you, and believe me, it's not a life worth living."

Once again, it's dark outside by the time we pull away from each other and although we haven't spent the evening kissing, I feel like we've moved so much further forward. There are still things we probably haven't told each other, but they can wait. The point is that she opened up to me at last… and she told me she loves me. And that's all that matters.

"It's late," Abbie murmurs, stretching her arms above her head. "We should go to bed."

Without waiting for my answer, she shifts off of my lap and stands, hesitating, and then holds out her hand to help me up. I take it and let her pull me to my feet, putting my hands on her waist and looking down at her.

"Shall I lock up?" I suggest and she nods her head, waiting while I go through to the kitchen, locking the back door and making sure everything is turned off, before I return to her. She's switched off the lights and is standing in the darkness at the bottom of the stairs, facing me.

"Ten minutes?" I say quietly, knowing it takes her roughly that long to get ready for bed.

She pauses and then shakes her head, leaving me confused.

"You… you don't want me to come to your room tonight?" I ask.

"No… I do," she whispers and I feel my brow furrow.

"In that case…"

"I don't want to get ready for bed first… either of us," she interrupts and very, very slowly, the penny drops.

"Are you saying you want me to come to bed with you?" She nods her head and, even though it's dark, I can see her blushing. My heart is beating loudly in my chest, but I know I have to be sure what she's saying – or not saying, being as she's gone quiet on me. "Do you just want me to hold you, or…?"

She shakes her head this time and moves closer, so we're touching. "I want more," she whispers, and without saying anything – because I'm lost for words – I take her hand, and lead her up the stairs to her bedroom door, where I pause, just for a second.

"Are you sure about this?" I ask.

"Yes." Her voice is a mere murmur, but it's clear enough, and I turn the handle, opening her door and letting her enter.

I follow her inside, shutting us in, and when I turn back, she's standing there, looking at me, the moonlight streaming in through the window behind her, giving her a magical, ethereal glow. I close the gap between us, capturing her face in my hands and kiss her, our tongues clashing in an instant as she moans into me. I move my hand down, brushing it across her breast and she trembles slightly to my touch, sighing and knotting her fingers in my hair as I walk her backwards to the bed and, when she hits it, I undo the zip at the back of her dress, leaning back and watching as I pull the straps from her shoulders and let it fall to the floor, revealing her perfect, rounded breasts.

I whisper her name, and lean down, capturing a hardened nipple between my teeth. She sucks in a breath and I kiss my way downwards, my lips stroking over her body, until I'm kneeling before her, my thumbs inside the top of her lace knickers. I lower them slowly to her ankles, my breath catching in my throat as I see her again.

"Y—You're still shaved," I manage to say.

"Not 'still'," she whispers and I look up at her.

"You mean… you shaved for us?"

"Yes," she says, "and I love the fact that you know it wasn't just for you."

I smile, leaning in and kissing that spot at the apex of her thighs. She shudders, her body quivering. "You think I could have forgotten that you found everything so much more intimate… more sensuous, when it was like this," I say, standing once more and lifting her onto the bed, laying her down and parting her legs with my hands.

She stares up at me and I let my eyes roam over her perfect body, which doesn't seem to have altered at all, despite the half a lifetime since I last set eyes on her, and I know I have to taste her again. Settling between her thighs, I run my tongue along her folds, discovering her swollen nub, flickering across it, groaning with pleasure as she raises her hips to me and starts to writhe and thrash beneath me. Within moments, she's trembling, moaning and whispering my name, her body close to surrendering, when suddenly she stops, deflating and sighing.

I look up at her and see she's staring at the ceiling.

"I—I can't," she murmurs, and I crawl up her body, raising myself above her.

"Because of what's in your head?" I ask and she nods, blinking back her tears and looking into my eyes.

"I'm sorry," she whispers.

"Don't be." I stand and pull my t-shirt off over my head, and she looks up at me, leaning on her elbows.

"It won't make any difference, Josh," she says softly, sounding frustrated now.

"Yes, it will. I can't talk to you when I'm doing that. But I can if we're making love."

I pull down my shorts and stand before her, naked, smiling as her eyes wander and she bites her bottom lip when they reach my very obvious arousal, her instincts intact, it would seem, despite her emotional barriers.

Crawling up her body once more, I pause to kiss her nipples, making her sigh, and then kneel between her legs, my erection finding her entrance, nudging against her… just like the first time.

"Do you want me to go and get a condom?" I ask, hesitating, on the brink of the precipice.

"Where from?" She looks even more surprised now.

"My room."

"You've got condoms?" The furrows appear above her nose as she frowns, just slightly.

"Yes." I can feel myself blush. "I—I picked some up the other day, at the supermarket."

"You did?"

"Yes. And I'm sorry if that seems arrogant, or presumptuous, but I… well, I hoped we might make love at some point, and after our conversation the other night, I thought I should be prepared."

Her frown fades in an instant and she smiles. "I'm on the pill," she says softly, and I lean down and kiss her, before raising myself up again and staring into her eyes, as I slowly penetrate her.

She sucks in a breath, raising her legs slightly, as I inch inside, feeling her warmth surround me, until we're locked together, and I'm finally back where I belong.

I start to move. I have to. And she grinds into me, our rhythm matched in an instant, as I keep my eyes fixed on hers. "You're perfect," I whisper, but she shakes her head. "Yes you are. You're perfect for me. Let your thoughts go, Abbie. Empty your head, don't think at all… just feel." I swivel my hips slightly, going deeper and she gasps, and then moans. "That's it… give yourself to me."

"O—Oh yes," she stutters.

I take her hands, holding them either side of her head, and I feel her body tighten, the memory obviously still fresh with her too, as the heat turns up a notch and we love each other with a deep, intense passion even I'd forgotten could exist.

"Josh," she whispers eventually, the desperation obvious in her voice. "Please… please, help me… I can't…"

"Yes, you can." I alter my position and take her slightly harder, and just like that, without any warning, she comes apart beneath me, writhing in ecstasy, her head tilted backwards, my name a constant murmur on her lips.

I don't know how I've held on through that, but I have and as she calms, I start to move again.

"More," I urge, thrusting into her. "I want all of you. Come for me, Abbie… only for me… now."

As I say the last few words, she clamps around me, her body rising up to mine, as a second wave of pleasure overwhelms her, her tight grip pushing me over the edge, driving me upwards, upwards, and into heaven.

Despite my breathlessness, I hold on to her, keeping her with me, not willing to let the darkness claim her, and I roll us onto our sides.

"I love you," I whisper.

"I love you." She sounds exhausted, satisfied… adorable.

"Go to sleep now, beautiful." She nods her head and nuzzles into me, her breathing changing almost at once, and I know she already has.

I wake early and find myself smiling before I'm even properly conscious.

But that's because Abbie's in my arms and my head is filled with memories. Only now they're not dim and distant memories, that I've clung on to through the passage of time. These are fresh, and new and vibrant, and best of all, we can make more of them. So many more. She feels soft and sleepy against me, her body cocooned with mine. She's got her head on my chest, her arm across my stomach and her leg is lying over mine. And it feels fantastic.

I twist just slightly, wanting to look at her, and she stirs, opening her eyes.

"Sorry, I didn't mean to wake you."

She smiles up at me. "Don't apologise." I notice that she doesn't move away. If anything, she snuggles even nearer.

"Are you okay?" I ask.

"Yes." She looks up at me. "Are you?"

"I'm a lot better than okay."

She lowers her eyes. "I—I'd forgotten it could feel that good," she murmurs.

"I know you had. But I promise, I won't let you forget again."

She nods her head and moves even closer still, almost lying on top of me now, and clinging to me.

"Hey, I'm not going anywhere," I say, to reassure her and she looks up, her eyes searching mine.

"But won't you need to go back to your own bed in a minute?" she asks.

"Why?"

"Well, Ben will come in soon – to one or other of us."

"He's been coming in here for the last few days, so I think it's safe to assume he's not going to break the pattern."

She bites her bottom lip, nervously. "And you're okay with him finding us together?"

"Yes. He's going to have to get used to you and I sleeping in the same bed sometime… and if I can manage it, then so can he."

She tilts her head. "What does that mean?"

I turn us onto our sides, facing each other and pull her close, letting her feel my arousal. "It means, that's the first time I've ever spent the night with anyone – other than Ben – and I don't think he counts."

Her eyes widen. "But… you told me… I mean, you said there had been other women," she whispers.

"There were. And like I said, there weren't very many of them. But the thing is, I never wanted to spend a whole night with any of them." She gazes up at me, still surprised, I think. "I always felt guilty," I confess.

"When?"

"Whenever I was with another woman, I always felt like I was cheating on you. We may not have been together at the time, but being with anyone else felt wrong." She reaches up and touches my cheek. "I meant every word I said last night, when I told you I could never cheat on you, because I know how it feels. As far as I was concerned, that was what it was like, every time I was with someone else… every single time, for the last eighteen years." I pause for a second, and then continue, "Do you know, I've never instigated anything, except when I've been with you. Not once. Not even a kiss." I gently press my lips to her forehead. "It was always you, Abbie. Always. You were the first woman I made love to… and you're the first woman I've spent the night with. And to me, that feels right, because you're the only woman I'll ever love." I hug her tight and she snuggles down, her head resting on me and I hold her, until I become aware of a dampness on my chest. She's crying, and I pull back and look down at her.

"What's the matter?" I ask. "Did I say the wrong thing?" She shakes her head. "Then tell me what it is. I want to help."

"You can't," she mumbles, trying to bury her head again. I'm not having that and I cup her face, raising it to mine, and see the pain behind her eyes. Something's very wrong.

"Let me be the judge of that," I urge. "Tell me."

"I—I was just thinking about Ben coming in here in a minute, and how normal that is… you know, for kids to come into their parents' bedroom in the morning, like he does…"

"And?"

"And then I had to remind myself that I'm not his parent. I'm not anyone's parent… and I never will be…" She lets out a sob. *Oh God.*

I try desperately to ignore her tears and her sadness, so I can speak. "Will you listen to me?" I say quietly. She pauses and then slowly nods her head, and I take a deep breath. "I'm not going to say that Ben isn't Lauren's son. He is. And I'll never try to take that from him. I'll never try to hide his real mother from him… but being a mother is about so much more than giving birth. I know that better than most, with the mother I was given. I didn't have the greatest upbringing…" I lean in and kiss her. "But I did have the greatest best friend, in you. And you got me through it, just like you're doing with Ben, even if the circumstances are very different." She sighs. "You must have noticed how he's taken to you?" I continue. "You must have seen how it's you he comes to in the mornings? It's you he wants to bath him now, not me. It's you he turns to when he's upset…"

"That's because I'm a woman," she interrupts. "He's associating me with Lauren."

I shake my head. "No, he's not. He knows the difference. He asks about Lauren, and he asks about you. He knows you're two separate people, Abbie, and he loves you for who you are."

"Loves?" she queries.

"Yes. Loves."

She stares at me for a moment and then starts to cry again, and I hold her, her body locked with mine, until eventually her cries subside and she starts to breathe more easily. I lean back again, capturing her face in my hands. "Be mine," I whisper. It's an impulsive suggestion, but it's the most sensible thing I've done in years… at least, since the last time I asked Abbie to 'be mine', anyway. But that was slightly different…

The little furrow creases above her nose and I kiss it. "Now?" she murmurs. "We can't. Ben could come in any minute… he can't see us…" She blushes.

I smile. "No, you don't understand. I wasn't talking about that. I mean… be mine, forever. Marry me."

She continues to look at me, in shock I think, which isn't that surprising. As I said… it was an impulsive suggestion. Right, but impulsive.

"I'm sorry," I say quietly. "I know that should've been more romantic and I should have bought a ring, and planned something special… and more than anything, I know I'm saying this more than eighteen years too late, but…" She clamps her fingers over my mouth, silencing me.

"Yes," she says.

"Yes?" *Yes' what? 'Yes', I should have been more romantic? 'Yes', I'm eighteen years too late…? God, I hope not.*

"Yes, I'll marry you," she whispers, smiling at me, through my confusion, and my heart quite simply bursts as I roll her onto her back, raising myself above her.

"You will?"

She giggles. "Yes, I will."

I lean down and kiss her. Hard. For quite some time. Eventually, I stop and look into her eyes.

"I want to spend the rest of my life keeping you safe. I want to care for you and protect you, and to try and make life better for you, if I can."

"I know you do," she murmurs, smiling. "And you already do make it better."

"I try. But I know you're still hurting," I add. "Grief is a journey, not a destination, Abbie... even I've managed to work that out. The pain you feel for Molly won't ever go away, any more than the pain of all the lost years... no matter what I do. So, we have to learn to accept that, and try to move forward... as a family."

"A family?" she echoes and I lower myself down again, so our lips are almost touching.

"Yes. A family. Don't you get it? That's what I meant earlier... when I was talking about motherhood. Ben may be Lauren's biological son, but he's become a part of you, because he's mine, and because you love me..." I pause and she slowly nods her head in agreement. "And Molly is a part of me, because she's yours and because I love everything single thing about you. As much as you love Ben, I promise you, I love Molly. And that means we're a family. So... we'll work things out; we'll talk, we'll cry, we'll laugh, we'll be there for each other when it gets tough, and we'll get through it... all four of us... together."

"All *four* of us?"

"Yes. Always."

"Together?" she whispers.

"Yes. Forever."

She smiles. The most perfect smile in the world and I lean down to kiss her, just as the door opens and Ben comes rushing in, and climbs up onto the bed, interrupting us – although Abbie's still smiling and neither of us minds in the slightest, because that's what families do.

Printed in Great Britain
by Amazon